LETHAL RED RIDING HOOD

Leonard and Ann Marie Wilson

ISBN-13: 978-1-7355525-0-7

Library of Congress Control Number: 2020917562

LOST IN THE WOOD PRESS

www.lostinthewoodpress.com

Conway, Arkansas, U.S.A.

DEDICATION

In memory of Gary Alan Wilson: brother, friend, game master, and the man who introduced us.

There are many people without whom this book would never have been written, but of all of them—and in defiance of the years since his passing—his was the biggest single influence on the shape it took.

ACKNOWLEDGEMENTS

Cover Design by Peter O'Connor
https://bespokebookcovers.com

Copy Editing by Elise Williams Rikard
https://www.elisewilliamsrikard.com

Editorial Assistance provided by
Fellowship of Conway Literati

CHAPTER ONE

WILD THING

"Wait! Don't go!" Tobias shoved his way through the crowd of revelers, struggling to keep sight of the young woman. Even if his words had reached her above the chatter and the lively airs of the musicians, though, they'd still have been drowned out by the deep, reverberating tones of the grand clock striking the hour. Tobias alternately cursed and apologized as he bumped into and dodged lords and ladies dressed in finery that would have turned every head on an ordinary occasion— but right here, right now, seemed eclipsed to Tobias by that remarkable blond girl in the dazzling ruby gown.

She'd riveted his attention from the moment she swept into the ballroom, and her every word and gesture had left him feeling they'd hit it off grandly. Then, bang, the clock struck twelve, and she was off with nothing more than an, "Oh, my! Look at the time!" and a hastily blown farewell kiss.

Tobias hit the doors running, bursting out from the ballroom and onto a landing that overlooked the great foyer of the mansion. He heard her before he saw her, her crystalline slippers clattering against the steps of the spiraling staircase that swept down to the main floor. In her wake, she'd already left an impromptu dam of servants who'd been on their way up from the kitchens with silver trays of roasted lamb and pheasant, now all tumbled together in a horrible mess by the abruptness of her passage.

"I don't even know your name!" he shouted. The girl finally turned just long enough to blow him another kiss and favor Tobias with one last merry smile before disappearing out the door.

He contemplated for a moment the dizzying distance to the hard marble floor below, and evoked more than a few gasps of astonishment from the onlookers as he went for it. Vaulting straight over the balcony railing, the athletic young nobleman aimed for the nearest of the room's high, arched windows, letting out a whoop of triumph as he caught the top of the drapes and began sliding quickly down. Then the rod holding them in place gave way on one end, and instead of sliding Tobias found himself swinging.

With a smash and a crash, he hit the windowpane. Shards flew everywhere, and visions of a life about to be abruptly cut short flashed before his eyes as he lost his grip and found himself flying out into the courtyard over very thin air.

Looking up at the stars glittering overhead as his momentum had its all-too-brief, stomach-churning fight with gravity, Tobias had time to think perhaps that this was a time ready-made to wish on one of them. What he didn't have time for was to actually act on the thought before he landed flat on his back in the mansion's decorative fishpond.

By the time they'd dragged him out and he'd recovered, of course, the girl was long gone. Tobias withdrew to his study to lick his wounds, change into some dry clothes, and escape the sudden murmurs of gossip buzzing about that the master of the house had gone completely mad.

As he stood before the fire, pulling on a fresh shirt and cursing himself for a fool, a knock came at his door.

"Your Highness," the man stammered after being bid enter. "I'm afraid she, er...got away..."

"Yes. Thank you," Tobias muttered testily. "You can go."

"But we may yet be able to find her, Your Highness. She seems to have lost a rather distinctive article on the front steps. Perhaps..."

"Yes!" Tobias perked up at once. "What? Where is it?"

The visitor beckoned to a footman waiting outside. "Here, Your Highness," he said, trying gamely to maintain an impassive expression as the footman held aloft the girl's ruby-red gown.

The rhythmic click of crystal on cobblestone echoed through the clean, quiet streets of Serylia, outside the mansion. Quite unfazed by her newly acquired lack of gown, Keely strode confidently through the flickering lamplight in nothing but those slippers, a short saucy white chemise, an eclectic collection of jewelry hanging from her throat and arms, and a self-satisfied grin. She'd yet to meet a soul on the streets at this hour, though the night wind did carry the clatter of a distant wagon drawing slowly nearer, and she angled off in the direction of the sound until she finally spied the cart crossing an intersection ahead of her.

The farmer driving it never spared a glance in Keely's direction. He drove on, staring straight ahead with his mind on his business without a clue as to what he'd missed. Even when Keely ran to catch the cart, the clatter of the cart's wheels drowned out the clatter of her slippers against the cobbles, and she was able to hop onto the back, undetected.

As the cart rattled on through the sleeping city, an old beggar resting in the shelter of an arch just around the corner stirred in time to see Keely perched there amid the farmer's load of pumpkins with her feet dangling off the back. Keely just grinned and winked at the man, holding a finger to her lips in a conspiratorial request for his silence, then slipped an expensive-looking bracelet off her wrist and tossed it neatly into the tin cup sitting beside him.

The beggar grinned back gratefully and returned the parting wave Keely gave him before shadow swallowed up the curious scene.

Keely felt the cart jerk to a stop and realized that she'd dozed off, but the smell of the river and the wisps of fog drifting through the night quickly reassured her that they'd come down into the market district. With that and the distinctive silhouette of the Swan Gate bridge against the moonlit sky, she had her bearings again even before she hopped to the ground. Landing on soft earth instead of hard cobbles, she walked away silently amidst the carts, tents, stalls, and snores of farmers who had arrived at a more reasonable hour.

Though scores of people surrounded her, none stirred to notice the barely clad woman in their midst, and Keely soon left them behind on her trek toward the bridge.

She'd gone halfway there before running into another waking soul— or, rather, before another waking soul ran into her. At first, she thought she was about to be assaulted as he burst from a dark alley in a headlong rush, and she raised a hand instinctively to claw at him. By the time she'd gotten her hand up, though, he'd already barreled into her, and they both went sprawling on the street. Then he scrabbled away, neither attacking nor apologizing nor paying her any mind at all.

The man couldn't even be bothered to spare a glance for her wardrobe, or lack thereof. He just grabbed for his small armload of books that had scattered on the ground when they collided, and as quick as that, he was off running again.

Keely dusted herself off, making a small face at how her nice chemise had been muddied, then quickly stepped off into the shadows of the doorway she'd just passed. Where a man was running like that, something was chasing him. The best she could hope was that it would be the city watch in pursuit of a burglar and even they would surely find excuses to detain her and wind up asking awkward questions, given the state they'd find her in.

She was pondering her options for if it turned out to be a pack of feral dogs when the pursuit arrived. Five riders came thundering out of the night so rapidly that she'd barely heard the horses' hooves striking the unpaved earth of the alley before the lead rider appeared, a shadow among shadows as the woman's midnight-black cloak whipped about her. The man riding a heartbeat behind also wore black, but alongside a brilliant crimson that left no chance of his being taken for a shadow.

The moment Keely saw that flash of red, she began wishing she was dealing with those feral dogs instead. Time slowed. Her heart sped up. She found herself fumbling to draw a non-existent cloak protectively around her as she shrank further back into her shadowy corner.

Now free of the confined space of the alley, the second rider spurred his charger forward, overtaking the woman's smaller horse by the time the last set of hooves behind them hit the cobbles of the street. A cudgel flashed out as he rode past the man with the books, connecting with a sickening crack. The echoing crack of the man's skull hitting the cobblestones sounded an instant later, no less sickening.

Blood glistened off the cudgel that had struck the man down. Its wielder wheeled his charger back toward the limp form on the ground and the books scattered about it. Keely held perfectly still, not daring so much as to breathe lest the movement draw eyes to the lamplight shimmering off the white of her chemise or glittering off the jewels she still wore.

Only when the riders had gathered up the man and his books and ridden off into the night did she finally gasp for air and collapse to the ground in the corner where she'd hid, tears rolling down her cheeks, silent but unrestrained.

With a start, Keely realized she'd been sitting there long enough for the chill of the ground to sink into her bones, though she had no memory of any time passing. "Page thirteen, girl," she muttered to herself. "Page thirteen." Angrily, she dried her tears with the heel of her hand, knowing as it came away with dramatic smears of the make-up she'd painted on for the ball, that her face must now resemble an artist's well used palette.

She got up and—moving a little unsteadily at first—followed the faint chattering of a fountain to its source. Perched on the fountain edge, in the shadow of a bronze likeness of the Child, Keely pulled off her blond wig and laid it aside. As she sat unwinding the long, silver braids she'd had tucked beneath, she gazed upward at the little girl who stood frozen in the act of reaching up for a large butterfly alighting on her finger while water cascaded around them.

"Fluff and faerie stories," Keely told the bronze girl earnestly. "That's what you are, you know. No disrespect, of course—we've got a lot in common—but while you're telling everybody you're all cuddles and comfort, the *rest* of you is out there sheltering this stuff behind her name. Behind *your* name? Whatever. It's not right."

Keely had given up believing in Seriena on the horrible night that had led to the creation of page thirteen, but that didn't stop her from confiding in Seriena's child aspect. It wasn't like that night had left her anyone else to confide in. Besides, who better to share your secrets with than a girl who didn't exist? The risk of them getting blabbed about seemed pretty close to zero.

Yet for all that, a little part of Keely felt sure she had just invited terrible retribution for daring to say a word against Seriena's second aspect as the protective mother goddess. Or was that the *over-protective* mother goddess?

Actually, Keely had come to think of the other aspect of Seriena less as the child's protective mother-self than as the child's petulant, tantrum-prone evil twin. Even an imaginary evil twin could do a lot of damage with an untouchable private army at her beck and call.

Keely splashed water on her face until she could no longer rub the colors off of it onto her hands, then she finished letting her hair down and began the calming ritual of combing it out with the little tortoiseshell comb she'd used to pin her long braids in place under the wig.

Keely was objectively aware that her face and figure were passable enough that she could bluff any man into thinking they were something special just by throwing around the right posture, props, and attitude. Despite the frequent necessity of concealing her hair, though, she didn't just accept it as adequate; she genuinely *liked* it.

The first step in getting anyone to give you anything in life—food, shelter, a smile, a kind word, money, flowers, jewels...*anything*—was getting them to notice you exist. Her hair got her noticed. One overly poetic young man had even gone so far as to describe it as "silky curls of liquid silver". That had been just before he'd become an overly ardent young man and she'd broken his lute over his head, but he'd hardly been unique in where he'd chosen to begin his flattery.

When Keely had finally finished combing out her hair, she stood up, straightened her chemise, and drew a deep breath. "Page sixteen?" she whispered to herself, to which she replied politely with a firm nod.

"There we go, then," she said, flashing the bronze statue a smile as bright and winsome as any she'd flashed prince what's-his-name at the ball. "All better, see? I told you not to worry about me. It's your other *self* that needs looking after. She's gone quite off her rocker."

As she peered down into the dark mirror of the fountain, Keely gave herself a final inspection as best she could around the ripples, then she climbed up gracefully and threaded her way through the cascading waters of the fountain to give the little bronze girl an affectionate kiss on the cheek.

"Thanks for listening." She dropped lightly back to the cobbles of the street, only slightly dampened from the experience.

"Oh, and..." She selected a glittering pendant from the jewels about her throat and tossed it into the deep waters at the foot of the statue.

"An offering from...the Countess Camdovan, I think?" Keely said as the pendant settled to the bottom amidst a scattering of small coins. "We only met the once. Short woman, brown hair, dark eyes, not a great dancer? Gets really...well, annoyed...with servants who have trouble reading her mind? You know who I mean, of course. Just count the donation as credit toward her place in the hereafter. I'm sure she needs it."

Madame Ophelia sat amid the clutter of her time-worn medicine wagon, thumbing curiously through a heavily weathered book with her equally weathered hands. The graying woman stopped short of actually reading any of the thing—not for lack of curiosity, but because she hadn't a bloody clue how. Decidedly and proudly a woman of the world, not a woman of letters, Ophelia nevertheless found it an occasional nuisance that objects such as this refused to volunteer their secrets to her.

Her two daughters, having grown up accustomed to maneuvering around the clutter, somehow managed to go about the business of changing their clothes without knocking anything over and without stepping or sitting on any of the half-dozen or so cats lounging about the wagon. They'd carefully stowed away the fancy ball-gowns they'd been wearing and were in the middle of slipping on more utilitarian wear when the door of the wagon opened. Keely climbed inside, nearly tripping over one of the cats as it scurried between her feet in a sudden rush to get outside.

Ophelia looked up from her book with an exasperated sigh. "Not again! Girl, that dress cost a fortune."

"And I'd have never been able to sell it, or to wear it again, after a high-profile job like that," Keely countered as she carefully removed a pair of diamond earrings and dumped them onto Ophelia's book along with an armload of glittering bracelets. "There. Paid for in full. The thing was an albatross."

"More like a calling card by now," Colette, the older of the daughters, remarked. A dark-haired young woman of about Keely's age, with a couple of decades just freshly behind her, Colette grinned mischievously as she tightened the laces of her bodice.

"Hey, it wasn't *my* idea to go crashing society parties. And those stupid gowns weren't exactly made for slipping away in. They're for making a scene in."

The younger daughter, Madeline—old enough to pass for a woman, but still young enough to pass for a precocious child—snorted. "If you wanted to get away unnoticed, you'd stash a dress to change into."

"I did the first time, and some ne'er-do-well stole it," Keely said, rolling her eyes. "Besides, I thought it was my job to be distracting. You got the book, didn't you?"

"Easy as one of those round, fruity confection thingies," Madeline grinned.

"You know, if you wanted to leave a calling card," Ophelia muttered, "you could try leaving an 'X'."

"I was fresh out of charcoal," Keely answered dryly.

"Or a glove," Ophelia went on. "Or a fan. Or a kerchief."

"You didn't pack me any," Keely countered.

"Or a slipper, for go'ss sake!" Ophelia said, throwing up her hands.

"Oh, no!" Keely shot back with a real display of temper. "*Nobody* messes with my footwear!"

"Those *are* some amazing shoes." Colette sighed, wistfully admiring the crystalline slippers.

"You like them?" Keely asked.

"You always find the best shoes," Colette said, shaking her head with a little smile of envy. "Where did you get them?"

Keely just winked as she began rummaging for a dress to pull on. "What about the book?" she asked. "Is it any different from the others?"

"I only judge a book by its cover," Ophelia said. "The binding's the same. I recognize some of the same symbols, and it's got that same cat front and center..."

"It's a lioness," Keely corrected her.

"It's an angry cat," Ophelia reaffirmed hotly. "But the point is I can't read any more than you can."

"Aren't you the least bit curious," Keely asked, "why she's willing to pay so much for this collection of books?"

"Not really," Madeline said, taking a brush to her hair as she studied it in a hand mirror. "From the gossip going on at all these parties, it's got to be some intrigue over—"

"Hush!" Ophelia cut her off. "Court politics is too nasty a business for any self-respecting criminal to get caught up in, so just keep your nose clean and your curiosity to yourself."

Keely finished taking off the rest of the jewelry and dumped it into Ophelia's lap before snatching up the book from her. "I'll be sure to stow that away with all the other advice I've pointedly ignored. I'm ready to bet she's paying a fortune for these things for the same reason that the Inquisition is chasing them."

"Here, now!" Ophelia grabbed for the book, but not nearly fast enough to reach it before Keely pulled back out of reach. Then she did a double-take. "The Inquisition?"

"Well, they rode down *some* poor fool with an armload of books tonight," Keely said, flipping through the pages as fruitlessly as Ophelia had.

Ophelia answered with a dismissive snort. "You know how many books the Inquisition has banned?"

"A lot," Keely conceded. "But the guy thought they were valuable enough to stop and pick them up after he dropped them, even with the Inquisition right behind. How much does a guy have to get paid to consider doing something that stupid? And how many *other* books do you think are floating around the city right now that could be worth that much to anyone?"

Ophelia gave Keely the wary frown of someone who suspects she's just heard a spurious argument but can't quite nail down what was wrong with it.

"You've always said I had good instincts," Keely said earnestly. "Trust them now. They're saying it's time to walk away from this job before we drown in it. Besides, isn't the rule that the moment the Inquisition shows up in town, we disappear?"

Ophelia snorted. "That's the small-town rule. Serylia's *always* going to have someone from the Inquisition wandering around, and it's big enough to lose ourselves in. For all we know, the job's over anyway. How many books could 'Lady A' need for her set?" Ophelia said, insistently holding out a hand for the book, but when Keely's only response was a stern glare, she relented a bit. "I'll sleep on it," Ophelia sighed.

"You do that," Keely said, tossing her the book before turning to duck back out into the night. "Heck, sleep on it a couple of nights. I'm going to get started tying up my loose ends." She adjusted the borrowed dress and walked off down the street, trailing a couple of the cats who seemed to have casually decided that if she was heading that direction, it might be because there was something interesting over there.

CHAPTER TWO

LOOSE ENDS

The sun rising over the Unclouded Vale a couple of mornings later shone upon an ironically heavy mass of fog rising off the lakes and off the broad silver ribbon of the Cornyssus River that wound its way among the picturesque green hills. The rest of the Vale's name had been saved from history's irony bin only by virtue of its relative vale-ness. The Cornyssus and her tributaries had long since worn deep, comfortable grooves out of the snow-capped mountains that towered to the north, embracing the vale with their southward-sweeping arms.

Getting from Point A to Point B through the vale's picturesque scenery generally consisted of forging across or around what residents of many of the civilized kingdoms would have unhesitatingly called mountains, but at least no one could accuse those particular mountains of being "alpine".

At the farthest navigable point of the Cornyssus, where the river poured down from a three-hundred-foot cliff as Seriena's Tears, the city of Serylia had begun the business of waking up. When a city the size of Serylia slept, it always slept restlessly, but Serylia at least did her diligent best at gathering strength for the new day ahead. Lights burned all through the night in those corners of the city dedicated to distracting the poor from the precariousness of their desperate lives. In the wealthy districts, the occasional celebration might drag on until dawn broke the horizon.

The substantial and devout middle class of the city, though, had gone piously to their beds by the time the Bell of the Final Candle tolled out across the city. There were, Keely had observed, some definite perks to that lifestyle around here—so the morning sun found her waiting sleepily in the open dormer window of her townhouse to greet it this one last time.

She sat perched there—wearing nothing but a blanket to protect her bare skin against the morning chill and a dark wig to cover her silvery hair—and sipped at a goblet of mulled wine while she waited for the bells to start. She didn't wait long.

The red glow of dawn had barely crept up over the mountains before the first one began to toll, its deep and somber chime rolling out over the city. It tolled ten times before the answers began to ring back from spires all across Serylia, and the dawn chorus had begun. How many centuries the city had been perfecting it, Keely had no idea, but the tones rang out clear, true, and intricate from at least a score of sites (and certainly no less than a hundred bells). The locals claimed they could tell the day of the year by the morning song of the bells, and Keely could at least testify that no song had been repeated during the month she had been listening—yet each of those songs stood out as a masterwork of beauty.

Keely closed her eyes and allowed herself the decadent luxury of drifting away on the sound until the echoes of the final chime came drifting back off the mountains. Then the vocal chorus swelled to take its place. Keely couldn't understand a single word of the old imperial tongue, but she couldn't deny the rapturous beauty of the voices. Countless priestesses throughout the city raised their voices in loving praise of Seriena, every woman of them blessed with a natural gift and a lifetime of training for exactly this.

Lack of belief or no, losing herself in the chorus each morning had soothed Keely's soul, and it had reminded her that Church and Inquisition were not one and the same—all of which underscored the truth that it was time for her to move on. All other dangers aside, Serylia was beginning to feel too much like home.

Hero joined her at the window just as the song was ending. She sighed contentedly as he stepped up behind and folded her into his arms, kissing her on the cheek. "What's that look in your eye, Fel?" he asked as she invited him into the blanket, savoring the feel of his bare skin against hers.

"Just have a lot to get done today, Hero," she said, smiling up at him. This week he was a tall man, and he'd chosen a good face this time. She liked the way it looked, framed in his long, brown locks. "I've got something for you, though." She slipped away from him, leaving him the blanket as she sauntered back away from the window, casting him a mischievous smile and a wink back over her shoulder. Fetching a key from the night table, she tossed it to him, then retreated behind the folding screen to pull on a clean chemise and her dressing gown.

"What's this to?" Hero asked, turning the key over in his hand.

"The front door," Keely said, as she began brushing out her hair. "Back door too, I think," she said, frowning thoughtfully.

"Oh, really?" Hero said with a flirtatiously cocked eyebrow.

"Yep. Run along now, but make yourself at home when you're done with your...thing today." She waved a hand in dismissive surrender to that hole in her memory where details on the matter might have been stored.

When Hero had dressed and gone—with a rather steamy farewell kiss—Keely headed down the stairs, humming cheerfully to herself. "Jenny!" she called loudly as she reached the bottom of the stairs.

"It's Raymentine, your ladyship," the young housekeeper corrected as she appeared dutifully from the back of the house.

"Of course, Jenny," Keely said, patting the woman fondly on the cheek. "Breakfast smells delightful. Is the alderman here yet?"

"Waiting in the parlor, your ladyship," Raymentine said.

"Best keep him waiting, then. Come help me get dressed?"

When Keely stepped into the parlor half an hour later, in addition to the dark wig of fashionable curls, she wore a dress of simple elegance and dark red velvet, and a slightly haughty—but otherwise welcoming—expression.

"Alderman Margar!" She greeted the elderly gentleman with open arms and a kiss on each cheek. "I hadn't expected to see you again so soon. To what do I owe the pleasure?"

"Lady Felicity," he greeted her, the stern expression fighting to maintain its place on his face at the warm greeting. "I find myself most vexed at you."

"At me?" Keely clutched a hand to her breast in the exaggerated manner of polite social theater. "Dear Margar, whatever for?"

"For not turning to *me* for help, that's what for," he said crossly.

Keely scowled pensively, biting her lip. "I can't imagine what you're talking about."

"You can't fool an old businessman," he said, raising a scolding finger at her. "I know you're getting ready to head back to Carabas, and I know why. I also know you're ready to be a fool about how you're doing it."

"Alderman!" she gaped at him as her scowl turned to one of offense.

"Your pride won't raise you an army," he said, meeting her offense with a steely resolve, "and your title won't get you much further."

"I will manage, sir," Keely said coldly.

"With that paltry sum Marviene Floron is offering you?" Margar raised a dubious eyebrow. "Look...Felicity," he said, softening, "I've never had a daughter to spoil, and I admire your courage. I could get two times what Floron is offering for that painting your father left you— maybe three, if I embellish its history just a touch. Let me send you home with twice the army to take back your lands. It will save a great deal of strain on my heart, knowing you'll have the upper hand when you leave. And if I'm lucky, I could still come out a bit the richer for it. What do you say? Personal favor to an old man?"

He gave her a smile clearly meant to be fatherly and charming but falling somewhat short of the mark.

"I..." Keely stammered, then cast him a suspicious sidelong glance. "How do *you* know how much Floron offered me?"

"I have my ways," Margar said with a canny wink. "Ignorance does not a rich man make."

"Twice?" Keely asked, in her best semblance of a woman doing some cautiously hopeful mental calculation.

Keely was humming happily as she entered the dining room. "Jenny!" she called.

"Raymentine, your ladyship," Raymentine said, appearing dutifully.

"I hope there's some breakfast still warm. I should have had more than those few bites before seeing the alderman."

"Of course, your ladyship." Raymentine nodded, then threw up her hands defensively to catch the small bag suddenly arcing across the dining table toward her.

"And sit down to join me," Keely said as Raymentine caught the bag with a clink of coins. "We're celebrating."

"Celebrating?" Raymentine asked curiously.

"I *told* you your Alonso will be a great artist someday. The alderman nearly twisted my arm off insisting I let him buy that painting off me," Keely said.

"And...this?" Raymentine asked cautiously, peering into the bag.

"The alderman paid me a *lot*," Keely assured her, carefully omitting the fact that—thanks to a little well placed misinformation—Alderman Floron thought he already had a buyer ready to take the painting off his hands for "a lot" five times over.

"Here's the thing, Jenny," Keely went on after Raymentine was settled. "That's, what, six month's wages you've got there?"

"Nearly a year, your ladyship," Raymentine said, picking at the food on her own plate.

"My life just got complicated..." Keely paused briefly, waiting for Raymentine to finish coughing up a bite of eggs. "...and I'm heading back home. I want to make sure you're taken care of, but I can't take you with me. So listen carefully: I need you and Alonso to deliver the painting to the alderman for me this afternoon. He'll pay you the other half of what he owes me. Follow me so far?"

Raymentine nodded, swallowing as she tried to guess the math of what 'the other half' might amount to.

"From there, the two of you are to go get married straight away."

"Married?!" Raymentine exclaimed, wide-eyed.

"I mean, if you want to." Keely smirked.

"Of course, your ladyship, but our families—"

"Will not be able to say a word against it," Keely interrupted her, "because you're going to take all that money the alderman will give you and head out to start life together in nice, cozy little city at least three days journey from here."

"I couldn't..."

"*Fine.*" Keely sighed. "At least a week's journey. The important bit is to change your names, so that the alde...I mean, so that your families can't find you. I wish I could say that if you'd rather not take the big, romantic adventure, I'd just give you a good letter of reference and let you take your chances. You'll just have to trust me; that would be a *bad* idea. Marry the boy and run away together. And do it tonight."

"What if he won't...?" Raymentine began.

"Jenny, he *always* does," Keely assured her.

"Always does *what*?" Raymentine asked, perplexed.

"You have my personal guarantee that he will, is what I mean. The boy is crazy about you, and not so crazy about his family. He'll do it. And if he *doesn't* do it, I'll come back and scratch his eyes out myself."

"What if...?"

"No! Jenny, life is short, and there's no end to the number of 'what ifs' you can bury your dreams under. You want this, so you do this, or I wash my hands of the whole lack-of-affair."

Whatever response Raymentine might have made was interrupted by the sudden, loud jangling of the front bell.

"That will be Lady Bellany," Keely said, allowing herself a final bite before pushing away from the table. "Please show her into the parlor."

Lady Bellany greeted Keely with a venomous scowl which twisted her otherwise pretty young features. "What are *you* doing here?" she spat.

Keely just sighed, holding up a placating hand. "Apologizing."

The venom on Bellany's face relaxed slightly in the direction of puzzled suspicion, and she left Keely the conversational space to go on.

"You're right about me. I'm no good. I've done bad things, and I feel awful for coming between you and Hero," she said with convincing contrition.

"Who's Hero?" Bellany asked, though a serious dent was appearing in her venom now.

"The guy who's supposed to be with you." Keely sighed, massaging her forehead in frustration. "Is there more than one of them?!"

"Please tell me we're talking about Perin?" Bellany sighed.

"Yes. Exactly. Him. You were right. I was wrong. I'm sorry for everything. No need to forgive me any of it, but if you promise me that you're willing to forgive *him* for my leading him on, I'll be out of his life before midday, and do my best to never be seen again. Can you do that for me?"

"I..." Bellany stammered, smoothing down her fetching red-and-white dress. "I don't know what to say."

"'Yes' will cover it," Keely assured her.

"Yes?" Bellany replied cautiously.

"Well said." Keely nodded. "Now I'm *also* here because this is actually my house. Well, *was* my house. Your house now. Turn it into a home for stray cats or whatever if you don't have a use for it. I'll be cleared out in a couple of hours. The key's on the mantle. Hero..." Keely winced and forced herself to carefully enunciate the name. "*Perin* should be by looking for me before dark. If I were you, I'd be here to break the news to him, and don't spare my reputation."

"I...Thank you, Felicity," Bellany said. Her words came out more confused than heart-felt, but at least the venom had gone. Keely readily accepted that as a win.

"Take care of him," Keely admonished sternly, then swept out of the parlor and up to her room, waving off Raymentine on the way. She locked the door behind her and fell back on the bed with splayed arms and a heavy sigh. Biting her lip so hard it almost bled, she screwed her eyes shut and lay there ferociously humming a nursery tune until the urge to cry had passed.

Crying would have been nonsense. They'd come back to her soon enough.

She went over to the flower box outside the window and dug around in the dirt until she found the leather pouch she'd put there. Gently upturning the pouch so a small cascade of sparkling stones poured into her hand, she satisfied herself that her little hoard remained intact, then she returned the stones to the pouch and carefully tucked it into the larger pouch full of coins Margar had given her.

A woman of her talents and selective morals never remained impoverished for long, but she'd found she quite enjoyed avoiding the business of poverty altogether. Always best to arrive at the next town with her pockets already well lined.

By the time she slipped out the back window, she'd abandoned the wig for her natural silver hair and traded in her noble's attire for the serviceable tunic dress and sensible knee-high boots of Serylia's working-class women. The dress may have been smartly fitted and dyed look-at-me red, and her soft black boots may have been adorned with several more straps and silvery buckles than strictly necessary, but the point wasn't to avoid attention. It was simply to avoid the wrong kind of attention.

She carried the wigs and other disguise essentials she couldn't afford to leave behind in a small pack on her back, along with the pouch of valuables. Everything else she'd owned was now someone else's problem to sort out.

She slid down the roof sloping away from the window and dropped gracefully down to the alley behind the house. She allowed herself a small sigh and one brief final glance at the place before turning her back on it and walking away into the city.

Keely found the medicine wagon parked in the shadow of the Swan Gate bridge, amidst a colorful array of other entertainers and vendors. How anyone could hear anyone else over the din of the marketplace escaped her, yet a brisk business seemed to be going on despite all the brisk business going on—and Madame Ophelia's traveling medicine show was certainly holding its own.

Consummate professionals who'd already been a seasoned team back when Keely had a home and a conscience, the three women worked the crowd without missing a beat. Ophelia hocked her wares, Colette played a thoroughly convincing "fine, upstanding citizen whom I've never met before", and Madeline cut a purse like nobody's business.

Keely caught up with Madeline inside the wagon as she sat counting her take.

"Hey, kiddo," Keely said, dropping down beside her. "Job all done? We ready to get out of this town?"

Madeline rolled her eyes. "Mum's still thinking. You spooked her enough that she's dragging her feet meeting up with Lady A to hand over the book, but not so much that she's convinced herself she won't. She's got a hard time letting go of that kind of money."

Keely sighed and nodded. "Speaking of money," she said, unslinging her pack and fishing out a generous handful of coins from her hoard, "here's your cut from the alderman. Thanks for helping with that one."

"It was fun." Madeline grinned, her eyes sparkling with avarice as she paused in counting the more modest morning's take to count the new treasure. "Never went after a mark that big before."

Keely watched the girl in silence for a few seconds before pressing on. "I'm out, you know, no matter what your mother decides. I don't mess with the Inquisition. When they show up, I disappear."

"You *can't* leave," Madeline protested with a frown.

"I can't *stay*," Keely assured her, "and neither should you. Just convince your mother, and let's get back on the road. There's a big, wide world to see out there."

Madeline rolled her eyes. "Like I could convince Mum of anything you can't."

"I appreciate you trying to take care of us, dear," Ophelia said, bustling into the wagon herself, "but we don't need it. It's you I'm not sure about, striking out on your own."

"I did just fine on my own," Keely assured her.

"I don't doubt it," Ophelia said with a conceding nod. "But 'just fine' can turn into disaster in a heartbeat when there's no one about to watch your back." She sighed, scooted a lazing cat aside despite its protests, and eased herself down onto the bench where it had been, trying not to antagonize any of the miscellaneous aches brought on by a morning spent on her feet.

"Look, you're young enough to be cavalier about money, but I can't keep this up forever, and I've got the girls to think about. You're asking me to walk away from a *lot* on nothing but a hunch that it's something sinister."

"You've already got enough money from this to buy your way into the gentry or to start a nice merchant house," Keely said with a frown. "That alone should be scaring you. Have we really put so much effort in or risked so much on this job for the payoff *not* to fall into the realm of 'too good to be true'? All we've done is lift half a dozen books from under the noses of half a dozen different nobles, plus sneak a couple more out of abbeys. So far we haven't come close to getting caught, and if anyone's started chasing after us, they're keeping it in the shadows. And don't get me started about 'Lady A' herself."

"Agreed. You're *not* to get started about Lady A." Ophelia scowled. "She's a legit black-market dealer in rare books, and a friend. That's all you need to know, and you'll respect her privacy—or we're quits."

"If she's such a friend," Keely said, returning the scowl, "why won't she just tell you what's in these books?"

"I said she's a friend, not a fool." Ophelia snorted. "This is business. She never says what's in a book, and she never hires anyone who can read. That'd be just asking for someone to re-negotiate the deal. And she's making me rich enough that I just don't care how much richer *she's* getting."

"Yeah. Okay," Keely said, drawing a composing breath and staring down at the floor for a moment. "It always comes down to the money. I know that." She got up slowly and gave Madeline a distracted hug and a kiss on the cheek. "See you around, kiddo. Tell Colette I said goodbye."

She left the wagon with all the poise and grace she could muster, but still couldn't help noticing the door she closed behind her sounded like it had been slammed.

She'd gotten about thirty yards through the crowd before Madeline caught up with her. The girl was clutching the book to her chest. "Keely?"

"Yeah?" Keely asked with the best poker face she could currently manage.

"Remember the postulant at that first abbey who reads aloud to herself?"

"Yeah?" Keely perked up slightly, glancing down at the book.

Smiling as she followed Keely's gaze, Madeline held the book out to her in a conciliatory manner. "Mum thought it might be nice to know what we're arguing over before you head out."

CHAPTER THREE

ENTER ELISSA

Belgrimm Abbey stood as a graying memory of a gleaming citadel, her once-proud, ivy-shrouded walls now in that twilight state somewhere between respectable old age and disgraceful decay. Truth be told, though, she wore her age very well indeed, considering she'd seen most other buildings in the city rise from the ashes of fallen buildings that had risen from the ashes of other fallen buildings, and so on, back into the hazy distance of recorded history.

It was only in the last century or two that the new round of gleaming marble edifices had begun to crowd in around her, blocking out the sun and leaving her to slouch in their shadows. The priestesses who roamed her halls could still hold their heads up with pride at the old lady's history, but the real power had moved on, and the world's eyes with it— so there was no one about to remark when an old medicine wagon rattled up to park outside her walls.

Keely stepped quietly out of the wagon, once more dodging a cat as it slipped out past her feet, and then another cat that had been trailing along behind the wagon, looking for an opportunity to dart inside. Keely stretched as best she could while clutching the weathered book, then crouched to scratch at the ears of the milling cats that were rubbing at her ankles.

"Sorry," she said. "No treats today. I've had a *lot* on my mind. But we'll see what we can hunt down after I'm done with this."

Strolling along in the shadow of the abbey walls, Keely stopped at one of the lowest spots—a simple garden wall only a couple of heads taller than herself—and leaned back against a bare patch in the ivy to wait. She whistled quietly to herself, inspecting and cleaning her nails as she waited, until the abbey bells began to chime. She straightened up, turned, and sized up the wall for a moment before carefully heaving the book up and over with just enough force to clear the wall.

The book landed neatly in the middle of a little gravel path through the abbey gardens. It lay there with no one around to witness it until a cat jumped up from back out in the street and peered curiously after it from the top of the wall. The little, white longhair wrinkled its nose as it glanced back and forth between garden and street, then perked up its ears at the sound of footsteps on the gravel.

"Hey, Bookend," the slender, dark-haired young woman coming down the path greeted the cat cheerily. "Nice to see you about. Did you chase all the butterflies out of the garden for me today?" The girl, who wore the simple sky-blue robes of an abbey postulant, gave an exaggerated shiver and a wink. "I always appreciate that, you know. Here..." She dug a scrap of bread out of the pouch on her belt. "It's not much, but all the more reason to enjoy it before any of your friends show up."

The cat hopped down, landing on the book on its way to sniff at the proffered morsel.

"What's that?" the postulant blinked, doing a double take, then scowled. "How could anyone leave a book just lying around in the garden? It'll be ruined in no time." She dropped the scrap of bread and left it for the cat as she ran to grab up the fallen book and dust it off carefully, inspecting it for damage. "And who'll catch the blame? Me of course. Thank you again little friend: bane of butterflies, savior of books."

She smiled at the cat, then peered around for any sign that other bits of literature might have been left lying around forgotten. At last she shrugged, sighed in disgust, and started to walk on down the path.

"How...curious," she remarked, her steps faltering for a moment as her finger traced the designs on the cover. She cracked the book open and peered inside, quickly scanning a couple of pages. "Very curious." She closed the book again and hurried on, clutching it to her chest.

Elissa slipped hurriedly into the grand gallery of the abbey library. In ages past it would have been brightly lit by sun streaming in through the windows, but today that same sun could only brighten the darkness to a gray gloom after dodging its way around the larger buildings that now stood outside the abbey walls. Paying more attention to the book in her arms than to where she was going, Elissa nearly collided with another woman as she rounded a corner in the gloom.

"Whoa! What's the rush, little sister?" The woman laughed, dancing aside just in time.

"Just a...a book to re-shelve," Elissa stammered apologetically. "I'm sorry, Miraculata." She gulped in surprise, recognizing the golden robes of authority the woman wore over a silk gown of pink and white even before she was able to make out the woman's face in the dim light. "So sorry."

"No harm done, Elissa." The miracle woman smiled gently. Short, beautiful, and slightly plump in a way that did little more than underscore her femininity, one could have imagined Miraculata Cosima—with her bright blond curls and her big blue eyes—to be the very picture of a cherub who had been allowed to grow up. "Have you been able to find any more of the books I wanted? I'm done with that last batch."

"A few, yes. They're in the south reading room."

"Excellent. Thank you for all your help."

"Do you mind my asking what it is you're looking for in all those old books?" Elissa asked.

"Even aside from its obvious significance, the first Serinian Empire represents a fascinating chapter in history," Cosima answered, "that offers interesting parallels to our own. I hope to find some wisdom that will guide us as the second empire is forged."

"So nothing to do with that lost book of prophecy the abbey is buzzing about?"

"Maybe a little," Cosima chuckled, giving the younger woman a shrewd look. "I don't believe for a minute that it actually exists, but it suddenly seems that a lot of people do. And once a lot of people believe something, that something takes on a sort of reality of its own. The rumor alone will be fuel for all sorts of political fires. So, yes, I want as many facts as I can find on what happened back then, so I'll be better armed to combat any hysteria that may arise."

"Makes sense." Elissa smiled. "Well, I'll just get this back to the shelves and see what else I can find for you, then."

Cosima nodded and moved on, leaving Elissa to scurry on to the sorting room. Once there, Elissa paused to trace a finger over the lioness embossed on the cover as she chewed on her lip thoughtfully. She was just starting to crack the book open and have a look inside when the voice of the head archivist cut the silence.

"Elissa!"

"Coming, Sister Shayla!" Elissa called back. She dropped the book heavily onto the nearest stack, and turned to head for the door, nearly tripping over the little white cat from the garden as she did.

"That's all I had," Elissa said, crouching down to stroke the cat. "But you're welcome to anything you can catch roaming the library, as always." She straightened back up and hurried out, pursuing the sound of Sister Shayla's voice.

The sun had completed most of its journey up the sky before Elissa was able to return to the sorting room, and she set right to work organizing the many stacks of books awaiting her attention.

"*Demons and Witches of the Northern Steppes,*" she read the title of one aloud. "You can always count on Sister Adalva to go for the heartwarming parables, can't you?" She flipped through the book to an eye-catching illumination of a wicked-looking giant of a woman with pallid green skin, standing amidst the mountain peaks as lightning from the swirling black clouds behind her struck down the diminutive figures at her feet.

"*Chooali the Troll Queen,*" Elissa read. "Chooali roamed the mountains between the headwaters of the Sanguine and Emerald rivers until slain by Agnar the Righteous in the ninth century of the modern era. The sword he used to defeat her was blessed by the sisters of Belgrimm Abbey, and bathed in the blood of..." She stopped reading in mid-sentence and snapped the book closed. "Oh, right: it's gory bloodbaths you can always count on Sister Adalva for," she said sarcastically, and slipped the book into its temporary home on the shelves.

Elissa returned to her work but paused a few books later to read another title aloud. "*Winterswort: Its History in Medicine and Ritual.*

"And what about its uses in Sister Shayla's mushroom soup?" she asked the book rhetorically. "But I'll bite. It's an interesting herb." She began to open the book, hesitated, then added it to the small stack she'd set aside for later reading.

Elissa shelved a few more books before her eye fell on the one she'd found in the garden that morning. "Oh!" she exclaimed quietly and hurried to retrieve the book. "Now where did you come from?" she asked it as she added it to the "to read" pile, then she slipped the whole pile into the pack waiting beside it.

With the pack slung over her shoulder, she stole to the door of the sorting room and peered furtively out, glancing all around to see if anyone was present before stepping out and pulling the door closed behind her.

Just before the door latched, she stopped and peered back into the room. There lay the little white cat in its favorite spot at the end of a shelf where sun from the high windows would always hit in the late morning, cleaning the little brown socks that made it look as if it had dipped its hind toes in mud.

"C'mon, Bookend," she whispered, slipping back in to reach for the cat. "Time for me to do some concentrated goofing off, and for you to *not* give me away by yowling because you got locked in." The cat hopped down before Elissa could touch it but was thoughtful enough to scamper out the door instead of hiding behind a shelf.

A few moments later, Elissa was quietly climbing the circular stairwell that led to the Chamber of Banality, the tower room at the highest and least accessible point of the library, where unwanted books went to die. There lay the final resting place of any old tomes too dry and trivial to ever be opened without risking death by boredom, but donated by some personage too important to ever offend—or even to offend the memory of.

More formally known as the Tower of Special Collections, it was nevertheless special enough to attract about as many visitors as a lecture on the nuanced difference between seventy shades of white—which, not coincidentally, the room contained a treatise on in thirteen volumes. There, amid the spectacularly unimaginative journals of a centenarian's daily life ("Hot today. Ate turnips.") and the world's most authoritative collection on how to classify mold stains, Elissa found her own little sanctuary in the form of a room no one else ever wanted to set foot in.

She settled at the reading table under the window and fished in her pack for the book she wanted. Laying it out in front of her, she spent a few moments studying the lioness on the cover before opening the tome, then she began to read aloud.

"The Goddess Chronicles: Being a True and Accurate Account of My Service to Seriena Since My Appointment as Protector General to Mother Church—Lord Vyncent Amberford. Volume the Fifth.

"Well, this ought to be entertaining, Bookend." She smiled at the little white cat as it came nosing curiously into the room after her. "Have you read any of Amberford's treatises? The man was a loon, but never dull."

Thumbing past the title page, Elissa continued her reading.

Nonus 22, 1389:

Today I resume and reaffirm my quest to recover the Grimm Truth, and beg forgiveness from the Goddess for my lapse in faith. I allowed the years of failure, frustration, scorn, and ridicule to wear away at my resolve, before finally, ironically allowing Pontifine Celeste to convince me it had been madness all along—the irony being it was Celeste herself who held the missing key in the form of a lost missive from Miraculata Antonia of Grimm.

The very existence of the letter is incendiary, as it was clearly dated three weeks after her martyr's death. Addressed directly to Emperor Marcus Lupus himself, the letter speaks of betrayal from within the church, and of Antonia's intention to meet up with his legions at Torresangrienta. Success in carrying out that intent would have placed her at the site of the emperor's famous last battle, more than a month after Antonia's supposed death.

"Oh, my." Elissa looked to the cat, wide-eyed. It just blinked at her from where it sat, so Elissa continued.

I have not confronted Celeste with my discovery. The fact that she keeps the letter so carefully preserved suggests that she seeks the Grimm Truth herself. Yet her refusal to acknowledge the existence of either the tome or the letter to me clearly implies she has some agenda other than simply reclaiming it for the good of Mother Church. Is she simply seeking glory of her own? Does she fear that the knowledge in the tome could undermine her own position? Or does she perhaps hope to find in it a weapon against her enemies?

In any event, two things are plain: I cannot trust Pontifine Celeste, and Miraculata Antonia did not die in the fiery siege that was supposed to have claimed her book of prophecies along with her life. For the glory of Seriena and Mother Church, I will not falter this time, and I shall find the Grimm Truth.

Elissa glanced over another page or two of the book, her brow furrowed, then she began to aggressively flip through the tome until she arrived at the last written page. She began to read again, but quickly faltered, and only mouthed the words silently for a few moments. Then her mouth fell open, and she was left uncharacteristically reading the page to herself.

"Oh, my go'ss!" she shouted at last. "Bookend, he found it! He found the Grimm Truth! And he..." Elissa frowned, flipping back and forth through the pages as if looking for more, even though she'd already determined that there was no more to be found. "And he..." At a loss for any more clues from the journal, Elissa rolled her eyes back and forth as if trying to peer into her own brain and track down some elusive memory that might help. "Bookend, I think he died."

Elissa grabbed the book and hurried down the stairs as quickly as she dared, back out onto the main library floor, where she began pacing the aisles until she was able to zero in on a specific book. Dragging it off to the nearest reading table, Elissa spent a couple of minutes thumbing through it before finding a page that satisfied her, then left the book lying open as she laid out the journal beside it and turned to the last entry.

"See! See!" she jabbed her finger at the dates in the two books, then looked around as if expecting to find the little white cat sitting there, waiting to share in her discovery. "Bookend, you silly cat. Don't leave me talking to myself!" Elissa bolted down the end of the aisle, where she spied her feline companion poking its nose into an aisle several rows down.

"Come on! You've got to see this!" Elissa took a deep breath and calmed herself enough to approach the cat in a manner calculated not to spook, then walked down and picked it up in her arms, stroking its ears as it purred. She carried it back to the table where she'd left the two books, and plunked the cat down beside them.

"Just like I said: Amberford died on the same day he wrote the last journal entry—the day he found the book everyone's been whispering about these days."

Elissa scooted up on the table beside the cat and put her feet up on the seat of the chair. "Right. This is big. You and I both know the cats are in charge, so maybe you haven't bothered following the gossip, but scripture has always said that a second *human* empire would eventually arise under the banner of Seriena.

"The Angelis has convinced all the Serinian kingdoms that the time is at hand. Now they just have to sort out who's going to be emperor, which seems to be a nightmare of a job. And by that I don't mean difficult—though I'm sure it is—I mean the kind of nightmare where certain noblemen have already met very...disturbing ends over the matter. We're talking the kinds of stories that Sister Adalva is probably clawing her way back from the grave right now in order to write down.

"Obviously, you're already thinking that someone killed Amberford over whatever's in the Grimm Truth, and that was a hundred and fifty years ago—before anyone was talking 'empire'. The kicker is the reason the Grimm Truth is on everyone's lips right now: They're saying that one of the prophecies Miraculata Antonia wrote down in it declares Seriena's own choice to lead the second empire. Every king this side of the mountains wants to get his hands on it in order to prove he's meant to be the undisputed holy emperor—or else to quietly burn it if he discovers it's filled with 'lies'."

Elissa sighed heavily, stroking the cat's ears as she stared blankly at nothing in particular. "You know, Bookend, I couldn't care less who's emperor. None of them can really muck about with the church. I'm much more concerned with the not-getting-dead thing that seems so hard to do for people who get caught up in this stuff. So let's keep this our little secret, okay? I'm going to go put it on the stack of books set aside for the miraculata and just pretend it showed up there as mysteriously as it showed up in the garden. She'll know what to do when she stumbles across it."

Elissa smiled a little as her eyes came back into focus. "Thanks for the advice, Bookend. You are a wise, wise cat." She hopped down from the table, re-shelved the reference book, and headed off toward the sorting room with the journal in her arms. Just as she was about to disappear around the corner, she took a step back and held up a finger to her lips as she tried to catch the cat's eye.

"Remember: *ssssh!*"

The cat just sat grooming its paw until Elissa had gone, then cocked its head listening, its tail swaying like a metronome keeping time with the sound of the postulant's retreating footfalls—until precisely at the count of ten, when the cat suddenly tensed. Then it disappeared like a flash through the library, headed in the direction of the garden.

CHAPTER FOUR

SHE DOESN'T KICK PUPPIES

Somewhere out in the abbey, a bell was tolling as Keely paused to tuck a telltale lock of silvery hair back under the hood of her borrowed postulant's robes. She peered into the south reading room of the library and upon finding the chamber empty, she slipped inside for a proper look around. A few books had been left scattered carelessly on tables about the room, but only one table held enough of a stack to require a proper search.

The other tables could be dismissed at a glance as not holding the book she'd come looking for. All that remained then was a quick scan of the stack on the last table to find her target—the journal with the distinctive lioness on the cover—buried four deep in the pile. She grabbed it and a couple of the other books for good measure and turned, quickly heading back for the door.

"Oh, hello. Are those for me, little sister?"

Keely hesitated just long enough at the unexpected appearance of Miraculata Cosima for the cherubic woman to reach out and take the armload of books from her.

"Yes. These should be excellent. Thank you," Cosima smiled as she inspected the titles on the two books that had them on the spine.

"*Actually*," Keely interjected hastily as she reached to pull the journal back out of the stack, "just those two. The abbess was wanting to see this one herself."

"Sorry," Cosima grinned apologetically, tilting her head to have a look at the face under the cowl. "I don't believe we've met, little sister."

"No, I...But, the abbess..." Keely held up the book meaningfully, managing to half-obscure her face in the process.

"Oh, right. Don't let me keep you."

31

Keely curtsied out respectfully and breathed a sigh of relief as soon as she was out of sight, then scurried off in the direction of the garden door. She passed a couple of priestesses hurrying the other way, but they strode on by with barely a nod of acknowledgment.

Arriving at the garden door, she tugged at the handle, only to find that someone had locked it since she'd let herself in that way just minutes before. She muttered a curse under her breath at the horrid timing and doubled back toward the front doors of the library. With the most direct avenue of escape cut off, she deliberately slowed her pace. Impatience now could only draw attention to herself—and for a change, that was something she wanted to avoid.

At a window just before she reached the doors, movement in the courtyard outside drew her eye. She looked up to see a flood of priestesses and postulants pouring out of one of the buildings, all very much in a hurry as they scattered in every direction. Keely smiled at the sight of fortune turning back her way, and pushed open the doors to lose herself in the throng. No matter what had sparked all this off, she couldn't have asked for a better hiding place than a crowd of people in too much of a hurry to even look at each other. She was even able to break into a bit of a run, and no one spared her even a first glance, much less a second.

Around the library Keely ran until she reached the garden gate—but even before she stepped through it she could plainly see that the garden was plagued with holy women rushing back and forth along the little cobblestone paths that wound among the flower beds. Keely hurried over to the alcove where she'd first tossed the book over into the abbey, and settled back into a corner, where she waited for a moment's privacy in which to toss the book back out into the street. Climbing over the wall herself with the book in hand remained out of the question.

"You there! Girl!" a stern-looking older priestess snapped, stopping just outside the alcove to glare at Keely. "What do you think you're up to, standing about like that? The wall can hold itself up. What is it you're *supposed* to be doing?"

Keely held up the book defensively again, but the priestess just continued to glare at her, clearly expecting some more explicit explanation.

"The abbess asked for this," Keely stammered.

"And she asked for delivery by way of hide-and-seek?! Quit lurking in the corner and go! If she asked to see it now of all times, you'd best have it to her five minutes ago. Run!"

"Yes, sister!" Keely ducked out of the alcove just ahead of an angry swat and dashed out the garden gate. A few paces into the courtyard, she glanced back over her shoulder. The glowering priestess had already parked herself in the gateway, intent on seeing Keely properly off on her made-up errand. "Do you know where...?"

The priestess jabbed a finger toward a building across the compound, and Keely took off running again, desperately scanning for any other way out as she re-prioritized haste above subtlety. The next time she felt confident she could reach the street with her prize before anyone would have time to interfere, she'd do it even if the whole abbey was watching.

Up the steps and into the appointed building, Keely ran between marbled columns and aging statuary as she dodged a steady stream of other robed women. As soon as she was sure she was out of sight of the garden gate, she ducked over to the first window she could find to orient herself and plan a path to the outer wall of the abbey. The chosen window looked out over the front courtyard, with the main gates clearly visible, but reaching them looked like it would be a trick. Though serene by comparison to the chaos that Keely had just stepped away from, the front courtyard of the abbey was still well-occupied.

First visible was the abbess that Keely had ostensibly come looking for, sedately descending the steps from the main chapel in her flowing golden robes. Flanking her came half a dozen sober-looking women in the silvery robes more typical of the clergy, and flanking them in turn came a handful of young women in postulants' robes.

The half-dozen representatives of the Inquisition present only came into view when Keely stepped right up to the window. The four black-robed priestesses among them had just dismounted in the courtyard and now waited impatiently to turn the reins of their horses over to the approaching postulants.

Keely was already muttering expletives under her breath when her gaze fell on the fifth member of their company, and the pure cognitive dissonance of him made her stomach churn. The tall, broad-shouldered man wearing the black-and-red livery of a knight of the Inquisition was just stepping down off of a spirited-looking horse. His long, dark hair framed a stern but handsome face with a neatly trimmed beard.

"Now *that*," Keely lamented quietly to herself, biting her lip as she studied the man, "is a real waste." Had she seen him in other clothes, another context, she'd have jumped at the chance to cast such a man as Hero. "I could have got worked up over you, sir," she sighed, "but the 'professionally sadistic zealot' outfit totally kills the mood."

"Really?" Miraculata Cosima asked as she calmly stepped up to lean against the windowsill next to Keely. Cosima studied the man for a moment herself. "From here it doesn't even look like the mood's seriously injured. Perhaps just had the wind knocked out of it. Shall I put in a nice word with Sir Riordan for you?" Cosima grinned impishly.

"No!" Keely blurted out before she could compose herself again. "I mean..." She stopped and furrowed her brow. "You're not upset about the 'sadist outfit' crack?"

"No point getting worked up over the truth, little sister," Cosima shrugged as she returned to looking out at the courtyard. "The Inquisition wages war on demons and witches so that the rest of us don't have to—but war is a cruel business, and letting it turn you cruel is too often the only way to survive it. So I count my blessings that it's not me down there dressed in black, but you'll never catch me pretending that the Inquisition is 'nice'. I'm quite sure our man Riordan isn't, anyway."

"And her?" Keely asked of the last member of the company, a slender priestess in flame-red robes who Riordan was just helping down from her horse. From this distance she looked quite lovely—in a severe, no-nonsense sort of way—but Keely could make out enough gray in the woman's dark hair to guess her for middle-aged, so the distance was probably flattering her a bit.

"Do I really have to tell you about Jane Carver?" Cosima asked, glancing sideways at Keely. "The Grand High Inquisitrix?"

"Ohhh..." Keely left her mouth hanging open as the little sound of realization trailed off. "She doesn't *really* go around kicking puppies, does she?"

"Goddess, no," Cosima shook her head, waving a hand dismissively. "She stabs them."

"Right," Keely said, defensively holding up the book in her arms. "I'd better just get this..."

"To the abbess?" Cosima raised an eyebrow. "That's one meeting you *don't* want to interrupt, little sister. Besides, we both know that the abbess isn't really expecting you or that book, either one. I'm fairly certain you haven't hurt anyone, and that you don't intend to, though, so let's make a bargain. I'll take you for a nice, quiet cup of tea where we can talk while this craziness blows over. You'll tell me what you're doing here and why you're so eager to get that one particular book out of Belgrimm Abbey.

"In return, I'll not only walk you neatly out the front gate with me, I'll cover to make sure that no one knows what you've done for—shall we say—at least three days? No more muss or fuss, and no worries about getting tangled up with the Inquisition."

"I don't know what..." Keely started, but cut herself off at the sight of Cosima's resolutely crossed arms and incredulous expression. "Yeah.

All right. But..." A sudden shiver ran down Keely's spine, and she turned back toward the courtyard to find the red-robed inquisitrix staring determinedly up at her. Even from this distance, there was no mistaking that those intense eyes never flickered toward Cosima as they held Keely's gaze.

"Don't look away from her, and just listen," Cosima murmured quietly as she turned to smile and wave cordially down at the High Inquisitrix and her entourage. "Keep eye contact like you're trying to stare down a barking dog. It'll buy you a few seconds. I've got enough connections she can't simply walk all over me, but unless you're accustomed to being asked round to dinner by kings and high pontifines, the worst thing Jane Carver can do is notice you exist."

Cosima continued to smile down at the gathering as more heads turned to see what the High Inquisitrix was looking at. All of them focused in on the miraculata in gold and pink—who greeted each with a little wave—ignoring the fake postulant standing frozen beside her. Between waves, Cosima slipped a key off her belt and discreetly slid it across the windowsill until it was nearly touching Keely's fingertips.

"That should open any door between you and the street. Please don't do *anything* to *ever* make me regret doing this for you. Now I'm going to pretend to send you down there so she won't rush to send anyone up here. The moment you're out of her sight, run, and don't look back for at least three counties. Take the key if you're ready."

Keely felt for the key without ever breaking gaze with the inquisitrix. As her fingers closed around it, Cosima turned to Keely with a pleasant smile, pointed broadly out the window in the direction of the gathering, and said, "Remember that's the fate worse than death everyone talks about, should you find yourself with a choice between the two. Now go, and Goddess guide you."

Keely nodded obediently as she took a step back, then turned and started off down the hallway, quickly breaking into a run. Rather than risk getting lost, she headed right back the way she'd come—down the steps, across the courtyard, and into the garden beside the library.

She was nearing the outer wall at a dead run when the side door to the library (that had been so inconveniently locked earlier) flew open, and a postulant with a massive armload of poorly balanced books came rushing out. They saw each other in time to avoid a collision, but when the girl came to a sudden stop, the upper half of her stack of books kept right on going, and Keely found herself pelted by a deluge of literature.

"Sorry! Sorry!" the girl stammered, setting down what was left of her load on a garden bench and turning to help Keely up—but Keely was already back on her feet and flinging a book over the garden wall. "I...Here now!"

"Oopsie! Lost my temper. Let me go get that for you." Keely smiled, patting the girl on the cheek. Without waiting for a response, she darted over to where an old fountain provided a few handy steps up, then pulled herself the rest of the way up and over to land neatly in the alley outside.

"Hey! This really *is* your book!" she called back indignantly, picking the thing up off the cobbles and scowling at it. "Where's *my* book?!"

"What?!" the confused girl called back.

"Heads up!"

The postulant ducked in alarm as a large book came sailing past her head, then went back to gathering the others from where they lay in the dust. A few moments later, breathing hard from the effort of crawling back over the wall without a convenient step up, Keely dropped back into the garden.

"There it is!" Keely said, scooping up the book from the ground and patting the lioness on the cover to reassure herself she wouldn't make the same stupid mistake twice. "Sorry for the mix-up." She tossed the book back into the alley and scrambled after it.

Landing beside it, she reached to pick it up again, and blinked. "What? No!" She rubbed her eyes with the heel of her hand. "Now I *know* you are *not* the book I just tossed out here." She groaned, shook her head to clear it, and looked around, but there was clearly only one book out here, and it wasn't the one she wanted. She left the book lying where it was and pulled herself laboriously back up and over the wall.

"You know, that's harder than it looks," she puffed to the postulant, who had finished re-stacking the books and was just trying to balance them again. Keely took a moment to peer out into the courtyard and make sure no one obviously attached to the Inquisition was headed this way, before catching the girl by the sleeve. "You've got a heretical book in there."

"I do not!" the postulant stammered, going wide-eyed as she tried to back away.

"Really. You don't want to get caught with..."

"You're with the Inquisition!" the girl gasped. "That's why I haven't seen you before!"

"Nnnn...yesss." Keely choked off the reflexive response and aborted the headshake she'd started, turning it into a nod. "Now..."

"This is just a pile we set aside to burn!" the postulant whimpered. "They found them in the cellars and...and..."

"Hush!" Keely laid a quieting finger on the girl's lips. "You swear you were just going to get rid of them?"

The terrified postulant nodded vigorously.

Keely gave her a glare of very convincingly feigned suspicion, then slowly allowed her expression to soften. "All right. I'll make them disappear before the High Inquisitrix sees them, but you owe me a big favor, right?"

"Right!" the postulant squeaked.

"Just help me toss them all over the wall, right here, and I'll go over and get them sorted out."

A short while later, when the last of the books sailed over the wall and into the alley, Keely crawled over one last time herself to land heavily on the dusty cobbles. She sat down and leaned back heavily against the abbey wall, breathing a sigh of relief, then began going through the books one by one.

"No. No. No," she said to herself, crawling over to the nearest one any time she'd gone through every book within reach. "No. No...Yes!" She hopped excitedly to her feet, only to let out a strangled, "Urk!" as someone grabbed her by the back of the collar.

By the time Keely could sort out what was happening, there was a massive hand clutched about her throat, pinning her to the wall, and she was staring into the menacing eyes of the knight she'd seen earlier in the front courtyard.

Keely clawed ineffectually at Riordan's gauntleted wrist, struggling simply to breathe. Then her blood tried to freeze in her veins as a slender figure in flame-red robes stepped into view from around the knight's eclipsing bulk. Jane Carver spared Keely a single impassive glance before returning to the business of slowly walking among the scattered books, kicking at them to examine their titles without ever bending down.

The High Inquisitrix clucked her tongue while shaking her head sadly. "I was going to ask who you are, girl," she said, finally turning her attention back to Keely, "but I'd say this is answer enough: You're someone whose screams I'm going to savor."

Keely launched a swift kick toward where she hoped Riordan's groin was, but never found out if that's what she really connected with, because the next moment he'd slammed her head back into the stone wall. Keely struggled momentarily in a disoriented sort of half-consciousness, in which the brilliant red robes of the woman beyond Riordan's shoulder seemed to take up the entire world—then she blacked out.

CHAPTER FIVE

En Memorium

Through the blackness of memory, Jenilee fled. Icy water splashed around her ankles and soaked the lower half of her skirts. Even with her arms thrown up protectively ahead of her, unseen branches scratched her face and tangled painfully in her hair. Her feet sank into the muck with each step. Things unknown squirmed or slithered away more than once beneath her feet. She could hear the others splashing through the mire ahead of her, breathing heavily, no more daring to slow their pace than she was to slow hers. Behind them, driving them on, came the screams of the dying and of those even less fortunate.

Then out of nowhere a woman came looming from the darkness ahead of them, all cape and cowl of such dazzling blood red that they seemed to light up the night with a fire of their own. For one brief, eternal heartbeat, Jenilee could see the girl ahead of her frozen in silhouette against that terrible red, then the woman's arm swung out like a scythe. The girl screamed.

Jenilee stumbled and fell, banging her knee on the tavern's hardwood floor.

"Jenny?" The dark-haired girl standing over Jenilee extended a concerned hand to help her up.

"Ow," Jenilee moaned half-heartedly as she accepted the hand, more disoriented and confused than in pain. The muck had gone. The trees had gone. Her skirts would now have been bone-dry were it not for the traces of sweat. Her scratches, blood, and bruises already felt like a half-remembered dream. Even the screams had faded into the raucous song and laughter of the sailors who frequented the tavern, and of their companions of the moment.

"Don't tell me you've got drunk just off the fumes in here," Jenilee's friend said wryly, dusting her off. "Are you okay? Can you stand?"

"I..." Jenilee bit her lip and tried to shake the fog from her head. "I'm fine, Keely. Just the *creepiest* feeling—like someone walked on my grave...maybe did a little dance...started hacking at it with pick and shovel. My skin's still crawling."

"Ah," the older girl said knowingly. "Nerves. Here." She grabbed a mug off a passing tray, replacing it with a couple of coins before the girl holding it could do more than offer her a dirty look, and shoved the beer into Jenilee's shaking hands. "Buck up before you embarrass us. We're hardened criminals, remember?"

"Right. Sorry," Jenilee apologized in her best emulation of a hardened criminal who was absolutely not a fourteen-year-old who'd always led a basically law-abiding life. She sipped at the beer and immediately wrinkled her nose in disgust, trying to inconspicuously spit it back out. She'd never much cared for the taste of what little beer she'd had in her life, but this particular mug of the stuff stood out as the uncontested worst of her experience. At least, she supposed, that helped it take her mind off of the nightmare vision.

"You're hopeless, you know." Keely chuckled, tousling Jenilee's hair before dragging her on through the crowded tavern. Jenilee bore the gesture with embarrassed good grace, though it reinforced how babyish and unsophisticated she already felt next to the lean and graceful fifteen-year-old with her mysterious dark eyes, elegant black curls, and curves that routinely got Keely mistaken for seventeen or eighteen.

Jenilee, by contrast, was lucky if she didn't get mistaken for twelve or thirteen, and on days when she was feeling particularly insecure, the voices in her head would try to convince Jenilee that Keely only kept her around as a sort of fashion accessory.

Her own silver-white hair did—according to a friend who would know about such things—offset Keely's raven curls nicely, enhancing the "femme fatale" aura she had going. Keely even made the ragged ensemble she'd pulled together for the occasion look like fashionably tailored pirate chic. Jenilee had the distinct impression that her own outfit simply said, "outdated ragamuffin".

Shouts at a corner table drew Jenilee's attention just in time for her to duck under the mostly empty mug that came flying from it, and the thing merely doused her with a splash of cheap beer rather than connecting with the side of her head. She stayed down, waiting for a fight to erupt in the corner, but whatever had caused the outburst quickly quieted down instead. When Jenilee got back up, she'd nearly lost sight of Keely through the crowd, and she hastened to catch up.

A tall, muscular youth stepped in front of Keely, blocking her way. His well-worn mariner's outfit looked like it had actually seen genuine labor of questionable honesty, splitting the fashion-difference between what the two girls wore. "How much," he was asking Keely salaciously as he brushed a long, unruly lock of dark hair out of his eyes, "for the whole night?"

Keely snorted at the young man, unperturbed. "You couldn't afford me for fifteen minutes, hero."

"Guess I'll have to settle for stealing a kiss then," he laughed, wrapping his arms around Keely's shoulders to draw her to him. She only objected inasmuch as a small laugh of her own could count as an objection and melted into a kiss that Jenilee was sure would be steaming up glassware halfway across the room.

"Hey, Jenny." The young man smiled warmly at Jenilee when they finally came up for air, and he tousled Jenilee's hair in a perfect echo of Keely's earlier patronizing affection. "Sure you're up for this, kiddo?" A current of genuine concern ran beneath his otherwise light-hearted tone.

"Of course," Jenilee assured him, though the butterflies in her stomach had been dancing such a lively hornpipe all day that she barely managed to take a bite of food, much less keep it down. "I've *got* to do this, Axy," she told him. "It's page one." It was also the only option left to her that she could even contemplate.

Axy nodded his sober understanding. He always made the effort to at least act like he was taking her seriously, whether he actually did or not, and she could have kissed him for it. Only, she *couldn't* have kissed him for it. Even thinking about being that forward nearly sent her into a panic. *And* it would have ticked off Keely and made things totally weird between the three of them. Cold, hard realities aside, though, she could have kissed him.

"Come on, hero," Keely said grabbing Axy gently by the ear and pulling him into step beside her. "Let's do this."

A door at the back of the taproom opened onto a sort of a sunken courtyard at the back of the Drunken Squid, where the more serious revelry seemed to be taking place. A rickety wooden fence stood as the only guard between one side of the yard and a forty-foot drop down a rocky cliff into Lake Etherea, while a crude wooden deck along the back of the tavern embraced the other three sides.

A few tables, weathered and mismatched, lined the edge of the yard, but the rest of it had been left open—save for one pink-veined marble statue the size of a horse, perched on a tall, stone pedestal at the center of it all. Though this was the first time Jenilee had laid eyes on the thing, she knew it by reputation.

Everyone in Hart Cove knew about the tentacled monstrosity of a statue that old Captain Hobbs had brought back from his days on the salt seas. He claimed it had been an idol worshiped by cannibals on one of those exotic islands where people wore leaves and feathers for clothes, when they wore anything at all. Now it sat looking out over their freshwater sea, every bit as disturbing as people said, though its tentacles now clutched an assortment of rusting tankards instead of the skulls and stone knives that Hobbs claimed he'd found it with.

The priestess of the local church had given him grief over it, but that was back when there'd been a priestess at the local church. Even at the time, her threats had been empty ones. Hart Cove faithfully served the church of Seriena in the same way that it faithfully served the king of Atiopryae: by saying nice things about it, sending it enough money to keep it mollified, and maintaining a low profile.

The real power in the town was currently carousing in the courtyard down below, the chaos of the scene swirling around her as if around the eye of a storm. Unlike the squid statue, Jenilee knew Blackwater Molly by sight as well as by reputation, and she would have been hard-pressed to say which of the two was the more flamboyant thing about the woman.

Molly moved through the crowd not merely like she owned the place, but as if she owned every soul in it. Dressed in a fine silk shirt of lemon yellow, tawny boots and breeches, and countless golden bangles that chimed as she moved, the pirate queen shone like a sun amid the more mundane persons of dubious profession who surrounded her.

As her long blond hair flew out in a corona about her, she swung laughing from arm to arm in time with the piper and fiddler who perched in windows above the courtyard, and she left a wake of dancing bodies in orbit around her. Not one of her rapidly changing partners— man or woman—passed through Molly's arms without an unchaste kiss, and not one—man or woman—seemed less than pleased by it.

Neither did any barmaid get within ten feet of Molly without the woman snatching a mug or a bottle from her and downing half of its contents—the other half invariably sloshing across the ground and her companion of the moment.

Jenilee had never seen Blackwater Molly in full revel before, but apparently the rumors were true that she could school a satyr in how to cut loose and live in the now. Perhaps, Jenilee reflected, it was only this expertise that held Molly back from becoming a more conventional sort of queen. Certainly no one in Hart Cove would have traded her de-facto rule for any actual interest from the man who wore the crown. She kept order up and down the coast, she levied fewer taxes than either king or church, and she made a body feel somehow like her companion off on a secret, magical adventure by the simple act of smiling when she passed on the street.

She could also stare down a belligerent drunk twice her weight, as Jenilee had seen for herself. The man had been itching for a fight, but whatever he'd seen staring into Molly's eyes for those few heartbeats had turned him white as snow and sent him stumbling over himself to get away from her.

If even a fraction of the stories circulating about Molly were true, the man had just been lucky she hadn't wanted to be bothered with him at that moment. Estimates of the number of men she'd killed never dropped below a couple dozen and ranged into the hundreds. Stories about *how* she'd killed them often featured in Jenilee's nightmares, even if Jenilee's imagination couldn't actually cast the lively and lovely Molly as the monster committing those atrocities. Whatever the truth of it, Molly's reputation carried such weight that no sober and sane person living on the shores of Lake Etherea would put it to the test without an army at his back. Reputedly, anyone who'd proved an exception could no longer be counted among the living, though, so that made sense—in a circular logic sort of way.

"Hey!" A gruff voice snapped Jenilee far enough out of her star-struck reverie to notice that Keely and Axy had started for the stairs down to the courtyard, only to be intercepted by a wall of scar-covered muscle. "Private party," the man growled. "I don't know you, you don't come in."

"You *don't* know me?" Keely replied archly without missing a beat. Her eyebrow arched. Her eyes narrowed. Her hands went to her hips. "*You* don't *know* me?" she repeated, her voice dripping incredulity. "Mister 'Do that thing with your tongue again' *doesn't know me*? How into your cups *were* you?" she demanded.

"Very...?" the man ventured, suddenly uncertain. "*What* thing with your tongue?"

Keely rolled her eyes but stepped up to the man on tiptoe. One hand snaked up the back of his neck to twine in his hair, pulling his head back, baring his throat. Jenilee was so busy gaping at what she couldn't quite see Keely doing with her face nuzzled up against the man's neck that she nearly missed Keely's unoccupied hand surreptitiously waving them on. Jenilee scurried down the steps, grabbed the hand of the still stunned Axy, and dragged him on down into the crowded courtyard without looking back.

Keely joined them a minute later, wiping her mouth on the back of her sleeve and making a little face of disgust. "First one of you to make a smart remark gets to bluff us past the next pirate," she said preemptively.

"Wouldn't dream of it," Jenilee replied, very nearly managing to keep a straight face.

"This way," Axy said, using his size to force a way through the swirling crowd. Though far from the largest man there, he stood tall enough and broad-shouldered enough to at least plant his feet and anchor himself to the ground when either of the girls would simply have been buffeted helplessly in the human tide.

So with Axy at point, they progressed in fits and starts toward the moving target of the pirate queen. Two near misses got him nearly within arm's reach before Molly danced away, oblivious to their attempts to attract her attention. The third attempt resulted in Molly emerging out of the crowd without warning, close enough to grab Axy by the arm and swing him around.

To Axy's credit, the young man kept his head enough to stammer out something about joining Molly's crew, but even knowing his intentions, Jenilee couldn't make out half of what he was saying above the din. She couldn't blame him, though. She could hardly stay focused on the job in this chaos herself, and she wasn't a young man suddenly swept up in the arms of Lake Etherea's deadliest nymph.

Molly had to be forty by now, but for all her hard living, she didn't look a day over thirty—even up close—and the raw energy and lust for life she radiated made it hard to remember she was even twenty. She came equipped with the curves of a nymph to go with the personality, too. And with eyes of sparkling blue. And with smiling lips, so full and sensual and...kissable? Jenilee blinked, shocked at the alien thought that had crept into her head.

Molly also paused in surprise at about the same moment. For all of half a heartbeat, she looked up into Axy's unfamiliar face. Then with an expressive shrug, she reached for his collar and dragged him into the undeniable proof of just how kissable those lips were. Unlike the other, passing kisses she'd been handing out, this one lasted so long that the dancers stumbling around her actually stood back and left her some room in a slowly widening circle.

Jenilee couldn't help but stare, mesmerized, until she realized that somewhere in that kiss the musicians had fallen silent. The whole party had fallen silent—arriving at a screeching halt while every eye in the room watched the kiss playing out.

At last Molly came up for air and stepped away, shoving Axy back a pace and straight into the arms of Keely, who'd gone red-faced from a mix of emotions that didn't seem to contain nearly the overwhelming percentage of jealousy that Jenilee had expected.

"So," Molly's cool voice chimed like a bell in the sudden silence as she looked the three friends over, carefully sizing them up. "You want in, right?"

The three of them nodded.

"Can you sail?" she asked soberly.

"Aye," Axy answered confidently, throwing on his best nautical demeanor, while Keely and Jenilee nodded. They'd never been on any serious voyage, but a girl didn't grow up in Hart Cove without learning her way around a sailing vessel.

"Can you fight?" Molly asked.

"Well enough," Axy said.

"I'm a fair shot with a flintlock," Keely said.

"I can learn," Jenilee said, stiffening her spine despite the voice crying in her head to run home and hide.

Molly gave a little snort that at least sounded more like mild amusement than open derision. She grabbed Axy firmly by the wrist, turned up his palm and studied it for several long seconds. Then she looked him square in the eye. "If I take you on, you'll most likely be dead within the year. If you're not dead within a year, you'll most likely be dead within two."

Axy paled slightly, but his face remained calm. "Her father's going to kill me anyway," he said, giving a backward nod toward Keely, "given that I'm not going to stay away from her."

"Ah...the runaway-young-lovers package deal," Molly said, turning her appraising eye on Keely. "My grandmother had a pair like you on her ship. I hear they worked out...delightfully. A threesome could be that much sweeter." She grinned at Jenilee, who felt sure she'd just gone redder than Keely.

"I...We're not," Jenilee stammered. "Just them!" she concluded with a desperate gesture toward her friends.

"Uh-huh," Molly said, slowly dragging the two primitive syllables out into an entire monologue of incredulity. Though she stood only two inches taller than Jenilee, the woman seemed to tower as she stepped closer and reached to tilt Jenilee's chin up to meet her gaze. "Can you honestly tell me..."

The touch was electric. Jenilee couldn't begin to put words to what she felt, but from Molly's faltering voice and widening eyes, she seemed to be feeling it too.

"You're in," Molly breathed, a grin spreading across her face. "Oh, girl, you are so in." Molly threw her head back and laughed exultantly while Jenilee blinked with astonishment. "You're in!" Molly declared, spinning to jab a finger at Axy. "And you're in!" She turned the finger on Keely. "Everybody's in! Now where's my music?!"

Molly grabbed the two nearest bottles—without concern for their contents or who had been holding them—and shoved them into the hands of Keely and Axy. "We sail whenever I bloody well feel like it," she declared, slapping them on the back simultaneously and shoving them on their way. "Be on the Siren's Song with everyone else, or be left behind."

Jenilee started to head after them, but Molly snagged her by the collar as she passed, busting a seam along Jenilee's shoulder in her haste. "Not you," Molly said. "Not yet."

"No?" Jenilee asked, not at all certain she liked being singled out for the pirate queen's attention.

"No. You and I, we have to talk."

Jenilee added the caves beneath the cellars of the Drunken Squid to the list of things she'd never seen before tonight. In this case, she'd not even been aware of their existence, but now she sat in one of them, alone with Blackwater Molly, the adorable blond scourge of that freshwater sea that lapped at the outer entrance of the cave.

Though they'd come down through a series of concealed stairwells, a longboat drawn up in the cave would easily have allowed them to depart straight onto the lake. The many crates and barrels piled up around the chamber lent it the air of a smuggler's hideout, despite the fact that Molly could have done open business with any man in Hart Cove, in any commodity she chose.

Between that and the nonchalant way Molly had led her down here, Jenilee had to conclude any secrecy was strictly for the benefit of locals like her, to allow them to plead ignorance should any more straight-laced authority figure come calling.

Molly kicked back casually on a crate, with her feet pulled up onto it. "First things first," she said. "Tell me about you."

"You...don't know about me?" Jenilee asked cautiously. "The way you reacted..."

Molly waved a hand dismissively. "Oh, I know who you *are*," she said. "And I dare say *you* know who *I* am. But just how much do you know *about* me? And how much of what you *do* know about me are you confident isn't just silly rumors?"

"Not much," Jenilee admitted.

"So tell me about you," Molly repeated. "No lies. No false modesty. No leaving out stuff because it sounds crazy or because I just wouldn't understand it anyway. Those are the juicy bits, and you're talking to Blackwater Molly now. Who are you really?"

"No one special," Jenilee started. Then she quickly backpedaled when she saw the glare coming onto Molly's face. "I mean, there's nothing about me I think sounds crazy or that people wouldn't understand. Except..."

"Except what?" Molly asked, cocking an eyebrow.

"The Rules," Jenilee said, shrugging sheepishly. "I keep this sort of book in my head. No one else seems to. Not like mine."

"A book?" Molly asked, wrinkling her nose.

"Well, sort of," Jenilee admitted. "I can't read properly. So instead of scribbles, I put other stuff in it: sights and sounds and smells...All sorts of things. When I have a memory I can't afford to forget, or just don't want to ever forget, I press it into the pages of my book, and it stays crisp and new and easy to find. I call it the Rules, because that's what's in it mostly. My mother told me I should make my own rules, and a rule's not a rule if you can't keep proper track of it."

Molly chuckled. "She told you that, did she?"

"Yes, ummm...Aye, Captain?" Jenilee ventured.

Molly laughed again, merrily. "What else did your mother tell you?"

"That's it, really," Jenilee said. "All I can remember. She died when I was very small."

Molly snorted. "She most certainly did not!"

"She...didn't?" Jenilee asked, guardedly studying Molly for any clues that the woman was having her on or simply misinformed. Jenilee had made peace with the death of her mother years ago, but it remained that tentative sort of peace where she simply didn't let herself dwell on what she was missing.

Even before her world had been turned upside down, allowing herself to start thinking she had a living mother out there somewhere, waiting to be found for a tearful reunion, would be inviting in a world of hurt when the hope of it died. Now...?

"Who told you she'd died?" Molly asked seriously.

"My Dad," Jenilee said.

Molly coughed. Then she laughed some more. She rolled her eyes. She shook her head. "Girl, we've got a mess to sort out. Your mother's very much alive and kicking and taking the proverbial names. It's your *father* that's dead. Or at least I thought he was. He didn't adopt, you, did he? Wait, no. It doesn't make sense regardless. But here you are! We'll let him tell his own story when I see him."

"He...*is* dead." Jenilee managed to force the words out through her constricting throat. "Four weeks now, I guess."

"I'm sorry," Molly said sympathetically. "Still, that's...what? A dozen more years than I'd thought he'd had? I'll call it a win for him."

"So how do you know..." Jenilee started, as an attempt to change the subject.

"Who you are?" Molly asked. "You felt it too, when I touched you. I saw it in your eyes. I don't know how you're here, or why. I thought you'd died as a babe along with your father, but there's only one person you *could* be."

"And who is that?" Jenilee asked.

"A force of nature," Molly grinned. "An untamed and untamable hellion to make men swoon and women tremble in fear, or whatever else you want them to tremble with."

"Ah. You've mistaken me for Keely," Jenilee said dryly. "I'll just go fetch her for you."

"No false modesty!" Molly barked, slamming her hand down with such force that it splintered the top of the barrel beside her—but her expression softened somewhat as she saw Jenilee cringing away. "Your friend seems a sweet and amusing little girl," Molly said, not unkindly, "but she's no niece of mine."

Jenilee blinked.

"I get it," Molly said. "But a panther raised among rabbits is still a panther. You'll come into your own. I promise. In the meantime, I've got three gifts to help you on your way, okay?"

Jenilee just nodded, not knowing what to say, not trusting herself to feel anything one way or another. Until this moment she'd hadn't a glimmer of hope she had any family left to her at all. Daring to believe Molly would be setting herself up for a blow she wouldn't *want* to recover from, should the belief prove unfounded.

Molly unbuckled the belt from her hips and held it aloft for a moment, making sure Jenilee's gaze fell on the dagger still dangling in a sheath on it. "First off, a real blade," Molly said, tossing the thing to Jenilee, who caught it reflexively. "That may not look like much, but it's tasted the lives of three men. Anyway, it's just a little something for emergencies, when things come down to try or die. If you like, we can get you some serious steel when you're actually learning to fight."

"Thank you," Jenilee said politely, still not trusting herself to actually feel anything. She could sense the emotions, though, circling like sharks just beneath the surface of her consciousness. When they struck, they'd be going into a feeding frenzy.

"Second..." Molly rolled off her perch and went to a battered, old chest at the back of the cave. The hinges screamed in protest as she forced it open, and she began rummaging around through old clothes and bits of other junk. Now and then she'd pause to look at Jenilee, somehow taking her measure again, until Molly arose carrying an aging pair of boots. "Try these."

Jenilee began to protest that she already had a perfectly serviceable pair of boots, but she stomped on the impulse and sealed it away before her mouth could form any actual words. Refusing the generosity of someone like Molly seemed like it could be a very painful mistake.

She shut her open mouth again, and smiled as graciously as she could manage, accepting the gift. She slipped off her old boots, which had sadly been the only part of her hardened-criminal costume she'd actually liked, and pulled on the stiff old leather with a bit of effort. At least they offered a decent fit, even if they'd seen better days.

"Again, not much of a gift, right?" Molly chuckled. "You don't have to pretend. I know they're dreadful."

"Just a bit," Jenilee admitted, feeling scandalously daring to say as much to Blackwater Molly, even with the prompting.

"But this time," Molly said, a conspiratorial smile spreading across her face, "there's a *lot* more to it than you'd think. Every girl should have a touch of magic at her disposal. Well...every girl in *this* family."

"You mean, *magic* magic?" Jenilee asked, staring down at the boots.

"*Magic* magic," Molly confirmed. "No metaphor about it. Wear those boots. Trust in those boots. Something good will happen. Don't ask me what. *Real* magic doesn't like to be predictable. That's what makes it magic."

Jenilee shrugged and nodded, seeing the sense of that. A giddy feeling of excitement and anticipation surfaced briefly from out of the swirl of her lurking emotion, but she danced back away before it could sink its teeth in. She was going to sail Lake Etherea and become a notorious pirate like Aunt Molly. She was going to see real magic. She was going to be reunited with the mother she'd never known.

She was...not going to dare to believe any of it until she saw it for herself. This was way too much, too fast. She trusted it about as far as— well, something that she trusted very little indeed, whatever that was. At the moment, she was too busy fighting down the urge to be giddy to recall a proper cliché for the occasion.

"And third?" she asked, to give herself something to think about besides all the anticipation she was definitely *not* feeling.

"Oh, nothing much." Molly shrugged. "It's just that I came to town to meet up with my sisters. If you'd like, you're welcome to tag along."

CHAPTER SIX

PAGE THIRTEEN

"No way!" Keely gasped.

"It's what she says," Jenilee said. "Doesn't make it true."

They sat on the only two chairs in the lonely little room above a cobbler's workshop that Jenilee had always shared with her father. Spartan in the extreme, they'd never had much money available to furnish it, and her father had never been one to allow clutter to collect. Even what little there'd been when her father passed from his illness had mostly been sold already out of necessity, or else packed to leave with on short notice.

All that remained aside from the little table, the chairs, a small cabinet full of necessities, and Jenilee's sleeping pallet, were a single tallow candle providing the room's only light, and the bag of things she planned on taking with her.

"Why would she say it if she didn't at least believe it?" Keely protested.

"Doesn't matter, really," Jenilee said doing her best to believe that. "Doesn't change anything. You're my family now."

"Yeah." Keely smiled warmly. "You and me and Axy against the world. But *still!* Around here, being blood to Blackwater Molly changes everything. Jenny, you're like a...a princess! And you're going to meet her sisters? I didn't even know Molly *had* sisters. No one talks about them."

"Not sure I *should* meet them," Jenilee sighed. "What if they realize I'm not who Molly says? We can't afford to have me muck this thing up."

"You worry too much, Jenny," Keely said. "You're a pirate now. Live hard, die young."

"I was kinda hoping for 'live smart, retire rich'."

Keely shrugged. "It could happen. But how much use do you think Molly has for a timid pirate? We've been over this."

"Page eleven." Jenilee sighed. "Thinking everything through is for people with time on their side, which won't be us. Get impulsive or get dead," she recited.

"Right." Keely nodded. "And when you set aside all the scary what-ifs, what's the only reasonable decision left?"

Jenilee grabbed her bag and took a last look around the place. It mightn't be much of a home, but it had been *her* home, and the only one she'd ever known. The ghost of her father hung over it, too. She still couldn't look at the door without expecting to see him walk in, shaking the rain off his cloak and hanging his battered watchman's lantern on its peg. She didn't even have to imagine the lantern as missing from the peg to start the scene. She'd buried him with it.

Part of her had wanted to keep it to remember him by, but in the end she'd decided he'd need it more than her, whether he used it to guide him to Seriena's isles or he decided to hang around here and continue his vigil over Hart Cove.

Drawing in a deep breath, Jenilee cracked open the Rules in her mind and carefully pressed the scene before her, ghost and all, into the first blank page available, along with the sound of her father's voice admonishing her to, "Fight for what you love," as he'd done so many times.

"Page twelve," she murmured, letting out the breath, and stepped out the door after Keely. She caught herself in the middle of locking the door, and she stopped to stare at the key. After a moment's reflection, she pushed the door back open and tossed the key into the little room, where it clattered across the floor. "Come on," she said, and walked away, leaving the door standing ajar.

The night had been warm when they'd gone upstairs, but as they stepped back into the open, an unseasonable chill swept over them. A stiff wind from off the lake had chased the blanketing clouds from the sky, freeing the full, golden moon to brighten the night to something more akin to twilight. The hush of sleep had settled over the town, broken only by the whisper of that wind, the sound of laughter from the nearby Goose and Goblet, and the clopping of a pair of horses disappearing down the street with their curiously cloaked riders. From this distance in the moonlight, Jenilee couldn't make out much about the riders save those cloaks—one so black as to make the night around it seem bright by comparison, one of bloody crimson so vibrant that not even the moonlight seemed to mute it.

The black cloak might have belonged to any number of people, but the red was the vibrant sort of color that few could afford, and fewer still could afford to wear casually around the streets of a backwater town, rather than saving it for special occasions at a royal court. It was the sort of red that burned itself straight into memory without pausing to wait for the eyes or the brain to process it, and left Jenilee with the absolute certainty that she'd never in her life seen that cloak before.

In a town like Hart Cove, where the only strangers' faces one saw tended to belong to ragged, unsavory mariners, that really narrowed the options of whose back she could be looking at.

"Do you think that's your aunt?" Keely whispered, her thoughts having clearly rushed down the same track as Jenilee's.

"My condolences if it is," Holt, the cobbler, said quietly from where he leaned in his doorway nearby. The door stood ajar, but the interior beyond it lay in darkness.

"What do you mean?" Jenilee frowned.

"Strangers in red and black?" the old man said. "That's the Inquisition come for Molly again." He took a slow drag on his pipe before continuing. "They've got no quarrel with a pirate for being a pirate, mind you. That's king's business, as far as they're concerned. But they take exception to an openly heathen pirate queen. The church loses face if they let that sort of thing go unchallenged, even out here."

"They've come for her 'again'?" Jenilee asked.

"They've sent a small army every few years since the days of Molly's mother," the cobbler said. "Of course, they still lost face. It's never gone well for them, and never been—"

Jenilee didn't realize at once why Holt hadn't finished his sentence. One moment she was standing there listening to him, the next she was picking herself up off the ground, wincing at the pain in her shoulder, and wondering why the only sound she could hear was the ringing in her ears. Before she could recover her bearings, she felt the second explosion, and saw flames erupt high into the night sky, somewhere on the far side of the Goose and Goblet, though its sound remained disturbingly muffled despite the violence of it.

Jenilee fought to recover her senses, and to sort out what had happened. The sharp, pervasive scent of burnt gunpowder filled the air, along with clouds of dust and smoke. The riders could no longer be seen, though she couldn't be sure whether that was because they'd gone, or because they'd been swallowed up by the sudden haze.

Down the street to the right, not thirty paces in the direction the riders would have come from, the shattered remnant of Finlay's mercantile now blazed brightly. Just beside Jenilee, Keely was staggering to her feet. Holt also tried to rise, but the older man was having some difficulty at it and looked like he might have hit his head.

Jenilee made sure Keely was steady on her feet, then the two of them went to help Holt off the ground, while Jenilee kept half an eye out for the riders to reappear. If they did, she wasn't sure whether the strangers would be more likely to offer their assistance or to kill anyone who might have seen them ride away from here. Could there *not* be a connection between them and the explosion?

People had begun emerging onto the street in alarm and confusion. Cries of, "Fire!" went up loud enough to faintly penetrate the ringing in Jenilee's ears. A bucket chain began to materialize as if out of nowhere. Holt's wife and grandson appeared, taking over the job of making sure the cobbler had not been seriously injured. Then a third fireball erupted over the rooftops, and a fourth. The crowd's quick foray into an organized response to the crisis began to unravel into panic.

Moments later, it fell apart completely as half a dozen men in red and black swept out of the darkness on horseback, randomly swinging their drawn blades at anyone within reach as they passed. The screams of the crowd took on a new edge of terror as blood glistened in the firelight.

Perhaps it was her near deafening from the first explosion that allowed Jenilee to approach the next few seconds with some measure of detachment. Not being able to properly hear the pain and fear of her neighbors certainly slowed the onset of her own panic and that might have been what bought her the precious clarity to see that one of the riders was on a deadly collision course with Keely, and to drag Keely out of the way a moment before the man's axe would have cut her down.

Jenilee kept right on dragging until she had the both of them off the street and into the shadows between two buildings that seemed—for the moment—to be securely not on fire. She paused then in the darkness, heart pounding, and tried vainly to communicate with her friend. She doubted they'd be able to hear a word from each other under the circumstances without raising their voices to a shout. Given the deadly attention that could have attracted, she gave up on communicating and focused instead on forcing down the threatening flood of emotion in an attempt to think clearly.

Whatever was happening, it had turned her brave new path in life into a nightmare before she could even set foot on it. For all she knew, there were going to be more explosions, and the building she had her back to could be the next powder keg on the list. For all she knew, some maniac with a blade was set to charge down this very alley, swinging at anything that got in his way. For all she knew...

"Page eleven!" Jenilee hissed to herself fiercely. She had to think clearly, not *thoroughly*. Thinking thoroughly would get her killed.

What *did* she know? She knew Holt had said this was the Inquisition come to do battle with Blackwater Molly, and that she—Jenilee— wouldn't be able to come up with a better guess of what was going on even if she racked her brain all night. Therefore, until proven otherwise, that's officially what was happening.

And while she was taking Holt's version of reality as cold, hard truth, accepting that the Inquisition had been trying for an entire generation to take down the pirate queens of Lake Etherea could put the events of the last minute into a terrifying but comprehensible context: the Inquisition had declared active war on anyone in the vicinity *not* taking up arms against Molly, and the explosions signaled the start of open hostilities.

Now she had a working theory that would have to stand in for reality, for want of time to explore other possibilities. It set her teeth on edge even trying to stop thinking it out there, but rules were rules and there were lives on the line.

So she was trapped in a war zone with her best friend, and still untrained in battle. That didn't leave much option but to run. But where to run to? Anything she'd normally consider "shelter" seemed likely to burst into flames without notice. They could head for the Siren's Song, but doing so would surely be heading into the thick of the battle. So leave town? There'd be plenty of places to hide in the swamp, but...

She closed her eyes and groaned, leaning back against the alley wall. "Page twelve?" she asked the sky. "Already? Seriously?"

So the question wasn't what she should do, but what did she love. Maybe if she'd been any sort of warrior, she would have said, "Hart Cove," or, "the people of Hart Cove". But she wasn't any sort of warrior yet, and she'd been ready to leave all that behind forever. All that remained to her that she *truly* loved were Keely and Axy—and now, *maybe*, her Aunt Molly?

Hart Cove would live or die without her. No bloody way could she save the whole town, so there lay her crystal-clear priorities: escape this chaos alive, take her friends with her, and save the pirate queen if it wouldn't endanger the other two.

Keely seemed to have finished ordering her own thoughts at precisely the same moment, and even amid the noise and in the scant light of the alley, they knew they'd announced a single conclusion together. "We've got to get to Axy!"

Keely pulled the flintlock pistol she'd brought with her when she'd said farewell to her own home earlier in the evening. The act reminded Jenilee of Molly's gifts. She reached for the new blade her aunt had given her, but imagined herself holding it as she hurried through the dark streets filled with panicked crowds, and abandoned the idea. Instead she settled for simply touching the hilt where it hung from her belt, to reassure herself it was there.

Then the two girls set out through the familiar back ways between the buildings, slowing only when billowing smoke drowned out the moon- and firelight as they ran toward the Drunken Squid. If Axy stuck to their plan for slipping away in the night, that's where he'd be waiting for them.

Hart Cove was no little village. It had the market. It had the garrison. It had the harbor. It even had a couple of streets with actual cobbles instead of dirt. No surprise, then, that even at a dead run, it took them a few minutes to get across town. While they ran, the ringing in Jenilee's ears began to fade, but she almost wished it hadn't. Screams of pain and panic dogged their heels, some raised from voices she recognized despite the emotion distorting them. The clanging of the garrison alarm bell competed with the ring of steel and the crack of musket fire.

Cannons began to roar. Three more powder kegs blew. One of them tore open the stone wall of the garrison tower that dominated the Hart Cove skyline, sending out shards of rock far enough to rain down on them as they ran. One sharp fragment glanced stingingly off of Jenilee's cheek—drawing blood—at about the same time they arrived at the clifftop overlooking the harbor. The three largest vessels in the harbor—two merchant ships and the Siren's Song—had all been set ablaze, as had half a dozen fishing boats.

Figures down on the pirate vessel could be seen rushing about, fighting the flames, even as her guns returned fire on the small fleet of black warships now blockading the harbor entrance.

This could be no simple raid or skirmish they were caught in, but a long-planned and vicious trap to catch up the entire town when Molly was in port. Agents of the Inquisition must have been in town for weeks or months to set those charges, to say nothing of the planning and coordination it would take to get that fleet to where it was right now without it being sighted well in advance. People were going to die tonight—lots of people. Most of them would be people Jenilee had known all her life. Hart Cove itself might be left as little more than a bloody cinder.

When they arrived in front of the tavern, it wasn't Axy they found waiting for them but Molly and a half-dozen hardened members of her crew, all standing with their backs to the door, blades drawn and discharged pistols discarded on the ground. Around them waited a ring of men in livery of red and black, at least three times their number but in no rush to throw themselves at the pirates' blades. Dead and dying of both factions lay tumbled in the no-man's-land between them.

Most of the remaining pirates had been bloodied, including Molly herself, but still she seemed to be holding the forces of the Inquisition beyond arm's reach as much with the intensity of her gaze and her ferocious, confident grin as by any threat of her blades.

"Blackwater Molly!" a knight of the Inquisition bellowed, stepping forward. He was a big man, armored in a suit of ornate steel that shone red in the firelight. "I am Lord Auron, Master at Arms of the Knights of the Inquisition, right hand of the Grand High Inquisitrix. You have been found guilty of countless heresies and other crimes against Mother Church and our lady, Seriena. Repent and surrender yourself, that your soul might yet be salvaged in her eyes."

"Wow," Molly said. "You people honestly talk like that?"

"Do not mock me, witch," Auron growled. "Personally, I'd as soon see you dead. I can't imagine there's anything worth saving in that shriveled little thing you call a soul."

"You're the one calling it a soul," Molly answered. "Personally, I call it Bosun Taggart. But be nice. Just imagine what *you'd* look like after fifty years at sea."

"It is, as they say, your funeral, but I shall offer leniency one last time. Any man who surrenders by a five count can walk free. Surrender yourself, Molly, and I'll spare your crew."

The offer met with a very ungentlemanly chorus of derision from the men at Molly's side.

"You're the outlaw here, sir," Molly spat. "You've broken my peace and killed my people. Surrender, and you have my word as the Queen of Lake Etherea that I'll not keep you begging for death for more than a week or two."

"Five!" Auron snapped. "Four!"

That was when Keely stepped out of the shadows, leveled her pistol, and calmly shot Lord Auron in the back from fifteen feet away. The man staggered a step forward, then failed to crumple to the ground like a puppet with its strings cut. What he did do was slowly turned around, glowering.

"It would seem it takes a bigger weapon than that to punch through steel plate, girl," he growled. Jenilee lost the fight to pretend she wasn't terrified, and simply froze wide-eyed in place behind Keely, who suddenly wasn't doing much better with the whole bravery thing. Keely let the empty flintlock clatter forgotten to the ground.

With a barely human howl, Molly launched herself like a wildcat, crossing the distance to the Inquisition in something akin to two heartbeats. Lord Auron, weighed down in the heavy steel plates that had saved him from Keely's gunshot, had barely begun to turn when Molly hit him in the back. The fully armored man might have weighed three times what Molly did, but what weight she had now came charged with fifteen yards of predatory acceleration, and she applied it with the express purpose of adding to the load on his shoulders. The net effect left him suddenly top-heavy while in the off-balance act of attempting to spin. She bore him instantly to the ground, and he landed hard on the shoulder of his sword arm.

Few of Auron's followers had actually taken their eyes off of Molly, but for that moment in time, all had at least been trying to split their attention in two completely different directions in the instinctive attempt to assess the new threat at their backs. By the time they'd re-focused themselves enough to intervene, Molly's men had come charging in behind her, and Molly herself had dropped her saber, pulled a stiletto, and plunged it with deadly, unhesitating precision under Auron's unarmored chin, into his throat.

When the first enemy blade came swinging at her, she was already rolling away and reaching for her saber. The brief moment of calm that the stand-off had bought amidst the swirling storm of chaos vanished.

"Run, girl!" Molly screamed at Jenilee above the renewed ringing of steel. "I'll not take getting yourself dead as an excuse to avoid meeting your mother!"

Jenilee ran, her buckling resolve to live up to the freshly inked "page twelve" happy for any excuse to do so. Keely ran with her. They'd barely gone fifty feet before Jenilee saw the tall, dark figure rushing through the shadows after them. With an involuntary shriek, Jenilee grabbed Keely by the wrist and dragged her once more into the deeper darkness between buildings, not daring to slow despite the danger of colliding with some unseen obstacle in the alley.

"Keely! Jenny!"

The girls skidded to a halt; then their momentum reversed. In a moment, Keely had flung herself at their pursuer, breathlessly kissing Axy all over the face.

"We're under orders to run and hide!" Jenilee blurted as she stopped a few feet short, letting her friends have their moment.

"Good," Axy said when Keely's assault had abated to the point that he could. "I'm under orders to..."

An ear-piercing shriek rose above the din, and the three friends turned to see Molly stagger. What remained of the Inquisition force around her seemed poised to break and run, but the shaft of an arrow protruded from her stomach—unmistakable even at this distance and in this light, thanks to the flames that had already leapt from it to Molly's clothes. The pirate queen screamed again, lashing out blindly with her saber as she spun in disoriented pain.

"Orders be damned," Jenilee snarled. As she charged back toward Molly, a small, logical part of her brain noticed with satisfaction that it was in no way being consulted about what should happen next, and she added a quick endorsement of herself for it onto page eleven of the Rules.

She found herself stopping to tear the cloak from the body of the first fallen soldier she came to; then she rose and resumed her charge toward Molly. She paused only to consider her best hope of dodging the wildly swinging blade while she adjusted her grip to spread the cloak, but in that moment of her hesitation, a figure in red and black swept in on horseback and a vicious swing from his axe connected solidly with Molly's rib cage. Molly flew ten feet through the air to land in a heap, the axe lodged firmly between her ribs. As Jenilee looked on in horror, the great war horse wheeled around and came back to trample the fallen pirate queen, her bones snapping under its hooves with sickening finality.

The impulsive part of Jenilee that had made her run to Molly's aid apparently divorced itself completely from the rest of her brain in that moment, and it began shouting instructions to her body while the rest of her mind just looked on in shock. She felt nothing, heard little more than the screams that seemed to be coming from her own mouth, but saw the eyes of the young knight on horseback, boring dispassionately into hers, taking her measure as they tried to decide whether this screaming girl posed enough of a threat to bother with dispatching at that precise moment.

She saw herself struggling to throw off the arms of Axy and Keely as they fought to drag her back away from the battle. She saw the volleys of flaming arrows streaking across the night sky, igniting anything that the explosions hadn't already. She saw Hart Cove burn in the cleansing, holy fire of the Inquisition's wrath.

At some point, she stopped screaming and resisting, and allowed herself to simply be dragged while she sobbed uncontrollably. Then she'd been flung over Axy's shoulder and bounced along there while her friends ran. As the first rush of horror ebbed, Jenilee's rational mind began clawing back to regain the control her emotions had vacated. The last thing her friends needed at the moment was to have her reduced to this senseless baggage. Her legs worked just fine. She only had to use them.

Jenilee began to struggle again, and told Axy to put her down, but her protests got drowned out by a new round of screams. Townsfolk surged past them in a panicked mob. Instead of being lowered to the ground, she found herself flung there when someone collided with Axy. It was all she could do to curl up into a protective ball and weather the crush of fleeing feet.

Somewhere beyond it all, a woman's voice rang out above the chaos, outraged to the point of sounding half unhinged. "No forgiveness! No quarter! You die tonight! You *all die!*"

When Jenilee finally dared uncurl—covered in bruises, and with blood trickling from her nose and busted lip—she looked up to find herself filled with a cold, horrible sense of déjà vu. Astride a black and dreadful charger sat the rider in the unforgettable red cloak who'd been there at the moment the world went mad.

Though she rode alone this time, she managed to radiate a level of menace which Auron and all his entourage together had failed to achieve. A bloody axe in one hand and a the reins of her charger in the other, she slashed wantonly at anyone the wheeling beast brought within her reach, and the blood-red cloak whipping about her seemed to blaze with a fire of its own, just as it had in Jenilee's nightmare vision back at the Drunken Squid.

A shot rang out. The rider jerked. She tumbled from the saddle, but somehow managed to land in a crouch rather than a sprawl. Even before she regained her feet, she hurled the axe and a man in the uniform of the town garrison went down with the weapon protruding from his throat, his spent flintlock tumbling from his fingers.

"You all die!" the woman screamed again, no longer sounding merely half unhinged. She grimaced for a moment as her hand touched her shoulder where the ball from the gun must have struck, and her fingers came away bloody, but she gave no other indication of feeling the pain. She just grabbed another axe that hung from the saddle of the horse and began to lay about her again like a woman possessed.

Another man from the garrison stepped between her and a fleeing girl, and he managed to parry the woman's axe before taking her knee in his stomach. Her axe flashed again, and the man crumpled before her onslaught. Then she spun on the man who'd been stepping up behind her, cut his throat with one neat slash, and hurried on, not even stopping to notice that her latest victim had actually been wearing the livery of the Inquisition. Jenilee had seen men in a drunken rage, but whatever insanity or religious ecstasy drove this woman had taken her past that and into levels of berserk fury that barely seemed human. Worse, she swung the axe like she'd been born with it in her hand—or perhaps with a meat cleaver. This certainly smelled more of butchery than of battle.

Jenilee realized she'd frozen again when Axy grabbed her by the arm and hauled her back to her feet, but she fought free of his grip and she staggered a step away. "No!" she shouted at him.

"No?" Axy gave her a puzzled frown as Keely appeared at his shoulder.

"I'm not doing this again! I *can't* do this again!" Jenilee said, tears streaming down her face.

"Jenny, snap out of it!" Keely screamed as the madwoman in red, drenched in blood, ran out of victims within easy reach and began stalking relentlessly in their direction. "We have to go! Now!"

"I'm so sorry," Jenilee sobbed. "You're both dead. You're already dead."

"Jenny!" Keely screamed desperately.

"Five...five hundred and...sixty-two," Jenilee stammered.

"What?!" Axy demanded.

"Five hundred and sixty-two," Jenilee managed more levelly, though she still felt like she was choking on the words. "The number of tally marks on page thirteen. The number of times I've...watched her...kill you."

The world dwindled into just one small sphere of light around the three of them at that admission, the sounds of the chaos reaching them, but slow and distorted and muffled.

"Jenny, I'm already plenty scared," Keely said. "You don't need to scare me more."

"At first, I saw it every time I closed my eyes," Jenilee sighed miserably. "It comes a lot less now, mostly when I let myself get stressed or scared, but that's still way too much.

"*I* was supposed to be the one to die, you idiots! Me!" she sobbed. "I was dead weight. You two could have saved each other and gone off on your happily ever after! What good is *me* alone?

"You know what's on page thirteen?" Jenilee demanded angrily. "You know what's on page thirteen?!" A well-worn and serious-looking tome appeared in her hand, and she flipped familiarly through it. "*This is what's on page thirteen!*" As she thrust the open book toward them, a vision unfolded within the vision, and there she was two days older on a gray and dismal morning in which it was impossible to tell lingering smoke from lingering fog.

Caked in mud and covered with bites from mosquitoes and leeches, she stumbled slowly up the hill from the swamp. Around her stretched a plain of mud and ash, populated with crumbling black timbers, fire-scorched stone walls, and the countless forgotten corpses of people she'd known her whole life.

Not a soul moved in the ruins of Hart Cove, only the ravens raucously feasting on the dead. Not a building remained intact. Not a ship or boat remained in harbor that hadn't been left scorched, broken, and mostly submerged. The choking air smelled of blood and death and ash.

Jenilee didn't actually vomit, having nothing in her stomach to lose, but it took quite some time for her to finish retching. When at last the spasms subsided, she pushed herself back up to her knees, and drove the heel of her hand fiercely across her cheeks, leaving streaks of muddy ash under her eyes.

"Dry your tears, girl," Jenilee's voice prodded contemptuously from within the pages of the rules. "Because *no one* is coming to do it for you."

CHAPTER SEVEN

INQUIRING MINDS

Keely woke disoriented, with her head pounding and her stomach churning, but managed to take some small comfort in the fact that she didn't have to—*never* had to—fight Jenny for control of her head after those nightmares. She loved her friend dearly, but the girl lacked the stomach to stick around in their aftermath, and would retreat into whatever dark corner of reality she liked to hide in.

Behind her she would leave nothing more than the fading dream, a body still overcharged with emotion, and another tally mark on page thirteen of the Rules. This time, though, the woman in red refused to fade with the rest of the dream—or at least the red she'd been in did. Through the darkness and haze and chaos and blood, Keely hadn't gotten a good enough look at the woman to recognize her if they'd been standing nose to nose, but that cape...

She shivered and realized about that time that she lay on her side in near total darkness against a cold stone floor, her cheek and her ear resting in a shallow puddle. She went to crawl out of it, only to discover that her hands hand been chained behind her back. She tried to twist her shoulders and roll away, but the effort set off a small explosion in her head, and with a little yelp of pain she let that go as a bad business too.

"I guess that means you're awake," a woman's voice asked out of the darkness.

"Only against my better judgment," Keely groaned. "Whatever it is you think I've done, you've got the wrong girl."

"Oh, yeah. *That* line *always* wows the Inquisition. 'Really? Gosh, I'm sorry. I wish you'd told us before we burned down your cattle and chopped off several of your limbs.' Skip the excuses and tell me what you thought you were up to, ransacking the library."

Keely kept her silence for a few moments while the gears in her brain began to sluggishly turn. "Elissa?" she asked at last.

It was her interrogator's turn to be silent for a moment. "All right..." she finally said hesitantly. "Let's skip the first question for now and ask who the heck are you and how do you know me?"

"You're with the Inquisition?" Keely asked incredulously.

"Yes," the postulant answered after another brief pause.

"No you're not." Keely sighed with as much relief as she could muster over anything at the moment. "Just tried that line myself, and much more convincingly—for all the good it did me. So either they've released me to the tender care of the abbey—which I'm *sure* didn't happen—or you're taking a huge risk by interfering with their business. And it's not like I have anything you want. They even took my boots," she said wiggling her toes in the cold, dank air. Then the realization hit her hard. "They took my boots!" she howled.

Suddenly oblivious to the pain shooting through her head, she thrashed around on the floor until she'd found a wall to beat her feet against to release the rage and frustration. "They *took **my boots!***"

"Hush!" Elissa scolded urgently. "You *don't* want them down here a moment sooner than they were already planning. Just count yourself lucky they didn't take your dress."

Keely calmed herself, but lay on the floor panting and seething for at least a full minute before she was able to speak again without shouting. "So what do I know that's worth risking your life to find out?" she asked at last.

"You're not in a position to be asking the questions here," Elissa said with a frown barely visible in the faint light, but clearly conveyed in her voice.

"On the contrary. I'm in no position to be *answering* questions. I've got nothing to lose, and the only card I have to play is whatever I know that you don't. So you do me a favor first, or I take everything I know to the infernal pits with me."

Elissa gave a frustrated sigh. "If you're going to..."

"Bring me my boots," Keely cut her off.

"What is it that's so special about your boots?"

"Just bring me my boots," Keely insisted.

"Do you have a key in them? A weapon? I won't..."

"They're *my* boots, and *nobody* messes with them. I'll get myself out of this just fine, thank you, but I'm not leaving without my boots—so this will all come off a lot simpler for everybody if you'll only round them up and bring them to me."

"That's it?" Elissa asked suspiciously. "Just boots?"

"*My* boots. Good, sturdy, comfortable, lived-in boots of great sentimental value," Keely said.

"Would I even recognize them if I saw them?"

"They've got a little paw-print design stamped into all the edging. Can't miss it."

"And if I can manage to find them and bring them to you," Elissa asked, "you'll what...?"

"Tell you anything you like."

"Will it be the truth?"

"If that's what you like." Keely shrugged as best she could while lying on the floor with her hands behind her back.

"All right. I'll see if I can find out what's become of them," Elissa agreed, and she disappeared quietly back into the darkness.

Keely just lay there in the timeless darkness, humming softly to herself and tapping her bare feet on the wall—for what could just as easily have been twenty minutes or two hours—before she heard the soft scuffle of Elissa's returning footsteps. "Found them?" she asked.

"Yes," Elissa said, crouching down to lay them in front of Keely's face. "I'm not proud of what I had to do to get them, but they're your rightful property, so here you are."

"Where were they? What did you have to do?"

"I don't want to talk about it."

"If you didn't really want to talk about..."

"Stop it!" Elissa snapped. "I was in a bad mood before and I'm in a worse mood now. You really don't want inside my head."

"All right," Keely said. "But I can barely tell these are boots, much less mine. Did you happen to bring any light with you?"

"How about some sunlight?"

"You carry that around, do you?" Keely asked, quizzically.

"Just hush," Elissa said shortly, helping Keely to her feet. "Follow me and keep quiet." She scooped up the boots in one hand and laid the other on Keely's shoulder as she led the way deeper into the gloom.

They'd only gone a few paces when Keely let out a half-stifled yelp behind Elissa, and started cursing under her breath.

"What?" Elissa hissed.

"Stubbed my toe. Could we maybe go ahead and get those boots on me?"

"Yeah. Trying to feel my way while leading you and holding them isn't working, anyway."

Keely leaned up against the cold, stone wall while Elissa helped her into the boots, then they continued cautiously on their way.

"Better?" Elissa asked.

"You have no idea," Keely whispered. "So, uh…What exactly are we doing?"

"Escaping," Elissa replied quietly. "You wanted that, right?"

"I told you I'd handle that myself."

"Are you trustworthy?"

"Not particularly, no."

"There you go then," Elissa whispered as they squeezed through a tiny space barely wide enough for them to fit sideways. At first Keely could feel stone on one side and wood on the other, but before long it was stone on both sides.

"But why?"

"Because I'm not as self-serving as you think. Because I don't care who you are or why you're here, what you've done or what you intend to do. For all I know you might deserve a headsman's axe, but no one actually deserves the Inquisition. They're everything a priestess should never be, and if I stand by and leave you to them when I could be saving you, I'm in the wrong line of work myself. No matter what you think, some people just do the right thing to do the right thing."

Keely accepted the answer without further comment, and they worked their way through a series of dank, claustrophobic, pitch-dark tunnels. "Isn't it customary to have guards on a prisoner? And locked doors?" she asked at last. "That sort of thing?"

"Yes. But keeping prisoners at Belgrimm Abbey isn't customary," Elissa said. "What *is* customary is building hidden passages and forgetting about them. Just exploring dusty corners of the library, I found three different maps to tunnels built during the abbey expansions in three different centuries, each seeming oblivious to the existence of the older tunnels. All we had to do to get out of your cellar was squeeze behind some barrels and out through a corner that the blackhoods never peeked into."

"Pity you weren't on hand *before* our lady Jane came looking for me," Keely said. "Wait, did you hear that?" She stopped suddenly.

"Hear what?" Elissa—who'd taken a step or two on—whispered as she groped back in the darkness for Keely.

"Sssh!" Keely hissed urgently.

"All I hear is your chains clinking," Elissa whispered.

"I'll ask for quieter chains next time someone throws me in a dungeon," Keely answered, but she managed to stop the rattling. "Maybe it was just echoes," she said after a few seconds of silence, "but I could have sworn I heard someone following us."

"Just keep moving," Elissa whispered. "Any blackhoods trying to follow us would either get lost in nothing flat or give themselves away with whatever light they've brought." Finally finding Keely's shoulder again, Elissa pushed on through the darkness and up a couple of flights of stairs.

At last they emerged, blinking, into the light of a disused, cobweb-ridden room with a small window overlooking an alley outside the abbey. "I'm the only one who's been here in years," Elissa said, pointing a toe at a set of footprints in the dust. "You've got your boots, there's a way out, and if we can manage to wrestle your chains under your feet..."

"Don't worry about that," Keely said, draping the empty manacles over Elissa's shoulder as she stepped past to peer out the window.

"But..." Elissa stammered.

"Oh, and thanks," Keely said, smiling with satisfaction as she looked up and down the empty alleyway, then she pulled her head back inside and leaned against the wall. "You really did me a good turn. I owe you, and I may not be trustworthy in general, but I do pay my debts. So what did you want to ask me?"

"Well, you can start by telling me how you got out of those chains!" Elissa said.

"Oh, blast!" Keely slammed her forehead into the heels of her hands. "I promised, didn't I?"

"You promised," Elissa nodded, with only a trace of smugness.

"Well, I'm not a witch or a demon, okay?" Kelly groaned.

"Did anyone say you were?" Elissa asked with a puzzled frown.

"Okay—maybe just a little. I don't know where you draw the line. The point is there are people who would turn me over to the Inquisition for the answer to that question."

"Even if I would, I'm in too deep to do that now. So tell me already."

"You're sure you wouldn't rather..."

"Just tell me!"

"Okay, okay..." Keely raised her hands in a gesture of surrender. "But I'd better just show you."

"This isn't going to hurt, is it?" Elissa asked warily. "Because if this is like one of those stories that ends with some horrible magic trick that..."

"Oh, hush." Keely took a step out from the wall, raised her hands high above her head with the palms splayed outward, then took a deep breath as she closed her eyes in concentration. A few moments passed, and just as Elissa began to ask if that was all that was going to happen, Keely began to shrink very rapidly.

In the blink of an eye, she'd simply vanished into her own dress, which then tumbled to the floor. While Elissa still stood blinking her eyes a few more times, whatever remained under that little red dress squirmed about a bit before emerging through the neck hole as a small, white long-haired cat.

"Bookend?!" Elissa gasped.

The cat gave a little acknowledging nod before raising up and making a small leap into the air, expanding in a rush as it did, back into the figure of Keely—a figure made all the more obvious because her clothes remained in heap on the floor. Elissa fidgeted awkwardly while she half-watched Keely sort unselfconsciously through the pile of clothes to reassemble her outfit.

"It's a pretty smooth transition, really, if you don't wriggle around and get everything out of place. So I just got down and went feline, let the chains fall off, and back human while I still knew I'd come popping back out in all the right places. You're not going to freak now, are you?"

"No...umm...No. But how come the boots...?"

"Changed with me when nothing else did?" Keely grinned, pausing in pulling her shift on over her head to hold up a still-shod foot for display. "Nobody messes with my footwear. Not even magic. Now are there going to be a lot of questions?" she asked as she finished tugging the hem of her shift into place and reached for her dress. "Because if this is going to take a while, I could really use something to eat first."

"How about a few questions, then we take a break if it starts to run long?" Elissa asked.

"Fair enough." Keely shrugged.

"Well, you've already answered one of them," Elissa said. "I was sure you'd come for just the one book, not that whole mess you left in the alley. Now I know *how* you knew about it, but...No, stop. If you're Bookend..."

"Keely," Keely said.

"What?!" Elissa asked.

"My name's Keely. You'll ask eventually, so let's get that cleared up."

"All right: Keely," Elissa sighed. "You've completely thrown off my chain of thought..."

"I do that a lot." Keely nodded.

"Look, do you do any other magic tricks," Elissa asked, "or just the one?"

"*Just* the one?" Keely replied incredulously. "*Just* the *one*? How many people do you know who can do even *one*?"

"Maybe a couple. Miraculata Cosima, of course—she *is* a miraculata—and..." Elissa stopped at the less-than-pleasant expression growing on Keely's face. "But I've never seen a trick in the same league as that one. Real show-stopper."

"Why, thank you," Keely said, her expression softening again.

"It's just, you know, witches are supposed to know lots of different spells, and some of them can turn into cats..."

"Pfft." Keely snorted. "All a witch can turn into is a pile of ash when the Inquisition's through with her. You ever met a witch?"

Elissa just gave an embarrassed little shrug.

"I'm not a witch. I'm not a demon. I'm a girl who lucked into exactly one magical talent. I didn't even sell my soul for it, so let's move on and stay focused. I'm hungry, remember?"

Elissa started to speak, but stopped suddenly, and held up a hand for silence. In the ensuing quiet, muffled voices could be heard filtering into the room. Quickly but quietly, she slipped out a dark little hall with Keely trailing cautiously behind. It soon brought them to a row of narrow window slits looking down into a vaulted chapel from high on the wall.

In the room below, Miraculata Cosima could be seen exchanging words with the High Inquisitrix, while Sir Riordan stood impassively nearby—the tension in the air between the two women tangible even from this distance, despite the fact that their voices remained level.

"I've got to hand it to you, Jane, dear," Cosima said, looking up at the slender, dark-haired woman who would have stood a head taller than the full-figured little blond even if she hadn't positioned herself atop the chapel dais. I know that finding conspiracies in every shadow is your life's calling, but this...this is a real piece of work. You've outdone yourself."

"*This* is *not* paranoia, Cosima," Jane said, pulling a book from the lectern—the same journal Keely had brought to the abbey—and tossing it to the floor in front of Cosima's feet. The echoes of it slamming into the stone floor reverberated through the chapel. "It's heresy. And we've pieced together the whole tangled, sordid story, with you at the center of the web."

"*Me*?" Cosima stifled a laugh only by turning it into a snort. "Jane, even if your accusations were the least bit plausible—which they're not—I'm *not* the woman you want to go picking a fight with. You can't touch me, and if you even try, I'll take you over my knee and teach you some of the manners you should have learned as a child."

"The parlor tricks you call miracles may have you in the good graces of the Angelis," Jane answered calmly, refusing to be baited, "but I wouldn't go betting my life on having her support once she reads the lies you've been passing around. I have witnesses who saw your little helper in the library pass this off to you, then saw you pass it off to your conspirator—who tried to smuggle it out of the abbey."

"She means us, doesn't she?" Elissa whispered. "That's it. My life's over."

"Tell me, Jane," Cosima asked, "did you tell your 'witnesses' what you wanted to hear before you had their fingers broken, or did they just make a lucky guess at what words would appease you?" Cosima asked, finally stooping to pick up the book and begin thumbing through it. "What horrors is this filthy thing supposed to contain, anyway?"

"You mean *besides* the supposed whereabouts of the Grimm Truth?"

This time Cosima totally failed to stifle her laugh. "A faerie story? Jane, you're ready to start killing people over a faerie story?"

"You didn't notice the blood you stepped in on the way in, did you?" Jane asked wryly. "Of course I'm not ready to *start*. The question is how hard you want to make it on yourself come your turn."

"No!" Cosima snapped, finally allowing a bit of temper to show. "No, the question is, do you *ever* think *anything* through, or do you just act on whatever impulse enters that messed up little head of yours? Antonia Grimm gave her life for the church. She did not slink off like a coward to write some damning book full of fool's predictions and scullery-maid gossip. No one is going to *find* the Grimm Truth *because it just doesn't exist*. And this..." Cosima snapped the book shut and let it fall back to the floor. "...this 'old' journal is some charlatan's cheap forgery. It's probably so new I could get ink stains just from handling it."

"Of course the book is full of lies," Jane countered. "That's exactly what makes it dangerous."

"What will make this book dangerous is *you* sending everyone into hysterics over it. You could have just tossed it in a random fireplace to be forgotten, but no; every person you bully, every person you torture, every person you kill over this book will add the weight of her own belief to its importance until it takes on a life of its own. There is no conspiracy, and this book means nothing. Burn it to ashes right now, Jane, and just let it die."

"Hysterics," Jane said matter-of-factly, "are the fire that cleanse. Why on earth would I want to avoid sending people into hysterics?"

Just then, the side door to the chapel opened, and a black-robed inquisitrix ushered a graying peddler woman roughly into the room. "Ophelia!" Keely gasped quietly.

"Ah! Now we get to it," Jane said with a predatory grin. "Tell me, woman, is this the mysterious 'Lady A' who hired you to find this abominable book?"

Ophelia's hands shook as she stared studiously at the floor. "Yes," she said quietly.

"Don't you think that might sound a bit more damning," Cosima asked, "if perhaps she'd actually *looked* at me? I'm bored with this charade, Jane. We're done here." Cosima turned away with a dismissive wave of her hand, and headed out the main doors of the chapel.

"Oh, no. You do *not* walk out on *me*," Jane snapped, hopping down from the dais to follow Cosima. "*I* say when we're done here." She paused at the doorway just long enough to call back, "Shoshona, get that vagabond locked back up."

The doors closed behind the four retreating women, leaving Sir Riordan alone in the chapel. He shook his head and gave a wry little chuckle as he crouched to pick up the fallen book. Holding it at arm's length, a bit gingerly, he began to dust it off, and was just looking around for a better place to set it down when he heard a loud clang from outside the side door. He stared at the door curiously for a moment, listening for some clue to the origin of the odd noise.

After several seconds of silence, he gave a mental shrug, and returned to his search, finally deciding to simply lay the book on the edge of the dais. Even as he did, the side door creaked open a few inches. As he straightened up and turned to face the opening door, a small, white blur shot out from the gap. The next thing he knew there was a little bundle of feline fury hurtling straight at his face with a menacing hiss, claws and fangs bared.

The startled knight threw his arms protectively across his face in anticipation of a collision that never came—or that at least never took the form he expected. Mid leap, Keely transformed back into a woman, slamming into Riordan with the full force of her essentially naked body, with one very precisely placed knee.

"Now *that's* how it was supposed to work," she smirked as Riordan folded up onto the floor. "You want a mastermind, here's your mastermind," she added, delivering a solid kick to his head before he could begin to recover. "Be sure and give your mistress my thanks for wasting so much time on the fools I duped. Now I've got a book to go find. The next time you see this little witch she'll be sitting with the

Angelis, going over the passage where it says what a phenomenally *stupid* idea it would be to establish an inquisition."

She gave him one last kick before grabbing the book from the dais and heading for the door. Riordan staggered to his feet just in time to see her blow him a kiss as she disappeared through it.

Riordan reached the door as quickly as he could manage on unsteady feet—but found nothing beyond it in the statue-lined corridor but a little white cat leaping over the crumpled, black-clad form of Sister Shoshona and out a window into the alley below. Riordan leaned against the windowsill, watching the cat until it had scuttled off around a corner. With a resigned sigh, he went to check on the fallen inquisitrix, then lifted the unconscious woman in his arms and carried her back into the chapel.

When they'd gone, Elissa slipped furtively out through a drapery behind a statue of a particularly pious looking miraculata, grabbed the book Keely had stashed there, then vanished back into the narrow stairwell behind the curtain.

"Please," Ophelia said plaintively as Elissa pushed past the older woman on her way up the stairs. "They've got my daughters."

"Where?" Elissa asked.

Night had long since fallen over the city as Ophelia pushed her way through the lamp-lit revelry of the working-class crowds on Dunley Lane. Behind her, Elissa clutched her traveling cloak tightly about her like a security blanket, both to shield herself from the unaccustomed chaos and to keep the postulant's robes under it from drawing unwanted attention.

Ophelia's daughters never lagged more than a step or two behind until the four women slipped at last through the door of the Rusty Mug Meade Hall. They stood for a moment, peering into shadows only marginally less thick than the ones on the street, until they saw Keely smiling at them from a corner table.

"What are you looking so smug for?" Ophelia glowered at Keely as she pulled up a chair across the table.

"What's *not* to look smug about?" Keely chuckled quietly. "Even forgetting any 'I told you so', when do you think was the last time four miscreants slipped right out from under Jane Carver's nose, much less walked off with her prize in the process?" She hesitated a moment. "You do have the book, don't you?"

Elissa pulled the book briefly out from under her cloak for Keely to see. "But what now?" she sighed. "That had to be me she was accusing of delivering the book to Cosima. I can't go back. And the four of you can only disappear into the city for so long before the Inquisition comes knocking. They have a nasty talent for finding people."

"Before I answer that," Keely said, "I've got a couple of questions of my own. Of all the women in the Inquisition, our High Inquisitrix is the only one I've ever seen who didn't dress in black. How many others are allowed to wear red?"

"None," Elissa answered with a shrug. "No other priestess wears red, period. It's her color of office."

"And who held the office..." Keely paused for some mental math. "Seven years ago?"

"Jane Carver's been leading the Inquisition for a dozen years or more."

Keely closed her eyes and nodded slowly, her expression briefly going stone cold.

"They took the wagon, too, you know," Ophelia groaned. "Everything was in there. I could have gone straight on the money from those heists."

"Not that you would have," Keely said, the unaccustomed sobriety on her face melting into a smirk.

"But I *could* have. I could be a respectable woman right now living in a respectable townhouse, leading a life of respectable debauchery. Instead I'm a pauper living a few steps ahead of the law, just like alwa—"

Keely interrupted her by sliding a leather pouch across the table toward Ophelia. "My share wasn't in the wagon. You can take it with my blessing and go buy that town house—in a town far, far away—or you can come with me and make some real money. I've got my next game all picked out."

"Bigger and more grand than any game we've run before?" Ophelia chuckled.

"Positively epic." Keely grinned.

"Then we'll take the money, thanks," Ophelia said, quickly scooping up the pouch before the offer could be withdrawn. "I'm tired, Keely, and you were right. That was one scare too many."

"Well, I..." Madeline started.

"Think carefully, girl." Ophelia raised a cautioning hand. "I know you've been having a lot of fun with Keely's 'bigger and better' things, but we just hit the limit. Do you really think you'll ever call it closer than we just did and still walk away with your life? When I walk out of here, I'm going to disappear forever, and the easy, comfortable life in this pouch is going to disappear with me. Do you want to be a shooting star on a grand adventure, or do you want some creature comforts and maybe live to see twenty-five?"

Madeline sighed. "Can I sleep on that one?"

"Of course, dear," Ophelia said, patting her hand. "I said I was tired. These aching bones won't be going any further before the sun comes up, and then with any luck they'll only have to take me as far as the nearest cart for hire."

"What about me?" Elissa asked with a little pout.

"You get to come with me," Keely beamed. "I can't ask Ophelia to split the money she earned before we met you, but I'm going to need a girl who can read and write. So come with me and together we'll get rich beyond your wildest dreams."

Elissa looked uncertainly to Ophelia, who simply rolled her eyes very eloquently. "I don't know," Elissa said hesitantly as she turned back to Keely.

"Did I mention we'll take down the Inquisition, too?"

CHAPTER EIGHT

MOVING MOUNTAINS

"Rise and shine, beautiful."

"*Mmph.* What gives, Jake?" Keely rolled over groggily at the prodding of a booted foot. She combed her hair out of her eyes with her fingers, spat straw out of her mouth, and tried to focus on the dimly illuminated figure standing over her in the loft. "Did you run out of drunks to hassle?"

"What have you been up to, girl?" the bouncer of the Rusty Mug demanded, waving a printed page in front of her face.

The other four women began to stir as Keely sat up and squinted at the page in the gray morning light. "Are you saying that's supposed to be me?" she asked dubiously. "That's not a very good likeness."

"The crier who was tacking these up says they're looking for a 'young, silver-haired witch by the name of Keely'. I kind of think it's supposed to be you. Not sure about the 'turning into a cat' part."

"Oh, absolutely. I also sneeze unicorns and turn lead into potatoes. Who comes up with this rubbish?" Keely asked, rolling her eyes.

Elissa, who'd come alert very suddenly, made a grab for the poster. "Keely, what did you do to get that book back?!"

"I just paid Riordan back for the headache," Keely said, still brushing straw from her face. "Oh, and I kind of taunted him about how I was going to find the Grimm Truth."

"What?!" Elissa gasped. "Are you suicidal? I knew we were going to have to move fast to keep ahead of them, but this is insane. Keely, you've leapfrogged yourself overnight from complete unknown to the Inquisition's most wanted. They kept some poor print shop up all night just to make these."

"Wonder how they knew my name," Keely mused.

"My fault," Ophelia answered as she climbed to her feet a lot more quickly than her body was happy with. "They were very persuasive. Come on girls, we're disappearing. Now. Sorry, Keely."

"Yeah. No, we're good." Keely waved a hand dismissively. "Get out of here while you can." She got up and quickly hugged Ophelia, Madeline, and Colette each in turn. "It's been fun. Don't think I won't track you down someday after the dust settles."

"Of course you will, dear." Ophelia patted Keely's cheek.

"I thought you said we'd never see her again," Colette said quietly to her mother as they hurried down the ladder to the stable floor.

"It's called manners, dear," Ophelia answered under her breath as she pasted on a cheerful smile and gave Keely one last wave from the stable door. "She's not going to last the week."

"Now it's time for *your* disappearing act," Jake said, turning back to Keely and tossing a dusty old cloak at her. "Way too many people know you were in the tavern last night, and you can bet your sweet little bottom more than one of them is already running to turn you in. If they find you here, we're *all* in trouble."

"You hear that, Jenny?" Keely asked even as she hopped to her feet and pulled the cloak around her shoulders. "He thinks my bottom's sweet."

"Keely!" Elissa gaped. "Wait...Did you just call me Jenny?"

"Come on, come on," Keely grinned as she waved Elissa toward her own cloak. "You're on the lam now, too. Start taking this a little seriously."

Elissa buried her head in her hand for a moment and took a deep breath before reaching for her cloak. "Whatever I'm doing penance for, please let it be over soon."

"And *you*..." Keely said, grabbing the big man by the collar and hitting him with a kiss that could have fogged windows at twenty paces, "...are pretty darn sweet, yourself. Thanks, Jake. I *really* owe you one." She scooped up the little pack she'd slept with, tucked her hair up under the hood of the cloak, and hit the floor of the stable while the bouncer was still shaking his head, trying to clear it. A moment later, she was out the door, with Elissa close behind.

The crystalline spires of Icehall Opera House soared above their corner of the city, shimmering with light and youthful energy as the early morning sun played across them. It stood quite literally as a symbol of a grand new era of wealth, power, and prosperity, erected in anticipation of the second empire about to dawn. The larger-than-life lioness perched dramatically above the front entrance had been carved with such exquisite care and detail that anyone staring too long might imagine they could see its muscles tense in preparation for the pounce.

The broad marble staircase leading to the doors swept upward in such grandeur that one could practically feel it pulling one's feet with it in defiance of gravity, and the light refracting through the free-hanging crystal prisms along the top of the front arcade showered the space below with chaotic swirls of color.

With all that splendor going on out front, the little white cat that was Keely had no trouble at all slipping in through an open back window and opening a door for Elissa to join her in the big, dark storage space beneath the stage—as well as to return Keely's clothes to her.

"So are you ever going to tell me what this big 'master plan' of yours is?" Elissa asked as Keely strolled like a shopper among the astounding assortment of props and costumes, pausing to examine a dress here or run her fingers through a wig there.

"I thought I said," Keely replied distractedly. "We're going to find the Grimm Truth."

"And which of the overwhelming problems with that plan did you want me to point out first?"

"Oh, amuse yourself, Jenny. Whichever one strikes your fancy." Keely stopped in front of a full-length mirror to try on a curly brown wig and ponder her reflection. She wrinkled her nose, shook her head, and returned the wig to where she'd found it.

"Okay. What if it doesn't even *exist*?" Elissa asked impatiently. "Miraculata Cosima seems pretty convinced it doesn't."

"Non-issue. Next objection?"

"In what conceivable world is this a non-issue?!"

Keely gave Elissa an exasperated look. "The one in which I don't give a fig what's in it. Don't let her baby face fool you. That miraculata of yours is a shrewd one—a serious politician. She knows how the game works."

"And how does the game work?" Elissa asked tersely.

"Like this," Keely said, pulling a set of three tin cups down from a shelf and laying them out upside down on a dusty tabletop. With a flourish, she produced a small ball, which she held up briefly before sliding it under one of the cups, then she began shuffling the cups quickly back and forth. "Now, which cup is the ball under?" she asked when she'd stopped.

"None of them," Elissa answered levelly.

"None of them?" Keely asked, cocking an eyebrow.

"You palmed the ball before you started. I saw it in your hand."

"Really? I could have sworn it was under the middle one."

"It's not." Elissa confidently lifted the middle cup and did a double take. Her brow furrowed as she lifted the other cups. "Okay, it was. But that proves...what?"

"It proves," Keely said, producing a twin for the ball on the table, "that you thought I was a cheat, so you treated me like a cheat."

"Well, you gave me reason to."

"And...?" Keely shrugged expansively. "The point is, it wasn't truth you reacted to, it was what you *believed* was true. That's what people do. Day in, day out, minute by minute, we make our best guesses about what's true, and we act on them. None of us can ever see the whole truth at once, so in the end, the only thing that makes one truth better than another is how much reality it can hold before it breaks. If a whole lot of us believe the same lie—if an entire kingdom believes the same lie—and the lie is solid enough, that lie can move mountains. So I don't care whether or not the Grimm Truth exists. I just want to drop a mountain on Jane Carver.

"Aha!" Keely suddenly shouted, a broad grin lighting up her face.

"What?!" Elissa asked, nearly tripping over herself to get out of the way as Keely danced past to grab something from the table behind her.

Keely spun triumphantly about, clutching the wig to her chest. "Today I'm going to be a red-head."

"I still think you're crazy, you know," Elissa said, holding the dress Keely had picked out for her folded close to her chest as she carefully picked her way along the steppingstones.

"It's a safe opinion to hold onto," Keely agreed, reaching dry ground on the far side of the little stream that wound its way through Rose Glenn, the public gardens behind the opera house. Among its many virtues, Rose Glenn offered an abundance of foliage to discretely mask the presence of those in its less-traveled corners from the rest of the city. "But back to business. Where will we find this wondrous tome?"

"That would be another one of those overwhelming problems I mentioned." Elissa sighed. "No matter what some little cuckoo told Carver, the journal doesn't actually spell it out. If we pretend that the miraculata is wrong, and the journal is genuine, I can tell you a few landmarks that are somewhere close to where the Grimm Truth was last seen—but even if I could get more exact, that last sighting was over a hundred years ago. It could be anywhere by now."

"Let me rephrase," Keely said patiently. "If you were Jane Carver, and you'd had only an hour or two to skim the journal, where would you go to start hunting for someone you were afraid had read it all carefully and was out to recover the Grimm Truth?"

"Oh," Elissa said, pausing to make the final hop to join Keely on the bank of the stream. "That's easy enough: The Wolf's Tooth."

"Oh? Where's that? *What's* that?"

Elissa sat down on a rock and rummaged through the small pack of belongings she'd salvaged from the abbey until she'd produced the journal. "That's the last place Amberford mentioned visiting," she said, cracking the book open and thumbing through its pages. "It also happens to be the place Miraculata Grimm said she was headed in that letter he discovered. Torresangrienta—the site of the first emperor's final battle—later came to be known as the Wolf's Tooth. It's a lone spire of rock at the edge of the Crimson Forest. It says here that..."

Elissa's eyes suddenly crossed as a large, bright-blue butterfly flitted just in front of her face.

"Oh, wow," Keely said. "I don't think I've ever seen...Elissa, why are you hyperventilating?"

"I...I..." Elissa stammered, recoiling slowly away from the colorful insect.

"They don't have stingers, you know." Keely sighed as she reached to gently shoo the butterfly away from Elissa's face. "It's just..." The journal Elissa had been browsing suddenly slammed shut, narrowly missing Keely's fingers.

"You killed a butterfly?!" Keely gasped in disbelief.

"It was going to bite me!" Elissa snapped defensively.

"They don't bite people!"

"How do you know?!" Elissa demanded.

"Never in the history of the world has there ever been a recorded incident of a butterfly bite! I don't think they even have teeth!"

"I don't like butterflies, okay?"

"Now that I'll believe." Keely shook her head. "And you call *me* crazy."

"Are there any more?" Elissa asked, looking around nervously.

"Let's see...Garden? Flowers? Yeah, I'm afraid we've still got lots of butterflies. I seem to recall seeing some back at the abbey, too."

"I know. They're everywhere." Elissa scowled, but she seemed satisfied at last that no others were coming to intrude on her space.

"All right: we're headed toward the Crimson Forest. Big target, right? I can work with that. Even as fast as the Inquisition is moving, I don't think we'll have any trouble slipping out of the city, but I'm sure they've already got people headed that direction. Do you fancy skulking through undergrowth like a fugitive for a couple hundred miles, hoping the Inquisition doesn't spot us?"

"Do I have a choice?" Elissa asked.

"Only if you want to split up, because that's not how I plan on doing it," Keely said. "If you want to do this the easy way, I'll need you to follow my lead."

"I can try," Elissa said.

"Good. Now are you a liar?"

"What? No!" Elissa answered crossly.

"Excellent!" Keely smiled. "Just the right tone of indignation. For a moment there you almost had me believing it. I think you've got the gift."

"I am not a liar!"

"Now don't ham it up," Keely cautioned her. "You need to keep the act understated if you want to pull it off for long. Just convince yourself that it's true, and the rest will flow from there."

Elissa let out a growl of frustration as she cradled her head in her hands.

"Look," Keely said, "there's a time and a place for playing nice. This is not it. If Jane gave a fig for the truth, you'd be home in your library cataloging books right now, right?"

"Yeah," Elissa conceded.

"She started this; she's one of the most powerful women in the world; and she fights dirty. Check your scruples at the door, or we've already lost. This is a no-holds-barred, take-no-prisoners, unapologetic fight for our lives. Can you get your head around that?"

"I...yeah." Elissa nodded slowly. "Yes. You're right. If there was ever a time to stop playing by the rules, this is it."

"There's my girl." Keely grinned proudly. "But we'll try to let you ease into this. Now, think...think...think..." Keely furrowed her brow in concentration. "Of course!" she laughed. "You're 'Lady A'!"

"I am not!...Wait, what? Who in the Blessed Isles is Lady A?" Elissa demanded.

"She's the woman who hired us to find this book—a whole set of books, actually," Keely said. "I never met her myself, but..."

"And now you think *I* paid you that pretty ransom to come ruin my life?" Elissa asked incredulously.

"Silly goose," Keely snorted. "You're going to *pretend* to be Lady A."

"Why can't I be 'Lady E'?"

"Because Lady A's already a player in this game. She's left tracks we can make point to you."

"That still makes no sense!" Elissa moaned. "What happens when the real Lady A shows up?"

"We stuff her in a sack and feed her nothing but cold turnips until she tells us everything she knows about this stupid book. Now here's what I need you to do..."

"You know, I don't even recognize this book," Tobias said, furrowing his brow as he flipped slowly through the pages of the journal. "Are you quite sure you got it from *my* library?"

"Well, technically..." Elissa began, then gave a bit of a jump as the little white cat in her lap nipped at the hand that was stroking its ears. "Yes. Yes, it's from your library.

"*Behave*, Bookend," Elissa scowled at the cat, shaking out her sore hand. She leaned out the window of the carriage as it rattled away down the road, taking a long last look at the retreating grandeur of Serylia's gleaming walls and towering monuments against the backdrop of the snow-capped Daneth mountains. Wherever life might be taking her now, this would be a hard act to follow.

"How did you even know it was there when I didn't?" Tobias asked, finally closing the book.

Elissa took a moment to glare down at the cat, as if daring it to play rough again, before pasting on a smile and looking back up at Tobias. "If I went around revealing my informants, I wouldn't have them anymore, but trust me: that journal wasn't easy to track down."

"And you're sure it's authentic?"

"Only one way to find out, really, but that witch is sure taking it seriously."

"You mean the one who, uh..." His pointed gaze finally forced Elissa's own to turn to the elephant in the carriage: a truly spectacular ruby gown draped upon a dressmaker's dummy. Half the bench Elissa was sitting on had been torn out to make room for it.

"Yes," Elissa agreed slowly. "The one who, uh."

"Are you sure your friend's all right?"

"Oh, yeah. Yes. I mean...Well, she should be. I think." Elissa spent a few seconds studying the neat, green hedgerow passing by outside the window. "She's fine. Just had to lead the witch away while I made off with the book. She'll be there waiting at Denecia."

"You're sure?"

"Not really. You ask that a lot, don't you?"

"Hmmm...Guess so. Sorry. I'm still not sure why you'd even show me a book you stole from me that I'd never have missed—especially one so potentially valuable. I mean, if the Grimm Truth really does exist, that could change everything."

"We were never after the book," Elissa said. "We were after the witch, but keeping the book from her was the best we could manage that night. Whatever happens, we can't let her have the Grimm Truth. Even if it was some crazy old uncle that stuck it in your library, this book is rightfully yours, and you'd be better able to keep it safe than we can. If you want it, keep it. If you're worried about the witch coming back for it, we can find another noble family to trust it to."

"I think I can manage," Tobias said with a wry little chuckle. "But if you're willing to trust me with this, can't we just drop the cloak-and-dagger stuff? You can't really expect me to go around calling you 'Lady A'."

"Would a different letter help?" Elissa asked without any hint of sarcasm. "A's not my favorite letter."

"I think I'll just let it drop," Tobias said, "before I fall any further behind, thanks."

CHAPTER NINE

GHOST STORY

What the smallish city of Denecia lacked on Serylia's grandeur, it made up for with a warm, lived-in feeling. Nearly as old, nearly as clean, but far less metropolitan, her residents had expended much less effort on building tall monuments and more on that subtle sort of landscaping that blends in with the natural terrain and leaves a community feeling like its got some elbow room.

Nestled into a valley on the shores of Nareyach Lake, Denecia's low, rustic buildings climbed up the surrounding slopes like the tiers of some giant's amphitheater looking down on the city harbor.

"You know, your accent's very good," Tobias said as the carriage crested a pass leading into the bowl of the valley, coming into sight of Denecia. A light, friendly rain outside the carriage window had taken the edge off what had threatened to become one of the last hot days of the dwindling summer.

"Accent?" Elissa asked, biting her lip as she looked up from the book she'd been reading.

"Almost didn't catch it. Thought you were a local at first."

"Who says I'm not?" she answered defensively.

Tobias cocked his head at an odd angle to get his best look at the cover of the book. "*A Pilgrim's Guide to Serylia*? Even if she needed it, a local girl would know that Marget's work is two hundred years out of date. Serylia's a whole different world these days."

"Oh." Elissa hid her face behind the still-open book, peering at him over the cover. "I thought we were done talking about this."

"Are you a cousin of the Brookshires?"

"Who?" she asked blankly.

"Are you even going to tell me what you and your friend are doing so far from home, chasing witches?"

"I don't think so," Elissa said earnestly.

During a break in the rain, the carriage finally stopped in the courtyard of the one edifice in Denecia that could, without room for argument or contradiction, be called "prominent". Palatial by comparison to its surroundings, the large stone building still somehow managed to pull off the vine-covered-cottage version of palatial.

"Jakob, you old scoundrel!" Tobias came bounding out of the carriage to greet the older nobleman who'd come to meet them, nearly knocking over the footman who'd opened the door for him in the process. "Do tell me you're still up to no good."

"Of course, Toby. Of course." Jakob chuckled. A little gray, a little soft, a little balding, he boasted the same friendly, comfortably worn-in look as the city around him.

"So good to see you again, Tobias." The youngish matron beside Jakob gave Tobias a familiar hug and a welcoming peck on the cheek. "To what do we owe the pleasure?"

"Well..." Tobias began, then suddenly ducked to avoid the red-clad dressmaker's dummy being swung out of the door behind him. "That, sort of. Watch it, Conrad. And mind you don't drag that in the mud!"

"A dress?" Jakob asked quizzically.

"Yeah. I'm looking for the owner. Oh, and..." He turned back to the carriage and urged Elissa outward, offering his hand to help her down. "May I present, uh, well...'Lady A', I guess."

"You guess?" the woman asked.

"If you can get more of a name out of her, you're doing better than me. You don't already know her by any luck, do you? Didn't think so. Anyway, milady," he said, smiling to Elissa and gesturing toward the couple, "Duke Jakob and his charming wife, Farada."

"Wild, wild guess," Jakob laughed, "but there's a story to tell here, isn't there? Come on, you two," he beckoned them onward toward the main entrance. "Any mysterious friend of Toby's is a mysterious friend of mine. I can't wait to hear what trouble you've invited into your life this time."

Elissa leaned back to let Bookend hop out of the carriage and into her arms before following the others inside.

A crack of thunder directly overhead rattled the windows of the mansion as the accompanying lightning cut through the deepening dusk. Even before the echoes had stopped bouncing around the valley, a powerful gust of wind snatched the doors to the garden balcony right out of the hands of the serving girl who'd been trying to struggle through them, and slammed them wide open with a bang. Silver service went scattering everywhere as the girl fought back the draperies suddenly tangling themselves about her.

In the midst of the confusion, a dozen half-drenched ladies and lords took advantage of the open door to come rushing inside, amidst much laughter and shrieking, as a torrential rain commenced to pounding at the windows.

"Lights! More lights!" Farada called to the staff, while Tobias paused to help untangle the serving girl, and a couple of the other lords forced the balcony doors shut.

"So much for dinner on the balcony." Jakob chuckled. "At least the heat's quite broken."

"Along with any chance we'll be meeting the more mysterious of your mystery women tonight, Tobias," one of the younger ladies said with a laugh. "I think it's safe to say no one will be coming late to dinner through this."

"Never underestimate what I'm crazy enough to do," Keely admonished the woman from where she stood in an interior doorway of the chamber. "I hope you don't mind my taking the liberty of reclaiming my dress," she said with a smile to Tobias and a happy little twirl into the room. The highlights of her flaring, shimmering skirts caught the light of the few candles that had already been lit against the approaching night.

"I'm afraid all I'd found to wear in the interim has been less than flattering." Even in the dim light, Keely could easily see Elissa melting with the relief that the crowd had just acquired a new focal point for its curiosity.

"You made it!" Tobias rushed across the room to sweep Keely up in his arms in a much more vigorous twirl than the one she'd initiated herself.

"Of course I did." Keely laughed. "So where's the marque...I mean—" she coughed. "Where's 'Lady A'?" She peered into the gloom as if she'd not yet seen Elissa.

"No no no no," Tobias demanded. "I've been fighting...the marquesa, here...to drop this whole cloak and dagger thing ever since she showed up. You already got through one entire evening without telling me your name, and you're not getting away with it again."

"Tobias is too right," Farada insisted. "We've been teased for hours with glimpses of a story, and hospitality demands you fill us in at once on all the juicy details."

"If only it was that simple." Keely sighed.

"Make it that simple," Tobias said.

"Give us a minute." Keely beckoned to Elissa, drawing her away into a corner where they whispered together for something closer to two or three minutes than just the one.

"I for one haven't had *any* dinner yet," Keely said when they broke the huddle. "Feed me, and we'll find a story for you."

The rain had settled into a steady downpour that beat against the roof, the thunder and lightning outside now offering only occasional punctuation to the evening's atmosphere. The chandeliers flickering over the dining table reflected endlessly back and forth between the long mirrors on either side of the chamber, amplifying the light, though it never quite seemed to banish the deep shadows from the corners of the room.

"Please understand," Keely said, when the last of the dishes had been cleared away and the last servants had been dismissed to go pretend they weren't listening at the keyholes, "whatever game it seems we're playing at, it's a dangerous game, and very high stakes." She spoke quietly, drawing her audience into a conspiratorial ring as they leaned forward onto the edges of their own seats, straining to hear her above the storm. "Witches, heresy, empire, forgotten secrets, corruption, the Inquisition...We may seem like a puzzle to you, but there are puzzles within puzzles within puzzles going on here. We've barely begun peeling them away ourselves, and already we've made some very powerful enemies. Over-sharing could not only put us in danger, but you as well. I'll try tonight to walk the knife's edge and satisfy your curiosity without saying too much, but I'd encourage anyone with enough prudence to outweigh her curiosity to retire for the evening and leave the rest of us to our folly."

No one budged from the table.

"I'll admit, as someone here has guessed, that we've come a long way to be here. A very long way, in fact. It's a testimony to our tutors growing up that we've been able to hide it so well, but no disguise is ever perfect, is it? I guess we do owe you names, be they real or imaginary, so will 'Chloe' suit me?"

"Well enough for now," Tobias said.

"And...'Alice'?" Keely looked meaningfully down the table to Elissa. When no one objected, she went on. "In any event, our home lies near the edge of Serinian lands, where enlightenment too often goes dark, and witchcraft can too easily become a very pressing problem. It pains me to admit the witch we've been chasing is one of my own cousins, though I expect that's the only reason I'm sitting with you now instead of scuttling around Serylia's sewers as a rat. She showed enough pity to turn me into a cat instead, and then only for a day or so. Not enough pity to transform my dress with me, mind you, which is how it came to be lying where you found it. It was quite the mortifying scene, I assure you, when my curse suddenly expired and I returned to my old self without warning."

A ripple of poorly stifled laughter went around the table, along with the telltale expressions of listeners trying to imagine exactly how that must have played out.

"That same connection is why I've been trying to keep this a family matter, though I fear it may be spreading out of control beyond that. We may soon have no choice but to accept the shame and the scrutiny of the Inquisition. She's on the trail of the Grimm Truth—close enough to convince me that it does indeed exist—and I'm fairly certain her plan is to bewitch the new emperor before he's even crowned, assuring her place as empress."

"That sounds a rather ill-conceived plan," one of the older men scoffed. "Not one man with any real support for the position is in need of a wife."

"Then I pity the queen standing between her and an empire," Keely responded coolly. "I doubt she'll wind up even so fortunate as the Countess of Elia."

"Elia?" the man asked. "Where's Elia?"

"Out west," Keely said with a dismissive wave that was more sort of south-ish. "Such a dreadful business."

"What's so dreadful about being out west?" the man's wife asked curiously.

"I mean, dreadful what happened to the countess," Keely answered with a shiver. "Hadn't you heard?"

"I hadn't heard of *Elia* 'til just now," the woman said.

"Well, for the sake of their digestion," Keely said, slipping out of her seat and around the table to the noblewoman, "I'll spare the others the re-telling, but..." As Keely whispered behind a cupped hand, the woman's eyes grew progressively wider and her mouth gaped open.

"Oh, my go'ss!" she gasped. "You can't be serious?!"

"Actually, I hadn't..." Tobias began.

"Oh, I hadn't believed it, either," Keely interjected. "I mean, I hadn't seen what the witch could do. Then I didn't want to believe she *would* do it, especially with some of the same blood in my veins. But it was all too real at the county court. I'm sure they'll still be telling the tale around the fire as a ghost story generations from now."

"It all sounds like rubbish to me," one of the younger women said, the irritation clear in her voice. With her pretty face, her long, brown hair carefully coiffed, and her rose-pink gown expertly tailored to accentuate a figure in little need of accentuating, there could be little doubt this was a woman unaccustomed to being upstaged at social gatherings.

"Then don't believe it," Keely said, easing on around the table to pat the woman familiarly on the shoulder. "I'm not trying to convince anyone of anything. I was asked to explain myself, and I am. Then, I'm going to go to bed, where I hope to indulge in one very deep sleep, completely un-plagued by questions of whether a hasty accounting of my life sounded plausible.

"I love that dress, by the way. I must meet your seamstress," Keely added before moving on.

"You said something about 'forgotten secrets'?" the lady of the house asked. "You mean the 'Grimm Truth'?"

"That's certainly the most sensational of them. I know it's fashionable to dismiss the thing as a nursery story, but if you can believe the man's own journals, it was apparently seen within the last couple of centuries by none other than the protector general of the church...just before he mysteriously died."

"Seriously?" The rakish young lord beside the woman in pink asked, sitting up a little straighter. "You've seen the journals?"

"I shouldn't have mentioned it." Keely sighed. "We're getting into 'can get you killed' territory here. But, yes, I have. And, no, it doesn't bother me if you don't believe that either. In fact, even if you do believe it, pretending that you don't might save your life someday, so knock yourself out. I'm used to it, anyway." She waved her hand with the weary, dismissive air of someone who was not so much "used to it" as "resigned to it".

"I've seen it to," Tobias spoke up sternly, and Keely flashed him a small smile of gratitude for taking the bait. "Whether or not the Grimm Truth is real, that journal is. And you can either believe in this witch, or you can believe Lady Chloe stood on my front steps during a very busy party, stripped herself naked where anyone might have seen, and left this exquisite gown she's wearing lying in the dirt—all so she could come here and be ridiculed tonight. You tell *me* which makes more sense."

"Whoa, there!" Jakob spoke up placatingly. "No one's ridiculing anyone. Well, maybe Sabina got a little snarky, but when does she not?"

The woman in pink shot Jakob a withering look. "And like the lady herself says, when a story gets this fantastic, you don't just go around expecting everyone to accept it without blinking."

"Well, our family's had its brush with witches," one of the previously silent lords spoke up—a man with the sort of neatly groomed, dark beard that looks a bit sinister by candlelight. "There's no other explanation for Uncle Henri. Like Toby, I'm a lot more willing to believe in the witch than, ummm..." He chuckled quietly.

"Whatever else is true, our Lady Chloe is a very intriguing young woman." A strikingly beautiful, middle-aged woman who had been hanging back from the table—watching the conversation from the edge of the candlelight—stepped forward with an amused little smile. "I'm bored with hearing about witches, though. Talk to me about books."

Keely was happy to note she hadn't been the only one startled by the woman's sudden entry into the conversation. She'd been hanging back so quietly, Keely had walked right past her while circling the table and barely noticed she was there—even though she wore a gown the same shade of look-at-me red that Keely loved so much. Indeed, most of the gathering seemed to have forgotten the woman was there at all, judging by the way they'd jumped at her voice. It all helped to cover up the fact that Keely had missed a beat in sizing up the woman, though.

"Books?" Keely asked, just to direct the spotlight back off herself while she re-settled her composure.

"These journals," the woman said, twirling a lock of her long, red hair in her fingers as she stepped up between Jakob and Tobias at the head of the table. "This...'Grim Tooth'...Witches can be wicked, *wicked* nasty, but books...In my experience, books are just downright evil." When Tobias gave a little laugh at this pronouncement, she reached to tilt his chin up with one finger while she leaned in close to his face and repeated very clearly and seriously. "Evil." She kissed his nose, sending a quiet ripple of laughter through the gathering, then straightened up and paced on around the table until she was facing Keely from across it.

"So if I'm following this, we've got one naughty little book telling us...what? That an even naughtier little book is on the loose somewhere, rampaging about the countryside?"

"I suppose you could put it that way," Keely answered guardedly.

"Is that first book helpful at all in saying where to find the second?"

"A bit," Keely said. "But that was over a hundred years ago."

"Then where *was* the second book?" the woman enunciated carefully.

"I, uh...Wolf's Tooth." Keely hadn't met many people capable of staring her down, but this appeared to be one of them. "Somewhere around there."

"What? That great big spike of rock over by the forest? I thought it would be in someplace exotic—like Trelgathra, or the Dead Mountains, or Little-Ox-Trough-on-Eastbrook. Any artifact so important as all that should develop some sense of style, don't you think?"

"I'm sorry," Keely said with a perplexed frown. "I don't..."

"Wait!" the woman interrupted her, hand raised for silence.

"What?" Keely asked with irritation as the silence dragged into seconds.

"Oh." The woman glanced around apologetically. "Isn't that where I was supposed to interrupt you? No matter. Is that all you can tell me about the books?"

"Pretty much," Keely said. "The witch is chasing the books. We're just chasing the witch."

"*This* witch?" the redhead asked, fishing in her bodice for a page that she neatly unfolded to display Keely's wanted poster.

"Uh...yeah," Keely nodded slowly. "That would be her."

The woman cocked her head, looking from Keely to the poster and back again, making Keely fidget despite herself. "I can see the family resemblance. Your eyes are much prettier, though. All right. I was kind of looking for her anyway, so I'll help you find her."

"You will?! Uh...wow. That's...great!" Keely pasted on a smile that she hoped looked more astounded than forced. "That would be just so great."

"Tomorrow, though. Tonight's no good for it."

"Yeah," Keely agreed slowly as another peal of thunder broke close outside. "I think you're right."

The woman smiled winsomely, then turned away and headed for the door, where she nearly knocked over one of the household servants in opening it. "Fetch me my cloak, dear," she told the girl.

"Where are you going?" Farada asked, perplexed.

"Out, silly." The woman gave a cordial little wave as she pulled the door shut after her.

"I'm really not sure, my dear," Jakob said, still staring at the closed door, "whether it's you or Toby who keeps the, er...more unique friends."

"Me?" Farada's confused expression deepened. "You're the one who invited her."

Jakob chuckled and shook his head. "So which of you did she come with, and who is she?"

All the guests just looked about the table expectantly at each other for several seconds before Jakob pushed away from the table and followed the woman out the door. A low buzz of whispered conversation overtook the gathering until he returned, dripping wet.

"I, uh...followed her to the gate," Jakob answered the stares. "That is, I followed her out the door. The porter says he hasn't seen anyone like her all day, wanting in or out the gate. Which of you even talked to her before just now?" he asked impatiently. "Did anyone *see* her before just now?"

CHAPTER TEN

WITHOUT A TRACE

Elissa lay awake, staring into the darkness—where she knew the bed canopy should be—long after the flickering lightning outside had stopped offering any chance to actually see anything. Soft and cozy as the bed she lay in was, she simply couldn't relax and get the anxious voices in her head to shut off, so she nearly jumped at the whisper of the bed curtain drawing aside.

"Storms over," Keely hissed in her ear. "C'mon, Jenny."

"Seriously? All those hours spying on me as a cat, and you can't even get my name straight? C'mon where?" Elissa whispered. She sat up and perched on the edge of the bed to stare at the darkness from a different angle. At least there was enough light filtering into the room to make out Keely's silhouette. "You're naked again, aren't you?" Elissa asked dryly.

"Of course," Keely hissed. "Now hush, and get your chemise off."

"My...?" Elissa gaped. "Oh, no. Naked is *your* thing, remember?"

"Then give my regards to Jane Carver, because those are our choices. I'm going to slip out that door and count to fifty, then I'm gone. I'm taking *nothing* with me, and neither are you, or you can figure this mess out on your own."

"But..." Before Elissa's mind could formulate a coherent question, the shadowy figure at her bedside had withdrawn to the door and slipped through it without making another sound.

Elissa sat stunned for a moment, then sat several seconds longer quietly pounding the heels of her hands into her forehead while she cursed incoherently under her breath.

"Fourty-three, fourty-four..."

"Oh, you were *not* counting outside your head all this time," Elissa whispered tersely as she slipped out into the gallery where Keely was waiting. The lighting through the windows was better here than in the bed chamber, but still left everything indistinctly wrapped in soft velvet shadows.

"Eh. The point is you were pushing it, girl. I thought I told you to leave *everything*. Is that a book you're carrying?"

"Are those boots you're wearing?" Elissa countered as she clutched the large journal protectively over her bare chest.

"I was wearing slippers last night. No one *saw* my boots, so they'll never miss them," Keely whispered. "Tobias was kind enough to overlook that I didn't leave anything but a dress behind back at Serylia, but if we don't do it right this time, somebody's going to start asking the wrong questions."

"Nobody saw my journal either," Elissa insisted. "And it's got my name in. My *real* name. We *have* to take it."

"Right, then," Keely nodded. "Good keeping your head about you."

"I'd rather've kept my chemise," Elissa muttered.

"Gah!" Keely rapped her knuckles on her forehead. "Almost forgot the wigs. Can't leave those, either." She slipped quietly back into the room and quickly returned with the two wigs she'd brought on the trip, then padded down the stairs to the foyer with Elissa following cautiously behind.

"How're we supposed to get out past the porter?" Elissa asked. "I can't exactly turn into a cat, you know."

Keely dangled a key ring in front of Elissa's face as they slipped out the front door and into a damp courtyard that was—even with only a thin crescent of a moon to light it—all too brightly lit for Elissa's comfort. "The lady of the house sleeps deeply, and any guards are going to be looking out, not in."

"But aren't *we* going to be outside in a minute?"

No guard actually stood at the wrought iron gate in the high stone wall that surrounded the estate—just a cottage a few paces away, which served as a guardhouse. Where the main house lay dark, flickering candlelight filtering out the windows of the cottage hinted that its occupants were awake, if not necessarily alert. While Elissa hung back in the shadow of the nearest convenient shrubbery, Keely slipped up to the gate and sorted through keys until one of them gave a satisfying click in the lock. She eased the gate open an inch to make sure it had been properly unlocked, then stole quietly over to Elissa.

"I've got to take these keys back, and to make sure our departure looks convincing," Keely said, shoving the wigs into Elissa's arms. "Hide here, then when I give the signal, look for your chance to slip out and latch the gate behind you. Don't worry about me; I can slip right through the bars."

"What's the signal?" Elissa asked.

About ten minutes later, she heard Keely's blood-curdling scream from somewhere inside the house. Within moments, two men in the blue and white livery of Duke Jakob dashed out of the cottage, each clutching an arquebus as he looked around for the source of the commotion. Just as Elissa was certain one of them had stopped to stare in her direction, Keely screamed again—as did two other women immediately after—and both men set off for the house at a run. By the time they were halfway across the lawn, Elissa was out the gate. By the time they made it in the door, Keely came darting around the corner of the house as a little white feline streak. In the blink of an eye she'd crossed the lawn and slipped through the bars of the gate to join Elissa—pausing only long enough to make sure that Elissa was hurrying down the dark street after her, as quickly as her bare feet would allow.

Elissa pulled the blanket more tightly around her shoulders to ward off the rain that had started falling again as she picked her way carefully up the slopes of the valley in the pre-dawn hours of the night. She didn't know where Keely had found the blanket for her, and—for once—genuinely could not have cared less. She just huddled beneath it, along with the book that was her only other possession in the world, and alternated between gratitude for that one small comfort and miserable contemplation of how her life had come to this.

"I still don't get it, you know. What went so horribly wrong that we had to vanish like that, right then?" she asked Keely, who—with the wigs tucked under one arm—walked beside her in a blanket draped much more casually, paying no attention to the rain.

"Our uninvited guest, that's what," Keely said. "She was as crazy as I am..."

"Close, anyway," Elissa admitted.

"...and at least as spooky," Keely finished. "You can't con crazy! Well, I mean you can, but it's like juggling knives blindfolded. She was already putting me on the defensive, and that's when everything falls apart. Whoever or whatever that woman is, she's a thousand kinds of trouble. Every instinct is screaming to get as far away from her as possible."

"I should have instincts like that," Elissa said with a roll of her eyes. "Scared of ghosts much?"

"Let's just call it a healthy case of professional respect. I don't bother them, they don't bother me. Not ready to call that woman a ghost, though. She didn't do anything I couldn't have."

"Yeah. She's definitely a thousand kinds of trouble."

"It was a good time to cut and run, though. With everything that's happened, we'll soon have...Ah! That's what we're looking for," Keely said, pointing off into the darkness.

"Clothes?" Elissa asked hopefully as she squinted in the direction Keely was pointing. All she could make out was the shadow of some large compound.

"With any luck. If you just want to wait here...?"

"Hey, I'm good with most any plan that involves me *not* going near populated areas without my clothes. You go right ahead. I'm just going to go sit under that tree and try to minimize this whole getting rained on thing." Elissa scooped up the other blanket and the wigs as Keely turned back into a cat and scampered off. "And don't forget the shoes!" Elissa called after her.

"You forgot the shoes?!" Elissa moaned. The rain had eased up, and the morning sun had begun to creep into the valley and bully its way through the clouds, but Elissa found it hard to appreciate that while she was contemplating setting back out on her tender feet. "How far do you think I'm going to get without shoes?"

"I'm sorry. I just couldn't find any. Not and hope to get out with them before the whole abbey woke up."

The compound Elissa hadn't been able to make out in the night was visible now as the local abbey—much more rustic and welcoming than Belgrimm. That'd be Bolberry Abbey, she'd observed, simply judging from the fact it lay on the outskirts of Denecia; but now she'd become rather more preoccupied with footwear than with geography.

"You couldn't find any shoes?" Elissa hissed accusingly. "*You* couldn't find any shoes?! You put your life on the line for a stupid pair of boots! I just rode for two days with a prince who couldn't go half an hour without mentioning the crystal slippers you wore to his party! Even when you're running for your life, you can't go half a day without changing out for a new pair you've scrounged from go'ss knows where. I could turn you loose in a garbage pit, and you'd come back with three pairs of silk dancing slippers, a half dozen pairs of fashionable boots, and a set of shiny, golden sandals covered with emeralds! But you couldn't find me one lousy..." Elissa stopped, glaring down at Keely's feet. "You did it *again*."

"Oh, uh...These?" Keely asked, lifting up one sandaled foot to study it herself, as if noticing the worn leather straps for the first time herself.

"I *know* you didn't leave your boots behind." Elissa fumed. "Give *me* the sandals, and you can wear your boots. Problem solved. That's not hard, is it?"

"Ummm...Well, yeah." Keely let out a long sigh. "Okay. This is a secret I've never shared with *anybody*. Ophelia knew about the cat thing, but even she didn't know *this*. If you ever tell another living soul, you'll wish the Inquisition had got hold of you. Got it?"

Elissa nodded cautiously, curiosity and apprehension gnawing at the edges of her anger.

"In the last five years, I've only ever worn one pair of shoes, and you're looking at them."

"What?" Elissa asked coldly.

"Here. Take my hands," Keely said, holding them out palms up. "Now look me straight in the eye...right...and count to three. Now look down."

When Elissa looked back to Keely's feet, she was wearing a gorgeous pair of golden sandals covered with emeralds.

"You said you could only do the one trick!" Elissa said, shooting Keely an accusing look.

"I lie. But technically it's not my trick. It's the boots. They're...magic. They'll change into whatever shoes I want. Sometimes they kind of even change without permission when I'm not looking, but always into whatever I'd have asked for if I'd thought to ask. And, no, I will never, ever, ever let you or anyone else try them on. If I ever catch you trying to get hold of them, I will push you off the nearest cliff. Then I'll push a very large rock off after you. After that, I'll get nasty. Okay?"

Elissa nodded, biting her lip.

"Right, then. We'll find you some shoes as soon as we can. In the meantime, here..."

"Clothes!" Elissa almost jumped out of her blanket as she grabbed up the silvery robes and clutched them to her chest with a squeal of delight. "Wait. I should have the blue postulant robes there," she said, pointing to the set Keely had kept for herself. "These are priestess' robes."

"And?" Keely asked quizzically.

"I'm a postulant."

"You're a fugitive."

"Oh. Right." Elissa blushed.

"I've spent years learning how to blend with the nobility—they're my favorite marks—but that mostly just takes attitude and mannerisms. Priestesses are expected to know things. Specific thing. Things like, you know...how to read? No one's going to buy two postulants wandering the countryside on their own, and I'd never pass as a trained priestess for long, but you...I admit you're a bit naive, but you're no dummy, and you've got enough book learning for three ordinary priestesses. So congratulations on your initiation, Sister."

Elissa blushed a little deeper at the assessment of her scholarship; and she blushed a little deeper still at dropping the blanket to pull on the priestess garb, but with no one else around and Keely already changing unselfconsciously in front of her, she would have felt even more awkward going to change behind the tree.

"You know, I never figured you for a tattoo girl." Keely grinned.

"What? Oh...yeah. It wasn't exactly planned," Elissa said, hastening to pull the chemise on over her intricately inked back.

"Girl, that's not the sort of design you wake up with after a night of drinking. I got a really good look at it last night." Keely tapped her temple meaningfully with one finger. "Cat eyes? And that's got to be the fanciest design I've ever seen. Some real artistry there. How many days did it take? And what's it a map to?"

"It's not a map *to* anything," Elissa sighed. "It's just...a map." She shrugged.

"A map of what, then?"

"The known world, pretty much. And yeah, it's good work..."

"It's amazing work!" Keely said.

"...but I wish I *had* got it when I was drunk. At least then I'd have an excuse. The truth is even more stupid and frivolous and embarrassing, and I'll tell you the whole story...the day you let me wear your boots."

CHAPTER ELEVEN

HARDENED CLAY

Down in the lowlands of the Verdmere river valley, summer had not been kind to Dydford, nor to anyplace remotely close to the little crossroads town. Even now, with the air cooling for a long, lethargic slide into winter, the ground lay baked and barren beneath a sparse layer of withered grasses. Here and there, large patches of ground even lay black where carelessness or bad luck had lit the tinder-dry grasses on fire.

On one particularly forlorn little hill on the outskirts of town, which offered a particularly depressing view of the sun-scorched countryside, there came a loud clang, followed by the loud report of cracking wood, followed in turn by the loud cursing of a man greatly dissatisfied with his current lot in life. At last, Clay Ambleforth—a wiry man, built into solid muscle by a lifetime of laboring, and presently coated in a muddy mixture of sweat and dirt—pitched aside the broken shovel handle and sank down to sit in the shady corner of the deep hole he'd been digging, where he fell into silence. He hadn't run out of epithets; his mouth was just too dry to continue.

Spying the head of the broken shovel lying just out of reach, he somehow found the will to scoot over a few inches and reach for it. With an enraged grunt, he hurled it out of the hole in a high arc, to be rewarded a couple of seconds later with the loud clang of the shovel head bouncing off a grave marker somewhere. Then Clay sat back in his corner once again and fished out a flask. He was still nursing it when a lovely young lady in pink appeared above him, peering curiously down into the hole as she held her skirts up to keep them out of the dirt.

"Ah, here we go," Sabina remarked with a satisfied smile. "Could you help us find, uh..." She paused, clearly dredging her memory for a name. "...Emery Ambleforth?" she finished at last.

On another day, under other circumstances, Clay would likely have fallen over himself to help such an attractive and clearly wealthy young woman. Here and now, all he could offer her was a bit of a suspicious glare and a terse growl as he pointed vaguely. "Under the ash tree, third grave out from the corner."

"Oh. Hmmm...He's, uh, dead then, is he?" Sabina asked, a frown crossing her pretty face.

"Just the three years now," Clay muttered, only half to Sabina.

"I...I guess I'm looking for his family, then. Someone who knew him, at least."

"I've got a *lot* of digging to do, your ladyship," Clay said tersely, taking another slug from his flask. "Way too much digging, and a shovel to go fetch."

"My friends and I are a bit pressed for time, too," Sabina sighed, scattering a handful of silver coins down into the hole with a casual wave of her hand, "so I guess none of us are in the mood for niceties, are we? The Ambleforth family *used* to be known as the Amberfords, and the name *used* to command a lot of respect. I'm in a position to prove that mad Lord Amberford wasn't so mad after all, and perhaps restore the family to its proper position. It'll be worth a lot to me to do so, so I'll make sure it's worth a lot to whoever helps me do it. I need to find out everything I can about the last years of the man's life. Where would *you* start looking?"

In a dark corner of the Thorny Tankard, Clay sat alone, nursing yet another ale and joylessly flipping a small silver coin through his fingers. He'd honestly tried to be excited to find himself carrying around enough wealth to buy half the town, but it was a town abandoned by Seriena. The brutal summer had been preceded by a nasty winter, which had been preceded by another summer that—if not so cruel as this one—had at least been stingy and downright rude.

For two or three years before that, the seasons had just been a bit callous and vaguely disappointing, but anti-social enough that they'd offered the locals no chance to hedge against the harder times now arrived.

Death didn't merely stalk the land anymore; it had moved into a pleasant little cottage on the edge of town and taken up a regular seat at the local pub where it knew everyone on a first-name basis. All of that kept Clay in steady work digging graves, of course, but far from death leaving its relationship with him crisp and professional, it had shoved its way into his personal affairs as brazenly as it had anyone else's.

Clay didn't really know anything about his great-great-great grandfather that any church archivist couldn't have said—but he'd discovered two things inside himself that morning when the lady in pink had come calling: a profound loathing for people who thought they could buy the world, and a ready supply of tall tales.

What he hadn't found in himself was enough faith in the future to care that a group of very rich, very angry young nobles would almost certainly come back looking for him. By his reckoning, he'd have plenty of time for a week of getting blind-drunk, then—since he had no family left himself—he'd stuff half of whatever wealth remained into the offering box for the other families the drought had devastated, and disappear in search of someplace, well...not here.

He was still contemplating that plan, and not yet entirely drunk, when for the second time that day—and, incidentally, the second time in his life—a very high-class sort of shadow loomed over him.

Back already? Clay groaned inwardly. Well, it had been a good...No, it had been a life. *Just* a life. Whatever good fate might have intended for him had clearly been misdirected to someone else along the way.

"Ambleforth, is it?" the man asked.

"I *told* you those were all just stories my grandfather used to tell," he muttered, not looking up. "Not like I was there myself."

"What stories?" Tobias asked, pulling out a chair and sitting down across from Clay, studying the man's face in an attempt to ascertain how much he'd had to drink.

"The...stories," Clay stammered. "The ones my grandfather used to tell. Look, sorry," he said, beginning to relax at the sight of the puzzlement on Tobias's face. "Thought you were with that pretty lady who came by earlier, asking about..."

"Your family?" Tobias asked excitedly.

Clay nodded cautiously.

"Yes! I was afraid the witch would be farther ahead of me by now." Tobias grinned coldly. "Your family wasn't easy to track down."

"She was a...witch?"

"Pursuing a foul quest, turning anyone who gets in her way into animals," Tobias growled. "It is vitally important that I find her—to stop her, and to save any of her victims that I can. Tell me quickly: what did you tell her, and where has she gone." He slammed a jingling sack full of coins down on the table. "Your help will not go unrewarded."

Clay had gotten to feeling quite a bit less awful by the time he stumbled out of the Thorny Tankard and into the muggy night air. Yes, the inebriation helped, but there was more to it than that. After all, he'd gone in with every intention of drinking until he passed out, and here he was staggering along home under his own power, still coherent enough to find his way by lantern light while singing a quiet tune to himself even if it was a funeral dirge. He almost felt heroic, knowing now it was an evil witch he'd fed lies to before taking her money.

In fact, he was sure he'd sensed it in her all along. Clever man that he was, he'd seen through the witch's disguise and sent her off on a wild goose chase, buying time for the pursuing prince to catch up and bring her to justice. Forget "almost"; he *was* a hero. What's more, he was a rich hero. He'd slain the monster, and he'd walked away with his pockets bulging with silver. Better still, it was starting ever so gently to rain.

Truly, it had been an un-bad day.

Clay was approaching the gate to the graveyard—on his way past to the cottage where he slept—when he saw the human skull lying in the path. It hadn't been there when he'd headed down to the Tankard, and no one but him would have had any proper business using the path between that time and this...but there it sat, neatly on the ground before the gate, like a dog waiting patiently on the stoop for some kind soul with a proper set of hands to come along and let it inside.

Clay stood, scratching his head, a little corner of his drink-addled brain filling up with ghost stories. Here it was, past the witching hour, on a misty, starless night—and he found himself standing alone, face-to-face with a skull that had no business being there, staring into its empty eye sockets.

How did those stories go again? If you weren't the hero, by the time you ran into something like this, your fate had already been sealed. If you ignored the warning, you were a fool, and whatever was lurking would cut you down. If you turned and fled, you were a coward, and whatever was lurking would chase you down. But he *was* the hero, wasn't he? At least for today? So what would a hero do?

Clay spent a few seconds frowning down at the skull before finally turning to unlatch the gate and swing it gently open. "All right, then," he addressed the skull, in a voice emboldened by drink. "In with you. No sense you wandering around out here all night."

Whether surprisingly or unsurprisingly, the skull failed to move. Then the snort of a horse in the darkness drew Clay's attention into the graveyard, and he saw red—the bold, billowing sort of red that stands out in lantern light against a black velvet night and screams for attention. This specific red took the form of long, flowing cloak draped around the shoulders of what was almost certainly a woman, although the red wouldn't actually let Clay take his eyes off of it long enough to explore the shadows beneath.

"Oh. Was, this...yours, then?" Clay asked, dry-mouthed, with a meaningful, sideways glance toward the skull.

Anyone standing about outside the graveyard that night would have testified they'd seen a whip lash silently out from the gates to twine about Clay's throat and drag him inward. Then they'd say they heard the lantern smash and the gates clang shut as the night went black. There being no actual witnesses to the event, all the townsfolk could say to the next important visitor who came calling for Clay Ambleforth was that he'd disappeared in the night, leaving behind no clue but a smashed lantern just inside the graveyard.

CHAPTER TWELVE

THE CALL TO SERVE

"Best of luck with your pilgrimage, sister!" Dame Eleanor bid a cheerful farewell as Elissa ducked her head to climb out of the coach. Their third benefactor since they'd fled Denecia, the elderly gentlewoman had proven keen on theological discussion during the ride.

She'd insisted that her captive audience satisfy her curiosity about such diverse riddles as, "How many demons can dance on the head of a penitent?" ("Probably twelve."), "If Seriena can do anything, does that mean she can make a brittlebeet stew so tasty you wouldn't have to hold your nose to choke it down?" ("I'd certainly think so."), and, "When the Inquisition's finally taken care of all the witches, do you think maybe they could do something about this ghastly weather?" ("I'll put it to the Grand Inquisitrix when I see her.")

In fact, the only definitive answer Elissa had to offer any of her questions was to how the women of heathen lands managed to bear children without Seriena's blessing of fertility. That one had actually been covered in a respected but obscure text she'd read, in which Seriena had mercifully shared her blessing of fertility with the unbelievers of the world; the catch being that if they were going to behave like uncivilized beasts, she would treat them like uncivilized beasts.

Rather than hang about to answer their prayers on a case by case basis, she made them settle for the same sort of blessing as the beasts, meaning anytime that they, well...did it...they just might wind up carrying their lover's child whether they'd meant to or not. That story had been new to Keely as well as to the owner of the carriage, and all three women agreed that it sounded like a dreadful and cruel business, especially to the child.

In the end, though, Dame Eleanor had seemed suitably impressed with the breadth of Elissa's vague and non-committal knowledge by the time she dropped them off at the crossroads, and they stood waving at her carriage until it had disappeared around a scraggly hedgerow.

"I should really have let you answer her questions," Elissa said, rummaging through her satchel to find her sandals, and slipping them on. "I don't think *anyone* would've had real answers for most of them, and you give non-answers with so much more conviction than I can."

The satchel had shown up at the same time as the sandals, and Elissa no longer asked Keely where she got anything from. The truth was, she couldn't afford to care, so she'd started placating her conscience with the observation that Keely really did prefer to take things from people who might never even miss them. After a few weeks on the road with absolutely no resources other than those which Keely managed to procure for them, Elissa's conscience had simply gone silent on the whole matter, and accepted that this was the way things worked now.

"Don't be silly," Keely said dismissively. "There couldn't have been a better time for you to practice, and I still say you've got the makings of an excellent liar. All we have to do is polish off the rough edges."

"Please tell me you were *born* without scruples." Elissa sighed. "It'll give me hope that I'll still have some left when all this is over."

"When all this is over, Jenny, you'll be able to afford all the scruples you care to buy." Keely grinned as they set off down the road, away from the route the carriage was taking.

"My name's *still* Elissa," Elissa said with a despairing sigh, then she stopped, staring off into the distance. "I think we're here," she said, pointing. Beyond a dry, thorny bramble that passed for a hedgerow in this part of the world, a chalky white spire of rock stood alone against a backdrop of forested hills midway through the act of trading its summer green coat for one of brilliant autumn red, accented with flecks of gold.

The northern slope of the spire rose in a graceful arc—climbing slowly at first, then more and more steeply as it neared the peak—while the southern slope fell away precipitously from top to bottom. A stone that got dropped off that side of the peak would surely hit something on the way down, but would just as surely bounce away and continue its journey rather then find a place to rest.

About two thirds of the way up the less severe slope, scaffolding and partial stone walls testified to some sort of construction or reconstruction underway on the spire.

"So, now what?" Elissa asked. "I'm still really vague on step two of your master plan."

"This would be step seven," Keely said. "Do keep up, Jenny."

"I'm still really vague on step seven, then."

"Step seven is finding the *Grimm Truth*."

"You couldn't perhaps be just a bit more vague, could you?" Elissa asked archly.

"I *mean*," said Keely, "we track down a book that someone who wanted to could believe was the Grimm Truth when she saw it from a distance—something old and musty and important looking, perhaps a bit on the holy side."

"You could have told me we needed a decoy back when I had a whole library full of them to choose from." Elissa sighed.

"By the time I knew we'd *need* a decoy, we were already on the run," Keely said. "We're smack in the middle of it now, and there's no time for crying over missed opportunities, is there? Just improvise. Where would you start looking for an old book?"

"Hard to think of any place better than an abbey," Elissa said.

"True," Keely conceded. "Which means that the Inquisition is probably already swarming over any abbey within a day of this place. If you've got any less obvious ideas, I'd like to hear them."

They walked on for a while in silence. "It only has to look right from a distance?" Elissa asked finally.

Keely nodded. "And not for long. It's to be a prop in a play, in a manner of speaking."

"Then for go'ss sake, just find the county market and take me shopping!" Elissa laughed.

"What? You think I have money?" Keely smirked.

"I think you're a woman on a mission, who is going to beg, borrow, or steal whatever she needs to get it accomplished—mostly steal, and mostly from victims who're going to say, 'thank you,' and then invite you around for supper after. And you *need* to take me shopping because, postulant or not, I was a librarian at Belgrimm. I've handled some of the oldest manuscripts in the world—*and I bind books*."

It turned out that the county market lay mercifully close by—less than an hour's walk down the road—in the less mercifully named little town of Weasel Gap, nestled in the shadow of a small stone castle atop a rocky hill. Rocky, in fact, seemed the order of the day, with the land immediately around the town suitable only for grazing animals and some haphazardly arranged orchards—not cultivated fields.

Westward past the town, the locals seemed to have given up on trying even to do that, cultivating only one of their thorny hedgerows to keep livestock from wandering into the ancient, shadowy forest beyond. A cannonball launched in that direction from the ramparts of the castle would probably have gotten into a fight with some five-hundred-year-old tree over who had a right to occupy that particular bit of space.

Nothing much recommended Weasel Gap as a site to build a town, except that the hill offered a reasonable place to put a castle, which then offered a reasonably protected place for craftsmen to set up business within a reasonable distance of all the outlying farming villages in the county.

"The tricky part," said Elissa as they wandered among a selection of little shops and stalls that one accustomed to the splendor of Serylia could most charitably think of as "disappointing", "is going to be finding proper metal fittings. They probably still use parchment out here, which is good for making an 'old' book out of, but either way, no one's getting close enough to tell, right?"

"If they do, we've got other things to worry about," Keely said.

"So a couple of boards, some leather, a nice dark stain for the leather...I can handle everything but the metal bits. We'll need those pre-made. But if we can find someone who deals in odds and ends, they might have..."

Elissa trailed off as she looked up to find a roundish, gray-haired fellow sitting on a donkey a few paces away, watching her with a patient-but-expectant—and slightly nervous—little smile, through a pair of pince-nez spectacles. His attire marked him at once as a member of the respectable middle class, and the ornamental arch inscribed on the craftsman's medallion around his neck hinted at his occupation.

"Ah, sister," he said, once he'd seen he'd caught her eye. "My apologies for putting you to the inconvenience of finding me. I was, in fact, just on my way to the castle with the ledgers."

"You...were?" Elissa asked, for want of any other ideas on how she should respond.

"Oh, straight-away," he assured her, dismounting a bit clumsily to rummage through the donkey's load until he'd produced a pair of well-worn books. "I was only delayed by a small emergency at the construction site. We can't allow any more setbacks, can we, after all that's happened? Speaking of which, as long as you've taken the trouble of coming to meet me..." He shoved the ledgers into Elissa's arms. "...I'll entrust them to you and return to my work. Far too much to be done, and the days are growing shorter."

"Oh, ummm...Fine," Elissa said, running her fingertips thoughtfully over the metal fittings of the top book.

"Thank you, Sister. And good day to you." The man tipped his hat respectfully and clambered back onto his donkey.

"Well," Elissa mused as she watched him ride away, "that was easy. Although it'll still need some serious work before anyone mistakes either of these for an ancient holy text. I'd hoped we could find something fancier for the metal bits, too."

"We'll see," Keely grinned. "But for now these books have more important job than playing decoy. They're going to make us an introduction."

"And what are we going to do with this introduction?" Elissa asked quietly, clutching the books to her chest as they lingered outside the great hall of the castle, waiting to be announced.

"Haven't a clue," Keely whispered, shrugging and biting her lip. "Well, that's not strictly true, but you don't think I planned *this* bit, do you? Every introduction presents an opportunity, and we're going to need all the opportunities we can get."

At that point, the doors to the great hall swung open, and the man who'd asked them to wait there slipped out, but he just shook his head as they straightened up expectantly. "I'm sorry, Sister," he apologized to Elissa, "it sounds like they'll be a while."

Elissa just nodded understandingly as the man moved on, but Keely furtively caught the doors before they had swung entirely shut, and casually propped them open a crack to spy on what promised to be an interesting conversation.

"Tosh! You can't seriously suggest that I go and tell the Angelis that Mother Church has been brought to her knees by the ghost of Weasel Gap!" a short but imposingly stocky woman bellowed, brandishing a gnarled old walking stick.

"Oh, my..." Elissa's jaw dropped as she peered past Keely and through the crack in the doors to stare at the speaker and her ornately trimmed golden robes. "Keely, let's just get out of here while we can. Trying to pass myself off as a priestess to a real priestess would be bad enough, but to a pontifine?"

"Oh, just relax and let me listen," Keely shushed her. "You'll do fine."

"Technically, Your Grace, she's considered the ghost of the Crimson Forest." Despite his considerable height and broad, muscular shoulders, the man seemed much less imposing at the moment than the woman beside him did.

"She's a band of bloody vandals is what she is, Haywood. Or do you buy into this heathen nonsense yourself?"

"Certainly not, Your Grace!" he answered indignantly. "But there is something...unholy...about the site."

"And what does one do about unholy ground, Haywood?" she demanded.

The man fumbled helplessly for an answer.

"You there!" the pontifine snapped as she spun about to face the doors where Keely and Elissa stood. "Whichever postulant is lurking at the door, come in here girl, and tell us what you do about unholy ground!"

Keely slapped Elissa's hand lightly to stop her from reaching for the door. "Keep your head, Sister," Keely reprimanded quietly. "She caught a glimpse of *my* blue robes."

With her head bowed in a demeanor of respectful subservience, Keely pushed the doors open wide enough to slip through.

"What do you *do*?" the pontifine demanded again.

"You, ummm...consecrate it, Your Grace?" Keely ventured uncertainly.

"See!" the pontifine declared, triumphantly banging her walking stick on the head table as she turned back to the original conversation. "Every postulant knows, and so would you if you ever attended services, Haywood. You consecrate it. And what could be more sacrosanct than a cathedral?

"We don't need another diocese in the heartland, Haywood," she said. "We need a diocese out here to deal with just this sort of nonsense. This cathedral has got to be built and it's going to be built, and if you can't control the heathen rabble long enough to get the job done, I'm sure King Gannon can find someone who can manage his lands properly."

"Yes, Your Grace," the man answered, tight-lipped.

"So who have we here?" the pontifine asked, beckoning both Keely and Elissa forward. "Why haven't you introduced us, Haywood?"

"This is the first I've seen of them myself, Your Grace," the man answered.

Elissa curtsied, mustering herself to play the priestess properly and take charge of the situation from her supposed postulant. "Sister, er..." She coughed, pointedly clearing her throat to cover the stumble. "Sister Jenny of Brookshire, Your Grace," she said, "and my charge is the postulant Chloe."

The pontifine scowled, peering closely at Elissa's face. "You're awfully young for a priestess."

"I hear that a lot, Your Grace. A happy circumstance for me that my looks are deceiving," Elissa answered so smoothly and with such a sociable smile that Keely had to fight to repress a grin. The girl was learning fast.

"Are they now," the pontifine harrumphed. "At least you seem to be training your postulant up right. You're in the presence of Pontifine Augusta, and this would be Lord Darby, Earl of Haywood. What business brings you here?"

"That would be these ledgers, Your Grace," Elissa said, holding them forward. "Some man down at the market shoved them at us and insisted we bring them up to the castle. I'm guessing now that he mistook us for part of your entourage, but he rode off before I could question him. We're actually just passing through on pilgrimage to Meissi." The ad lib caught Keely by surprise. Up to now they'd been telling everyone that it was Aeladia they were headed for, and by Elissa's own suggestion. Of course, she'd also been introducing herself as "Sister Alice". There was no question the girl was more nervous than showed on her face.

"Ah, there's a good lass." Augusta finally smiled as she stepped up, flipping open one of the proffered books and glancing inside. She nodded with satisfaction and gestured for Elissa to lay them on the head table nearby, then began pacing about, leaning heavily on her walking stick. "I started my own pilgrimage to Meissi the day after my ordination. Too many people put it off. Too, too many. Then they get to be old and hobbledy like me, and the next thing they know, they're begging their children to drag them there in a donkey cart. Or else the plague comes and, well...It's a fine, fine place, Meissi. Well worth the trip, even without its spiritual benefits."

"So I've heard, your Grace," Elissa said.

"Now what's holding up dinner, Haywood?" Augusta demanded. "Our pilgrims must be as famished as I am."

"I'll inquire after preparations at once, Your Grace," Darby said with forced politeness.

"Now, then," Augusta said, settling at the head table. "Sit! Sit! You must tell me everything. Where have you come from? What adventures have you had this far?"

"Well, uh..." Elissa glanced pleadingly to Keely—her supply of cleverness apparently wearing thin—and Keely replied with an accepting nod. "Postulant Chloe's quite a bit more eloquent than I am, and she really inspired me to take up the pilgrimage. Perhaps she should be telling the story."

"Certainly. Certainly," Augusta said agreeably. "I do love the enthusiasm of youth."

"Actually, I have to give credit to the Miraculata Cosima for inspiring the journey," Keely began.

"Oh? Do you know her?" Augusta asked.

"We met just the once. I'm sure she doesn't remember my name, but she entreated me to travel far. 'Go, and Goddess guide you,' she said."

"Lovely, dear woman, Miraculata Cosima," Augusta nodded. "And wise beyond her years. You did well heeding her advice."

"Of course, I wouldn't have got far on my own," Keely went on, "so I harangued the Sister into leading me on a proper pilgrimage, and she'd always sung the praises of..." Keely took her turn at coughing to buy a moment to search her memory. "Sorry. Sung the praises of the place," she bulled onward, having entirely failed to recall the name Meissi, "so before long, there we were on the road, without the slightest clue how very far we were getting in over our heads..."

Keely wove the rambling tale of a natural storyteller concerned more about keeping her audience engaged than in sounding plausible. She threw in mention of the now notorious witch "from far off Sabracar", of course, and of the enigmatic "Lady A" who seemed to be chasing her across the continent, but they featured alongside such other highlights as a narrow escape from highwaymen in a desolate swamp, an encounter with a once-holy inquisitrix gone mad, a bloodthirsty ogre, some pirates, and a terrible flood.

The timeline did begin to wander and grow fuzzy after a while, and it became increasingly difficult to tell which bit happened when in relation to what, or even if—perhaps—several of them mightn't have happened simultaneously. Still, what she lost in coherence she made up for in raw energy. She also stitched the whole thing together with a thread made of pious determination and of good fortune visited by the grace of Seriena, which appealed to the current audience most thoroughly, and kept the narrative from falling apart into irredeemable silliness.

"My, my," Augusta chuckled when Keely had finished the epic fabrication. "With a glib tongue like that, you're going to make a fine priestess, child. I suspect this is one of those tales that grows larger with each re-telling," she said with a sideways glance at Elissa, who answered with a little grin and a tiny nod of confirmation, "but you re-tell it well. I've half a mind to put you on the pulpit preaching the joys of the pilgrimage, only I'm afraid you'd make it sound *too* adventurous.

"You know, I do believe I sense Seriena's hand in our meeting," Augusta went on, addressing her comments once more to Elissa. "This weary old body has a favor to ask, and you'll find she can be most appreciative of those who come to the aid of her diocese."

"We'll do what we can, of course, Your Grace," Elissa said, "though I hope it won't keep us long from our pilgrimage."

"Of course, of course, dear. Service to the Goddess can be most inconvenient at times. No one knows that better than I. But I must insist you stay on for a couple of months as a spiritual guide for the locals while they're working on my cathedral. The woman I had installed in the position met a rather foolhardy end, I'm afraid, trying to fend off the ruffians who sabotaged our progress. It was a noble gesture, but one that should have been made by someone else entirely." Augusta cast a dark look across the hall in the direction of their host.

"Anyway, you're smarter than that, and I dare say that Haywood shan't make the same mistake twice, or his whole family will pay for it. All it will take is two months for me to line up a suitable replacement and return. The you're off again on your merry pilgrimage, and with a very handsome position waiting for you in my diocese when you're done."

"Well, I don't know..." Elissa began.

"How to thank me? No need, child. Just do your duty," she punctuated each word of the sentence by rapping her walking stick lightly on Elissa's shoulder, "and perhaps bring me back a trinket from Meissi.

"Haywood?!" she bellowed. "I just saw that man. Now where has he gotten to? Ah, there you are. Haywood, Sister Jenny and her postulant here will be ministering to the area in my absence. I will not find them dead when I return. I will not find them mysteriously missing. They will be right here, alive and well, and smilingly showing me the intact progress that's been made on my cathedral, or I shall have a trophy room built, just so I can hang your head in it. Do I make myself clear?"

"Yes, Your Grace." It was the most polite growl either Keely or Elissa had ever heard.

CHAPTER THIRTEEN

IN SERIENA'S EYES

The eyes of Seriena looked out reflectively over every congregation in every chapel throughout the kingdoms. That was, in fact, how you knew it was a chapel: her gaze manifested as a matched pair of large mirrors behind the altar. In the early days of her church, Seriena had only kept one eye on each chapel (or so it seemed to Elissa from her studies): one grand and perfectly circular mirror of reverently polished copper, from which the Goddess was said to look out from behind the altar, and in which pious worshipers would occasionally claim to catch some glimpse of the Goddess herself.

As the centuries passed, the metaphor of the mirror as the eyes of Seriena evolved into a more literal translation, which eventually resulted in the current custom of the paired mirrors in the stylized shape of a woman's eyes. In a modern grand cathedral, the mirrors would be huge and baroquely ornate, framed in precious stones and metals, with polished marble for the whites of the eyes; glass backed in gold-leaf for the irises; and polished onyx for the pupils. Perhaps the only thing that hadn't changed about the mirrors was the reported sightings of Seriena within them.

The chapel in Castle Haywood was no grand cathedral, and the mirrors behind the sturdy wooden altar could have been centuries old, hearkening back to the simplistic style of the earliest paired mirrors: just two slightly distorted and skewed ellipses of bright, unadorned copper, smooth as glass and mounted on a wooden backing carved with decorative scrollwork. A pair of fancy iron candelabras and a series of tapestries depicting the lives of miraculatas—many of whom not even Elissa could recognize—finished the trappings of the boxy, spartan room that had been the domain of the recently departed Sister Petra.

Behind one of the tapestries lay the alcove where Sister Petra had slept, and it was there that Keely and Elissa found themselves now, getting settled in as they pointedly failed to say anything meaningful about the situation that had befallen them. Though there was much to be discussed, they had already agreed—through a dozen different non-verbal signals—that an unfamiliar old castle like this was no place to go saying anything they shouldn't care to have public knowledge.

There was no guessing what odd acoustics might carry their voices where, nor what secret spy holes might have been left by centuries of courtly intrigue. Their own eavesdropping back at Belgrimm Abbey had left them keenly aware of that possibility, so they wordlessly resolved to maintain their charade as if under surveillance the whole time they were in Castle Haywood. Tomorrow, they would go out and "minister", as they had been charged to do, and they would sort the whole thing out then.

Most of Sister Petra's personal effects had long since been removed, but Elissa did inherit her cot, and they'd also been given a straw-filled pallet for Keely to sleep on. As Keely laid that out on the floor near the cot, Elissa busied herself by going through what had been left behind in Petra's writing desk and on the alcove's one little shelf. It didn't amount to much.

"Looks like I was wrong about the parchment here," Elissa said. "Sister Petra, at least, was using paper."

"Is that going to be a problem?" Keely asked.

Elissa bit her lip thoughtfully as she shook her head. "Parchment would be better for...some purposes, but either one should get the job done." Catching a shadow of movement out in the chapel, beyond the tapestry, she quickly added, "The point is simply having something to write on." She paused expectantly, but whoever it was out in the chapel seemed to be neither sneaking around nor approaching closer, so Elissa finally brushed the tapestry aside herself and peered out. A brown-robed girl of ten or so, with pinned-up, curly red hair and ears that looked like they were waiting for her to grow into them, sat in the corner with a wooden tablet in her lap and a look of intense concentration on her face. The tip of her tongue peeked out from the corner of her mouth as she slowly etched meticulous lines into the wax on the surface of the tablet.

Her curiosity satisfied for the moment, Elissa turned her attention back to going through the desk, but Keely slipped on out past the tapestry and approached the girl. "And what are we doing here?" Keely asked, peering down at the girl's tablet.

"Practicing my letters," the girl answered without looking up. "The church won't take a postulant who doesn't know her letters."

"Well, you're doing a fine, fine job," Keely assured her. "Your letters already look better than mine do."

"Do they really?" the girl asked, engaged enough by the compliment to make eye contact—after she'd finished out the letter she'd been working on, of course.

"They really do. Though it's fair to warn you, I managed to get into these robes despite my penmanship, not because of it. Safest to keep practicing, in case they're stricter with you than they were with me. I'm Keely, by the way."

"Addie," the girl said simply, returning to her letters. "I'm the chapel attendant."

"So you worked for Sister Petra, then?"

"Yes. And she was a good woman, no matter what you hear anyone else say." Addie looked up from her work again, defiantly this time. "The ghost shouldn't've killed her."

"Is someone saying it should have?" Keely asked, not having to work too hard at sounding aghast.

"A lot of folk didn't like her," Addie said, not exactly answering the question. "She didn't always understand the way we do things here, and she got into some real rows with our own priestesses. But she took an interest in me when no one else cared, so don't go bad-mouthing her to me."

"Of course not," Keely assured the girl readily. "Not a local woman, then?"

"Sent by Pontifine Augusta, just like the sister in there," Addie said, nodding toward Elissa in the alcove, "and don't expect to be winning any friends for it. It seems we don't care for strangers much here."

"Then it's an excellent thing," Keely said, grinning conspiratorially, "that I've never been a stranger anywhere. And Sister Jenny's all right; certainly more interested in her books than in butting heads with anybody."

"Oh, we're used to butting heads, Miss," Addie said. "Course there was plenty of grumbling about it with Sister Petra, but it wouldn't have got her killed. It was her *books* that did that."

"Her books got her killed?!" Elissa asked, suddenly appearing at the edge of the tapestry.

"Books are bad luck," Addie said. "Cursed. Everybody knows that."

"And tablets aren't?" Elissa asked, staring pointedly at the girl's work-in-progress.

"Not if you smudge out the writing when you're done," Addie said.

"Then what's the point of writing at all?!" Elissa asked in exasperation. "Look, I thought you said it was the ghost that killed her, anyway."

"Bloody Scarlet *killed* her. The books *got her killed*," Addie clarified, with the exaggerated patience of someone who wasn't really showing any. "Like falling under the wheels of a carriage'd kill you, but you never would've fallen if you hadn't broke that mirror last week. Books are bad luck."

"Why is everybody rushing to tell me this *now*? Wouldn't it have made sense to bring it up *before* I accepted a post at the abbey library? Just once?" Elissa withdrew back into the alcove behind the tapestry with a growl of frustration.

Keely gave Addie an apologetic smile before following after Elissa, to find her face down on the cot, her arms splayed carelessly to the side as if she'd simply collapsed there and couldn't be bothered even about making herself comfortable. Keely started to speak, but Elissa interrupted her before she could get a word out.

"I have never traveled so far," she said, her voice muffled by the bedding. "I have never walked so far. Every day we do things that keep me wound like a spring. Every night I'm too on edge or in too much pain or we have too little time for me to sleep right. You run off and do whatever you want. I'm going to lie here and try to find the energy to care which horrible death will catch up to me first. With any luck, I'll fall into a coma before I manage it. Good night."

Leaving Elissa to lie in bed, Keely persuaded Addie to take her on a tour of the castle, and to get her up to speed on the area and its inhabitants. Remaining in one spot for two months was putting down some serious roots, as far as Keely was concerned, and she would really need to do her homework if she was going to pull it off. The circumstance would have been challenging even if she hadn't been sending out all those open invitations to follow her here.

The thought of cutting and running certainly held its appeal, but she would have to plan that carefully if she wanted to keep Pontifine Augusta from taking out her anger on the Haywood family. Leaving them to their fate without first being sure they warranted it would be a serious violation of the Rules.

She'd seen for herself, in a very close and personal way, just what became of people who tried to live without rules. For one thing, it couldn't really be done. For another, the closer you got to achieving that goal, the less human you became, until you were nothing more than some feral beast that no sane person would have anything to do with—one that society would eventually hunt down and rid itself of.

To the casual observer, it might seem as if Keely lived without rules, but that's just because she was rigorously selective about which ones she would follow. Those she kept all bound up together in the well-worn mental scrapbook that she'd pieced together from fragments of thought that she'd collected over the years. She couldn't actually recall the business of starting it, but page one offered its own hint as to why she had every time she opened the book.

The page had been given over to an audio clip of a woman's voice sternly demanding, "Do *not* spend your life playing someone else's game. *You* make your *own* rules, and *you* enforce them." She'd no other memory of her mother to corroborate who that voice belonged to, but it had to be her. Nothing else made sense.

So to stay true to her mother, she'd begun recording the Rules for herself. And to stay true to her mother, she'd rejected the petty little life Hart Cove had planned for her and...gone...That was, Jenilee had gone...

Keely slammed the book shut on that thought and bit her lip hard as she began singing a bawdy drinking song in her head at the top of her mental lungs. Thinking too hard about Hart Cove always got her confused, and always brought on the nightmares. She could hardly remember it anyway—couldn't even remember how the three of them had escaped. The nightmares about *not* escaping had burned themselves into her brain over and over until that's the only way she could recall it. Yet here she was.

"Are you okay?" Addie asked, looking up with concern on her face.

"Couldn't be better," Keely answered with reflexive sincerity, banishing her introspection. "So that's where they're building the cathedral?" she asked, pointing up to the construction on the Wolf's Tooth.

"Yeah," Addie confirmed. The tour had taken them up to the top of one of the castle towers, and it offered an excellent vantage point from which to take stock of the surrounding countryside.

"It looks like a better place for a castle than a cathedral," Keely observed. "In fact, it *begs* for a castle. I can't imagine why anyone would put one down here when they could have put it up there instead."

"Someone did," Addie said.

"Oh?" Keely asked. "That sounds like a story begging to be told."

"There was an Imperial fort up there that Emperor Lupus used as his headquarters during his final war against the barbarians. He burned with it on the Night of Skulls, and the rock has been cursed ever since."

"No one's tried rebuilding in all that time?" Keely asked.

"Oh, sure," Addie said. "There've been three or four more castles up there. They always fall into ruin. The last one just blew up."

"It blew up?" Keely raised an eyebrow.

"It was one of the very first castles to be outfitted with cannons. Earl Jedrick wanted to turn it into a mighty citadel and bring some glory back to this place. They say for weeks you could watch gunpowder being carted up the hill by the ton. Then one day...boom. Farmers still turn up shards of old castle wall in their fields, miles from the Wolf's Tooth."

"Sounds like quite a colorful history." Keely smiled grimly, shaking her head.

"We tried to tell the pontifine not to build there, but people from the heartlands always know better than we do," Addie said, her eyes challenging Keely to come out and declare herself one of those patronizing foreigners—or even sympathetic to them. "And now everything's going wrong before her cathedral can even be built."

"What about this castle?" Keely asked. "It looks too old to have been built after that."

"It wasn't, I think," Addie said, leaning out over the battlements to enjoy the cool evening breeze on her face. The sky was gray, and the wind smelled of distant rain—no small delight to experience after the long, dry summer. "I don't know much about its past, but I'm pretty sure it's been around a good, long while. I think the other castles just weren't around long enough for this one to ever fall out of use."

"Is this one cursed or haunted or anything?"

"Not that I know of," Addie answered earnestly. "Just the Wolf's Tooth and the forest."

"I think Earl Haywood made some mention of that." Keely nodded.

"So that's all you really need to worry about. Oh, and the books, of course."

"Of course."

"And maybe the Inquisition." Addie nodded down toward a small procession being led through the streets by a black-robed woman on a courser—black with white markings—that even at this distance and in the fading light of oncoming dusk, radiated an aura of barely restrained power and temper. Flanking her rode another priestess of the Inquisition on one side, and a red-and-black clad knight of the Inquisition on the other. Trailing along after them marched half a dozen footmen in the livery of the Inquisition.

"Oh, yes," Keely said, biting her lip as she watched them cut a wake through the thinning crowds of the marketplace on their way toward the castle. "Them."

When Keely woke to the pale morning light filtering in through the narrow window of the little alcove, she yawned and stretched, digging her claws into the blanket and twisting this way and that, working the built-up kinks and stiffness out of her spine.

According to Addie, Sister Shoshona—the inquisitrix—and her entourage had arrived at Weasel Gap a couple of days prior, in the company of Pontifine Augusta. She'd been charged with the business of rooting out whatever "loathsome heretics" were responsible for sabotaging progress on the cathedral, and for the death of a holy woman.

Previously, that had been Earl Haywood's responsibility, but the incident in which Sister Petra had died had regrettably been the most recent, not the first. The pontifine had—and most charitably, she seemed to think—decided that the earl was incapable of conducting the investigation and providing proper security for the site at the same time, so she'd decided to free him up to focus on preventing further setbacks.

Keely had returned to the chapel to find Elissa still lying face-down on the cot, in what could have been the exact same position she'd left her. Satisfied that the Inquisition wasn't likely to drag them out of their beds in the night, Keely had opted not to disturb the exhausted young woman and save any news that might disrupt her badly needed dreams for the morning.

Keely had not been so satisfied, however, as to curl up peacefully in her own bed. Instead, she'd folded up her clothes neatly, transformed into a cat, and curled up on a pile of blankets in the corner beneath Elissa's cot. There, hidden from view from anyone who might burst suddenly into their rooms, she'd finally realized how exhausted she herself had been, and she'd slept.

And it was there, under the cot, as Keely lazily roused herself the next morning, that it dawned on her that something about the floor beneath the blankets didn't feel quite right.

Curiously, Keely poked her nose beneath the blankets, and sneezed at the whiff of mold up her nostrils. She sat back for a moment, rubbing her nose with her paws, and then when she'd quite recovered, held her breath and tried again.

This time she discovered she'd spent the night lying on top of a small, weathered book. The thing lacked the air of ancient respectability—even in its metal fixtures—that she was looking for in a decoy, but it had somehow arranged for itself to wind up in what might be the only place no one had bothered to look while cleaning up Sister Petra's personal effects, so Keely liked the odds that it contained some secret worth knowing.

When Elissa at last stirred in her bed, it was to find Keely up, alert and dressed and sitting, watching her patiently.

"Ready to face the day?" Keely chimed cheerfully.

"Maybe," Elissa grunted, rolling up onto her side. "Will it involve running from anyone or pretending I'm more charming than I am?"

"Only if we're lucky. We can start it off with a job I think you'll actually like, though." Keely slid the little book across the floor to Elissa.

"Where did you get this?" Elissa asked with surprise.

"Never you mind right now. Just have a look and tell me if there's anything worthwhile in it."

"If you want to brush up on scripture, there is," Elissa said, scooping up the book and beginning to thumb through it. "It's a copy of the *Exemplar Serinitas*. If you mean anything other than that, though..." She shrugged, and as she did so, a sheaf of neatly folded papers slid out. Elissa picked up the papers and gave them a cursory scan, then stopped and began to study them more closely. As she did, an odd array of expressions played across her face, such that Keely couldn't decide whether their sum total meant good news or bad by the time Elissa folded the papers crisply back into the book, snapped it shut, and declared, "We *really* need to get out and do some ministering."

They were most of the way across the main courtyard, headed for the castle gates, when a sharp, stern voice drew them up short. "Where exactly do you think you're going?"

The two young women turned slowly about to see Earl Haywood glowering at them from about fifty paces away, where he'd been talking with an inquisitrix. The black robed priestess remained silent, but stared at them implacably.

"I'm...supposed to be ministering," Elissa answered. Her voice faltered at first, but she quickly rallied after that first stammer, pulling herself up straight and delivering the rest of the answer with an indignant edge.

"Not without an escort you're not. Ulric! Nolan!" The nobleman shouted to the two men who'd been standing by the gate, at ceremonial attention in the presence of the inquisitrix. Excusing himself with a quick word to the black-robed priestess, Haywood stalked over to Elissa and Keely, where the guards joined them.

"Our honored guests will be wanting bodyguards," Haywood said, his tone forbidding any attempt at contradiction. "Consider yourselves assigned to them until the pontifine returns. Their lives are worth more than yours and your families' put together. Don't forget that for a minute, and never let them out of your sight."

"Such a fuss," Elissa grumbled as they headed out. "Will you please stand back?! Just twenty paces? Okay, ten! Or do you think the weasels are liable to jump out and maul us to death before you can get that far?"

Keely stifled a laugh. "They're just doing their job," she said quietly after the men had given them some room.

"It won't do them much good if I suffocate," Elissa said. Then, lowering her voice, she added, "I guess this will have to do for privacy."

"So what was in the letters?" Keely whispered.

"I think the girl was right: Sister Petra's books did get her killed." Elissa cast a glance over her shoulder, satisfying herself that the men were almost certainly out of earshot of hushed conversation. "It looks like she was corresponding with 'Lady A'."

"*Our* Lady A?" Keely asked.

"There's no signature, but the wax seals were imprinted with an 'A', and they're definitely talking about Amberford's journals."

"That's got to be her," Keely agreed.

"They don't come right out and say it, but if I'm reading correctly between the lines, I think they were convinced that Amberford found you-know-what up on the Wolf's Tooth itself, and Petra had started searching for it up there," Elissa said.

"Then it's settled," Keely said with a satisfied grin. "That's where it'll be found. Add those letters to the history of the place, and you've got a story that everyone will be wanting to believe."

They quieted down after that, then began to discuss inanities in normal tones, concerned that too much whispering would arouse curiosity in their escorts. When they'd set out for the morning, they'd had no more plan than to get somewhere off on their own where they could dare to make plans. Now, with even that plan spoiled, they floundered a bit, trying to figure out their next move without being seen to do anything that looked too overtly like the scheming that needed doing. Mercifully, the market just down from the castle gates offered an obvious first stop, and casually browsing its stalls amid the morning bustle gave Keely time to process the latest developments, formulate a plan, and whisper enough of it too Elissa that she could uphold the charade of being in charge.

"I should like to start by having a word with the architect of the cathedral," Elissa announced to their shadows. "Any reason to think I won't find him at the construction site?"

CHAPTER FOURTEEN
SABINA'S BREAKDOWN

It was mid-morning by the time a rather splendid carriage came rattling along the rutted road toward Weasel Gap, only to make an abrupt, unexpected stop at the fork in the road where Keely and Elissa had found themselves dropped off the day before. Beneath the layers of road dust, which now rendered the carriage various dingy shades of brown, lay paints of vibrant red and white and appointments of shining silver—all of which could probably be restored to their original glory at some point through the auspices of a vigorous cleaning.

In the meantime, their muted hues only served to hint at the truth that the carriage had been designed with the thought of transporting fine ladies and gentlemen through the relatively clean, cobbled streets of the respectable parts of a respectable town. In fact, much more thought had gone into its construction as to the business of arriving in style than in the business of arriving at all, which might be why—after weeks of abuse, traveling between kingdoms and often along what only the most charitable soul could call roads—the carriage hit one particularly deep rut, and something in the front axle splintered with a resounding crack. The left front wheel sheered away, and the carriage pitched in that direction so suddenly the coachman flew from his seat to land in what would have been mud had the parched ground not been so thirsty to drink up the rains that had come in the night. As it was, the rains had at least softened the dirt, so perhaps he achieved the most merciful landing possible under the circumstances. Nonetheless, he was still picking himself up and taking stock of what damage might have befallen him, when the occupants of the coach began to emerge.

"So sorry, sir," the coachman apologized as he hastened to help a handsome, brown-haired young gentleman, who was squirming out the window of the coach on account of the door being wedged nearly shut against a large rock protruding from the ground. The rakishly dressed gentleman gave only a curt nod, neither thanking the coachman for his help, nor venting his displeasure at the situation.

He left that to the young woman in rose pink that they together helped out of the coach after him—or at least she handled the part about venting displeasure. Sabina Elettra Marini muttered a string of very unladylike oaths, in defiance of her very ladylike appearance, until they'd made sure she was fit to stand on her own. Then, as they turned to assist a second lady from the carriage, Sabina spied exactly what had happened to the coach, and the epithets began anew.

"What go'ss-forsaken land have you stranded us in now, little brother?" Sabina asked the young rake sharply when she'd finally exhausted her ready supply of curses, but Baldassare had long since learned not to let his sister bait him. He was not the same rakish gentleman who'd accompanied Sabina at the disconcerting dinner party where she'd been treated to Keely's ghost story.

Sabina knew whole boatloads of young, rakish gentlemen. A few of them had even fought duels over her. Baldassare distinguished himself from among those other gentlemen chiefly by being the very least concerned of them about her opinions of him, and by two small-but-noticeable notches in his left ear—one left by a pistol shot, one by a rapier. Remarkably, the scars had been left as reminders of two separate duels, neither one of which had had anything at all to do with Sabina.

Giving his sister's question no more acknowledgment than a dark, sideways look, Baldassare called out to one of the horsemen who'd been riding in entourage. "The county market can't be far ahead, Lanzo. We're all right here. Ride ahead to find if they've someone with the skill to fix this mess."

The horseman, who'd been about to rein his horse and dismount to assist, now nodded his head instead, and rode off at a brisk pace.

"And this go'ss-forsaken land," Baldassare said, finally acknowledging his sister as he looked about the landscape, "would seem to be the one in the shadow of the Wolf's Tooth, just as you planned. Though how you hope to find anything here is still beyond me."

"No one's pretending it's not a long shot, Baldassare," Sabina said with a smirk, "but compared to the time and money you routinely waste gambling, I'd call the investment in this little expedition both modest and sensible, wouldn't you?"

"Slain once again by your rapier wit," Baldassare answered without any trace of sincerity—but Sabina had already turned her attention to the little girl she'd just noticed watching them from her perch on a nearby gate. Off in the orchard beyond, several other children could be spied darting in and out of view, engaged in some manner of game involving wooden swords and hobby horses. More than half of the children sported hair in various shades of red, but even among them, the long hair of the little girl stood out as the most striking and vibrant shade. A very pretty little thing, perhaps eight or nine years of age from the look of her, all fair skin and freckles, she sat with a little grin on her face as if she were watching a parade passing by. Around her shoulders hung a brilliant red cloak, much finer than the rest of her rough garb.

Sabina took on a rather bright red hue herself, blushing to think of the language the child would have just overheard her use, but she took a moment to compose herself, and all her harsh edges vanished. Her smile when she addressed the girl, whether it was genuine or not, would at the very least have given the most jaded onlooker pause to think it must be. "Hello, dear. I'm sure you've noticed we're in some need of help. Are we close to the market town?"

The girl nodded and pointed into the orchard. "Just a quick walk," she said. "The road goes the long way."

"Is there an inn?" asked the blond woman who'd climbed out of the coach after Sabina. Or perhaps it would be better to say she'd "unfolded" out of the coach, for despite her elegant, fashionable attire, her build could best be described as "amazonian", and she stood at least half a head taller than any of the men attending them. Her face and figure remained pleasantly feminine, but if one were to put her in the right clothes and put a sword in her hand, she'd have made a very plausible barbarian queen of ages gone by, from the frozen mountains of the north.

As to the presence of an inn, the girl gave a look that hinted she thought this a daft sort of question to be asked, but the look had vanished in an instant, to be replaced with a more amiable one. "The Golden Crescent," she said politely. "It's rather nice."

"I do hope so," the tall woman replied. "After this journey, I'll not be fit to be seen at the county court before I've had at least half a night soaking in a hot bath."

"Can you show us the way?" Sabina asked the girl. "I must admit that sounds like an excellent idea."

The girl shrugged but hopped down from the gate and headed unhurriedly off through the orchard, looking back after a few paces to see if they were following.

Baldassare took a moment to advise the coachman that they'd have a wagon sent back for the trunks, and that the rest of the expedition should join them at the inn once the coach was seen to, then he hastened to catch up with the women.

"We've been roaming the countryside looking for old books to publish," Sabina was saying to the girl. "The older the better. In the age of the printing press, no book should ever have to truly die, you know. Yet every year an appalling amount of scholarship is lost to us forever. Of course, any abbeys about should have their share of books, but do you know anyone else around here who might collect them?"

"No one," the girl answered simply.

"Ah, well," Sabina said, not having pinned any real hopes on the question to a child. "Perhaps they'll know at the inn."

"Of course they know," the girl said. "Everyone knows. No one around here would be silly enough to collect books."

"Oh," Sabina frowned, partly at the news, partly at what it implied about the girl's opinion of her. "What's so silly about collecting books?"

"Scarlet would never let them keep them."

Around them, a brisk autumn breeze stirred the branches of the apple trees, heavy with fruit for the harvest, and dislodged the occasional droplet of water that had managed to elude the light of the morning sun. The clouds had withdrawn before daybreak, but the air still smelled of rain, and another darkening cloud bank had just begun to threaten.

"Then it sounds like this 'Scarlet' is the one we should be talking to. Does she hoard the books for her..." Sabina trailed off as a flash of red and a flutter of movement caught her eye. Neither one would have attracted attention on its own—the red was weathered and muddied, not so bright as the girl's cloak, or even so bright as the apples in the orchard; and the fluttering barely exceeded that of the leaves on the trees—but together they did the trick, and gave Sabina a start to think that someone was standing there watching them.

After a moment, though, the figure resolved itself into a scarecrow in a badly tattered red cloak. Sabina breathed an almost-inaudible sigh of relief just in time to get her second start, as the wind-tossed hood fluttered aside to reveal the face of the scarecrow. Atop the thing's crudely constructed shoulders sat an actual human skull.

"Ugh." Sabina's tall, blond companion wrinkled her nose at the sight.

"It's a scarecrow," the girl said, as if speaking to someone very slow and stupid.

"It's a scarecrow with a *skull* on," emphasized Baldassare.

"Yeah?" the girl responded. It was the impertinent sort of query where one could practically hear her throwing up her hands and arching her eyebrow simply from the tone of her voice, begging to be told why this was not the stupidest observation she had ever heard. Indeed, it was so impertinent that Sabina found herself reaching across Baldassare to block his use of one arm and restrain the wrist of the other when she saw the look on his face—for concern he was about to strike the child.

All moral concerns and protective instincts aside, there was no telling whose child this might be—certainly not some nameless pauper, given the quality of her cloak—and antagonizing the locals could end their search before it had begun.

Sabina considered trying to redirect the conversation back to a more productive subject, but decided they'd be better off waiting to discuss such matters with adults—rather than risk another conversational spark that might set Baldassare off—so instead she began chattering with her tall companion, Evadne, about fashion, court gossip, and other random inanities that they'd already rehashed many times on the long journey, while Baldassare and the girl simply allowed them to chatter.

After a quarter mile or so, with the laughter of the other children fading in the distance, they reached the far side of the orchard, where the girl ducked through a large but rough gap in the hedge. Sabina paused for a moment, peering into the dark opening before ducking in, but from somewhere beyond came the reassuring sounds of wagon wheels on cobbles, horses snorting, and voices competing with each other to be heard, in the manner of marketplaces everywhere.

Halfway through the opening, Sabina's cloak snagged on a brier. It took her a few moments to untangle, and she pricked her finger in the process, so she was a bit cross when she emerged sucking the blood from her fingertip and found that she still couldn't see the market—and that their guide hadn't waited.

This was a wood, dark and ancient, grown up right to the hedge with trees so tall and so twisted that they'd surely been old when Sabina's mother had been born. Their canopy so blotted out the sun that, with her eyes still trying to adjust, she could barely make out the little girl's red cloak disappearing into the gloom ahead. Sabina called out as she stood waiting for the others to get through the opening in the hedge, but if the girl heard her, she showed no sign of it. Evadne, with her great size, had gotten well tangled by the briers, where Sabina had merely snagged, so by the time she'd carefully extricated her skirts and cloak, their guide had completely disappeared.

"Small wonder most people stick with the road," Baldassare remarked, but Sabina was craning her neck to stare up into the leaves of the dark forest, gazing around raptly like a sleeper who had just awoken to find herself in an unexpected and wondrous place.

"We're on the right track," Sabina murmured. "So old. So wild. So powerful. This is a place where magic happens. Can't you just feel it?"

"All I feel is tired and sore and hungry," Evadne said. "Maybe a little creeped out, I guess. If I found myself here alone, I'd be not here just as quickly as I could manage it. Is that magic?"

"Even granting your instincts the benefit of the doubt," Baldassare said, "why would you think it's the right magic? One does not generally store books in the middle of a forest."

"Do either one of you have an *ounce* of poetry in your souls?" Sabina answered crossly, planting her hands firmly on her hips.

Evadne patted a hand experimentally around her face and chest before shrugging. "No. I don't think so."

Sabina threw up her hands in disgust and turned to march off down the trail the girl had taken through the wood, in the direction of the sounds of the market. "This entire journey is a quest of faith. Even the church likes to think the Grimm Truth doesn't exist."

"And you know better because...?" Baldassare asked.

"Because it bloody well has to!" Sabina rounded on him so viciously that the larger man tripped over a tree root in his haste to back away from her, and he sprawled backward onto the ground. "Because you're a damned wastrel and because our father is just as much a politician as I am a blacksmith!

"Get it through your head, little brother: Our fortunes—maybe even our lives—are hanging by a thread. We have until the new emperor is crowned to set things right; I'm the only one trying to do anything about it; and this is the only go'ss-forsaken plan I have! So you will stop questioning me at every turn and you will start having the good grace to pretend you believe in me, or I'll be going my way without you, and I *will* conveniently forget we're related when I come out all roses and you're being thrown in some debtor's prison to rot."

Sabina didn't wait for her brother to answer. She didn't wait for him to climb to his feet, much less to dust himself off. She just turned on her heels and stalked away down the trail, still seething. Red rage blinded her, driving out every other thought from her head and obliterating the passage of time, so that it might have been but a moment later that Sabina found herself sitting on a fallen log, somewhere in the shadows of the forest, with tears streaming down her face.

Perhaps she should have been alarmed that she seemed to be quite alone; perhaps she should have been alarmed that she saw no sign of a path and heard no sound from the market—nor any other sound at all, save the gentle rustle of the wind through the trees—but however fleeting it might prove, at that moment she felt only gratitude for the concealing embrace of the forest.

Eventually, when the anger had completely drained from her and she had once again began to ponder a future that involved something other than sitting on a log, Sabina roused herself to stand and look around the still forest, to truly take stock of her situation. It was then that she had to admit to herself that she'd no idea which direction led out of the forest and which might lead further in. No sight, no sound offered her the least clue.

Ah, but smell! It suddenly dawned on Sabina that the subtle-but-enticing aroma of something baking was being carried to her on the breeze, and despite her history as a life-long urbanite, it didn't take her long to orient on which direction it must be coming from. If following it did not lead her straight to the inn, it would certainly lead her straight to someone who knew the way. So it was a short walk later that found her standing in front of a rather fine little cottage in the woods.

The building sat by itself, beside a little brook in the middle of a sunlit meadow, surrounded by a pastel rainbow of wildflowers. Ivy twined about white stone walls in a most picturesque and friendly embrace; sweet-smelling wood smoke curled out from the brick chimney and wafted about the clean thatched roof before being lifted by the breeze and carried away over the treetops. To it all clung the tantalizing perfume of fresh, hot apple pie. Even before she'd set out to cross the meadow toward the little building, Sabina found herself dearly hoping that this would be the promised inn, despite the lack of signage advertising it as such.

As she reached for the door, a sound from the edge of the trees behind her drew her attention before she could knock, and she paused—with her hand still poised—to look over her shoulder. In the split second it took her to turn, her mind painted a picture of her tall friend and her contrite little brother emerging from the forest to join her here for a welcome rest, but whatever had caused that loud rustling was nowhere to be seen. Biting her lip in disappointment, she turned her attention back to the door, only to find herself interrupted once more.

This time, it was the door itself that interrupted Sabina, swinging inward just before she could rap at it.

"Oh, just come in already," the young woman behind it greeted her with good-natured vexation.

"I'm sorry," Sabina found herself apologizing as she stepped into the little entry alcove. She'd gotten a fleeting impression of the woman as being yet another red-head, and possessed of a very pleasant countenance, but that was quite all she'd noticed before the interior of the cottage itself commanded her attention. Along the walls of the room just past the entryway, she could see shelf after shelf lining the walls, all crammed floor to ceiling with dusty old books.

CHAPTER FIFTEEN

CAT AND MOUSE

"I hate to have to tell you," Keely said quietly, "but the Inquisition's not far behind us."

"I know." Elissa sighed. "I saw that inquisitrix back at the castle. Did she bring company?"

"Yes. That is...Well, she did, but that's not what I mean. Look..." Keely nodded toward the side of the road, just off of which the ground fell rather precipitously away toward the lower end of the switchback they were climbing. Not thirty feet away, as the stone drops, rode a knight of the Inquisition and a black-clad priestess, urging their mounts patiently up the long and winding road that led up the Wolf's Tooth to the cathedral site.

"I spotted them the last time we stopped so you could catch your breath," Keely whispered. "At this rate, they're going to reach the top well ahead of us." The obvious problem wasn't so much who should arrive first at the cathedral site, though, as it was the proximity it would force when the riders passed them. The long and winding road up the northern face of the Wolf's Tooth offered almost nothing in the way of cover or places to duck off to, and even less in the way of forking paths.

It was also sparsely traveled. They'd been passed a couple of times by carts full of building supplies, and a few more by travelers riding or leading donkeys, but there would be no bustle of passersby to blend in with. Nothing could look more suspicious when the riders passed than if the supposed priestess and her entourage failed to look them in the face and offer some manner of respectful acknowledgment.

"Can you walk faster?" Keely asked.

"I can try." Elissa nodded.

"Do that," Keely said. "Because that knight..."

"I saw," Elissa assured her. "It's Riordan."

The women exchanged glances that silently agreed it would be a very poor sort of grudge for a knight of the Inquisition to hold should he not know Keely by one glimpse of her face after the way she'd made a fool of him back at Belgrimm. Perhaps they might have found a spot to hide from him still, were it not for their bodyguards, but the very presence of the two men would serve to confound all manner of otherwise clever plans.

The little group continued on without altering its overall pace until the riders were safely out of earshot, then Elissa announced—directing her remark toward no one in particular—that this climb was taking entirely too long, and at this rate they would never reach the top. So saying, she set off with the speed of determination, though her legs ached and her breath grew short. Life in a library had not much prepared her for such a climb.

Together, they rounded another switchback, and Keely watched as the riders passed just below them again, but even if Elissa could manage this pace all the way to the top—which Keely sincerely doubted—it was becoming alarmingly clear the riders would still overtake them before they reached the plateau of the construction site. And while a couple of carts could be seen in the distance on the long tail of a road that fell away toward fields below, no sight nor sound offered any hope that someone would be descending from above that Keely might be able to turn into a distraction for the riders.

Watching over her shoulder as the riders once more headed away from them down the switchback, Keely finally snorted.

"What?" Elissa asked a little worriedly.

"I can't do this," Keely answered in a hushed tone of disgust. "I've let myself get cornered into playing someone else's game by someone else's rules, and it'll lead me into mistakes that will get us both killed— if I don't die first from the sheer boredom of trying to blend into the rocks, or from mortification thinking about what my mother would say."

"What are you going to do?" The look of concern on Elissa's face noticeably deepened.

"I don't know. But *you're* about to fall and twist your ankle."

"I am?" The prediction did nothing to make Elissa look less apprehensive.

"If you think you can pull it off convincingly," Keely said.

"No," Elissa said with incredulous certainty.

Keely shrugged. "Let me know when you come up with a plan, then."

They arrived at the next-to-last switchback before reaching the top, and paused for an appraising look up and down from the curve. "They *are* going to catch up to us, aren't they?" Elissa sighed.

"Yeah." Keely nodded.

"Maybe I could..." Elissa began—but whatever she was about to say as she started on up the trail got cut short when she tripped over something she would later come to suspect was someone's foot—and she went sprawling onto the rocky ground.

"Omigo'ss!" Keely gasped, bending over Elissa and rolling her over onto her back as their escorts came running up from the discrete distance they'd been following. "Sister! Are you hurt?"

"No. I don't think so," Elissa said.

"Are you sure?" Keely asked, glaring pointedly. "It looked like your ankle took a *very* nasty turn."

"Oh, I...aaaah!" Elissa yelped, involuntarily wrenching her foot away from Keely's cruel but surreptitious pinch. "Ow...ow...ow...Yeah, it's bad," Elissa said. Her gaze flickered darkly back at Keely for only a moment before she looked pitifully to their two escorts, who were crowding around her now. "It might even be broken," she whimpered with a convincing grimace, biting her own lip so hard that her eyes began to tear up.

"Let me..." Ulric began, but Keely quickly cut him off.

"Here; help her up. One on each side...There we go. There must be *someone* at the site who knows how to deal with injuries like this and someplace she can have a proper lie-down. Let's just stay focused on getting her there."

Keely followed closely behind as they set off, helping the limping Elissa up the trail, chattering advice a mile a minute as she went. Gradually, though, she let the chatter dry up and allowed herself to lag further and further behind, until she stood watching with satisfaction as the trio climbed laboriously away without her. After a few moments, she turned and walked unhurriedly back down to where a leafy bush up against the rocky inner wall of the switchback actually grew higher than her knee, and she stepped carefully behind it. Taking a deep breath, she wriggled her shoulders to loosen them, then vanished into the depths of her robes as they collapsed with her wig in a heap behind the bush.

"...And so the abbess leads us to this little empty room that looks like a pantry that's had all the food pulled off of the shelves and carted away, and Jane just turns and looks at her. You know, the look?" Riordan said. The big, broad-shouldered knight would have towered over his petite companion even if they'd been standing side by side. With the priestess astride her sleek, black courser and Riordan seated on an enormous chestnut destrier that might have been bred for the sole purpose of making people look up nervously at its rider, her head barely came up to his rib cage.

"The, 'Seriously? Don't you think your own life is worth a little more effort than this?' look?" the priestess asked.

"That's the one. Anyway, Jane gives her enough time to start squirming, then says all slow and deliberate, 'I said take me to the *library*.' And the abbess squeaks, 'This *is* the library.' Of course, Jane comes back with, 'I thought it was generally customary for libraries to have books in.'"

"She used 'the voice' there, too, didn't she?" the priestess laughed.

"Oh, yeah," Riordan nodded. "The voice."

"I can just hear it."

"And so the abbess says that all the books are out just now, being read. The entire library. Whatever *Jane* was thinking at that moment, *I* was tall enough that I could actually see a wheel of cheese that had gotten pushed to the back of a top shelf and forgotten, so..." Riordan reined up his horse, suddenly realizing that there was a little, white, long-haired cat, with brown socks on its hind toes, sitting there in the middle of the road, placidly watching them approach.

"Oh!" the priestess cooed, her attention drawn now to the cat, too. "What a..."

"Hyah!" Riordan spurred his horse forward again, urging it to trample Keely, but she was gone over the edge of the road in a flash, already having scouted out a series of cat-sized ledges she could use to hop down to the stretch of road beneath in four easy bounds. She paused to look back at the knight, only to see the silvery flash of Riordan's great battle axe hurtling toward her. That might have been the end of her had the thing been balanced at all for throwing. Instead, Riordan had thrown it as the only weapon that came immediately to hand, trusting that even a wild impact from the heavy wooden haft would do a cat grievous harm, but it struck the ground beside her and bounced harmlessly away.

In a flash Keely was herself again, wearing only her boots and blowing Riordan a kiss, before hefting the heavy fallen axe and leaping with it off the ledge toward the next lower stretch of road. In mid leap, she shoved the axe away to fend for itself, and melted into feline form just in time for a dagger thrown by the priestess to pass through the air where her human shoulder-blades had been. Graced with the body of a cat and the mind of a woman who'd spent much time testing that body's

132

many advantages for making rapid exits, Keely landed completely unharmed and scrambled away down the road.

Above her, the priestess spurred her courser to race back down the road as quickly as it dared, while Riordan abandoned his destrier to come clambering down the cliff face, following Keely as directly as he could—but it proved a chancy and slow business. Until the slope and the switchbacks gentled out, they had no realistic hope of catching her—and by then the foliage would be thick enough for her to disappear into. Keely lured them on as best she could while trying to not be too obvious that she wanted them to follow.

"What the...?" Ulric looked up from helping Elissa limp along, and he watched the courser and its black-robed rider galloping recklessly down the road below them. He had noticed the riders earlier—with some resigned and wary hostility—but had thought nothing particular of it. He'd known the Inquisition was in town. This sudden change in their behavior, though, could not herald anything good.

Immediately, Ulric shifted his burden completely to his comrade, Nolan, and started to un-sling his arquebus as he spun about—in his gut, expecting he would see the knight who'd been riding with the priestess come charging up the road at them—and hoping he would have time to load the gun and fire it. All Ulric spied was the knight's warhorse pacing restlessly about on its own—and that only after some searching. Then Ulric noticed his own party was short one postulant.

Elissa learned several new curse words at that moment, and she turned an impressive shade of red as Ulric swept her off the ground and practically threw her over Nolan's shoulder.

"Get her to the top and *sit* on her," Ulric demanded, then he charged off back down the slope, scanning all around for any sign of Keely. When he arrived at the switchback, he peered with dread over the long drop-off there, with little hope there was any place else she'd have had time to vanish to. Not seeing her lying broken at the bottom offered only limited relief, in the same manner as a brief stay of execution.

Ulric paused for a moment, searching in every direction for some new clue to the puzzle. Spying none, he turned his attention back to the inquisitrix. Whether she was riding to something or away from something in such haste, she clearly had information right now that was probably a life-or-death concern for him. So he slung his rifle back over his shoulder and scrambled down the rocks to the road below.

It was not a pleasant or easy sort of shortcut, but taking it three times did allow him to get ahead of the rider before she could reach the open lower slopes of the Wolf's tooth. He muttered to himself as he unslung the rifle again and began loading it. The process felt like it took forever, but by the time the inquisitrix drew near, he was ready and waiting— taking careful, steady aim at her horse.

The inquisitrix gave some serious thought to trying to ride Ulric down, but apparently decided she liked that horse enough not to risk it, and she reined up short of Ulric by a couple dozen yards as they sized each other up in silence. The petite, blond-haired woman in black, sitting imperiously astride a fiery courser, made for a striking contrast to the dark-haired, roughly shaven veteran blocking her path.

In the end, it was the priestess who blinked first. "Out of the way, fool!" she shouted. "What do you think you're doing?"

"Questioning the Inquisition. The way I have it figured, I'm a dead man just for pointing this thing at you. I'll get more of a head start if I kill you where you are before I start running, too, so you might want to convince me your death would be a waste, and not a blessing. This is nothing personal, but I have to have answers, and I have to have them *now*."

The woman continued to glare at Ulric for several long seconds, still sizing him up, and then her expression finally began to soften. "I'll not fault your courage," she said at last. "Convince me that killing *you* would be a waste, and perhaps I'll forgive both the insult and the interference."

"What am I interfering *with*?" Ulric said, lowering neither his weapon nor his guard. "You'd been almost up the Tooth before you changed your mind and took off like a shot."

"What? Is that all that's worrying you?" The woman gave an easy laugh. "I'm chasing a witch. I'd be more angry with you, but I'm afraid she's already got away. Unless Sir Riordan's already caught up with her—in which case he may be in need of some assistance. She's got the best of him before. So if that's all...?"

"I saw no one else on the road but the two of you," Ulric answered.

"Not even a little white cat, about so big?" the woman asked, gesturing demonstratively with her hands. "That's how she met us on the road. It seems to be her favorite animal form."

Ulric shook his head but accepted that the inquisitrix might be speaking true. *Something* he didn't understand had happened, and there were plenty of places along the road that a cat could have hidden.

"I'm Sister Shoshona, by the way. We've been following the witch across the kingdoms and thought we might catch up to her here, but it was only a guess until just now. Now that we know she's here, I've got something you really ought to see. May I?" she asked, tilting her head toward her saddle bags.

Ulric considered for a moment before nodding his assent, and Shoshona climbed carefully down to rummage through the horse's load. "Here," she said producing a folded paper and holding it out to him.

"I can't read." Ulric shook his head.

"That's okay," Shoshona urged. "Just look at it."

"Open it," Ulric said.

Shoshona shrugged and obliged him, unfolding the wanted poster. "You've seen her?" she asked. The man had a pretty good poker face, but she'd seen through better.

"Maybe," Ulric said. She might have caught his subtle reaction to the image, but he'd caught *her* subtle reaction in turn. The inquisitrix may have put away her claws, but she wasn't done mousing for the day. "I've seen a stranger in town who could be her."

"Silver hair?" Shoshona asked.

"More red."

"Where have you seen her? What caught your eye?"

"She's pretty." Ulric smirked. "A man remembers a pretty girl. We barely spoke, though, and I haven't a clue where she'd be right now. If it's the woman you're looking for, you've seen her more recently than I have."

"Well, now, aren't we a fine pair of fools to have nearly killed each other over a simple misunderstanding?" Shoshona laughed. "Just leave me to go rescue Sir Riordan, say you'll let me know anything you learn about the witch if she eludes us, and I'll forget any of this ever happened. Everyone wins but the witch. Fair enough?"

"Fair enough." Ulric nodded. He laid the gun on the ground and took a step to the side, leaving the courser ample room to pass—but beneath his cloak, his hand lay anxiously on the hilt of his sword until horse and rider were well clear and on their way, disappearing down the hill. "I'm dead," he muttered, watching them go.

"Yeah. Didn't see that coming. What were you *thinking*?"

Ulric spun to find Keely standing behind him, wrapped in a tattered red cloak—and probably nothing else—with the wind tousling her silvery-white hair.

"She didn't *forget* to ask what was so important for you to question her at gun point," Keely went on. "She let it drop because she's not done with you, and she'll come looking when she can finish it on her own terms."

"I know," Ulric said grimly, stooping to pick up his gun.

"I feel kind of guilty," Keely said. "Like it's sort of my fault."

"It's *all* your fault," Ulric glowered, though Keely showed no sign of hearing the accusation.

She had been thinking she'd cop to being the witch and then play the card about the postulant being her cousin in pursuit, but now that the moment had come, she knew just by meeting Ulric's gaze that this man would not be buying it. There was no bewilderment or doubt or hopefulness to play on there—only anger and resolve.

"Thanks for not ratting me out," Keely simply said instead.

"This isn't our first dance with the Inquisition around here," Ulric answered, "and they'd stomped on plenty of feet before the music stopped. Anyway, I had to save the pleasure of killing you for myself."

"Pfff." Keely brushed off the threat as the hollow thing it was. "You know, some farmer down there actually hung a skull on his scarecrow? A real skull?" she said, adjusting her tattered cloak.

"They all do," Ulric said.

"What? Why?"

"I am *not* going to let you change the subject!" he snapped.

"Where do they get them all?" Keely asked, biting her lip as a perplexed and disturbed expression crossed her face.

"This isn't just the usual business of the Inquisition seeing witches everywhere," Ulric pressed her. "When I go back up the Tooth, I'm going to find paw prints picking up where your footprints leave off, aren't I?"

"I don't know." Keely shrugged. "Are you a good tracker?"

"Good enough."

"Then probably." She sighed. "Look..."

"No, *you* look," Ulric growled. "I don't care what you *are*. I care what you *do*. What you've done is written me a death sentence, and you've shoved a bunch of other folk toward the headsman's axe!"

"I'll fix it," she said quietly but with conviction, her jaw set.

"Will you now?" He laughed bitterly. "Now that's magic I'd like to see. The last time the Inquisition was here, Haywoodshire went through two bloody slaughters. The first came when the Inquisition rounded up their 'witches'. The second came right after they left, when 'Bloody Scarlet' went on a rampage."

"Bloody Scarlet again?" Keely asked, morbidly curious. "The ghost who tore down the cathedral?"

"Bloody Scarlet is the local scapegoat—the bogey of the Crimson Forest," Ulric explained, shaking his head. "She's the legend parents use to keep children in line. Wander off into the forest or forget to do your chores, and she could come 'a slinkin' and a creepin'" to take your head and put it in her cupboard. People generally outgrow believing in her, but whenever something goes horribly wrong, we won't hesitate to lay it at her feet. So when folk who'd testified against the 'witches' began meeting with unfortunate accidents or disappearing from their beds..."

"People started saying it was the work of Bloody Scarlet, rather than point a finger at the families of the witches?" Keely finished for him.

"The Inquisition left town just before the fall harvest, and before the first snows fell, anyone who'd allied himself with the Inquisition was either dead or missing. Perhaps some of those who went missing simply left all their possessions and fled for their lives, but I've never heard of any of them turning up. So even *if* I could appease the Inquisition by turning you in, and *if* you could convince them to patiently treat you as an honored guest until the pontifine returns in a couple of months, and *if* she didn't hold us all responsible when the Inquisition still roasted you alive despite her best efforts, I'd still wind up mysteriously dead within a fortnight."

"Oh. Yeah, that does sound sticky, when you put it that way. But you know..."

Ulric was about to cut her off again, but not before they were both cut off by the sound of someone crashing and cursing through a nearby thicket. "Riordan," Keely explained with a lopsided smile. "We'd better get moving."

Ulric laid a hand on her arm as she started back up the road toward the peak. "Not that way. The knight left his horse up there. Someone's going to come for it—probably on horseback—and there are too many ways this could all end in them running us down on that slope today. We do need to get up to the cathedral site, but there's a safer way, and a quicker one. You'd never get a cart or a horse up it, and I'm not even sure about your Sister Jenny, but given the run you just gave the Inquisition, I think you'll make it."

CHAPTER SIXTEEN

CROSSING PATHS

Tobias' horse reared in alarm, and he struggled to keep from being thrown as a spirited black courser burst from around the hedgerow in front of them. The courser's hooves kicked up great clods of muddy earth as the animal raced past, the cloak of its black-clad rider billowing out behind it. As if all this wasn't enough to deal with by itself, Tobias realized with another note of alarm that this was a priestess of the Inquisition who'd just come hurtling past him like a dark bolt of retribution from a vengeful Seriena.

By the time Tobias brought his horse under control, wiped away the grime that had spattered his face, and taken a moment to silently thank Seriena that he was at least no longer choking on dust from the parched earth he'd spent so many days riding through, the inquisitrix was already disappearing around the next bend in the road.

Glancing to Conrad, his only companion to have accompanied him out of Denecia, Tobias was pleased to note that the young squire had managed to keep ahorse himself and appeared only moderately muddied by the incident. He grinned at the boy, who grinned back as he used his fingers to comb dark, dank soil out of his fair hair.

The prince's grin was one that Conrad knew well, and it meant something exciting and totally reckless was about to happen. Conrad didn't mind a bit. Those were his favorite moments in Tobias' service, and he'd yet to come out the worse for them. His eagerness to embrace those moods was exactly why it was Conrad that was here with Tobias now, and not some more-seasoned squire who might be better with arranging logistics or at swinging a sword. He was, in fact, the least likely person in all the world to suggest that Tobias might wish to think before acting.

With not a word exchanged between them, Tobias spurred his horse after the inquisitrix, and Conrad started after him. Considering how far they'd come from the heartlands, and that the Inquisition was after the same quarry he was, Tobias could not imagine that this woman was not close on the heels of the witch.

They rode hard, now kicking up their own share of earth, but even Tobias's best horse would have been hard pressed to keep pace with the courser—much less overtake it—and this was not his best horse. The inquisitrix was long out of sight ahead, and Tobias was just wondering if he should slow before Conrad fell out of sight behind, when he came upon the carriage. He reined up, partly from curiosity over whether the misfortune that had befallen the carriage had had anything to do with the witch, mostly because it sat at a fork in the road, and he could not be sure immediately which way the courser had gone.

Standing apart from the men who were working to lever the carriage up onto a block so the damage could be inspected, Baldassare Marini watched with cool interest as Tobias stopped in front of him. "I've seen strange things today," Baldassare finally said, raising an eyebrow, "but the *Inquisition* is on the run from *you*? Perhaps I should just go back to the inn and have a lie down until the natural order of the world reasserts itself." Despite the rake's willingness to make light of the situation, it did not escape Tobias' notice that Baldassare's hand lay ready on the hilt of his blade.

"We're merely chasing the same witch, and the Inquisition is doing it faster." Tobias smirked, casting a glance over the coat of arms painted on the side of the carriage. It looked vaguely familiar, but he couldn't actually say he recognized it, and he decided that it must belong to a local branch of a family he'd encountered back east.

As for Baldassare himself, Tobias had twice attended the same crowded ball and once been at the same tournament, so it wasn't fair to say he had never laid eyes on the man. Four times, in fact, his gaze had passed directly over Baldassare without ever stopping to focus on him.

Baldassare had actually looked directly at the prince once from a distance, and might even have recognized his coat of arms had he been displaying it—but as it was, he recognized only that the finery of a wealthy and important nobleman lay beneath the dirt on the horseman in front of him, and Baldassare decided belatedly he was probably addressing the local earl.

"So...there really is a witch?" Baldassare asked, an unaccustomed look of concern creeping onto his face.

"Absolutely," Tobias assured him. "I've been chasing her for weeks."

"I'd thought I was only humoring my sister's foolish imagination," Baldassare said, scowling at himself. "And now she's gone missing, with a genuine witch on the loose. We were taking a shortcut through the forest, and she ran off in a fit because I didn't believe her. When we didn't find her, I figured she'd just come back when she cooled down, but..."

"Yes, you'd best find her, and quickly," Tobias nodded. "And pray that it's not too late. The witch has a penchant for turning people into animals, so I'd advise tracing her footsteps, and look for signs of something else leaving the spot if you find that they suddenly stop without her in them."

"I've never been one for the hunt," Baldassare said. "All I see when I stare at the ground is...well, ground. Any chance you could..."

"I wish I could help," Tobias said sincerely, "but I can't leave one woman to face down the witch herself. Nor would you thank me if your sister's been turned into a hedgehog and I allowed the inquisitrix to kill the witch without first making sure she wasn't needed to restore her victims. That is..." Tobias paused, his eyes shifting uncertainly from side to side for a moment, "...unless perhaps you have a particular fondness for hedgehogs, I suppose."

Tobias coughed uncomfortably, then chewed his lip for a moment as he stared at the ground. It took only a few moments for him to decide which direction a horse had just gone galloping through, tearing up the soft earth as it went. "Best of luck, and I shall keep your misfortune in mind."

Baldassare, left somewhat at a loss by the comment about the hedgehog, watched silently as Tobias offered a respectful salute of departure, and took off with Conrad trailing behind. When they'd gone, Baldassare's spirits began a relentless slide from the annoyance they'd been harboring for weeks, down into a bog of guilt, anxiety, and genuine concern. No matter what differences he had with his sister, she *was* his sister, and that meant enough that he'd come along on her fool's errand just to see she didn't get herself killed on the road.

Now he might even have failed at that, a thought made all the worse by the knowledge that she'd been not so insane after all. And if she'd been right about the witch, had she been right about the book, too?

"Lanzo," Baldassare snapped, "return to the inn and ask where we can find a huntsman. Once you've found him, rouse Evadne out of her bath and bring them both back here as quickly as you can. Oh, and be sure that Evadne brings her claws. We may have want of them."

For the next several minutes, Baldassare paced and brooded, unaware that's what he'd been doing until the sound of hoofbeats once again drew his attention. As before, the thunder built, only this time it built into a massive wave, until everyone backed nervously up against the hedges—and none too soon, as what must have been a score of riders in the black and red of the Inquisition came barreling past.

Baldassare was fairly sure he recognized the inquisitrix and her horse who'd come through before, now leading the unnerving charge. In her wake rode a half dozen more priestesses, a few knights and their squires, and a smattering of other retainers whose roles he couldn't be sure of.

Lastly, just when he thought they'd all gone, came one grim little dwarf of a man astride a wild-maned white pony that cocked its head as it passed. Baldassare could have been wrong, but he imagined the fierce-looking little beast to be just listening for any whisper of laughter as an excuse to kick in someone's head.

Baldassare was watching the tail of the pony disappear around the curve of the road when he heard the sound of a throat being cleared and turned to find Tobias and Conrad sitting there on their horses.

"I'm going to say that the Inquisition has this one well in hand," Tobias said. "Let's go find your sister."

CHAPTER SEVENTEEN

THE DEAD POOL

"This is safer?" Keely asked dubiously, craning her neck to look up at the towering southern rock face of the Wolf's Tooth. "And quicker? I mean, I can see how it would be quicker to get down, provided you weren't concerned about getting back up again. Anywhere. Ever. But 'up' doesn't seem to even be on the table as an option."

"Which is exactly why it's safer," Ulric assured her. "Hardly anyone knows it's possible, and certainly not your friends in the Inquisition. At least not yet."

"So how *are* we supposed to get up?" Keely asked. She turned to follow him as he led on, ducking under a low-hanging limb of a particularly old and gnarled apple tree. This could have once been an orchard he was leading her through, but in the here and now it was just a wild and overgrown copse, sandwiched between the edge of a pasture and the cliffs. "I certainly hope you don't expect me to turn into a raven and fly. I don't do ravens." What she did do, however—and with some satisfaction—was notice Ulric pretending not to notice when her makeshift dress fell away from her leg as she maneuvered through the foliage.

"Skull Crevice," Ulric said, then continued when Keely prompted him with a dubious look. "At least that's what the young ladies call it."

"The young ladies?" Keely asked.

"Earl Darby's girls. I've spent more than a few hours watching over them while they explored this rock. I was tagging along with Minda when she discovered it."

"So is Skull Crevice where the farmers dump the leftovers when they take down their scarecrows?" Keely asked. "And are you having me on with that? I can't imagine where they'd get that many skulls. Or, rather, I *can* imagine it, because I am. I just wish I wasn't."

"Condemned criminals," Ulric said. "The farmers say the nastier the criminal, the better the scarecrow. Most of the present lot came from an old peddler woman who travels the kingdom, collecting them from the headsmen. It's illegal to trade in them without a license from the king, and I doubt there's a black market for them. Hard to accept that Bloodthirsty Alfred's head on a spike will protect your garden without also accepting that Grandma might come throttle you in the night if you accidentally buy her skull off of some grave robber who dug up your family plot."

"And what do you accept?" Keely chuckled.

"I just try not to think about it." Ulric shrugged. "I hear that Seriena frowns on killing people, and I've done that more than once. Only when I had to, of course, but still, nothing in the official rules about, 'Don't kill people except when it's an important part of your job', is there?"

"Not that I've ever heard." Keely shook her head.

"So all in all, I try to pretend that the next world is a bit more...murky?...than we give it credit for. And in the meantime, I'll let the farmers sort out the bit about the scarecrows.

"Ah, here we go." Ulric paused at a fissure in the rock no more than three feet across, and slipped inward between the massive walls of stone.

"You know you're not nearly in such an impossible spot as you think," Keely said, pulling the cloak about her a little nervously as she stepped into the crevice. Although she'd never thought of herself as claustrophobic, something about staring up at the distant sliver of sky overhead left her feeling the weight of the rock closing in from either side.

"Do tell," Ulric prompted her as he carefully picked his way up a wall of debris where large slabs of rock had sheered away from the cliffs high above some decades or centuries back, and now choked the crevice to a height of fifteen or twenty feet. Behind him, Keely carefully studied the climb, then looked down and contemplated how she'd look from above as she climbed with no hands available to hold the tattered cloak closed.

A few moments later, the balled-up cloak came sailing past Ulric to land at the top of the climb, and a little white cat came bounding lightly up after it. By the time Ulric reached the top, Keely had squirmed under the cloak, transformed back, and was pulling it about her shoulders with what little modesty the situation would allow—which, as coincidence would have it, was about all the modesty she had to scrounge up anyway.

"Yes, you're boxed in," she continued as they squeezed one after the other through a narrow opening left by two particularly large slabs of rock, "but a box is only as strong as its lid. In this case, that's our inquisitrix. The moment she loses interest in your insult, you're back in the clear."

"What? No warrant for my arrest...?" Ulric asked.

Keely waved the thought off. "You hurt her pride. It's personal, and she means to deal with it personally, for the sheer pleasure of indulging her anger."

"You know her that well?"

"Not really. Witches just know things."

Ulric fixed her with a skeptical stare before beginning the climb down the other side of the rubble.

"It was all over her face," Keely admitted with a smirk. "In her voice and her eyes and her bearing. That wasn't some church bureaucrat who wants you to quake at the massed power of her flunkies. That was a woman who wants you to fear *her*—personally—and who loves getting her hands dirty. I've only laid eyes on her twice, already underestimated her once, and it very nearly cost me a dagger in the back. I promise, she's not dreaming of having your head served up on a plate right now. She's dreaming up the way she'll catch you where that gun and the size you have on her will both be worthless."

The cloak came floating down past Ulric, followed by the little white cat again, and he paused to watch with some interest as it wriggled under the cloak and arose as a woman.

"But that's all to your advantage," Keely went on, "because people do stupid things while nursing their anger and defending their pride. And the moment she gets more worked up about something else than she is about you, all you'll have to do is give her time and space to forget the insult. Provided you stay out of her line of sight, eventually she'll leave town, and odds are you'll never hear from her again."

"And what do you think she's going to get so worked up over?" Ulric asked.

"Me, probably," Keely said.

"Not an option," Ulric said sternly. "You're not getting anywhere near that woman again, and she's not getting anywhere near you."

"Then I'll just have to upset her from a distance, won't I? Send her a stiff note, maybe. Or help someone else find the book she's looking for."

"She's looking for a book? Around here?" Ulric laughed incredulously.

"I said she was dangerous. I never said she was sane." Keely shrugged as they arrived at a point where the crevice began to climb sharply up and away, the rock underfoot carved into a twisting flight of stairs—ancient, weathered, and covered in moss, but still serviceable.

"This used to be someone's postern gate," Ulric said, "but I think it was forgotten centuries ago."

The scuffing of Ulric's boots echoed up and down the narrow stairwell as they climbed, now passing intricate scrollwork designs carved into the walls as high as twenty or thirty feet above their heads. Scattered at random amidst the abstract carvings, hundreds of realistic human skulls had been carved, jutting out where natural extrusions of rock must have existed for the sculptors to reshape. Their cold, empty stares fueled the unease Keely had already been feeling from the weight of the walls around her, and she shivered despite herself.

"This place is almost as cheery as your scarecrows," she said, failing to deliver the observation in the usual cavalier tone she reserved for such comments. A sense of wrongness had descended on her that couldn't be explained away by a bit of morbid sculpture.

"I think we can thank the Tuatha," Ulric said.

"The what?" Keely asked.

"The barbarians Emperor Lupus died fighting. This would have been their land back then. They were..." Ulric stopped, staring down at the step in front of him. "Now that's curious."

Keely followed his gaze to where a few shards of broken glass lay. "And potentially nasty," she said, thankful that whatever else might go wrong with her wardrobe, she never had to deal with the mishaps of wandering barefoot.

Ulric crouched down and carefully picked up one of the shards, turning it over in his fingers, and examining the step where it had lain. "Apparently this stair isn't as forgotten as I'd thought." He rubbed a finger across the ground, then held it up to study the glistening stain on the tip. "Lamp oil."

"The 'young ladies'?" Keely ventured.

"Possibly," Ulric agreed. "I'm definitely going to have to ask, but it's no less likely that it was our vandals. Even some chance it was the Inquisition after all. Whoever it was, we're going to pretend they're still up there, so stay behind me and keep your voice down."

Keely fought a brief skirmish with her natural state of contrariness before simply nodding her acquiescence. Her gift for reading people hardly limited itself to knowing when an inquisitrix wanted to chain someone to the wall and torment him with branding irons; and however calm and collected this man might seem, it was the calm of a soldier already committed to a suicide mission, determined to see it through to the end. If he needed to feel he was in charge at this moment, it was an illusion she owed to him.

They'd climbed a hundred steps or so before the stairs ended at a stone arch, decorated with the same skulls and abstract designs as the walls. Above the arch, the crevice continued, but rising so steeply and narrowing so quickly that it might as well have ended to anyone but a seasoned rock climber.

The arch, for its part, opened into a tunnel—not a particularly large one, but still broad enough that they could have comfortably walked side by side, and tall enough that no man would have fear of banging his head. Ulric stepped inside without hesitation, and Keely followed.

They'd only gone a few paces in when Ulric stopped, listened to the fading echo of his footsteps, shook his head, and leaned against a stone skull to take off his boots. Even before he'd finished, Keely realized with gratified surprise that her eyes were already adjusting to the underground environment.

Far from being a descent into a world the sun had forgot, this was just a hole bored straight through a wall of rock to come out the other side, perhaps a hundred yards away. There remained plenty of deep shadow toward the middle that could easily be hiding some dark pit or side tunnel, but Ulric showed no sign of concern—so if the shadows held any hazard at all, it was probably more broken glass. Ulric did take his time traversing the tunnel, clearly mindful himself of the potential dangers that unseen objects could offer bare feet, but they emerged from the far side without incident, and Keely craned her neck around to take in the sight.

The place turned out to be a circular pit, open to the sky hundreds of feet above, and broad enough that while Keely could have hit the far wall by throwing a stone at it, she would have had to put some real effort into the throw. The mid-day sun was doing a fair job of shining down the shaft from above, but would probably have faltered long before reaching the bottom were it not for the numerous little cross-shafts bored in at an angle from the south—too small to climb through, but letting in light.

All around the outside of the main shaft wound a spiral stairway, cut back into the rock as if by the threads of some monstrous screw. The pit extended down from here, as well as up, though how far down was impossible to guess because it seemed to have collected rain like a cistern. The black, mirror-smooth surface of the waters lay near enough below that Keely could have safely dived into them, but far enough below that she would have thought twice even if she'd known no surprises lurked beneath.

"The barbarians did all this?" Keely asked quietly.

"Probably," Ulric whispered. "But let's save the history chat, okay? We'll be passing more than a few side-chambers on our way up. Any of them could look like a very nice hideout to the sort of people who'd tear down a cathedral." They'd barely begun the long ascent when he held up a hand for Keely to stop, and he pointed out the muddy boot prints on the stairs—faint but unmistakable, even to an untrained eye. "Not the young ladies," he assured her. "Big, rough boots. Someone's been through in just the last few hours."

"Should we turn back?" Keely asked.

"Depends. Fancy your chances out there with the Inquisition scouring the countryside for you?"

Keely actually fancied her chances far better than his. A cat could disappear into the hedges and evade dozens of determined humans, but Ulric...No matter who they might meet in here, he'd be better off taking his chances with them than trying to avoid the woman leading that lot out there.

And page twenty-five of the Rules—which not coincidentally happened to smell like a rather savory stew and feel like a bit of warm and well-used blanket—clearly stated, "Take care of the people who take care of you." Whatever Ulric's motives might be, he was making it his personal mission right now to keep her alive. That made it her responsibility to return the favor, and *that* made turning back completely out of the question.

"Good point." She smiled, shooing him ahead of her, and they continued cautiously on up the stairs.

Smoke floated above the orchards in the shadow of the Wolf's Tooth—not the fine sort of wisp that might rise from a chimney or a campfire, but the thick, roiling black cloud that only comes from a serious blaze. Sister Shoshona had smelled it before she spotted it, and now she contemplated the cloud as she sat astride her horse, waiting.

A couple of the other black-robed priestesses waited with her in the shade of the trees, atop a small rise with a commanding view of the crossroads where the trail up the Tooth started. The rest of their company had dispersed in pairs, beating the metaphorical bush in the hopes of driving the witch back this way. If she was seeing this, then so were they—most of them, at least. So were many of the locals.

Would they be drawn to it to investigate? Would the witch? Had the witch started it herself? And if she had, was it a ruse to distract them or to draw them out, or was it the incidental effect of some wicked magic?

"I'm going to check it out," Shoshona decided at last. "Don't leave this spot except in direct pursuit of the witch."

She rode off quickly and alone, down the road that led most directly toward the billowing smoke. When that no longer seemed to be getting her closer, she found a gate in the hedges and cut through field and orchard. Along the way she passed more than a dozen panicked locals—men, women, and children all scrambling toward the blaze.

The summer had been dry enough that despite the recent rain, even an intentional and supposedly controlled fire of that magnitude would be courting disaster. One wafting spark that landed in the wrong place could set fire to countless acres of crops before they could be harvested and devour orchards that had been decades in the growing.

When she arrived at the blaze, she found it busily devouring a farm cottage. A mercifully barren plot of dusty earth surrounded the cottage, but the flames had still found enough traction among the sparse tufts of grass to spread to a nearby chicken coop. The few people already on the scene had clearly given up the cottage for lost, but they were running around trying to smother any flames that spread, and a line had formed passing water from the nearby well to the chicken coop. Shoshona doubted they'd be able to haul water fast enough to salvage the coop, but that would have to remain their own concern. Her concern lay with the witch.

While everyone else remained too focused on dealing with the fire to even acknowledge the presence of an inquisitrix in their midst, Shoshona looked around for any sign of the story behind the fire. What she spotted was a man in the distance, standing on a rocky outcrop on the lower slopes of the Wolf's Tooth, watching the proceedings. He wore red and black, and seemed to incline his head in acknowledgment of her gaze. From here, it was hard to make out any other details, but the man had to be Sir Riordan. Spurring her mount to skirt around the heat of the fire, she headed off toward him.

She rode through a quiet pasture, leaving the scene of destruction behind only to discover a whole new scene of destruction awaited her. An enormous bull lay dead in the middle of the field, it's skull cloven in by one powerful blow, its blood still pouring out to pool on the ground. Shoshona paused only a moment to take in the scene before riding on.

At last she came to the point where her horse could go no further, so she dismounted and climbed the rock up to where Riordan stood waiting patiently. He'd managed to find his axe on the trip down the

Wolf's Tooth, and he cradled it now, the blade crimson and dripping with blood. Blood covered his face and clothes, as well, in great spatters all over. He'd made no attempt to clean any of it.

Wordlessly, Shoshona stepped up beside him and just stood for a minute, watching the cottage burn. "It happened again, didn't it?" she asked at last.

Keely and Ulric had circled the pit a couple of times and passed a couple of side tunnels—one rough and natural, the other smoothly carved from the rock—when they heard a loud clang of metal on stone, reverberating up and down the shaft. They both jumped from the suddenness of it, then froze listening until the echoes had died away. A heartbeat passed in silence. Then five. Then...clang! C-clang! And silence fell once more, at least until they'd climbed halfway round again. Klump, klump, tlang! Klump, klump, tlank!

At last they spotted the source of the noise: a man in filthy workman's clothes on the far side of the shaft, still some ways up, but descending noisily. After every couple steps with his heavy boots slapping against the stone, he'd swing the shovel in his hand carelessly around, striking the wall or the steps, and occasionally sending off sparks. His scraggly beard, unkempt hair, and erratic gate suggested, if not an intimate familiarity with alcohol, then at least a passing relationship with some state of mind other than "sound".

While both Keely and Ulric remained frozen, lest a sudden movement attract the man's attention before they'd decided what to make of him, they watched his unsteady progress around the arc of the pit until he'd gone almost out of sight again.

Then as one particularly vigorous swing of the shovel rebounded off the wall, the shovel slipped from his fingers and began to tumble away. He lunged after it, and Keely let out an involuntary gasp as the man stood tottering on the rail-less inner edge of the stair. He'd succeeded in grabbing the shovel, and for a very long second, he swung it around with the rest of his weight in the fight to control the direction of his imminent fall. At last he got it right and sat down hard on the stairs.

"Are you all right?!" Keely called up to the man, instantly earning herself a scowl from Ulric.

The man whipped his head around in surprise, bobbled the shovel again, and this time succeeded in overextending himself as he grabbed for it. Keely muttered a single expletive under her breath as the shovel clattered off the stone then went whirling away into free-fall, followed immediately by its owner. Both plummeted past, hit the pool with an awkward splash that violently disrupted the smooth, black waters, then disappeared beneath them. The shovel was gone in an instant, any buoyancy in the handle overcome by the weight of the blade. The man resurfaced after several seconds, just long enough for his flailing to make it clear he didn't have a clue how to swim.

Keely made a move to start down the stairs, but she drew up short—coughing—as Ulric snagged the hood of her cloak and it caught around her throat. "I'll go down," he barked. "*You're* going up." She rounded on him viciously, with a slap that left his face stinging and blood trailing down his cheek from the instinct she hadn't quite been able to overcome to claw at him. Then the cloak fluttered limply in his hand and she was a little white cat, launching herself off of the stairway and out into open air, falling, falling...

She closed her eyes, trying to trick herself into forgetting the onrushing experience of wet fur, and just went limp. The water still hit her like a brick, but she had done the mental arithmetic and chosen it as better than attempting a graceful high-dive as a woman, hoping she'd actually pull it off and *not* run straight into some barely concealed pile of rubble in the process.

Then the initial shock of hitting the water was over, and she was a woman again. With long strokes, she made for the surface, but found she'd gotten turned around. Irregular shapes loomed out of the dark water ahead of her until she realized abruptly that she was going down, not up.

At the same moment, she also realized what it was she was seeing, and in the shock of it nearly inhaled a lungful of water. She fought again for the surface, this time getting her bearings right, and broke into the air, gasping. Above her she could hear Ulric cursing her, and the sound of his bare feet slapping against stone as he hurried after her in the best semblance of a run one can manage while descending a stairway.

Orienting on the point where the staircase met the surface of the water, Keely made her best guess to where the man had gone down, and she stroked quickly over to it before steeling herself and diving once more beneath the surface. Her guess proved true, and there he was, still struggling ineffectually to reach for the surface.

He went wide-eyed when he saw her, and Keely saw in those eyes a reflection of how she must look to him: a naked woman, floating above him, surrounded by a halo of long, silver hair—back-lit and extending a hand downward to him as he hovered on the doorway of death. He was having a religious experience, and she couldn't have been more grateful, because it stilled his thrashing. Not wasting a moment for his panic to reassert itself, she grabbed him by the wrist and dragged him toward the stairs for all she was worth.

Ulric was there to meet them as Keely pushed the man, coughing and gasping, up out of the water. Ulric had never let go of Keely's ratty red cloak on the way down, and she grabbed it gratefully as he dropped it now to help pull the man up. She was out of the water and wrapped in it, trying to escape the chill of the water and the vision of what she'd seen in its depths, well before Ulric could get the man settled to rest on solid ground.

Leonard and Ann Marie Wilson

CHAPTER EIGHTEEN

LIVING A NIGHTMARE

Sabina pulled another dusty book off the nearest shelf and dropped it with a satisfying thud onto the table next to the growing pile. She opened it reverently, and carefully turned the brittle pages, to find more of the ancient, indecipherable text. Or, to put a finer point on it, the text was indecipherable to her, given her personal ignorance of the old imperial tongue, but this was the stuff: tome after tome that reeked of age and authority, each one a musty exemplar of what a fifteen-hundred-year-old holy text should be.

Behind Sabina, a light flared as her hostess lit a candle, then placed it on the table, and it was only then that Sabina realized how dark the cottage had become. Was night falling already?

"Where did you get these?" Sabina asked the woman excitedly. It was the first words either of them had spoken since Sabina had been invited in. Instantly entranced by the collection, Sabina had never even spared her hostess a second glance, and the woman had seemed in no hurry to break the spell.

"Oh, the usual places." The woman answered in the hushed tones of a librarian—though there was no one else about for her voice to disturb—before gliding off again into the gloom. "Salvaged from the deepest pits of despair, wrestled from out of the darkest nightmares. That sort of thing."

"That's...usual, is it?" Sabina asked. Finally taking an active interest in her hostess, Sabina peered into the darkness, but could see no more of her now than a shadowy silhouette as she moved about, pulling a book off a shelf here, sliding one onto a shelf there.

"Where else?" The woman still whispered, though her voice carried like a bell in the cold silence of the library. "Seriena trains up women to

152

read and to write so that when they die and she drags their souls screaming down into the pit, she can chain them up in dank little cells to make books for her for all eternity. When they're not being poked with red hot needles, of course. That would make them jump, and smudge the words."

"Oh," Sabina said, not knowing what other answer she could give to that story.

"Books are evil, dear. Poison. They're how Seriena spreads her hate and her venom to every corner of the land."

"And yet you surround yourself with so many..." Sabina observed, trying against all her natural urges to not sound judgmental.

"Oh, these aren't mine," the woman whispered. "These are for you. That's what you came looking for, isn't it? Forbidden knowledge? Power at any cost?"

"Who *are* you?" Sabina asked, shivering suddenly. She found herself whispering in imitation of the woman.

"Oh, I know Seriena has this whole 'sweetness and light' thing going," the woman continued. "But that's just a mask for the rubes. Helloooo? Inquisition? You think she doesn't condone their methods? She's no better than the rest of us."

"I think I'd better go," Sabina whispered nervously. "My brother's looking for me."

"Of course," the woman said. "Show yourself out. Sometimes the power's not worth the price, is it?"

"Sometimes," Sabina agreed, a note of uncertainty creeping into her note of uncertainty. But she stood up slowly and started edging toward the door. "You're the witch, aren't you?"

The woman laughed loudly, the suddenness of it startling in the quiet darkness. "I've been called a witch," she murmured finally. "I'm not."

"Then what *are* you?" Sabina asked earnestly.

"Famished," the woman answered with a thoughtful nod. "And perhaps a bit melodramatic. It's hard to be sure, though. Is this Tuesday?"

"I...no," Sabina shook her head, now at least as perplexed as she was nervous.

"Pity." The woman sighed wistfully. "I have a theory about days of the week, you know. Melodrama is so much easier to recognize on a Tuesday. But look, we're not here to talk about me, are we? This is all about...*you*." The woman finally stepped into the candlelight, and for a moment there was something unnervingly familiar about her manic grin. Then she leaned over and blew out the candle with one quick puff of breath and the room plunged into utter darkness.

Sabina screamed. She screamed until—stumbling backward in the darkness—she tripped over a chair and fell flat on her back, at which point she found there was no more air in her lungs to scream with. Then as she lay there gasping and helpless, a dazzling burst of light blinded her as thoroughly as had the darkness before. And then all was stillness and silence except for Sabina's own gasping, and she lay there with her head swimming until she'd recovered enough first to breathe, and then to see. The first thing to come into focus was her hostess bending over her.

"Ah, you see?" the woman said enthusiastically. "Now *that's* melodrama. You're really quite good at it. Consider me impressed." The burst of light seemed to have come when she'd pulled back a very heavy drapery from one of the cottage windows, and now she stood there illuminated by it, looking all sincere innocence. Then she gave an amused little smile, and Sabina remembered where she'd seen that smile before—or, rather, one very much like it.

It had resided on the face of the mysterious lady who'd crashed the party on that stormy night in Denecia, where this whole thing had started. And this, Sabina thought, must be what that lady had looked like fifteen or twenty years ago. That the two women were of a blood, Sabina had no doubt. Had the face not instantly convinced her, the mannerisms would have.

"Up you go," the lovely redhead said, extending a hand and helping Sabina effortlessly to her feet. "So...melodrama? Check. Tuesday? We'll reserve judgment on that one. Famished? Yes, but not a state we want to maintain. Apples are in season, if you like that sort of thing. Or I've got a basket of goodies around here somewhere..." She began rummaging around, shoving aside books and looking under tables.

"Did I say I was hungry?" Sabina asked.

"Aren't you?"

"I...guess," Sabina said, realizing suddenly that she was. How long had it been since she'd last eaten? How long had she been in the forest, for that matter? How long had she been in the cottage? "But it can wait. The books..."

"Oh, right...Books." The woman bit her lip, eyes glazing for a moment in thought, as if it had entirely slipped her mind that not only were they surrounded by the things, but that she'd just delivered a diatribe against them. "It's not here, you know." Sabina started to ask her what wasn't there, but the woman fixed her with a reproachful, don't-be-silly gaze, and the words died unformed. "And none of these are going to help in finding it. To be brutally frank, they're all rubbish—every single one."

"Well, if you don't want them..."

"I *said*," the woman enunciated slowly and impatiently, "they're all *rubbish*." With that, she picked up the doused candle from the candle holder and jabbed it wick-first into the pages of the book Sabina had left open on the table. The dark red wax, still soft from the heat, squashed and splattered across the page, leaving it looking for all the world like the book was oozing blood for being stabbed with the candle.

Sabina let out a small, distressed yelp. "What are you doing?!"

The woman sighed as her only answer. Then in defiance of Sabina's estimate of how long a doused candle could remain a fire hazard, the page erupted into flames. Sabina shrieked, thinking even as she did so that this was suddenly turning into a bad habit, but the woman dispassionately picked up the flaming book and tossed it into the nearby fireplace.

"That was worth..." Sabina could feel a tear rolling down her cheek as she watched the fire greedily consume the book. "...a lot," she finished weakly.

"It really wasn't," the woman said, casually grabbing another grand-looking tome and tossing it into the fireplace with the first. "They're not even as old as you'd think. Anyway, what's wealth to *you* but a road to power? You didn't buy that fancy dress you're wearing because it's comfortable," she laughed. Indeed, Sabina did squirm uncomfortably, though it would not have been fair to blame it all on the dress. "You bought it to impress; to convince everyone you're a noblewoman to be reckoned with and to help seduce foolish men into your thrall. Am I wrong?" The woman arched a questioning eyebrow, but Sabina just stared back at her uncertainly.

"Do you want power, little girl?" the woman asked. By all rights, the words should have come out sounding patronizing—or, at best, like a fresh round of marginally coherent babbling—but somehow they managed a sincere, motherly tone that wrapped itself like a warm cloak around Sabina's shoulders and attempted to dry her tears. When Sabina looked into those ice-blue eyes now, they gazed back at her like a steady rock of sanity in a tumultuous sea, and they whispered of a wisdom that had no right to exist on such an unblemished, girlish face.

"I...yes," Sabina answered.

"The church was foolish to turn you away." The woman beckoned, and she opened her arms, truly embracing Sabina now and smoothing down her hair. "Such a strong and clever girl. No doubt Seriena would have turned you into a pontifine before she was through with you, but some jealous little tart of a priestess denied her the chance. Their loss."

"How...how do you...?" Sabina's voice cracked, denying her the chance to finish the question.

"I know all about you, dear. I've been watching you. Watching over you."

"Like a...faerie go'ssmother?" Sabina asked.

"Sure, dear," the woman answered with a glint of kindly laughter in her eyes. "Like a faerie go'ssmother. Now let it out. I'm here."

No more tears came, despite the invitation, but Sabina did bury her face in the woman's hair.

"So there you've been," she went on, gently patting Sabina's shoulder, "stuck playing politics in a man's world, grabbing for whatever scraps of power you could find, knowing like a cursed prophet that the whole world is about to collapse into ruin, but that no one will listen to your warnings no matter how loud you scream."

The detached, dispassionate corner of Sabina's mind idly noted that perhaps this summary of her life was a bit on the melodramatic side. The exhausted, overwrought majority of Sabina's mind responded by slapping the other bit in the face and telling the little weasel to shut up. That's when the quiet tears started up again.

"Maybe if you'd become a power in the church, you could have restored some sanity, but that's not going to happen now, is it? We've got to find you another way. We *will* find you another way. Just leave it to Scarlet."

"What are you even doing here?" Ulric's voice echoed down from above. He'd accepted at this point that they were past any pretense of stealth, and that anyone who might have come out from a side-tunnel to confront them would have done so by this point. So he'd put his boots back on, and agreed that it was better for Keely to follow at a discreet distance than to have the rescued workman wondering about either the silver-haired woman or the curious cat trotting along with them.

He'd hauled the man bodily up the stairs to where he wouldn't see Keely (or a set of wet footprints on the stairs ahead) before he could regain any semblance of his senses.

Even now, that semblance of his senses remained limited, but at least he was able to stumble back up the stairs under his own power, provided Ulric assisted him with issues of balance. He'd also been able to speak clearly and coherently enough to share that his name was Clay Ambleforth, but not much else yet.

"C'mon!" Clay protested, ignoring Ulric's question, and not for the first time. "You *saw* her! Y'had t' see her! She was standin' right at your shoulder!" His speech came slow and slurred and stammering, as from someone who was having a great deal of difficulty forging thoughts into words, and even more difficulty recalling how to operate his tongue.

"I wasn't looking over my shoulder," Ulric told him. "I saw you fall. I ran down to help. By the time I got there, you'd already got to the edge of the stairs and I just helped you out."

Keely fidgeted, drumming her fingertips silently against her own arm as she climbed the stairs. Keeping track of the two men by the sounds of their voices and footfalls alone was not the least bit difficult, but slowing her pace to match Clay's so she was always one rotation directly below them had already become wearisome.

"I didn' jus' *get* t' the edge of the stairs. I haven't swum a stroke in my life!"

"Whatever happened, whatever you saw, I can't tell you I saw your mysterious lady, okay? And the Inquisition's around," Ulric said. "They tend to frown on folk having unsanctioned visions, so I'd just keep it all to myself if I was you. But what are you even doing down here?"

There followed a long silence before Keely heard Clay finally answer, slowly and deliberately and surprisingly clearly, "Living a nightmare." She heard them start walking again, but the conversation seemed to have died from Ulric not knowing how to respond to that. Eventually, it was Clay who broke the silence again. "Acshully, 'm more sure she's real 'n I'm sure you are."

"Well, if it helps any to hear, I'm not sure I'm real either," Ulric said sympathetically.

"Least y'haven't turnt into anythin' dreadful yet," Clay sighed in exhaustion. "I do 'preciate that."

"Well, we'll get you back up to the construction site and..."

"No! I've got to find the book!" All at once there came a scuffling and cursing, and Keely leaned outward as far as she dared in the hopes of seeing what was going on above her. For a heart-stopping moment she saw Ulric's feet dangling off of the stair, scrabbling for purchase, before he managed to pull himself back up—presumably with a strong grip on Clay, because there wasn't much else on the stair that one could hold onto.

After only a moment's hesitation, Keely was a cat again, leaving her cloak to flutter once more to the stair as she dashed madly around and upward. It wasn't just the thought of Ulric's near fall that panicked her. It was the thought of diving in after him if he didn't recover gracefully on his own. Her mind was still trying to come to terms with what she'd seen down there, and it was in no way ready for round number two.

Caution was no longer an option, and her feline body had it all over her human one for accelerating up those stairs.

The sight of the two men struggling as she rounded the stairwell did nothing to put her mind at ease. Ulric had the clear advantage in training and in having his wits about him, but Clay had the clear advantages of being berserk out of his wits and of being muscled by a lifetime of heavy labor. By going from marginally coherent to completely unhinged in the blink of an eye, Clay had also started off with the advantage of surprise, and Ulric was clearly still fighting to recover from that. Still, Clay seemed more panicked than angry, and Keely couldn't help thinking he'd have run off after an initial shove if Ulric hadn't been forced to grab him to keep from falling. Now the two men seemed only to concern themselves with overpowering the other in order to gain control of the situation.

Given a few more moments, Keely might have found a way to play peacemaker—but Clay had found a good-sized fragment of rock that had chipped off of some part of the architecture and was trying to smash it into Ulric's skull. Without breaking pace, Keely came bouncing off the wall and the steps and landed squarely in the middle of Clay's back, her claws sinking straight through the filthy cloth of his tunic and finding purchase in his flesh. Clay howled, reflexively dropping the stone to grab for the yowling demon just out of his reach behind him.

The result wasn't all good, as the falling rock still struck a glancing blow off of Ulric's forehead, the jagged edge cutting a bloody line across his temple before bouncing away.

Ulric was able to shake off the painful distraction more quickly than Clay could shake off his, though, and Ulric laid the man out with one solid punch to the jaw. Then all was still and silent except for their heavy breathing and the once-more naked Keely asking Ulric if he was all right as she peered out from behind the man who'd collapsed backward on top of her. Then like the final punctuation to some morbid punch line, the splash of the offending rock finally hitting the water echoed up the shaft to them.

"Are you okay?" Keely finally asked.

"How is it," Ulric said, eying Keely's feet where they stuck out from under Clay, "that you never lose those boots no matter how many times you turn into a cat, but you can't keep a cloak on for anything?"

"Nobody messes with my footwear," Keely assured him. "Besides, if magic just made sense, we wouldn't call it magic, now would we?"

As soon as she'd satisfied herself that all was as well as could be, Keely became the cat again and, wriggling out from under Clay, went trotting off down the stairs to fetch her cloak. She was most of the way to it when she realized there was an odd sound whispering at the edge of her hearing, and she peered over the edge of the stair, down into the depths of the shaft, trying to pinpoint its source.

The sound came as gurgling, she realized; a bubbling, as if the dark waters far below had begun to lazily swirl and churn. The thought froze Keely in her tracks as the recollection of what lay beneath forced its way back to the front of her mind.

The pool was one big watery graveyard. The dead lay in careless heaps across the bottom, dragged down by chains and by metal weights and by large rocks that made it clear they'd been interred there quite intentionally. Naked rib cages and femurs and all manner of other bones that Keely couldn't name lay strewn about both in bits and in mostly intact skeletons, like the hoard of some macabre aquatic dragon. They lay so thick and ancient that there was no seeing the actual floor, and no telling how far down the mounds might go.

As if that all weren't dreadful enough, not all of the corpses were bare bones. Some lay in varying states of stomach-churning decay, and Keely couldn't help but wonder how long a corpse could last in that water before being reduced to pure bone, even if there was nothing lurking down there, cleaning the flesh from them. Certainly, there was no way that all of those bodies could be blamed on some long-dead cult.

Then in one final insult to Keely's view of living in a world possessed of some passing acquaintance with safety and sanity, there was the business of the heads. Or, rather, there was the business of the lack of heads. Not once in surveying that wreckage of what had once been a living, breathing mass of humanity—carrying all the hopes and joys and fears and beauty and ugliness that went with it—did Keely spot a single head or skull; not so much as a jawbone.

Now something down there had been disturbed in those awful black waters, and Keely thought she could see a faint, flickering swirl of red meandering through their depths. She tore herself away from the sight and fought to shove all those unsettling thoughts back into the little box she reserved in the back of her brain for anything that made her suspect for even a moment that she might not be in charge of a given situation.

For the first time in years, though, Keely found she was shoving too much into that box, and she couldn't close the lid. Things were going wrong. *Lots* of things were going wrong, and one of them even had her wondering whether there might be some point to the Inquisition beyond terrorizing the innocent.

Whether by the hand of man or demon, something unspeakable had happened here—was probably still happening here—and as Miraculata

Cosima had said, war is a cruel business. If this was even close to typical to the things the Inquisition was fighting, it would explain how hard their hearts had become.

Keely reached the cloak she'd left on the stair and stopped, staring at it. In her mind she was seeing it as she'd originally found it, draped across a scarecrow, the hood half concealing a weathered skull gazing back at her with empty eyes.

Then she was seeing that over and over as imagined scarecrows in every field loomed nightmarishly closer and closer in her mind's eye, each one of them pointedly not sitting on the shoulders of one of the bodies in the watery grave below. Keely backed away from the cloak, hackles raising and a feline growl coming unbidden to her throat.

"Keely?!" Ulric called down, concerned.

Keely, turned back into a woman and swept the cloak off the edge of the stairs with a quick swipe of her hand, recoiling from it even as she did so. "The cloak fell!" she called, watching it flutter away down the shaft. "I'm going to need your tunic unless you want me to just stay a cat!"

CHAPTER NINETEEN

BILGE GLYPHS

"This day gets better and better and better." Countess Violet Haywood sighed as she mounted the last step out of the great shaft and onto the very pinnacle of the Wolf's Tooth.

A severely dressed middle-aged woman, tall and trim and fit, Violet could have passed for a rather stern governess who'd softened just enough to charm the lord of the castle, married him, then had her existing wardrobe sensibly altered into something with adequate panache and sparkle to be taken seriously at court. Whatever her actual story might have been, she was in no mood to offer it.

A watch tower had once stood on this spot, many centuries ago, but now lay in a jumbled ruin of cracked, moss-covered stone beside the pit, all traces of it invisible from below. That no one had bothered to rebuild it certainly seemed more sensible than that it had ever been built in the first place, given that placing a watchtower here seemed rather like offering a step stool to a giant so he could see over the kids at a puppet show.

Even without it, the pinnacle offered an unobstructed view of the fields and pastures and orchards and streams and villages spread out in a patchwork far below, and far off to the hazy horizon. Only the thickly forested slopes to the west created any blind spot, and in their case, another forty or fifty feet wouldn't have made much difference. If nothing closer had blocked the view, the stark white line of cliffs rising some miles back among the trees would have managed it.

Time and weather had taken their toll here not just on the ancient watch tower, but on the mouth of the pit, as well. Huge cracks had formed in the stones of what had once been a courtyard, radiating out from the pit like fractures in a glass mirror that had been struck with a rock. A few chunks of stone about the size of a grown man had sheared away and fallen into the pit some time long ago, and a couple of even larger shards looked poised to take the plunge should anyone step on them carelessly.

Violet crossed the remains of the courtyard, the wind of the heights tousling the few loose strands it could find of her dark, neatly done-up auburn hair as she picked her way carefully over the rocks and around the scraggly grasses. Behind her trailed Nolan and Elissa, the latter of whom seemed quite anxious and uncertain. They skirted the pit, leaving it a wide berth, until they arrived at the edge of the rubble where Keely sat with Ulric upon the fallen stones.

Keely now wore a rough workman's tunic that fell off one shoulder and hung to her knees—having been made for someone much larger than herself—and a pair of scuffed, sturdy leather work boots that fitted her perfectly. Ulric had acquired the tunic for her when they'd paused most of the way up the stair, and he'd slipped out the side passage that came out behind some rocks near the cathedral site. He'd quickly found someone he could trust to deliver a message to Nolan, then borrowed the tunic from a friend on the work crew.

How they'd wound up with the boots, why they fit Keely so well, and why she'd traded in the much-nicer pair she'd been wearing for these old things were details that Ulric had managed to miss.

"This morning," Violet began calmly, "I ate my breakfast across from the crocodile smile of an inquisitrix who clearly thinks her friends should have killed me the last time they were in town. Then I had to go off and leave my husband to dance with the Inquisition on his own and hope he'd still be there when I got back, because someone had to come up here and sort things out at the cathedral site. Since then, I've learned that the damage to the cathedral was twice what anyone had been admitting, that the workers think the site is cursed and they're nearly ready to walk off, that the county has become infested with a plague of witches, and that someone's house is on fire down at the bottom of the hill. Oh, and that half the players in next week's Allanaves pageant have just declared they'll never take the stage with the other half because of some business about a pig and three bolts of silk.

"So now I've got to broker peace between them, or else decide which of the county's two most influential families I'd rather insult. I've already got an army's worth of people beating on my door, demanding I solve all of their problems yesterday—if not sooner—so please, please tell me that..."

Violet stopped suddenly, staring at Keely through narrowed eyes. "Your hair is white. Why is your hair white?" She'd had only a perfunctory introduction to Keely and Elissa when they'd been drafted to take over where Sister Petra had left off, and honestly hadn't given them a second look, but she was sure she would have remembered that little detail.

"I like to think it's more a 'silver'," Keely offered helpfully. Then before the countess could slap her for being so helpful, she added quickly, "This is its natural color. I covered it to hide from the Inquisition. They're here looking for the Grimm Truth, a very old text that..."

"I know what the Grimm Truth is," Violet said curtly, waving a hand to hurry her on. "Why are they looking for it *here*, and why are they looking for it *now*, and what have *you* to do with it?"

"They're following a trail left by someone calling herself 'Lady A'. Sister Petra was working with her, convinced they'd find it here on the Wolf's Tooth. I'm pretty sure that's what got her killed, and the cathedral vandalism was just to cover someone's tracks. I hope that the someone was associated with the Inquisition, or we've already got another player involved who'll stop at nothing to get the book."

"We can show you the letters we found in the chapel," Elissa interjected.

"And there's probably a workman still sprawled on the stairs halfway down," Ulric added, because Keely's explanation had already been interrupted, "who seems to have been involved, too. Going by what he babbled, he's been searching the catacombs for 'the book'. Drunk or insane or both. Got violent and forced me to deck him. Too big to shift up the stairs very far without help."

"Oh, and the Inquisition thinks I'm a witch," Keely finished helpfully. All set with a pithy reply for when Violet asked whether the Inquisition was right in that regard, Keely felt a vague sense of disappointment when the countess evinced not the slightest curiosity.

"So what you're trying delicately to tell me," Violet ventured instead, "is that Pontifine Augusta has charged my family on pain of death with keeping the two of you alive while all the forces of the Inquisition are trying to make you both considerably dead?"

"Pretty much," Keely admitted. "Sorry."

With no visible change in her expression, and still appraising Keely, Violet reached back in the general direction of Nolan. At first Keely thought she had moved to point to him for some reason, but the countess held her hand out expectantly with open palm.

"Your ladyship?" Nolan asked, as puzzled by the gesture as anyone.

"Nolan, what do you have on your person that you don't think I *know* you have on your person," Violet said, "but which you'd suppose I might find very useful just now?"

The man puzzled for a couple moments more, then light dawned in his eyes. Wordlessly, he dug in his tunic, produced a small metal flask, and dropped it into Violet's waiting hand. She accepted it just as wordlessly, uncorked the container, and took a healthy swallow before re-sealing it and returning it to its owner.

"Thank you," Violet said levelly before returning the full force of her attention to Keely. "So the Inquisition is here chasing a legend?"

"Yes." Keely nodded.

"And you actually came here trying to find it first?" Violet asked.

"Yes."

"And I should trust you about all this because...?"

"Damned if I know." Keely shrugged. "But since you're probably not ready to turn me over to the Inquisition anyway, I'm not actually invested in you believing any of it. You asked, I told."

Violet bit her lip thoughtfully, in her first display of any emotion other than exhaustion.

"Oh, and the Inquisition thinks I'm a witch because I can turn into a cat," Keely said. "Ulric's seen it. Now if you think it's worth the time, I'm willing to tell you the entire story. Otherwise, I'm just going to count on your sense of self-interest to keep us away from the Inquisition and alive, and be happy for it."

"You're certain the Inquisition is willing to kill over this book?" Violet stopped herself and made a face. "Of course they are. What I mean is, is it really important enough for them to interrupt all their other bits of killing and maiming to chase it across the kingdoms? And then..." She dug the heels of her hands wearily into her forehead. "I'm too tired for this."

"Jane Carver personally threatened a miraculata with death for conspiring to find the book," Elissa said. "We were there."

"The High Inquisitrix threatened to kill a miracle woman?" Violet asked incredulously. Her shell of composure had developed some serious cracks at this point.

"I don't know if Carver wants the book for herself," Keely said, "or if she just wants to burn it before anyone else can read it, but the woman is obsessed."

"So if we were to find it before she did, and—say—track down a printer willing to publish it...?"

Keely nodded. "You'd be able to hear Jane Carver cursing a blue streak from any corner of the kingdoms."

"Well, this isn't the least bit odd or suspicious." The young noblewoman brushed back her long, dark-auburn hair and looked down appraisingly from the back of her sturdy, sure-footed, chestnut pony. Perhaps it was just a trick of the forest terrain, but she somehow seemed to be looking down quite a bit farther than she had any right to from the back of such a small mount.

Like her companions—two men and a woman of about her age—she wore hunting leathers. She also cradled a fine wheel-lock hunting rifle in her arms. Every surface polished and gleaming, the gun screamed craftsmanship of a sort Tobias couldn't recall seeing outside of the heartland before, and perhaps not even there. Across the back of her pony hung the gray carcass of a recently deceased wolf, the victim of a single clean shot to the head. "Should I start by asking who you are, or by asking what you're doing here?"

While Tobias was still mustering his response, the local huntsman that Baldassare had brought along stepped forward. "I brought them, your ladyship." He made a broad gesture toward the trio of nobles and the squire behind him. "They were on their way to make their introductions at court, but their companion ran off into the woods and seems to have gotten herself lost."

"And with that witch the..." Tobias began.

"Do *not* talk to me about witches." The woman fixed Tobias with a cold glare, ice clinging to every word. "Just be out of the forest by nightfall or you'll be lost yourselves. And do find the courtesy to present yourselves at the castle, with or without your friend. If she's still lost, we'll see what we can do to help look for her in the morning."

"Thank you," Tobias said, but the woman only nodded curtly in response before turning and riding away with her companions.

"Lady Minda," the huntsman explained after they'd gone, "Earl Haywood's oldest girl. And I'd listen to her about the forest. She knows it as well as anyone."

It dawned on Tobias then that he'd probably jumped to conclusions in taking Baldassare and Evadne for locals, and that in all the excitement they'd made only the most cursory of introductions to each other. Then the thought slipped away as quickly as it had come when Conrad announced, "She rested here." Crouched next to a nearby fallen log, the boy nodded at the soft earth in front of the log, and the footprints Sabina had left in it.

As Tobias and the huntsman stepped in to join Conrad in examining the ground, and Baldassare looked on hopefully from behind them,

Evadne quietly shifted the matched set of daggers she'd drawn under her cloak when Minda had appeared, and she slid them back into their sheaths.

Leaving the others to their task, the towering woman devoted her attention instead to scanning the ancient forest around them for any sign of Sabina or...well, anything that might be dangerous, though the possibility of lurking wolves had pushed its way to the front of her mind after the encounter with the hunting party. As a true child of the city, she didn't know what else to expect from a forest, but one always heard stories about the wolves.

The proof that there were indeed wolves out here redoubled her concern for Sabina, and Evadne cursed herself for not running after when her friend had bolted. Sabina being useless in fight was the whole reason Evadne had managed to escape the wretched slum where she'd been born. The rich girl had come to relish having a streetwise friend to literally watch her back.

The years and Sabina's generosity may have replaced the backstreet tomboy with a refined young gentlewoman, but it was a refined young gentlewoman who knew all the most telling places to bury a knife in a human body, and all the best ways to get one there.

"But which way did she leave?" Evadne asked impatiently.

It was Tobias who finally pointed the way, and they set off through the woods again, tracing Sabina's footsteps until they emerged into the late afternoon sunlight and something that passed for a meadow, so choked in thick brambles that a body could hardly cross it without first descending into the dry, stony stream bed that wound its way between the thorns. In the midst of it all stood an abandoned old hovel, clutched in the thorny embrace of the briers and collapsing in on itself from many years of neglect.

They paused while the three hunters spread out around the edge of the brambles, looking for signs of Sabina's passage. "Nothing," Tobias said at last. "Which means she followed the stream bed. It's the only way to get through this mess without leaving a trace."

"We've got to check the old cottage," Evadne said firmly.

"If you want to wade through those brambles, be my guest," Tobias answered her dismissively, "but *she* didn't. Anything bigger than a wildcat would have to force its way through, and nothing has for weeks."

"Stop being clever for a moment and think," Evadne said. "You're chasing a witch who turns people into animals. I assume she counts as a 'people' herself? This place may be a bit run-down for even a witch to call home, but it'd be an excellent spot to rest her head without fear of being taken unawares. And if she *was* here when Sabina showed up..."

"Here now!" the huntsman said crossly. "That wasn't just Inquisition-scare-talk about a witch you started to prattle at Lady Minda? You're actually chasing some'n who changes decent folk into actual animals? And she might be out here anywhere?"

"Yes!" Tobias said. "No one told you?"

"No, no one bloody told me!" The huntsman glowered. "His man showed up," he said, pointing accusingly at Baldassare, "pounding on my door and offering to pay me to help find a lass lost in the woods! No one said a whisper about no witches!"

"If you're that worried about witches," Baldassare said with menacing calm, "you might want to stop shouting to them that we're here."

"*I'm* not here. I am *not* here!" the huntsman said, rounding on Baldassare. "*You* may be here, but I am already on my way back home to a stiff drink."

"Even if I double your pay?" Baldassare asked with a cocked eyebrow. "We've got other trackers now, but I'll admit your knowledge of the woods is worth something beyond that."

"My knowledge of these woods tells me this is no 'woods', lad. This is a forest—big and deep and dark and old, full of things no man living understands. I'm sorry about the lass, but she was a fool to be runnin' off into it. You're welcome to follow me out, but I'm leavin', and I'm doin' it now."

"At least my dear sister will have the comfort that I'm not wasting money on her," Baldassare said as he watched the man stride off back through the trees, but the others were already forcing their way carefully through the brambles toward the hovel.

When at last they reached it and stepped inside, what became immediately apparent was that "inside" seemed an overly generous term. Barely enough of the roof remained to call it a roof, and the walls were all rotting and falling in. With space limited and the whole business looking unsafe, Baldassare didn't bother pushing in after the others, but stood peering about outside while Evadne poked around the collapsed remnants of furnishings that had been humble in their prime, and Tobias and Conrad studied the dirt floor for any signs of passage.

Out of the corner of her eye, Evadne caught a sudden, sinuous movement at her shoulder where there should have been none. Without a thought, she spun with the speed of a serpent, small silvery blade flashing in her hand. The blade sunk deep into decaying wood, but not before trapping an actual serpent against the wall and beheading it.

Big around as an ordinary woman's arm if not Evadne's, the body of the beast flopped down from the beam it had been coiled around to lay writhing on the floor in a macabre and disturbing dance of death amidst a shower of rotting debris that had been shaken loose by the force of the giantesss' planting her dagger in the wall. Evadne wrenched the blade free and was backing toward the door, away from the snake, when they heard the structure creak and saw the support beams begin to shift.

"Out!" Baldassare shouted, though the others hardly needed the warning. Evadne dove for the door. Conrad squirmed quickly through one of the larger holes in the wall. Tobias simply threw himself at a rotting wall with as much running start as he could manage. All three rolled clear as the aging structure fell in on itself in a cloud of dust and mold.

"I hope condolences are not in order," Tobias said, brushing himself off and plucking gingerly at the thorns he'd acquired in his landing. "Dame Evadne was right: someone was in that house very recently— probably more than one someone—even though there was no way they could have gotten in. Pray that the witch didn't turn your sister into a snake."

"No," Baldassare whispered, waving them to silence with a hand. "That's her over there. That's got to be her." At the tree line behind where the old hovel had been, a small-but-regal, snow-white doe stood watching them.

"I found something!" Nolan's shout echoed through the tunnels beneath the Wolf's Tooth, bringing everyone within earshot hurrying to join him. The younger—but the larger—of the two guardsmen who'd been assigned to babysit Keely and Elissa, he sported the medium-red shade of hair so common among the locals—closely cropped, but making a fair effort at appearing unkempt given the meager length it had to work with.

They'd been joined by half a dozen other guardsmen, who'd been trusted with no more than the knowledge, "We're looking for a book in here somewhere. No one goes home until we find it," and the search party had fanned out through tunnels that ranged from ancient to merely very old, in hopes they'd return with a legend.

Keely had eyed the waters at the bottom of the shaft nervously when they'd first come back down from the peak, but whatever had stirred in their depths had since settled, and their surface had returned so completely to its original mirror calm that Keely began wondering if she'd imagined the whole thing. Perhaps she'd even imagined the dead she'd seen sleeping beneath.

It was a tempting story to tell herself, but a much harder one to believe than the one about imagining the unsettled waters. For now, she simply held onto the hope that they'd find the book somewhere in the upper reaches of the tunnels.

Many of the little and not-so-little chambers that Keely discovered by flickering lamp light had probably been re-purposed multiple times over the centuries. A handful still seemed in active use as storerooms or armories, and one had been set up as some sort of council chamber. The room where she found Nolan and Elissa—whom he still dutifully refused to allow out of his sight—had been stocked with barrels marked "gun powder" and with a few racks of cannon balls, reminding Keely of young Addie's story about the castle blowing up.

By Keely's guess, the Haywoods had decided after that last visit from the Inquisition they'd best be ready for a siege. Not that the one little county could ever weather a serious siege driven by the Inquisition, but she could understand the appeal of going down fighting instead of getting dragged off begging for a mercy that would reputedly never come.

"A book?" Violet asked hopefully, appearing at Keely's shoulder with her own lantern.

"Sorry, no." Nolan shook his head, extending a single torn and muddy page. "But isn't that an 'A' this was sealed with?"

"Lady A?" Violet grabbed the page quickly and unfolded it, her brow furrowing as she smoothed it out and inspected it.

"It was wedged in-between the wall and one of the crates," Nolan said. "Looks like Sister Petra must have hidden it in a hurry the night she died."

Violet just shook her head dismissively, tucking the page away in her bodice as she waved the searchers back to work. As the others filed out, though, she quietly grabbed Elissa, Keely, and their escorts, and led the way back up the stairs to the peak.

"I'm accepting notions on what to make of this," she said, pulling out the page again once they were safely out of earshot of any men whose lives might yet be spared by not knowing what they were up to. "I read tolerably well, but I can't make head or tails of this." She extended the page to Elissa, who studied it as the others peered over her shoulder.

"I shouldn't wonder!" Elissa exclaimed. "These are bilge glyphs."

"Bilge glyphs?" The countess raised a questioning eyebrow.

"A code of symbols developed during the Crusade of the Sea Lords. Actually, there were three or four codes that used similar techniques, but they developed a reputation for being easily decoded, so they fell out of use as trash—bilge glyphs."

"Can you decipher them?" Violet asked.

"Maybe," Elissa said. "Probably, if I had my library. Not sure without it, but I can try."

"All right. You stay here with Nolan and work on that." Violet nodded. "The rest of us will get back to searching for the book."

"Actually," Keely said, "I've been doing that too long already. We need more time. With the Inquisition on the hunt down there, they're going to find this place sooner or later. My guess is it will be sooner, and the only thing that's going to stop them is if they stop searching around the Tooth."

Lady Violet nodded slowly. "And what do you propose?"

"They're searching for two things: me and this book. We have to convince them that both are someplace else."

"And we would do this by...?" Violet prompted.

"I lead them away while the rest of you keep searching."

"*You* lead them away?" Violet asked with an arched eyebrow. "You're not some expendable pawn in this game, girl. *You* may be able to forget that if anything happens to you or Elissa it's check and mate for my entire family, but I can't."

"I'll go with her," Ulric said.

Violet frowned. "Ulric, this isn't protecting her against two or three thugs, this is protecting her against twenty knights of the Inquisition and..."

"And sometimes the most dangerous thing you can do, milady, is fight defensively," Ulric insisted. "Don't forget how hard even putting together a plan to deal with the vandals has been with the Inquisition on our backs. We can win the battle of keeping our guests safe and still lose the war. We have to get the Inquisition out of here, this is the woman who can do it, and I'll be right there with my last breath saved just for getting her back to you alive. I'm a marked man anyway."

Violet's scowl deepened.

"It's a good plan," Elissa said quietly. "If I've learned anything traveling with Keely, it's that she knows how to make a quick getaway and how to play a good shell game."

"That is *not* the most reassuring thing you could have said." Violet turned her dark look briefly on Elissa, then back to Keely before finally sighing. "All right! You're right. Getting the Inquisition out of the equation would change our situation from impossible to merely precarious. We have to do it, but if you aren't back with us safe and sound before the pontifine returns, I will personally hunt you to the ends of the earth. If I find you alive, I will introduce you to tortures that would give Jane Carver nightmares. If I find you dead, I'll invent ways to make you wish I'd found you alive. Do we understand each other?"

"Perfectly." Keely nodded. "Now to do this con right, we're going to have to break into two teams. Ulric, if you're with me, this is going to graduate you from 'marked man' status to painting a big bullseye on your chest for the whole Inquisition. Are you really up for that?"

Ulric answered with a curt nod. "I hear that dying of old age is over-rated."

CHAPTER TWENTY

A TRAGEDY OF ERRORS

Minda stared down the muzzle of her long hunting rifle, watching carefully as the wolves sniffed among the trees. She'd counted seven of them, about two hundred yards upwind, and suspected more. The Crimson Forest was by no means generous when it came to clearings or clean lines of sight for any distance to speak of, but she knew it well enough to have learned a few rocky outcroppings that commanded a reasonable view, and she lay stretched out on one of them now.

A few yards away, Doryne Pendleton—daughter to one of the local barons—crouched patiently behind a rock, cradling a loaded crossbow. Their other companions had either spread out along the low ridge or remained behind with the horses once they'd spotted the fresh set of tracks.

"That's not the same pack, is it?" Doryne whispered.

Minda shook her head. "Definitely seeing different alphas." This also definitely marked the first time she'd seen two distinct packs in a single day. It was rare enough to encounter one pack this close to the forest's edge, and those usually came at night in the late winter months, looking for an unnoticed break in the hedge and some farmer's untended flock. This just served as one more reminder that they lived in strange, unsettled times.

Then the wolf she'd been waiting for wandered back out into view: big, black, shaggy, and scarred, at least a quarter again as tall at the shoulder as the next largest wolf in the pack. Much as Minda loved her hunting rifle, it would give her exactly one shot at the wolves, then they'd disappear back into the forest before she could even start to reload.

Her back-up rifle lay on the ground within easy reach, but even that would only afford her a second shot if the wolves hesitated in confusion before deciding which way to bolt. And her friends might bring down one or two of the animals, but in Doryne's case, it would take a lucky shot from this distance, and Minda couldn't be sure any of the others would have line of sight to try. Not a farmer in the county would thank them for leaving that overgrown beast alive to come looking for livestock, and Minda had to assume it was up to her to take it down in one clean shot.

The alpha stopped and cocked its head, suddenly listening, and Minda took her aim. "That's it," she murmured. "Hold that pose." Then another of the wolves came loping directly in-between her and the alpha before she could steady, and the moment was gone. The alpha started moving again, and it disappeared back behind a tree before the other wolf got clear. Then the whole pack was moving. Something had spooked them, which surely meant *someone* had spooked them. One of the other hunters had gotten careless, and in moments the wolves would be gone.

Minda muttered a curse under her breath and gave up on the concept of careful aim. Her eyes scanned the trees in the direction the wolves were heading, until she spotted a couple of the wolves darting past a break in the foliage. She leveled the gun at it and held her breath. Then a flicker of black fur emerged into the break. Even before Minda's mind had processed what her eye had seen, her body had adjusted its aim a hair to the left, and her finger had squeezed the trigger. The alpha tumbled suddenly over its own unguided feet and went down without a making sound.

A chorus of shots cracked from somewhere off through the trees to the right. Minda noted with satisfaction that it elicited yelps from at least two of the wolves, but she kept her unblinking gaze fixed on the spot where her own quarry had fallen, and she reached for her backup rifle to be ready if the beast stirred.

Out of the corner of her eye, Minda saw Doryne step out from behind the rock and quickly fire off her crossbow. Doryne muttered something and grabbed for another bolt. "Minda?" she murmured.

"Let it go," Minda said, still keeping her eyes fixed on the spot the wolf had fallen.

"It's not *going!*" Doryne insisted with quiet urgency.

"What...?" Minda finally dragged her gaze away from the fallen wolf to glance in the direction Doryne was staring as her fingers fumbled to reload the crossbow. A black blur below came darting closer through the trees.

"I almost got her!" Doryne stammered. "She looked up at me and snarled and..."

"Wolves don't act like that!" Minda snapped, but even the brief glimpses through the foliage told her it was the female alpha—as black as the male—charging up the hill straight toward them, and in fury, not in panic. Keenly aware of how little effort it would take an enraged wolf to bound up to their rocky perch, Minda instantly forgot the fallen male and leveled her rifle at the spot where the female should break out of the thicket below in three...two...one...

The snapping of branches allowed Minda to refine her aim even before the blur of black broke out of the greenery twenty paces away. Her rifle cracked. Then everything happened so fast Minda's brain couldn't start piecing it together until it was all over.

The first thing that had happened was the woman: brown-haired, brown eyes, dressed all in black. She staggered back from the shot, glancing down at her gut where she'd been hit.

The second thing that happened was the wolf. It came barely a heartbeat behind the woman and barreled into her back, forepaws striking the woman's shoulders and driving her into the rocky ground, but the wolf never stopped. It barely slowed. Rather than tear into the fallen woman, it simply used her falling body as a springboard to launch itself up at Minda.

Still dreadfully short of having the crossbow ready to fire again, Doryne dropped it and pulled her own back-up weapon from her belt. The pistol cracked. The wolf yelped and tumbled backward down the rocks to land just a few feet from the woman in black, where it lay whining piteously.

With that whining boring into her head, Minda couldn't begin to manage a coherent thought until she'd taken the pistol from Doryne's quavering hand, reloaded it, and finished the wolf with a clean shot. It was only then that her mind re-engaged and began piecing together the seconds it had lost. Finally coming to the panicked realization that she'd just shot a woman, Minda scrambled down to rocks with Doryne close behind.

The stranger lay face-down and unmoving. How much of the blood that covered the ground was hers and how much was the wolf's, Minda could not immediately say—but when Minda rolled the woman over, it instantly became clear that too much of it was hers. The wolf had done her a mercy by slamming her head into the rocks, probably not killing her, but at least rendering her insensate to the lingering death of the gut shot. She was beyond help.

Minda sat down unsteadily, closing her eyes and lowering her head, leaning on her hands while she tried to still the nausea in her stomach. The wounds were not pleasant to look at, but she'd seen her share. It was more the shock of the whole situation and the coming down from the adrenalin rush that had her feeling woozy.

The wolf had been smart enough to understand not just that some human with a gun had killed her mate, but to identify Minda herself as the offender through all the trees and the chaos. That realization itself was unsettling. Add in the realization that the wolf had been more enraged than scared—willing to charge not just a human, but apparently three humans, in its need for vengeance—and it threw everything Minda thought she knew about wolves into question.

As for the woman, what had she even been doing there? Dressed all in black as she was, Minda's first thought had been "inquisitrix", but she lacked the robes—instead dressed quite sensibly for an outing in the woods—so...

"I recognize her," Doryne said shakily. Minda's brief ray of hope vanished as Doryne tugged at the gold chain around the woman's throat and fished out the single claw that hung from it. Sharper than a wolf's claw and larger than a wildcat's, it came from no creature that Minda could identify, but she'd seen its like often enough, hanging about the neck of agents of the Inquisition.

"She's the inquisitrix I saw talking to your father before we left this morning," Doryne hissed.

Ulric started at the sound of rustling at the edge of the copse, and he raised his crossbow—relaxing only slightly when he saw it was Keely scurrying back toward him as the little white cat.

Before they'd left the tunnels, he'd traded in the power of his arquebus for the silence of that crossbow, and the distinctive livery of the Haywoods for nondescript workman's garb. He'd also pulled on a wide-brimmed hat and a woolen scarf that together could do an effective job of hiding his face. The effort to guard his identity had evoked a discrete, satisfied smile from Keely, who took it as a silent admission that he wasn't quite so doomed as he liked to say.

For her part, Keely had gone back to wearing red. When Elissa and Nolan had gone scrounging supplies for them, Keely had been as particular about that as she'd been about the fact she'd have nothing scrounged from a scarecrow this time. Out of the options they'd brought back, she still went for a ragged, old, red cloak and a ragged, old, red tunic that hung down nearly to her knees.

Then—apparently not satisfied that they were ragged enough—she'd ripped off the arms of the over-sized tunic and deliberately torn and slashed at both garments until a scarecrow was all they looked fit for.

Now that outfit lay on the ground beside Ulric where Keely had left it, but rather than darting into it, she drew up short and started hacking and wheezing like she was having a disagreement with a hairball. Out of the corner of one eye, Ulric watched Keely with concern while the rest of his attention remained alert for any pursuers that might be coming fast behind her. None had appeared before Keely quieted and crawled back into her clothes.

Human again, Keely pushed herself up unsteadily on her arms. "Eeeeewww," she moaned. "Eewww, eewww, eewww…"

"Are you being followed?" Ulric asked quietly, not allowing himself to be distracted from priorities.

"I seriously doubt it," Keely managed.

"Did you find our friends?" Ulric lowered the crossbow and allowed himself to divert more of his attention to Keely.

"Oh, yeah," Keely said with an emphatic nod that she immediately regretted, as it seemed to set off another spasm in her stomach.

"Torturing someone, were they?" Ulric asked grimly.

"Sorta. Kinda." Keely looked up with a sour face. "Not really. I don't know." Ulric just stared at her until she volunteered more. "Seems Riordan and Shoshona managed to tear themselves away from the hunt while everyone else is out beating the bush, and… You know, even when people notice a cat, they're not terribly concerned how they behave in front of it?"

"So they were…?" Ulric smirked.

"I think they'd call it that." Keely looked dubious. "I've seen a lot of weird stuff and a lot of sad stuff and some funny stuff. A couple of times, I've even seen stuff that made me tingle to my toes and back again." She managed a weak grin. "More often, I've seen stuff that I just wish I could forget."

"And this was one of that last lot?" Ulric's smirk didn't falter.

"This is the new reigning and undisputed monarch of the last lot. If I ever see anything more grotesquely horrible than…" Keely faltered as visions from the watery graveyard floated up in front of her eyes. "I mean, something that's…supposed to be fun, but it's gross…"

"You're stammering," Ulric said.

"People stammer!" Keely shot back defensively.

"People stammer," Ulric agreed. His smirk had gone now without a trace. "You don't stammer."

"I…"

"Have you ever stammered in your life?" Ulric asked.

"Yes!" Keely huffed, but her eyes wandered as if scouring her own thoughts. "Prrrrobably...Must have...I'm sure I have."

"When?"

"Sometime! What's your point?!"

Ulric studied her impassively for a moment before finally shaking his head and looking away to scan the trees. "No point. What now that we've found them? This is your show."

Sir Riordan emerged from the orchard-facing back exit of the old barn, gripping his great axe as his gaze swung slowly about, searching the trees. At last satisfied that he would see nothing from here but the lone wisp of straw dangling in front of his eyes, he brushed that away and swung the axe around casually enough that an observer might have thought it accidental when the haft thudded into the barn door. He strode out slowly toward the orchard, still scanning his surroundings for any sign of movement, absently combing his fingers through his long, dark hair in search of any other debris that might have caught in it.

Only the leaves of the orchard and the tattered red cloak of a scarecrow, fluttering in the wind, stirred in the lengthening shadows of the early evening.

"Feeling better?" Shoshona asked quietly without looking at him as she emerged from the barn herself, straightening her robes.

"Much," he answered, returning her lack-of-gaze with his own. When he finally did turn around, he quirked a bit of a smile and stroked meaningfully at the side of his chin. "You've got..."

"Oh." She mirrored his action, and her fingertips came away red. She grinned and blushed faintly, wiping at the corner of her mouth until Riordan nodded that it was gone. "At least it was only blood." She giggled girlishly. "Has anyone told you how hot it is when you turn into a berserker and set fire to stuff?"

"Well, Jane seems to get a kick out of it," Riordan answered wryly. "I'm really going to have to take your word, though, given what memories I have of it are always like shards of a shattered mirror."

"Yeah, well...Oops. Stern-face," Shoshona whispered, nodding toward the corner of the barn, around which could be heard the muffled thud of hurried footsteps.

When the gray-haired farmer rounded the corner moments later, he was met by the all-business scowl of the inquisitrix, the all-business scowl of her knight companion, and the all-business shimmer of the sun off her knight-companion's very large axe. The man's plumpness and decent clothes marked him as a freeman, wealthy as farmers went, but well enough acquainted with his place in the world that he went to his knees at once upon seeing them, despite an arthritic twinge.

"Sister!" he seemed only half surprised to find them there. "There's a ghost in my house! Or a witch! Something...! She..."

"White hair?" Shoshona snapped. "Young looking?"

The farmer nodded. "She..." But before he could get two words out, the inquisitrix and the knight had disappeared back into the barn. Moments later, they returned, mounted, and it was all the farmer could do to scramble out of the way of their spirited horses as they came charging out. "Follow," Shoshona commanded him before they disappeared around the corner of the barn.

"Flush her out!" Shoshona said, drawing up near the man's anxiously waiting family within sight of the well-kept, two-story cottage. "Just give me a minute to swing wide around back."

Riordan nodded. Glancing back as he counted to himself, he could see the old farmer just puffing into view behind them. The man hadn't covered half the distance before Riordan decided it was time to make his move and spurred his destrier forward. The big man vaulted from the saddle to land on the boards of the front stoop of the house with a heavy thud, then kicked the door in.

"You're mine, witch!" he bellowed, punctuating the declaration with a swing of his axe that splintered the chair by the door into kindling. Only then did he stop to listen and look, his gaze rapidly drinking in the whole room. From somewhere toward the back of the house, he heard a scuffling, and he made his way that direction with a mixture of haste and caution, as he wanted neither to arrive too late to assist Shoshona, nor too quickly, lest he blunder into a trap laid by the witch or allow her to escape should this be a ruse to distract him.

The scuffle had quieted by the time Riordan reached the kitchen and saw the back door standing ajar. Then from outside a cat screeched. A small white blur bolted into the room at floor level, chased by a flurry of billowing black, and Riordan swung his axe with deadly accuracy. Blood flew in all directions. The little white head bounced away, rolling to a stop in the ashes of the fireplace, and the body stumbled. The black cloak that had been trailing behind fluttered down over the fresh new corpse.

For one brief moment, all went still. Then out of the corner of his eye, Riordan saw the cat. It had frozen, wide-eyed and mouth open, just inside the doorway, staring at him and the blood and the axe and the corpse.

As the witch-cat stared, the wheels of realization began to turn in Riordan's brain. He'd gotten so far as to comprehend that it was the severed-head of a long-eared white rabbit now laying in the fireplace when the cat bolted between his legs and back toward the front of the house. It took a few more heartbeats to process that he was looking down at the cloak of an inquisitrix pooled on the floor, and that it had been trailing the rabbit because it had been fastened about the creature's throat with Shoshona's ivory-and-onyx brooch.

Horror-struck, Riordan crouched over the wreckage he had wrought, and clutched the blood-spattered brooch with numb fingers. Then as the ice gripping his heart boiled away into steam, he tore the brooch from the cloak and closed his fingers tightly about it as he rose to his feet with slow determination. Fire flickered in his eyes—not figurative flames, but literal ones—and as he threw back his head and howled, every scrap of cloth in the kitchen burst into flames at once, and every board and beam began to smoke and smolder.

Through the doorway to the front room, he caught sight of the witch-cat standing on the splinters of the door he'd come in by, staring at him wide-eyed once again. Then Riordan launched himself at the cat, and he knew nothing but burning rage.

Ulric slammed Shoshona hard into the rabbit hutch behind the farmhouse, dancing back a step to take the crossbow well out of her reach and level it at her again as she fell to the ground. She lay for a moment, recovering and watching him cautiously while Ulric listened to hear if her shout had attracted Riordan's attention—but the same chaos inside the farm house that had distracted him long enough for her to rush him had either drowned her out, or was keeping the knight too busy to respond.

"I knew you were in league with that witch," Shoshona growled. In the struggle, she'd managed to pull the scarf from his face, and the recognition had been instant.

"Lady, have you ever heard of a self-fulfilling prophecy?" he replied calmly. "You know, my life would suddenly get ten times less complicated if you happened to stop breathing, so you just used up your escape attempts. Now shut up, get face-down on the ground, and put your hands behind your back, or this quarrel goes straight through your gut."

"You'll..." Shoshona began.

"Now!!" Ulric snapped, taking careful aim. The little fair-haired inquisitrix shut up and complied.

"It's not too late to find your way back to Seriena's grace," Shoshona said as Ulric pinned her under his knee and roughly bound her hands with a cord. Her tone had shifted from imperious to motherly with a disturbing lack of transitional state.

"I really think it is," Ulric answered without emotion. "If she's on your side, I hope it is."

"Of course she is," Shoshona said, showing no concern for the rough handling. "Why do you think your witch resorted to trickery instead of actually turning me into a rabbit like she would anyone else? The goddess protects me from her dark magic."

Ulric snorted as he wrapped the scarf back around his face, then pulled Shoshona back to her feet. "Believe what you like. Just get moving. If I can't get you out of here without anyone being the wiser that you're *not* a rabbit, you're still a dead woman."

As he hurried Shoshona away, Ulric glanced uneasily back over his shoulder at the thick, black smoke that had begun pouring out of the farmhouse.

CHAPTER TWENTY-ONE

BURNING RAGE

"Tell me that doesn't *look* more powerful than some silly old book," Scarlet said, gesturing expansively up at the sheer southern slope of the Wolf's Tooth, towering into the darkening sky above them. The voluminous, crimson, traveling cloak the lovely redhead had pulled on as they'd left the cottage fluttered in a wind damp with the promise of rain.

Sabina—who'd just taken a healthy bite out of an apple from the orchard they were standing in—chewed thoughtfully before answering. "Very majestic," she admitted, craning her neck to stare up at the cliffs. "But even if it was mine to build a castle on, it's not a fortress I need." Her own pink cape fluttered about her shoulders stylishly but lacked the length to lend it the sort of grandeur that Scarlet's cloak achieved.

"*Everyone* needs *some* sort of fortress." Scarlet shrugged. "But that's beside the point. There's magic stirring in that big rock—magic old and deep."

I thought you said you weren't a witch? Sabina just managed to not ask, biting her lip and staring sideways at Scarlet instead.

Whatever retort Scarlet might have come up with was lost in her obliviousness to what Sabina had almost blurted out. "You wouldn't have known it ten years ago," Scarlet said instead. "The magic's been...sleeping. But it's shaking off the cobwebs now, and whoever harnesses it is in for a lovely wild ride. That someone could be you."

The next comment Sabina avoided making was, "Or you," but so loud was the thought that at first she wasn't sure she hadn't given it voice. She wanted to believe this whole "faerie go'ssmother" thing—she *really* wanted to—but in her experience, no one ever just *gave* you anything.

She'd received her share of so-called gifts, to be sure, but they'd always come with a price attached.

Right now, for example, there were no less than half a dozen young men who she was diligently avoiding because each thought of her as bought and paid for by things they'd done for her or given her. Keeping them all deluded was the increasingly difficult juggling act that had brought her to the realization of how precarious her family's position had become.

Now a complete stranger was offering to mother her, and to hand her the future on a platter? Even Sabina's own mother hadn't mothered her, on account of being dead for as long as Sabina could remember. All the woman had ever given Sabina was her curvaceous beauty and— not coincidentally—an extravagantly wealthy father. Admittedly, that was more than most people had to work with, but she *had* worked, and that was the point.

A girl of a different temperament in Sabina's situation might have grown up realizing that she was perfectly positioned for an easy life as some man's trophy, even if that meant marrying down a bit. A girl of a slightly different temperament might have resented that idea. A girl of a *very* different temperament might have embraced the notion and devoted herself to looking for just the right man for the job—but Sabina being Sabina had spent her life resolutely staring right past the option, oblivious to its existence, no matter how many matchmakers waved it in front of her face.

Always in her private, girlish fantasies, from a most tender age, she had known that when she married, she would marry for power, and would pull her husband's strings like a puppet master playing with an especially well crafted and responsive marionette. As the result of it all, the exhausted young woman found herself to be, in equal measure, both ready to look for miracles and thoroughly mistrustful of them.

"This is where you step in and say, 'Wow, really? How do I do that?'" Scarlet prodded her—then stopped and cocked her head, sniffing the air as a scowl crossed her pretty face.

"What...?" Sabina began. Then she smelled it too. "Something's burning?" She followed Scarlet's gaze skyward and saw the thick black smoke billowing up behind the treetops. Something *big* was burning. Only a contrary wind had kept them from smelling it earlier.

Scarlet sighed heavily and shook her head. "What *are* these people doing?"

A little white blur, low-to-the-ground, came speeding through the orchard and directly between them, leaving the grasses rustling in its wake.

"Now that," Scarlet said, glancing thoughtfully over her shoulder to watch the little cat go, "I do believe was your witch."

Sabina was still watching the cat go, trying to decide if she should believe the woman's pronouncement or chalk it up to mental instability, when Scarlet struck her in the shoulder with a sudden, straight-armed shove of startling strength that nearly pitched her into the trunk of a tree. Sabina yelped, sprawling in the dirt, but before her mind could decipher what had happened or why—and before her body could choose between fight and flight—a towering, terrible figure in black and red came barreling through the space she'd just been standing in, slinging about a very large axe with murderous intent.

"And that would be a very bad man," Scarlet pronounced, her eyes narrowing as she watched Riordan disappear after the cat.

"Isn't he trying to kill the witch?" Sabina managed to ask, spitting out dirt and grass as she tried to clean up her face.

"That's what I said," Scarlet replied with a sharp nod. Then she added, "Oh, bother," as a flaming cinder settled on her cloak, and she extinguished it with a quick slap. Both women glanced around to find the flames behind the smoke they'd smelled spreading quickly through the orchard and heading their direction, contrary to the contrary wind. "Now would be a good time to run," Scarlet said quietly but firmly.

As a woman of decisive action, Sabina froze. Her accustomed arena of decisive action had nothing to do with matters of bodily harm, and everything to do with social and political maneuvering. Had the onrushing flames seemed amenable to some manner of negotiation, she would have sprung to the offensive, convincing them that all the really *good* combustibles lay somewhere off in the opposite direction, probably behind a hedge or two, while all they'd find over here was an ill-tempered rainstorm known to haunt the region. But it didn't, and her finely honed mental reflexes failed her.

Scarlet grabbed Sabina by the wrist and pulled her roughly to her feet. "Run!" she repeated, giving Sabina another little shove toward the towering rock wall of the Wolf's Tooth.

"Please tell me this wasn't part of her plan," Elissa murmured.

"You think I'd know if you don't?" Nolan asked.

In truth, Elissa didn't know which thought scared her more: that Keely might be so out of control to think that playing with fire was a good idea, or that the fire itself was out of control. To their left, the red glow of the setting sun had nearly faded into night, but ahead and to the left, the red glow above the treetops had only intensified.

Above them, the night sky had briefly turned to dark blue velvet shimmering with star dust, until encroaching storm clouds had rolled across the great silver moon and begun dousing the other lights one by one. Then the ominously expanding cloud of smoke had gotten in on the act, and what had first whispered promises of becoming a beautiful, clear night had begun to rapidly devolve into something dark and dreadful.

Knowing they might not arrive before dark at the crossroads where they'd planned to leave Elissa's handiwork for Keely and Ulric to find, Nolan had prudently brought along a lantern. He'd been in no hurry to light it—not knowing where the Inquisition might have spread its net looking for Keely, and neither of them really caring to attract its attention themselves—but given the current turn of events, he did so now. Stumbling along blind in the neighborhood of a wildfire could easily have lethal consequences.

Elissa fully expected Nolan to simply turn back at that point, claiming it was too dangerous for her, but to her mixed relief he simply urged her to make haste.

Other lanterns appeared out of the dark ahead of them—one at first, then two and three. The first of the lanterns swung wildly as it approached, illuminating a soot-stained farm boy of perhaps twelve, scurrying down the road as fast as he dared. "Bryn Pencaer's whole farm's burnin'!" he coughed excitedly. "They're needin' every man who can to come help, and all else t' get clear."

Nolan exhaled sharply, shaking his head in disgust and disbelief, but rallied quickly. "Off to warn the castle, cousin?" When the boy nodded, Nolan sent him on his way with an encouraging clap on the shoulder. "There's a lad. Mind your feet in this dark!"

"Nephew of yours?" Elissa asked as she watched the boy disappear into the gloom. She'd noted the word "cousin", but figured decent odds he'd simply meant it as "relative", especially with the age difference between the two of them.

Nolan shrugged. "Maybe. Can't throw a stick around here without hitting *someone* in my family. Let's get this done, then we'll figure out whether I'm dragging you along to carry buckets or dragging you up on the Tooth to keep you out of harm's way."

More and more lanterns appeared from the gloom as refugees from the flames hurried past—mostly women with children and the elderly— all either making for the rocky heights of the Wolf's Tooth or the stout stone walls of the castle. The general consensus seemed to be that they'd been sent away only as a precautionary measure. They retreated from the flames in an orderly fashion rather than in a panic, and Elissa found herself able to relax a little.

At last they arrived at the crossroads, and Elissa unslung the large satchel she wore, removing the newly bound book from inside to give it one final inspection.

"It's fine," Nolan prodded impatiently. "The first two attempts were looking fine as far as you took them. It only needs to fool folk for a quick glance from a distance."

"That's no excuse not to get it right!" Elissa said defensively.

"It's the *perfect* excuse." Nolan chuckled.

"I just wish I knew what the real Grimm Truth looked like." Elissa sighed, fidgeting with the crisp new pages. At least they were the only bit that didn't look respectfully aged.

"Breathe, girl," Nolan prodded her. "That's battle-jitters talking, because once you let go of that thing and walk away, it's all real. No taking it back and starting over. But you did your bit, and you did your bit good. You got your friend exactly what she asked for. It even looks old and important to me, and I saw you binding the thing. If anyone sees through it, it'll be Keely's fault, not yours. It's her battle now. Let her fight it."

Elissa sighed again, but nodded, and she slipped the book under the hedge directly behind the old, whitewashed signpost at the crossroads, not allowing herself time to think about it any further.

"Come on now," Nolan said. "Let's get you up on rocky ground where it's safe. Up on the Tooth it'll be easier to see how bad the fire is, anyway."

"Oh, you have *so* much to answer for, young lady!" Keely snarled, slamming Shoshona back up against the trunk of an old apple tree with a hand around her throat. Keely had emerged from the dark night so swiftly and silently that neither Shoshona nor Ulric had been aware she was there a moment before, and now she stood naked and soot-stained and furious, back-lit by the fire raging three fields away, her nails gouging deep enough to draw blood from the neck of the bound priestess.

Ulric cleared his throat but backed off cautiously when Keely waved him away with her free hand. "You demonize me, and you chase me across, what...five kingdoms?" Keely hissed. "For turning myself into a fluffy little *cat*? Then you have the nerve try to bring me to justice by unleashing the human inferno into the world's biggest apple-scented tinderbox? Or is that 'man' even human?"

"I don't know what you're talking about," Shoshona rasped.

"That!" Keely snapped, throwing Shoshona roughly to the ground as she pointed back over her shoulder at the blaze. "Your man Riordan did *that*! I *saw* him do that! He didn't knock over a candle. He didn't kick up embers from a fire pit. He just got *mad,* then the whole farmhouse went up, and the flames came chasing with him like a hound at heel. *How many people has that bloody demon already killed for you!*"

"Liar!" Shoshona shouted back vehemently. "He's a good, holy warrior! You..."

"*I,*" Keely interrupted the inquisitrix, crouching down to return her hand to Shoshona's throat, "will do any shouting that needs to be done around here.

"He was there, wasn't he?" she demanded. "When you people killed Blackwater Molly? When you burned Hart Cove to the ground?"

Shoshona made a faltering attempt to laugh past Keely's tightening grip on her throat, and her eyes grew hard and cold. "*Blackwater Molly?*" she gasped. "Sir Riordan slew that witch-queen *himself.*"

"That witch queen was my blood!" Keely screamed, releasing Shoshona's throat only to seize her by the hair and slam her head mercilessly into the ground. She'd slammed it a second time before she felt Ulric's arms wrap under hers and pull her forcibly off the woman. Keely struggled for a moment before a flicker of actual self-awareness caught her attention through the haze of rage, and she forced herself to stop fighting him, if not actually relax into his grip. No one spoke as she hung there for several seconds, seething.

"Let's get moving before I kill her," Keely spat, when she'd finally composed herself enough to speak. "We'll probably *have* to if someone comes poking around because of my screaming."

"I wouldn't worry too much," Ulric said, cautiously easing his grip on Keely until he was satisfied she'd really regained some semblance of control. "That fire's going to demand a lot more attention than a little yelling, and it's causing its own share of yelling, too." He unslung his pack and dug out the clothes he'd brought along for Keely, tossing them to her. "Do we still..."

"No. With that *thing* chasing me, I had to swing around a couple of times to find it," Keely said, melting back into the darkness to get dressed, "but I *did* find it. Let's just get moving."

"We'll be needing to take a detour," Ulric said, watching the fire with a bitter sigh, painfully aware that every field or orchard those flames devoured would make it that much harder to feed the county through the winter—and that much harder for it to recover after—but all this had officially escalated beyond any semblance of control. The house of

Haywood had declared a covert war on the Inquisition, and whatever happened from here on out, it wasn't going to be pretty. Innocent bystanders were going to get hurt—were already getting hurt.

For their own safety, though, he had to pretend he didn't care. Some twisted fate had landed him as the Haywoods' field commander, and from what *he'd* seen, a commander who struggled to protect *everyone* generally wound up endangering more people than he saved. The best way to save lives was to win the battle and end the war as quickly as possible.

Keely was a clever girl, and she *thought* this was her show, but the woman was a con-artist, not a warrior. Some part of her clearly believed that if she couldn't see the damage she'd wrought, it had never happened. Worse, her complex schemes were *not* surviving contact with the enemy, and her only "plan B" seemed to be concocting more elaborate schemes as she went.

If all that wasn't bad enough, she'd also just tipped her hand at how deeply personal this whole thing was to her, and that he couldn't expect her to keep a cool head when confronted with her own emotions. Whatever trust he'd chosen to invest in Keely, she lacked the discipline for any meaningful sort of command.

Ulric's career to date had always focused on the comfortable role of "competent right-hand". He was good at it, and it allowed a certain level of privilege while dodging all the real responsibility. Those days had just come to an end. This was *his* war now. No one else able to take charge of it was in a position to.

"Come on, though," he said, pulling on his best suit of emotional armor and buckling it into place as he pulled the still dazed priestess to her feet. "It won't be far."

Keely reappeared, looking a little less wild now that she was dressed and relatively calm, but she still made for a rather convincing witch, moving fluidly through the dark night with her ragged cloak and tunic and her silvery hair only half tamed. She allowed Ulric to lead the way, lingering behind and prodding Shoshona as needed.

At last Ulric led them through a gap in the hedges and into a dark so deep that they had to feel their way along with each step.

"Is me tripping and breaking my neck part of your plan?" Shoshona asked quietly. "Or are you just hoping I'll smash my face into something?"

"Either would work nicely," Keely said sweetly. "You're alive out of a rather questionable sense of courtesy, not because I expect you to be useful."

"Just sit tight," Ulric said, his voice muffled by some light banging and clattering sounds. "I think I'm going to have to step back out to get this lantern lit after all. Can't see *anything*."

"Of course, I could just turn you into a stoat or something," Keely went on.

"Could you now?" Shoshona answered mockingly. "You have no power over me, witch, or you'd have already done it."

"I'm sure it's comforting to think that," Keely said.

"And you *do* need me—for something," Shoshona said. "I don't know what it is yet, but I will soon enough. You're terribly transparent. You went to far too much trouble prying me away from Sir Riordan for this to be a whim or an accident, so you can stop pretending you'd just as soon kill me."

Keely let out a long, deep sigh. "Fair enough. I do expect you to come in handy getting the book, but don't think you can't be replaced. You were just the most promising candidate at hand. Now be a good girl and shut up again."

"Here we go," Ulric said, ducking back in through the gap in the hedge with a glowing lantern in hand. Its light revealed an old, half-overgrown track leading away among the great, gnarled trees of the Crimson Forest. He headed off down the track without hesitation, and the others fell in behind him.

Keely gave one last look back at the hedge wall that so sharply marked the line here between civilization and wilderness, and she watched as the shadows of the night—chasing the retreating lantern light—swallowed it without a trace. Somewhere off in the distance, the hooting of an owl was answered by an unnerving screech that Keely couldn't identify.

Little could be seen as they walked quietly along amidst the trunks of the towering trees, but the bitter smell of smoke from the fire already hung heavy in the air, mingling with the earthy aroma of decaying leaves and the damp scent of rain on a wind that had begun to rustle through the branches. In that wind, in those shadows, those ancient trees seemed to crouch together, whispering conspiracies to each other in the night, and Keely found a personal appreciation for how the forest could inspire ghost stories.

"Won't this be a really bad place to be if that fire spreads?" Shoshona asked, still trying to sound cavalier, though her voice had finally taken on its first hint of nervousness—either from actual concern over the fire, or because night in the forest was working on her imagination as it was on Keely's.

"If you'd rather, we could climb the Wolf's Tooth or head for the castle," Ulric said without looking back. "But if we run into any of your people, I'll kill you on the spot. Think we can make either one without that happening?" When Shoshona offered no answer, he went on. "There are no 'safe' places to be right now, but this is the least un-safe of them. Just stay close, because you *will* get lost in the dark without me. Then if the fire jumps the road and reaches the forest before morning comes, you *will* die—if you haven't already been torn apart by wolves."

They were perhaps twenty minutes back into the forest when the path opened out into a clearing. At first the only thing visible there was the lack of trees, but as they crossed, the lantern light fell on a curious little building nestled up against a natural rock wall at the far side. Half-obscured as it was by a particularly ancient and gnarled oak that embraced a corner of the two-story cottage, one had to wonder at the age of the building itself, given that the tree couldn't have been there at all when the foundations were laid.

By all rights, the cottage should have cracked and collapsed long ago, as the tree intruded on its space, but it seemed to have undergone a major restoration sometime within the last century, orchestrated by someone who had gone to great trouble to leave the tree intact. While the place didn't seem much used, neither did it look entirely neglected.

"Come on, then," Ulric said, opening the door and leading them into a comfortably appointed sitting room. "We'll be good here while I settle on the best way around the fire. I should probably..."

"Ulric?" a perplexed female voice called from up the stairs at the back of the room. "What are you even doing here? Don't my parents..." Minda Haywood stopped halfway down the steps, casually holding the hunting rifle she'd obviously grabbed out of caution before she'd identified Ulric's voice. Everyone in the room stared at everyone else in the room in various states of surprise and alarm.

"It's okay!" Keely said hastily before anyone else could recover, noticing that Minda's grip on the gun was tightening. "Ulric, be a dear and tell her it's okay."

"Who are you?" Minda snapped suspiciously, bringing her rifle to the ready—pointing the weapon toward Shoshona, even though her gaze and question had been directed straight at Keely.

"Minda, it's okay," Ulric said. He could have done a more convincing job of it, though, and Minda showed little sign of being reassured.

"Who *are* you?" Minda repeated.

"She's a witch," Shoshona volunteered. Her shock having come from the sudden belief that Earl Haywood's family had masterminded her kidnapping, she recovered swiftly now that Minda had dispelled that notion. "You might want to point the gun at *her*, not me."

"She's not a witch," Ulric said reassuringly, as he moved to join Minda.

"I am so a witch!" Keely protested hotly.

"*Maybe* she's a witch," Ulric conceded with a shrug.

"And that's...Sister Shoshona, isn't it?" Minda gaped, her own shock not dissipating so quickly. "And she's...tied up? Ulric, what...?!"

"Who else is here?" Ulric brushed off the question.

"Just Doryne."

"Come on," he said, pushing past her and up the stairs, despite the arm she held out trying to block him. "I only want to tell this story once."

"But you're holding an inquisitrix prisoner!" Minda shouted, chasing up the stairs after him.

"And she's *not* happy about it!" Shoshona yelled after them.

"Ah, well. Maybe he can still sort things where we don't have to kill you," Keely sighed wistfully. "Looks iffy, though, don't you think?"

Shoshona glowered at Keely, who responded by whistling idly while the seconds passed, until without warning, a shot rang out upstairs. A woman screamed. Another shot followed, then silence. As the heavy thud of boots started down the stairs, Keely realized she'd been standing, gaping, and began edging back toward the door to the cottage. The inquisitrix was still gaping when Ulric came into view—a smoking hunting rifle in each hand, and streaks of blood on his shirt and hands.

"All sorted," he said grimly, tossing the rifles to the floor as he arrived at the bottom of the stairs. "Now it's your turn." He fixed his gaze on Shoshona as he advanced, and the priestess' demeanor finally broke. She shrieked and flinched away as he grabbed her by the collar and threw her face down to the floor.

By this point, Keely had reached the door and quietly cracked it open. She swallowed hard as she stood contemplating how insane the man had gone, and whether it was time to bolt and forget her entire scheme. Then Ulric, with his foot on Shoshona's back, keeping her pinned, turned his gaze on Keely. With a strange little smile, he mouthed the words, "It's okay," and pulled up a sleeve, gesturing first at the bloody gash on his arm, then sweepingly at the blood on his clothes. "They're fine," he mouthed.

"The other girl had a crossbow," he said gruffly. "Go upstairs and get it so you can keep an eye on this one," he gestured to the hyperventilating priestess, "while I search around to make sure there was no one else."

With one wary eye still on Ulric, Keely swung wide around him and scurried up the stairs to find the two young women sitting on the bed there, biting their knuckles to suppress an impulse to laugh. The rifle blasts had damaged one of the walls, but the scene seemed otherwise intact.

Keely gave a long, involuntary whistle. "Quite a mess you made up here!" she shouted down to cover for it. "You'd better not be thinking I'll clean it up!"

"Just leave it!" Ulric shouted back.

"Wow," Keely whispered appreciatively to Minda. "He's good. Where's the crossbow?"

Doryne hefted the weapon but waved Keely off from taking it. "I'll take guard duty. Just give me that cloak in case she catches a glimpse."

As Doryne headed downstairs, Minda grabbed a lantern and tugged Keely toward a door at the back of the room. As they passed the bed, Keely noticed a single black boot sticking out from under a blanket. It caught her eye not for its own sake—it was certainly a reasonable cut and quality for a young noblewoman to be wearing out into the forest— but because it looked to currently have a foot in it, as well as a similarly occupied mate somewhere under the blanket, and probably an entire person attached as well.

Keely looked up from noticing all this to find Minda noticing she'd noticed all this, and that all trace of merriment at Shoshona's predicament had vanished. Keely began to form a question, but it died unasked as she read on Minda's face that there would be no answers forthcoming.

The two women stepped out into the forest, this time at the top of the little cliff the cottage had been built against. Down below, Ulric appeared, carrying his own lantern, and Minda waved down to him. Through nods and hand-signals, the two agreed to head further on down the cliff until, about a hundred yards later, an easy climb presented itself. Ulric joined them at the top, where he returned Minda's prized hunting rifle to her.

"Oh, you scuffed her," Minda said with a little pout, examining the weapon. "Now what the blazes is going on?!" she demanded of Ulric. Her voice torn between the need for quiet and the urge to shout, it came out as a furious whisper.

"With all respect, milady," Ulric said, "I should be asking the same. Can we please start with the dead woman, and then move on to the captive one?"

Minda looked suspiciously at Keely. "I don't think..."

"Right. Okay. Lady Minda, this is Keely, the postulant for the new priestess. Remember?"

"Hi," Keely said with a friendly little wave. "You might have heard me called 'Chloe'."

"Oh, uh..." Minda peered at Keely in the lantern light. "Yeah," she said noncommittally, looking more puzzled than ever. "Your hair wasn't silver, though. Was it?"

"I really shouldn't tell you anything about what's going on," Ulric began, cutting off Minda's protestations with a raised hand, "*but* I'm still going to. Your parents will probably have my head, if I can keep it long enough for them to find out. This is a lose-lose situation for me, but I'm starting to get used to those. As of today, we are at war with the Inquisition."

"Yes!" Minda responded so exultantly that she barely managed to choke it off from becoming a shout. "Yes!" she repeated with more composure. "It's about bloody time."

"*But this is not a game*," Ulric hissed fiercely. "People are going to die. People are *already* dying," he corrected himself, thinking back to the corpse of the inquisitrix he'd stumbled on when he'd barged upstairs in the cottage. "Now tell me *why* they're already dying, or that's all you get, milady."

"It was a hunting accident!" Minda blurted. "She just ran out between me and a charging wolf from out of nowhere. Doryne saw it. She's the only one who saw it. But you *know* the Inquisition isn't going to care how it happened."

"A *charging* wolf?" Ulric interrupted.

"Yes! I know. It's crazy. The thing wasn't even rabid. I shot its mate, and it charged right at us."

"What was an inquisitrix doing in the forest?" Keely asked, perplexed.

"None of it makes sense," Minda said, clearly flustered. "But it happened, and I shot her, and she's dead." She took a deep breath before continuing. "We'd also met a group of strangers out here earlier—foreign nobles. Said they were looking for a woman who got herself lost in the forest, so I sent the others to take the wolf pelts back, and tell my parents we were out looking for the lost woman, to buy us time to figure out what to do. When I said we'd hole up at the old hunting lodge for the night if we took too long, I never thought anyone would actually come looking for us."

"And what did you figure out?" Ulric asked.

"I didn't want to leave the body there, in case someone knew where she was and came looking, and it was getting late fast. I figured we'd go in the morning to find a ravine back in the forest to bury her in."

"We may want to give her a funeral pyre instead, if they don't bring the fire Sir Riordan's sparked under control quick," Keely said.

"That's a thought." Ulric nodded, then pressed on before Minda could ask what they were talking about. "I'll help you clean up your mess, milady, but the less you know about my mess, the better, unless— and let me be very clear on this—you just sign on as a marksman in the war effort, and don't go pulling rank on me. You could be a *huge* help, but I *can't* be responsible for your safety if you're trying to be in charge."

"Ulric, if there's a war against the Inquisition going on, you cannot *keep* me out," Minda said. "But, yeah, I've been trusting you to look out for me since I barely came up to your belt, and up 'til right now I've been a hunter, not a warrior. If you want to call my shots, the job's yours. Now, spill. What is up with your captive? And *why* are you dragging around a postulant dressed up like a scarecrow?"

"I'm not a scarecrow," Keely protested. "I'm Bloody Scarlet!"

Elissa looked at her askance. "You *do* know that Bloody Scarlet's a nursery story, right?"

"I sure hope so," Keely said. "I'd hate for her to really exist and decide I was mocking her. The point is she's got a mystique I can borrow to spook the Inquisition. They've already decided I'm a witch. Might as well ham it up for all it's worth."

"*Are* you a witch?" Minda asked.

"I don't think so," Keely answered, biting her lip thoughtfully. "Kind of a complicated question."

"She's a witch," Ulric assured Minda.

"Wow. Really?" Minda smiled, abruptly looking at Keely as something other than a ragamuffin being dragged into her presence. "That is so excellent."

CHAPTER TWENTY-TWO

SO NOT GOOD

"We'll catch up with her in the morning," Tobias assured Baldassare, leaning back against a tree to watch the dancing flames of their campfire.

"I still can't believe she didn't know me," Baldassare sighed, rubbing his eyes.

"I still can't believe you're so blasted certain it's her," Evadne muttered. "What if it's not? What if..."

"Then we don't have a clue *where* she is, is what," Baldassare snapped. "You were the one so quick to remind us the witch changes people to animals."

"What if the deer *is* the witch?" she asked him, pulling her cloak up about her shoulders and turning to step away from the fire.

Although the doe had been bold by most standards, it had bolted before Baldassare could get halfway across the clearing to it, and they'd spent hours tracking it before the shadows of night took the forest very quickly. Even had they been paying closer attention to the time, and even had they been willing to abandon the pursuit, they would have been hard-pressed to retrace their steps to safety before the light completely failed them. Now, with the ground so rocky and uneven, pressing on through the forest in the dark would have been an invitation to fall and break something.

It hadn't helped matters that even the most experienced huntsman among them thought of exploring the woods as a "day trip" sort of thing. Not that Tobias had never spent a night in the wilderness, but he'd never met a wood so thick or dense he couldn't leave just by walking in the same direction for a couple of hours. He'd set out to find the lost woman confident that, whatever the outcome, he'd be back under the open sky before nightfall—back with his horses and all the traveling gear they carried.

Though the local ponies that hunting party were riding had seemed sure-footed and confident, Tobias hadn't been about to trust his own good horses to this treacherous terrain. He *had* made sure Conrad brought enough food and drink along that they weren't going hungry, but they'd brought no light, and bedding down for the night would mean looking for the least uncomfortable patch of ground by the fire.

"What is that awful screeching?" Evadne asked as the sound pierced the night yet again. She shivered slightly at the encroaching chill of the evening.

"You mean the owl call?" Tobias asked.

"No, right after the owl."

"Pretty sure they're both owls." He shrugged. "The screech answers the hoot."

"I don't like this place." Evadne sighed. "I don't trust this place. Deer or human, I really hate to think of Sabina out there alone in the middle of this, without even a fire for comfort."

"Wait," Tobias said, pieces finally clicking into place inside his head. "Sabina...Marini? You're the Denecia Marini's?" He kicked himself for not placing the accent earlier.

Baldassare nodded, eying Tobias a little warily.

"She dragged you all this way chasing after that silly book, didn't she?"

"Which book?" Baldassare asked with poorly affected innocence.

Tobias snorted. "Look, it's okay. I've got three older brothers and a father all playing the politics game, but that makes it way too crowded in there for me. And even if old Amberford wasn't delusional, and even if the Grimm Truth is full of dead-on accurate prophecies, I don't care *what* happens to it. Have you ever heard a story with a prophecy where the prophecy actually helped anyone? They all have some naive lad or lass running around blessed with the luck of ignorance, fulfilling their glorious destiny by simply following the dictates of a pure heart, while the powerful lord or lady who knows exactly what's going on sows the seeds of his own destruction out of fear, trying to keep the prophecy from ever coming to pass. Prophets rush in where even demons fear to tread."

"You *know* about the Grimm Truth...and you're following the Grimm Truth...but you don't want it?" Baldassare asked, arching an eyebrow.

"All I want is a girl who happens to be mixed up with it somehow," Tobias said levelly. "Or to avenge her if she's past help. I'm after the witch. You can keep the book."

"You do realize," Evadne said, returning to tower over the fire with a wicked grin, "that makes you the pure-hearted lad naively fulfilling his glorious destiny?"

"Oh...my...go'ss," Elissa gasped, almost forgetting the weight of the old woman leaning on her shoulder as she stood gaping at the devastation spread out below her.

Nolan lowered the littlest of the woman's grandchildren to the ground and shooed the family on back from the edge of the trail to where they might find a rock worth sitting on, and he stood behind Elissa, muttering something unintelligible under his breath. Things had been looking rather grim from two switchbacks further down the Wolf's Tooth, where they'd come upon the woman and children struggling with the climb. By Nolan's best guess, he was seeing half a dozen farms ablaze. After that, the trail had taken them away from the side of the Tooth with the fires, and they'd lost sight of the flames for perhaps half an hour, slowed as they were. They couldn't be sure how much looked different now because of the added height, and how much had actually changed in that half hour, but right here and now it looked to Elissa like half the world was on fire.

"This is so not good," she whispered.

The lights of lanterns strung out on the winding trail below them betrayed the increasing flow of refugees from the fire—as did the clop of hooves, rattle of wagons, and complaints of various livestock. Somewhere off in the night, a bell began to toll.

"Nolan? Nolan!" A brown-haired, top-heavy young woman suddenly appeared out of the darkness behind them to wrap herself around Elissa's escort. The woman didn't say another word, but buried a face stained with soot and tears against his chest.

After watching for a moment as Nolan rocked the woman in his arms and patted her back soothingly, Elissa turned her attention politely back to the fire. She studied it numbly for another minute or three, watching the flames engulf the silhouettes of trees while lightning flickered across the sky behind it all, before clearing her throat. "Nolan?"

Nolan carefully detached himself from the young woman's embrace, though she didn't relinquish his hand as he stepped over to where Elissa beckoned.

"See all those lanterns?" Elissa pointed to the main cluster of lights visible on the farmland below. The cluster had sprouted a tail of lights making its way slowly down the road this direction, but many of them remained fanned out slightly ahead of the flames, their owners likely attempting to construct a fire break. More lights were converging toward the cluster from the surrounding lands, as well, as the able-bodied rushed to assist in containing the blaze.

Nolan nodded his acknowledgment.

"Then see there?" Elissa pointed off to the right, where an arm of the blaze had jumped ahead to a closer orchard. "And there?" She pointed off to the left, where the fire was clearly racing along a dry hedge row it had ignited.

Nolan continued to stare for most of a minute himself, watching the flames advance, then swore under his breath. "That bell's tolling the wrong alarm.

"Nessa," he said suddenly to the woman still hanging on his arm, "take charge of this road. Anyone who's made it this far needs to keep going up, but we've got to get everyone else headed toward the castle."

Nessa released his hand reluctantly, but nodded, then put on a no-nonsense face as she turned to face the mostly grown girl and the clutch of children who had arrived just behind her. "You heard him," she told them. "We've got a job to do." As she started barking instructions to the children, Nolan grabbed Elissa's hand and started dragging her back down the way they'd come. He didn't break into a run, but Elissa nearly had to in order to keep up with his long, urgent strides.

"We're headed for the castle," he explained. "They've got to change that alarm now. That bell will get everyone out of their beds, but it's also going to send a lot of them scurrying off to help."

Neither Nolan nor Elissa wanted to say it aloud, but both had seen what that meant. Those far-flung arms of the fire had begun to close in on each other. The main line of defenders was in serious danger of being cut off in a ring of flames, along with anyone who joined them. "It's time for everyone to just go to ground and pray to Seriena that storm's going to hit hard enough and soon enough to drown that fire tonight."

"So I'm guessing that was your niece?" Elissa ventured with a little grin as they hurried down the road.

"Nessa?" Nolan chuckled. "Not so much."

"Kid sister, then?" Elissa asked. "She did mash that chest up against you in a very sisterly way."

"More like 'drinking buddy'. Probably a distant cousin. If you're trying to draw up my family tree, I promise it will be a heroic task."

"Just looking for a smile in all this," Elissa said. "Back at the abbey, drama was what happened when somebody put a book back on the wrong shelf. Nessa seems a lovely and sensible girl, and I do wish you many a happy drink together."

Their chatter ended abruptly as they both looked up and realized that the lanterns now approaching weren't held aloft by the sort of refugees they'd come accustomed to seeing, but by a mounted procession of black-robed women and of armed men in black and red.

"You're going the wrong way little lambs," the woman at the head of the procession said tiredly. "It's dangerous down there. Best shelter for the night up at the work site."

"Thank you, Sister, we'll be fine," Nolan answered with gracious good nature. "We're headed away from the fire, toward the castle, to share our news of how it's spreading."

"Oh? And how *is* it spreading?" One of the knights rode forward, towering over them on his destrier. It took a moment for Elissa to recognize Riordan in the darkness, but when she did, she shrank an involuntary step back. "Actually, I can't imagine you having a thing to tell the earl that he really needs to know. *All* of this is the fault of the witch we came here to find, and she's down there running amok. She's already murdered our most revered sister in cold blood this night. *No one* is safe down there, and the fire is the least of your worries."

"She...murdered...?" Elissa asked in aghast disbelief. The man spoke with such passionate conviction that she had to remind herself not to accept his words as unvarnished truth.

Riordan stared suspiciously down at Elissa for a long moment, then swung out of the saddle and stepped toward her. As he did, Nolan stepped bodily between them. Steel rang through the night as a dozen swords and knives unsheathed behind Riordan, but the knight calmly stared Nolan down. "Stand aside, man. I have no intention of harming a holy sister."

Nolan studied the drawn blades at length before stepping hesitantly back, his posture still anything but relaxed. Elissa bit her lip, but stood her ground as the big man reached out to tilt her chin up and stare down into her face. She met his gaze and held it as he continued to stare at her and the seconds ticked by, until at last his stern countenance began to relax. "Brookshire?" he asked. "Elissa of Brookshire?"

"Riordan?" Elissa asked with a note of surprise so perfectly feigned it would have made Keely weep with pride to hear it.

"You...know her, sir?" Nolan asked.

"*Know* her?" the big man answered Nolan with a rumbling laugh. "There was a time it seemed I'd never be *rid* of her! Go'ss, you're a welcome sight on a dark day, Littlebrook. And you've *made* something of yourself! A priestess? Still so young?" Riordan swept Elissa up and swung her around in an enormous bear hug, which her arms returned with enthusiasm while her face registered barely contained panic—though mercifully registered it only where Nolan could see it from over Riordan's shoulder.

"Wow! It's been so long!" Elissa gasped breathlessly—an effect easily achieved when caught up in the sort of embrace she was experiencing.

"What are you *doing* out here in the middle of nowhere?!" Riordan demanded good-naturedly.

"It sort of came with the ordination." Elissa smiled sheepishly as he finally set her down. "Pontifine Augusta got it into her head I should take over here after the tragedy with Sister Petra. Maybe she needed someone expendable, in case it happens again."

"It will *not* happen again. I just have a certain witch to wreak holy vengeance on," Riordan said with a snarl, "then I will personally see that these vandals are brought to justice before they can cause any more harm. I owe you that much, after the business with my family."

"You've got me tearing up, big guy," the tired priestess at the head of the procession said, "but can you save your little reunion for the top of the hill?"

"But we're going down," Elissa insisted.

"I can't let you," Riordan countered firmly. "It's too dangerous." Then he frowned. "Tell me what you saw. It...wasn't Ryan, was it?" he asked, his voice falling near a whisper.

"What? No!" Elissa gasped. "How could...? What are you...?" she stammered, then composed herself. "Riordan, your brother's dead. You know that." The last bit almost came out as a question, and indeed her eyes searched his face for some confirmation that it was true.

The big man sighed and shook his head almost imperceptibly. "Should be dead. *Would* be dead, Goddess forgive me, if not for my own folly," he said quietly.

"But I saw..."

"What I wanted everyone to see," Riordan said. "I will tell the tale *later*. But he's alive and he's free and he's gone completely mad and...it seems he's here. Since you're here, too, he can only be looking for revenge. You're in danger. So climb on the back of my horse and let's get you up someplace safe."

"I...No," Elissa finished firmly after an initial hesitation. "My ordination may have been a farce, but I accepted these robes and a responsibility for these people with them. Many will die if we don't let them know that the fire is out of control. *My* safety doesn't matter, but I've got the best swordsman in the county as a bodyguard anyway." She pointed emphatically back toward Nolan, who straightened visibly at the sudden attention. "I'm going. And the only way you're stopping me is by throwing a kicking, biting, scratching, and screaming holy woman over your horse while you're fighting off *him*." She pointed again, and Nolan obliged by throwing a confident scowl in Riordan's direction.

"You heard the sister," the spokeswoman said sharply without leaving Riordan a moment to protest. "She's not our problem, and we've got responsibilities of our own. Now let's move."

"Yes, sister." Riordan withdrew reluctantly, nodding his assent to the woman. "Be careful, Littlebrook."

"I will," Elissa assured him with a small smile, and she stood back with Nolan to let the procession ride on past.

"I'm really not much more than passable with a sword," Nolan said quietly as they hurried on down the road. "Now give me a nice, sturdy cudgel and maybe..." He trailed off, noticing that Elissa was hyperventilating.

"He's going to kill me," she gasped.

"No, he's not," Nolan said, gently grabbing Elissa's shoulder and bringing her to a stop. "Just breathe. No matter how big or nasty or crazed this Runyan is, I can handle him. We're on *my* turf, I fight dirty, and..."

"Not *Ryan*," Elissa hissed. "Riordan!"

Nolan looked back and forth between Elissa's face and the darkness that the riders had disappeared into, trying to reconcile what he was hearing with what he'd just seen.

"How long do you think I could hang out with Keely and not know when I'm being conned?" she hissed. "Yes, we were sort of kids together, and Riordan wasn't faking the whole nostalgia thing, but his brother is *dead*! Not sort of dead! Not mostly dead! Not maybe dead! He's as totally, completely, gruesomely dead as dead gets! Riordan made sure of it, and I was too much a frightened little mouse of a girl to stop him."

"Then...But..." Nolan tried a couple of times to make enough sense of the situation to form a coherent question or protest, but the efforts went for naught.

"Riordan doesn't know how much I saw," Elissa said. "He thinks he can come up with a plausible story to make me doubt. And there's only one reason he would try to resurrect his brother."

"Guilt?" Nolan ventured.

"Scapegoat!" she blurted, then it all came out in a rush. "Even when it was just kid stuff, Riordan had a knack for letting his brother take the fall. 'It wasn't me! It was Ryan!' They were twins, and Riordan was better at telling a convincing lie than Ryan was at telling a convincing truth, but Riordan finally taught me his own tells. Back there, he thought we'd seen something he didn't want us to see. He's covering up something about the fire. The man sacrificed his twin brother to ambition, and the Inquisition's had *five more years* to harden him since then. He's not going to blink at getting rid of some kid he used to know. And he's not going to blink at getting rid of some stranger he's barely laid eyes on, for that matter," she finished, staring at Nolan meaningfully.

"Do you think he'll find an excuse to double back before they reach the top?" Nolan asked, warily eying the darkness behind them.

"How hard do you think it would be for him to sort of drift back in the line until everyone had passed him by?" Elissa asked.

"Ever handle a flintlock?" Nolan asked, pulling a pistol out of his belt.

"Not once," Elissa answered. "I fancy my chances better with running. But you're on your home ground, right? And you fight dirty...?"

"Oh, yeah," he said, grabbing her wrist and pulling her on down the trail. She quickly matched his step, and they broke into as much of a run as they dared by lantern light on the dark slope. "I can take him. Don't you worry about a thing."

"I told you I'm learning to spot a con, right?" Elissa asked.

There had to be a metaphor here, the detached corner of Sabina's mind mused—some sort of allegorical summation of what had become of her life—as the rest of her mind stared in fascinated horror at the wall of flames not twenty feet away, licking at the mouth of the crevice she'd taken shelter in. She already had her back pressed up against the rock behind her, and the sides of the fissure closed in so tightly she couldn't spread her elbows without touching both. Sweat covered her body and drenched her hair and clothes, the heat so intense that she thought the fire would roast her even if it couldn't come any closer.

A gust of wind blew a fresh cloud of smoke her way, and she coughed painfully, her throat already raw, until her head swam, and she fell to her knees. Then even her knees didn't work, and she collapsed flat on the ground, gasping like a fish.

"You'll be safe in there," her guide had told her before almost shoving her back into the crevice, but Scarlet had conspicuously passed up sheltering there herself. Sabina had tried to chase after the woman, but had quickly been forced to agree that her makeshift shelter looked like the least flammable spot in a world quickly transforming itself into a hellish inferno.

She didn't know how Scarlet found the courage to even try to escape through it. She didn't know if Scarlet had made it through alive. All she did know was she'd soon heard some dreadful screams that threw the woman's survival into even more serious doubt. Well, she also knew that "safe" had become a relative term, translating into "not burned alive as such".

Somehow down against the ground, Sabina found herself breathing a pocket of relatively cool and clean air, and her head stopped swimming long enough for her to realize she would be dead as soon as that small respite gave out. Rolling onto her back as she weighed her lack of options, it dawned on her that the wall she'd been up against might be climbable. The side walls soared smoothly hundreds of feet overhead, but only a rough blockage of fallen stone walled her in behind. Climbing had never been Sabina's thing. Laborers and pesky little brothers might climb, but climbing would never even crossed the mind of a well-bred young lady.

Were the lady, perchance, only mildly well-bred, thoughts of climbing *might* just come flitting through her mind at random moments, seductively representing themselves as the only alternative to a fiery death—but even then the lady in question would recoil in horror and carefully glance around to be quite certain that no one was watching before making eye contact with said thoughts and formally acknowledging their existence.

Amidst the heat and the smoke and the unyielding stone, Sabina drew a long, deep breath that she hoped would not be her last, scrambled to her feet, and—with all the dignity possible to muster while climbing frantically in a fine gown utterly spoiled by soot and sweat—pulled herself up and into the welcoming darkness of Skull Crevice.

CHAPTER TWENTY-THREE

WAKE UP

"Now ride!" Nolan slapped the back of the horse, and it sped out of the farmyard as best it could given its advancing age and the inexpert guidance of the girl on its back. Lightning danced through the clouds, briefly illuminating mount and rider in its flickering strobe before the night fell once more to black. The bobbing glow of the girl's lantern lingered, dwindling in the distance, until they passed through the gate to the road and disappeared around a hedge.

He and Elissa had made it down off the Tooth without sounds of pursuit, but neither of them took that luck as more than a badly needed head start. The specter of being ridden down before they could reach the castle had still loomed large, so Nolan had detoured at the first farmhouse where a flicker of light had offered hope of someone to pass the proverbial torch to.

Unwilling to risk that Riordan might pass this girl on the road and take her for their co-conspirator, he had sent her off on the long route to the castle, despite the precious minutes it would cost. As she'd disappeared into the night, he was still silently cursing the Inquisition for forcing him to walk this knife's edge between the safety of an innocent girl, the safety of dozens of his friends and family, and the safety of the young woman he'd been charged on pain of death to protect.

"One more problem out of our hands," Nolan said resignedly, forcing himself to take a deep breath and let it go. "Now we head *this* way." Turning away from the road, he grabbed Elissa's hand again and led her quickly around the back of the old barn.

He helped her over a stile into a pasture, prepared to prod her into using whatever reserves of speed she might still have after their rapid descent, but instead found himself running to catch up with her and the lantern she carried before she could unthinkingly leave him behind in the dark. He steered her off to the left, and she flushed at the realization she'd just taken the lead without any real notion of where she was going.

A chill, damp blast of wind cut across the pasture, carrying with it both the hope of a serious storm about to be unleashed on the wildfire and the threat that unless—and until—those rains arrived, the winds would be out there spreading sparks and fanning flames. Behind them, the farmyard and stile vanished into the night, leaving them lost in a bubble of lantern light floating through a sea of sunbaked grasses that had been cropped short by grazing livestock.

When she would glance behind them, Elissa could make out a horizon glowing infernal-red behind a haze of smoke, but ahead of them, only occasional flashes of lightning proved that the grassy sea didn't stretch on forever into the darkness.

They'd gone perhaps halfway across it when Nolan grabbed her wrist and stopped her, raising a finger to his lips for silence. Then he carefully reclaimed the lantern from her and doused it.

Just before the light went out, he'd tilted his head off toward one edge of the pasture, and Elissa's gaze had naturally followed. There, the light of another lantern bobbed beyond what must have been the bordering hedge of the pasture. With it came the determined clop of hooves from a horse unmistakably more robust than the one the girl had left on.

It mightn't be Riordan, Elissa knew. On a night like this, with so much chaos and so much hanging in the balance, anyone could legitimately be out and about, and whatever had brought them out would most certainly demand urgency. But it could be Riordan. She couldn't say that whoever it was was coming from the wrong direction to be Riordan, and—apparently—neither could Nolan. And if it *was* Riordan, that meant all her nightmare imaginings had been spot-on.

If it *was* Riordan, the one thing they could not possibly afford was to attract his notice. So they huddled there together in the blackness, with Nolan's dark cloak pulled protectively around her to hide any glimmer the lightning might catch of her silvery robes. And they held their breath, and they listened and they waited.

When at last the sounds of hooves and jingling harness had faded in the distance, they breathed a mutual sigh of relief. Nolan moved to relight the lantern, but Elissa grabbed at his cloak and pulled it back tightly around her. "Wait," she whispered.

"What is it?" he asked, peering around them into the darkness, and straining to hear anything but the wind rushing through the grasses.

"Just cold." She giggled quietly, pressing her back up against him. "That wind's picked up a bite. Give me a minute more to warm up."

"Sure." He chuckled, folding his arms around her. "No one will be rushing to search for us here in the night. But don't get too comfortable. We've got a lot of ground to cover before the storm breaks, if we can."

"Where are we heading?" she asked.

"Into the forest."

"What? With the fire?" He could hear her worried frown even if he couldn't see it.

"Blackmoon Lake's not too far in," he reassured her. "I'm not taking you anywhere near the castle tonight, and we both know the Tooth's off limits, but there's an island..."

"Someone's watching us!" Elissa hissed suddenly.

Nolan released her with one arm to ease the flintlock out of his belt. "Where?" he whispered.

"Off to the right," Elissa whispered. "I don't know...maybe fifty yards away? I saw him standing there when the lightning flashed."

"Did he move?"

"No." She shook her head. "Just...watching."

Nolan edge around to get Elissa behind him, and stood listening, waiting for the next flicker of lightning. After the better part of a minute, it finally came, its light dancing across a tall, shadowy figure in a tattered red cloak that whipped wildly in the wind. "Scarecrow." Nolan sighed in relief, wrapping his arm comfortingly back around Elissa's shoulder. "It's okay."

"Really?" Elissa asked, not completely mollified. "That is so odd."

"Odd?" Nolan chuckled. "The farmer's put them up all over."

"To protect crops?" Elissa asked.

"Of course." Nolan nodded. "Works, too."

"What crops?"

"Apples. Grains. Anything that's..."

"No, Nolan," Elissa hissed impatiently. "*What* crops?"

The fragments of what he'd just seen clicked into place in Nolan's head, and the red-cloaked figure appeared again in his mind's eye, standing alone amidst the short-cropped grasses—not in an orchard, not in a field, but in a pasture, without a single thing for it to protect. "Oh," he said finally, his mouth going dry. "I guess I should make sure, shouldn't I?"

He considered shouting across the distance, but didn't want to risk attracting attention from outside the pasture, and honestly didn't fancy finding out later that he'd been shouting at a scarecrow. He considered walking toward it, but didn't fancy either leaving Elissa standing alone behind him or dragging her closer to anyone who might be insane enough to be standing out here in the middle of the night, in the middle of everything that was going on, just silently watching them.

Finally, he settled on raising his pistol and leveling it at where he thought he'd seen the figure standing, but it quickly became clear his hand wasn't steady enough right now to make that a good option, either. Still, he kept the gun leveled just in case, but concluded aloud, "No. No point getting any closer. We're just getting out of here." He wrapped his hand around hers again. "But I'll keep an eye on it while you lead, to be safe."

Even so, Nolan felt foolish keeping an eye on what could only sensibly be a scarecrow, but he refused to let that cow him into carelessness, given it couldn't sensibly *be* a scarecrow, either. So he kept his eyes on it. "No light yet," he hissed when he heard the rattle of Elissa picking up the lantern.

"I can't see a thing!" Elissa protested quietly.

"Nothing to see. We've got at least another hundred yards of open pasture ahead of us. Just take it slow and careful, and make the most of the lightning when it comes. But if you light that thing, it'll..."

The lightning came, directly overhead. The thunder rattled the lantern and their teeth alike.

"You know what? Forget it," Nolan said hastily. "Finding shelter just became top priority."

"You saw something!" Elissa said. Fumbling with the flint and tinder Nolan handed her, before she finally pushed the whole mess back at him. "This is *your* lantern. I can't figure this out in the dark."

"No, I didn't!" Nolan reluctantly accepted the duty of relighting the lantern and began fumbling with it himself as quickly as he could.

"What did you see!" Elissa demanded of him again.

"Nothing!"

"Stop treating me like a child and just tell..."

The lightning crackled again, and Elissa saw for herself. "I..." she began slack-jawed.

"I told you!" Nolan snapped.

Out in the pasture where the watcher had stood, she'd seen it clear as day: no shadowy figure, no tattered red cloak whipping about in the wind, no place for it to have run, no place for it to hide. Just...nothing. Elissa stood shivering in the biting wind, with the first tentative drops of rain rolling down her cheeks, until the lantern finally sprang back to life. Then she let Nolan take her hand again, and they ran with the storm howling at their heels.

"Don't move, dear."

Clay roused himself from dreams at the sound of the familiar, friendly voice, but allowed himself to be restrained by the firm hand pressing the cool cloth against his forehead.

"It was a bad fall," Grace told him. "You hit your head on a gravestone. What were you doing up on the Harrison Mausoleum, anyway? It's not like there's any Harrisons around anymore to complain of its condition. Not a soul would have cared if you'd waited 'til there was help, and you know those old slates are treacherous."

"I'm sorry," he apologized with heart-felt sincerity. He was paying for the indiscretion liberally, his body aching all over, but his head most of all—like he was suffering from the worst hangover ever, and then got hit on the head with a shovel for good measure. "I..." He tried to make excuses, but it was hard enough to remember having gone up there in the first place, much less recalling why.

"You scared me witless, silly man," she said with the sort of brave little smile used to plaster over slowly fading fear. "You know we need you alive and whole."

"Sorry," he apologized again. He tried to sit up a little only to be rebuffed by a firm-but-gentle hand, and he sank back into the bed.

"Just apologize by making a full recovery." She kissed him on the forehead, and her smile turned genuine as she gazed down at him. "I hope you're feeling up to a bit of dinner."

"Definitely," he assured her as his eyes followed her across their cottage to the crackling hearth. "I'm starving, actually." From the smell of it, she'd gotten a rabbit from somewhere while he'd been oblivious. The aroma of the bubbling stew filled the cottage, along with the scents of wood smoke and roasting apples.

Folk did not generally accuse Grace Ambleforth of being a beauty, with her plain, shoulder-length hair the color of damp sand, and a face still bearing some blemishes from a childhood pox, but Clay couldn't imagine a more lovely sight to wake up to—after so many dark and disturbing dreams—than that familiar smile.

"Aidan? How's Aidan?" Clay asked, a sudden fear gripping his heart. "I dreamed..."

"Our boy's fine, dear." Grace looked up from stirring the kettle to smile reassuringly. "He's just out to the plots, digging a splendid hole. Took it t' heart that he's the man of the house while you're abed—and he's doing a fine job of it, all things considered. It may not be near right, but I dare say it'll be easier for you to make it right than it would be to've dug the whole grave yourself. Old widow Dawson finally moved on in the night. The family will be needing it as soon as can be managed."

Clay breathed a relieved sigh, and began flexing his fingers experimentally to begin a catalog of how badly he'd been hurt where. He'd gotten as far as deciding he still had five working digits on each hand when Grace appeared back at his side with a steaming wooden bowl. "Now, let's try to get some strength back in you," she said cheerily, but Clay's attempt at refocusing his attention on her got derailed by the rattling sound still coming from the hearth— specifically, by the distinct tapping of a ladle on the rim of the pot. When he looked, he could see Grace standing there across the room with her back to him, still tending the stew.

"Can you sit up?" Grace-at-his-side asked, setting the bowl down on a stool by the bed and trying to wrestle him to a sitting position. Clay offered no help, but instead lay staring toward the hearth, lost in the sudden certainty that he was still dreaming. Then the woman at the fire began to turn. Not Grace, he realized with a rush of relief. Her sister.

"No? Too much too soon?" Grace asked him worriedly. "Dear, you're shaking like the bangles on a heathen dancing girl." It was a friendly jab that brought him instantly back to her. They'd actually seen a heathen dancing girl once, the year the traveling show had stopped for a night at Dydford, bringing wonders from across the sea, and Clay had studied the girl with a bit too much interest for Grace to ever entirely let him live it down.

"I'm okay," he reassured her, struggling to work with her now. "Just weak." Still, something plucked at his mind, about Grace's sister and that traveling show. As much as Ivy would hang on the storytellers' tales of distant shores, Clay had always thought it a shame she'd missed that show, with its strange people and exotic pageantry. Sadly, she'd died just the winter before.

No, Clay told himself firmly. That had been one of the nightmares. Ivy had died in one of the nightmares—just like Grace. Just like Aidan. Those were nightmares. Those had all been nightmares. Just like the shadowy figure pulling itself out of the pot behind Ivy was a nightmare. It had to be a nightmare, because already more of it had come out of the pot than could have ever fit in.

Its great bulk towered over Ivy now, and still the rotting nightmare beast kept coming—some huge, deranged amalgam of man and ox and rabbit, with broth and unsavory bits of carrot and things less identifiable all pouring off its matted fur like rain off of a gargoyle. Already it so filled that corner of the cottage that it had to stoop beneath the rafters, but neither of the women had noticed, and Clay's voice caught in his throat when he tried to warn them. He watched helplessly as claws the size of scythes sprang forth from its hooves and its fixed its malevolent gaze down upon Ivy.

"No!!!" Clay finally screamed. "Run! Get out! Wake up!"

Turning and seeing the beast, Grace and Ivy both screamed in terror. "Not again! It can't happen again!" He shouted, but Ivy's blood was already everywhere, and Grace stood rooted to the spot. "Wake up, damn you!" he screamed at her. "Wake up! Wake up! Wake up!"

In one brief glimmer of mercy, Clay did break out of the nightmare before the thing could cross the floor to Grace. He found himself somewhere cold and seemingly alone in the pitch-black dark, his arms restrained and his cheek pressed up against rough woolen cloth that must have been spread out atop unyielding stone. He lay there, sobbing and quietly cursing to himself, "Wake up. Wake up. Wake up." Had there ever been such a thing as reality, or had he dreamed that as well?

"Who is responsible for this rabble?!" Sister Maritine shouted. The howling wind there on the Wolf's Tooth echoed her demand, and the lightning underscored it. She was exhausted. She was angry. She was even starting to feel the unaccustomed roiling of fear in her stomach, though anyone who lasted long in the Inquisition would reflexively respond to fear by stoking that into anger, too.

"Which part of it, Sister?" A man with pike and musket, wearing the Haywood livery, stood his ground while the rest of the crowd shrank back. He mostly managed to keep his voice level. He also made a fair point, given the motley assortment of workers, guards, and refugees from the wildfire that had roused themselves from trying to sleep in order to come see what the latest commotion was about. "I suppose I'm as responsible for the lot as anyone actually here right now."

"Congratulations," Maritine snapped. "You're now an acting representative of the Inquisition as well. The witch we're hunting is on the Tooth, and growing more brazen by the hour. If we don't find her before dawn, I'm making no promises that *any* of you will have homes to return to. Single out the most trustworthy of your men, and use them to separate everyone the lot of you can vouch for from everyone who might be suspect. Anyone not above suspicion needs to be confined wherever you can safely put them.

"I'll leave an experienced detail to guard and question the prisoners, but we'll need most of our strength to go back out hunting the slopes. You'll organize whoever you haven't detained into groups of half a dozen each to scour the cathedral site for anyone who might be hiding or anything suspicious. Do well, and you'll be rewarded. But if I find the witch was up here and you let her slip through your fingers, I'll make sure you wish she'd turned you into something vile and stepped on you, so that you didn't have to deal with me. Is any part of that *not* clear?"

"No," the man answered in a tone that could have been taken for any number of meanings, though enthusiasm was certainly not among them. "I believe I understand, Sister."

"Then get started!" Maritine bellowed, and she fell back away from the crowd toward where her followers waited. How, how, how had the witch snatched the strongest of their knights right out of their own ranks without being seen?! She ground her knuckles into her forehead in frustration. Unbelievable enough that the witch had slain Sister Shoshona with Riordan standing so close he'd actually seen it happen, but this was far too much.

Maritine had fantasized often enough about the arrival of some sudden field promotion, but now that it had actually happened, she'd found it less exhilarating than in those fantasies. She'd always imagined herself as more prepared for whatever evil she happened to be fighting at the time. Despite their wily reputation, all the witches she'd faced to date had proven rather predictable and by-the-book. Vicious, certainly, but when it came right down to it they'd lacked the power to resist a trained, organized expedition of inquisitors, and most of them had even had the good sense to simply accept their fate when faced with the might of Seriena's chosen. This witch not only seemed to possess unprecedented power, but she was using it to actively stalk her own hunters.

The world as Maritine had known it was being turned on its head, and that was the last thing she could admit to anybody. This was the trial that would make or break her as an inquisitrix, and the moment she admitted to weakness or a loss of faith, all would be lost.

"Tetch," she beckoned to the dour little man on his vicious-looking white pony. "You're the only one I can trust to stay alert through the night and take charge of the prisoners as they're rounded up. If the witch is among them, a moment's inattention could mean disaster."

"I could just break all their ankles t' be safe, Sister," he nodded respectfully.

Managing to suppress a groan, Maritine shook her head. "The cathedral's had enough setbacks, and men with broken ankles can have trouble raising walls. Try not to break any bits you don't really need to."

"As you say, Sister."

Maritine picked a couple of other knights to stand watch, and ordered the rest of the company to dismount and grab what sleep they could where they were, while the prisoners were being rounded up. They'd all had a rough day, and were in for a rougher night. A catnap before attempting to hunt down a powerful witch on the slopes of the Wolf's Tooth by lantern light seemed like the bare minimum nod to sanity. It would also give her fatigue-addled brain some precious time to dream up a strategy on how to go about this.

When they woke, she'd leave behind their two sentries to help Tetch, and a couple of the sisters to begin interrogations. For now, though, she laid her head on her cloak against the rocky ground and slipped into an uneasy sleep that wavered back and forth between dreams of heroically dragging the dreadful witch of the Wolf's Tooth—beaten bloody and in chains—before the grand high inquisitrix, and nightmares of being turned into some tiny animal or other who inevitably found herself pounced upon and devoured by a monstrous, white cat.

The cycle of dreams didn't break until after one particularly gut-wrenching transformation into a field mouse, Maritine found herself picked up by the tail, instead, dangling upside down and staring into the face of the still-more-or-less human witch. In her dream, the witch took on the likeness of one of those macabre scarecrows she'd seen over and over while searching field and orchard that day—draped in the tattered red cloak, hood framing a skull with flowing red hair.

"I am *not* well pleased, little mouse," the witch hissed. "I try and I try to play nice. I haven't killed *anyone*...important...very recently. But just look at what you've done!" The witch gestured widely with her free hand to the wasteland of ash and burning trees that surrounded them.

Maritine tried to hurl the witch's accusations back at her, to condemn her of setting the fire herself, but it all came out as frantic squeaking.

"Leave it to your insane little cult to fight its battles with fire," the witch said. "If you really want me, stop mucking about and just come and get me." With a casual toss, she sent Maritine tumbling through the air to land amid the ashes, which flew up about her in a choking, blinding gray cloud.

When Maritine's vision cleared, the witch was walking unconcernedly away across the wasteland toward a wall of raging fire. The hood of the tattered red cloak had fallen down about her shoulders, and at least from this vantage point no sign of the dreadful skull that had stared out from it remained. At this moment she could have been any pretty young thing in a long, black tunic with a swaggering sway to her step.

Lightning danced crazily across the midnight sky, shimmering off what Maritine suddenly realized was a large carving knife held casually in the retreating woman's hand, dripping blood. Thunder pealed like it would never quite stop, through a world of smoke and cinders and flames and darkness. Ahead of the witch, the wall of flames guttered and gave way to the smoldering black remnant of a hedge.

Beyond it rose the forest, its canopy alternating—by whim of the lightning—between inky black silhouette and bold, bloody autumn red. Ancient, weathered marble columns flanked by stone wolves framed the gap in the hedge that the witch was heading for. Passing between, the woman reached out to nonchalantly bury the knife in the eye of one of the wolves, the blade sinking into the stone as effortlessly as if it had been parchment.

As the witch vanished into the shadows of the forest, blood began to well from the stone, streaming down the cheek of the statue to collect in a dark pool at its feet.

The sharp report of thunder directly overhead snapped Maritine out of her dream in an instant, and she was sitting up before she even knew she was awake. The next moment, she was on her feet, fighting with the wind to secure her cloak about her shoulders with fumbling fingers. The roiling of fear had turned to knots of dread in her stomach, and that made her very angry indeed.

"Tetch! Where's Tetch?!" she shouted to be heard above the wind and the thunder, wondering if this accursed storm was ever going to break, while also praying to Seriena it would hold off an hour more. The closest of the watchmen pointed off into the darkness toward where their suspects were being gathered. "Wake everyone! Now!" she bellowed before grabbing his lantern from him and hurrying off across the construction site.

She found the dwarf in a large tent that had served as a workman's dorm before the spartan furnishings had been hastily dumped outside the entrance and replaced with a motley assortment of rope-restrained men she had no doubt had been rounded up as much for garnering the disfavor of the guards and the foremen as for any actual likelihood they could be connected with the witch—but better a net too wide than a net too small.

"Tetch! The goddess has sent me a vision. I need to know where to find the one-eyed wolf, and I need to know immediately. We're racing to get down off the Tooth before the storm makes the road any more treacherous than the night already has."

"The one-eyed wolf, sister?" he asked, snapping to respectful attention but presenting a questioning eyebrow.

"It might be an old statue. It might be some beast in a menagerie. It could be the name of a tavern. It could be some old bandit with a scarred face. All I know is if we find the wolf, we find the witch. Question anyone you think might know. Drag him to the nearest inquisitrix if he gives you any trouble. Just get me the information *now*.

"And," she stared pointedly over at the captives who were doing their best to fade back into the canvas of the tent, "break as many ankles as you like."

CHAPTER TWENTY-FOUR

INTO THE WOODS

"Rain already!" Elissa screamed at the sky.

"Save your breath for running!" Nolan scolded her, tugging at her hand. "If you can yell, I haven't been pushing you hard enough."

He *had* been pushing her. That a soldier still more or less in his prime who lived on the edge of civilization could outrun a young woman who'd spent her days cloistered away in a library pretty much went without saying, but Elissa still found it galling to have her body screaming out so many complaints when her escort wasn't even breathing hard.

Still, a quick glance over her shoulder was all the confirmation she needed that Nolan could be right. Their race against Riordan had turned into a race against the storm that had turned into a race against the wildfire.

They'd seemed well ahead of it, but the rising winds had helped it leap a road, then race down a network of hedgerows, and in a matter of minutes the flames had gone from a distant concern to a looming menace dogging their heels. It had completely cut them off from returning to the Wolf's Tooth, and was making it look a very dicey proposition to veer off toward the castle at this point.

Their only hopes of salvation lay in staying ahead of the fire until either a downpour drenched it or they reached this lake Nolan had offered. Either way, Elissa knew she'd be in for a wet and miserable night, but that it would be immeasurably better than the alternative.

The good and bad news was that the closer they got to the forest—and the lake therein—the rockier the ground became. On the one hand, that gave the fire less vegetation to grab hold of. On the other, that made the footing more treacherous, and a turned ankle at this point might make all the difference between life and death.

Raindrops had begun to fall, at least, but just enough to make Elissa's robes damp and the rocks slippery underfoot. A fire that out of control would never be tamed by such gentle persuasions. What it needed was a merciless pummeling from some drunken brawler of a deluge to knock the fight out of it, *then* a lulling rain to gently soak the parched earth and convince the fire that it had nothing to return for.

They ran again, as best Elissa could manage. Off in the distance, in the direction of the castle, the warning bells that had been ringing off-and-on for hours rang again, but to a different tune, and Nolan gave Elissa a nod and small, encouraging smile. It might be too little, it might have come too late, but they'd accomplished something in all the chaos. If worse came to worst, Elissa could convince herself now that at least one family had made it to safety that wouldn't have otherwise outrun the flames, and her last hours would have counted for something.

The next lightning flash lit up the forest close enough to make out the branches that had grown out over the thorny hedgerow. "This way! This way!" Nolan steered them off to the right, and they began to skirt the edge of the forest. "No, wait! That way!" he grabbed her before they'd gone twenty paces and tugged her back the other direction.

They continued far enough along the thorny, unbroken hedge that Elissa had begun having serious doubts about the competence of her guide, when they finally encountered a spot where a rusting iron gate guarded a small gap that had been left for a little-used track leading into the forest.

"What fool chained this thing?!" Nolan slammed a frustrated boot into the gate, which rattled noisily but gave only a couple inches before pulling up short. Unlike the gate, which had clearly been standing there for decades, the chain and lock securing it couldn't have accumulated a year's worth of weathering. Still, this was not an insurmountable obstacle. Not much more than head high on Elissa, the gate with its narrow bars had clearly been put there to deter the passage of largish animals, not people.

"Boost me over," she said, already grabbing the bars and looking for footing to scrabble up. The footing wasn't abundant, but lifting Elissa didn't prove a terrible challenge for Nolan, and before long she was rolling over the top of the gate. She landed with a fair amount of grace, and with a small tear in the sleeve of her robe where it had caught on one of the gate's ornamental spikes.

Nolan passed the lantern over to Elissa, then followed himself, minus both the grace and the torn sleeve. At least, Elissa noted, he'd had the decency to do some grunting and some heavy breathing to show he'd put an effort into the climb.

They took only a few moments to recover, then set off quickly along the trail into the deeper darkness of the forest. Behind, them, the red glow of the wildfire quickly became lost from sight behind the hedge and the forest canopy. The trees also provided shelter from the winds, blocking the most biting of them, even as the leaves in the upper reaches—tossed about in the oncoming storm—whispered to each other like a mob of crazed conspirators.

Few drops of rain had worked their way down through the foliage yet. Far more often Elissa would see bright autumn leaves came fluttering down into the lantern light than feel cold water splash against her skin now. The one thing they didn't seem to be leaving behind was the smoke from the fire, which remained thick enough here to evoke the occasional small coughing fit from each of them.

"It's like we stepped into another world," Elissa said, staring around them into the dark, at once comforted by the sheltering embrace of the forest and disturbed by the strange sounds and shadows crowding in around her.

They walked briskly for fifteen minutes or so, encountering a few forks in the half-overgrown trail, but each time Nolan led them on confidently. Either he knew exactly where they were going, or he was invested in making it look like he did.

Something felt a bit ominous to Elissa about the mad whispering of the leaves and the limbs that would reach out of the darkness as they swayed in the wind, but she didn't get truly spooked until a loud creaking overhead gave way to the sharp report of a heavy limb breaking under the strain of the storm. It crashed down through the forest canopy to rain a heavy shower of leaves and twigs on them, but drew up short somewhere still out of reach of the lantern light, leaving Elissa to wonder if the branch had been as big as it had sounded, and how close it might have come to falling on them.

After that, every groan and creak in the forest canopy set her on edge, straining to listen for the sound of cracking wood. At one point, looking up when she should have been looking down, she caught her toe on a rather solidly placed rock, and sat down heavily, stifling curses that would have been most unfit for the robes she wore.

"I'll bet this forest has seen a lot of stories," she said as the pain ebbed, and she eased herself back to her feet. No good letting herself think about how dangerous the trees—or the shadows—could be while there was no escaping them.

"They say it was already old before the first emperor was born," Nolan agreed. "The trees out here on the edge are babes. People used to fight with it, trying to tame the forest, but the hedge is where they gave up and built a wall to keep it in. They say in the deep forest there are trees so old and so big you could get lost just trying to walk around one." He met her dubious look with a mischievous grin. "I said they say it. Didn't say it was true."

"What else do they say?" Elissa asked earnestly.

"Well," Nolan said, peering around into the darkness, "the Oobly Yech lives just over there." He pointed through the trees to the left.

"The Oobly Yech?"

"A slimy, child-devouring monster that lives at the bottom of a sinkhole," Nolan said. "The ground over there's unstable, and after a rain, you can find yourself sliding down the mud into a cave you'll never get out of on your own, even if you survive the fall. People who've gone in after lost children say there's the ruins of a pagan temple that the ground swallowed up down there. Lots of story, even discounting the Oobly Yech itself.

"They say the whole forest's full of ghosts and goblins like that," Nolan went on, "and hill folk that have been worshiping demons so long that you can't tell them from the goblins."

"Have you seen any?"

"Of which?" Nolan grinned again. "No. None that admitted it. I do know a few folk who live back in the forest, but they're same as anyone else. Never even met an outlaw out here, come to think of it. Still, no telling what we'll run into after dark, eh? No one crosses into the forest at night without a good reason, and even the people who live out here won't bed down without barring their doors."

"Because of the goblins?" Elissa asked, stepping carefully over a large and gnarled root that intersected the path. Her toe thanked her for being more alert this time by not screaming in pain.

"Never asked. They've never said. Probably more folk wisdom than fear of anything in particular—like how people say its bad luck to spill salt on a weasel, but never mention what's like to go wrong."

"It's bad luck to spill salt on a weasel?" Elissa asked.

"That's what I hear." Nolan nodded. "Can't recall ever being around a weasel while I had any salt to spill, though. Not sure how anyone found out."

"I expect the bad luck is weasel bites," Elissa said thoughtfully, and Nolan found himself forced to agree.

"Well, something's likely to bite you," a woman's voice floated out of the darkness, then clucked warningly as Nolan reached for his sword. "Just stop right there unless you fancy learning how good a shot I am. Who are you?"

"Uh...Lady Minda?" Nolan asked the darkness uncertainly. "Is that you?"

"I asked who *you* are," the voice insisted. "Raise the lamp up where I can see your face."

"It's Nolan, and my charge, Sister Elissa, milady," he said as he complied, growing more confident the more he heard the voice. "The fire cut us off from the Tooth and the castle, so we're headed for the lake to get away from it. It's getting dangerous-close to the forest."

Minda Haywood walked out of the darkness on the path ahead of them, lowering her hunting rifle as she came. "Doryne and I are headed that way, too," she said with a nod. "We'd been at the old hunting lodge for the night when the bells changed. Better a night in the storm than to risk a dance with a forest fire."

"Where's Doryne?" Nolan asked.

"I sent her off with our lamp when we spied yours coming," Minda said. "There are folk abroad these days I wouldn't care to dance with, either." She stepped aside and waved them on. "I'll round her up, but hurry on now. Don't wait for us. We'll find you at the lake."

"And that was...?" Elissa asked as they hurried on down the dark path.

"Lady Minda's the earl's oldest girl," Nolan said. "Heir to county and castle, and a better shot with that rifle than any man in her father's guard—including myself, to be sure. Stay on her good side if you can."

"I'll remember that," Elissa said.

"Not that I mean she's likely to shoot you with it or anything," Nolan added hastily. "The Haywoods are good folk. No King Crogan for the minstrels to be singing about in a thousand years, I guess, but the sort that most people are glad to have sitting up at the castle sorting things out. Hard to ask more than that."

The storm seemed to think otherwise, choosing that moment to loose a crack of thunder particularly close overhead. Then the real rain began—not a downpour yet, but enough that it could be heard steadily pattering into the leaves of the forest canopy, and enough that the droplets filtering through to land on Elissa finally outpaced the falling of the leaves. It offered every hope that they'd not see the forest turn into an inferno around them, but still managed to renew their sense of urgency to find what shelter they could for the night.

When the forest finally opened ahead of them, it did so without warning, and Elissa slipped on the muddy embankment. Only Nolan's timely grab at her arm kept her from tumbling headlong into the dark waters fifteen feet below. It was a tumble she surely would have regretted, given the number of rocks that protruded above the surface of the water. On another night, that surface might have been a finely mirrored one, but now the wind and the steady rain pattering down kept it churned into ripples that could reflect only disjointed fragments.

The trail split here to skirt the edge of the lake in both directions, and once Elissa regained her footing, Nolan paused a moment to orient himself before setting off to the left. At times, the trail would wander off back into the woods a bit, putting some distance between itself and an untrustworthy bit of embankment. Even when lightning would flicker across the sky, the rain would obscure the otherwise-open expanse of water, making it impossible for Elissa to judge the extent of the lake, but it quickly proved to be more than a pretentious little fishpond.

Ten minutes later found them still walking its edge as they arrived at a relic of a stone bridge. The old structure must have dated from that time when people were still fighting with the forest over where it ended and their own domains began. Once a fine and sturdy thing built to accommodate the width of a cart, it couldn't have seen more maintenance in the last hundred years than someone coming in occasionally to hack back whatever growth threatened to block access to it.

"Is it safe?" Elissa asked dubiously when Nolan seemed intent on crossing the bridge.

"Safer than staying on this side of it tonight," he assured her, "and a lot dryer than trying to swim. Don't trust the railings, though, and stay in the center."

The forest still sheltered them from the worst of the winds, but once on the bridge they lost all protection from the rain, and taking care with their footing made it impossible to run. By the time they'd traversed its fifty foot length, Elissa's robes weren't soaked through, but they'd safely achieved the status of unpleasantly damp.

The shore they stepped onto was forested as well. "It's an island," Nolan assured her. "Maybe twenty acres worth. Can't promise we're far enough offshore to be impregnable to the fire, but the moat and the rain together should keep us safe."

"Is there any place to get out of the rain?" Elissa asked worriedly. "I've got that page with the Bilge Glyphs in my robes, and a copy of the

Exemplar Serinitas. If you think spilling salt on a weasel is bad luck, just imagine letting a holy book get ruined."

"I can find a place," Nolan nodded, "if you're not too picky."

The path began to climb steeply up and away from the shore, heading toward the center of the island. Soon it passed between the remnants of what had been a pair of stout stone gate posts, though whatever the gate had been guarding seemed to have been long-since reclaimed by the forest. "Stay close," Nolan cautioned Elissa, "and watch your footing. We're going to have to leave the path and hunt around a bit."

The warning about the footing proved well-justified. Slabs of moss-covered stone lay everywhere, cracked and scattered among the trees. Most lay flat against the ground, or leaning against the trees, but when Elissa spied a few of them standing more-or-less upright, she realized the ruin she was walking through was the ruin of a graveyard.

"Suddenly I'm feeling a bit picky," Elissa said warily. "Where exactly are we taking shelter?"

"Over there." Nolan pointed. "I think the roof's intact. It's the only one on the island that might be."

No one could have called the mausoleum that loomed out of the darkness a welcoming sight, but it did seem creditably intact for a structure that had surely seen more decades than Elissa had seen years and had probably gone untended for half of them.

They paused at the door sill, and Elissa bit her lip as she studied the facade apprehensively. Even before the years had taken their toll and the forest had swallowed the graveyard, this building had been no cheery testament to a better life waiting in the embrace of Seriena. It had been—and remained—a harsh and blocky perch for scowling gargoyles, and a canvas of dark-red granite onto which countless skulls had been etched.

Even the watchful eyes of Seriena carved above the doorway seemed they must have looked down in grim judgment back before some very-determined vandal had taken a chisel to them. Now all that remained of those eyes was a pair of black pits so deep that by lantern light there was no knowing they didn't pierce clear through to the chamber beyond.

"The trees will keep us fairly dry if the storm doesn't get too bad," Nolan offered when Elissa hesitated.

"No." She shook her head as resolve replaced the doubt on her face. "No book dies on this librarian's watch."

Corroded iron fixtures hung askew in the entrance to the mausoleum, a rust-red memory of a door long-since vanished, and the building stood open to the night. Elissa started determinedly up the three stone steps to where the deeper darkness swallowed the light of their lantern, but Nolan wordlessly held out a restraining hand and pushed past to enter first himself.

The skull motif continued on the inside of the building, down to engravings on the floor tiles underfoot, half-hidden by dead leaves that had blown in through the open doorway. Stone sarcophagi flanked the central aisle to the left and right—four in all—their lids lying askew next to them as they probably had for decades. Some brackish water had collected in one of the sarcophagi, but anything else they had ever held had been claimed by grave robbers or wild beasts, or else simply fallen to dust.

At the far end of the aisle, a cowled figure carved from rose marble and leaning on a headsman's axe loomed over a flight of stone steps descending into the bedrock of the island. The thing's tattered robes and skeletal face immediately put Elissa in mind of the scarecrows scattered about the fields and orchards. That in turn reminded her of the watching figure that had unaccountably vanished, and she shivered, her eyes falling on marble blade of the headsman's axe.

"Miraculata Carmine," Nolan told her, noticing Elissa's interest in the statue.

"Miracu...lata?" Elissa asked falteringly. "That's a holy woman?" Studying the statue, she could imagine there might have been what the sculptor intended as a hint of hip and breast beneath the robe, and the figure did possess a certain gaunt slenderness that seemed unfit for wielding the huge axe. At first glance, she'd just dismissed that as suggesting the skeletal nature of the headsman, but perhaps the artist had meant to suggest something else by it.

Or perhaps not. Elissa suspected she was at least a hundred years too late to question him on the matter. "I've never heard of Miraculata Carmine." That puzzled Elissa more than anything. Impostor priestess though she was, she was a well-read impostor priestess.

"Patron of the condemned," Nolan said. "They say that if she touched a man who had been wrongly executed, he would return to the living."

"That's...quite a miracle," Elissa said.

"Or black magic, depending on who's telling the story," Nolan conceded. "You heard more of the 'miracle' stories back before the last visit from the Inquisition."

"Ah." Elissa nodded as understanding dawned.

"Nowadays, she's the witch who gave a spark of unholy life back to the vilest murderers and bent them to her will. My grandmother told the stories differently, and some of the folk who live out here still call her 'miraculata' among themselves, and pray to her for the souls the Inquisition took during their last visit."

"Still a rather macabre protector," Elissa said, moving forward to study the statue more closely.

"What do you want from the champion of last resort?" Nolan asked. "Butterflies and rainbows?"

"No!" Elissa blurted. "Not that! Skulls and axes are good, I guess," she finished weakly.

She followed Nolan down the steps into a chamber of similar size, where more sarcophagi lay open and empty, and black scorch marks on the floor and ceiling bore witness to fires past. They would clearly not be the first travelers to take shelter here, but for now they seemed to have the place to themselves.

"Lady Minda knows the area well enough to check for us here," Nolan said, leading the way back upstairs. "No need to go out looking for her. Curl up and try to get some sleep. I suggest you claim that corner." He pointed to one near the door. "Doesn't look like the roof leaks there, and it's not so much in the shadow of the statue." He gave a small smirk. "Even I have to admit I'd sleep better without it standing over me."

Elissa couldn't argue. She wasn't a short woman, but he wasn't a short man, so she stood up on her toes to give him a weary hug and a grateful peck on the cheek. "Thank you, Nolan," she said sincerely. "For everything."

He answered her with a reassuring smile, then settled down with his feet braced against one side of the door frame and his back against the other. No sooner had Elissa curled up with her back in the corner than all the fatigue of the long day washed over her in a relentless tide. It couldn't have taken more than a minute for the wind and the rain to lull her into a deep, deep sleep that no thunder or lightning could shake her from.

The only time she stirred was from a fleeting dream in which a grinning white skull sat atop a moss-covered tombstone on a desolate hilltop. Then a single, blood-red butterfly came flitting down to light gently atop the skull, and Elissa woke with a start.

"You're insane," she muttered to herself. "This whole quest is insane. What do you really think you're going to accomplish?"

Outside, the wind howled and the thunder crashed. The rain came down in relentless sheets, pounding against the roof of the mausoleum, splashing and spattering through it in places. At least none of that splattering was reaching her, she noted with a grateful glance to Nolan where he still sat silhouetted in the doorway. While Elissa had slept, someone had spread what seemed to be a ratty old cloak atop her, and the warm body of something small and furry had curled up against her head, purring gently in her ear.

There in the most unlikely of places, she found herself feeling suddenly, inexplicably safe, in a way she hadn't felt for a very long time. Amidst the dark and the cold and the chaos of the storm, Elissa of Brookshire drifted gently back into a contented and dreamless sleep.

CHAPTER TWENTY-FIVE

COLD, HARD MATH

"You're getting ready to spoil everything, aren't you?" Elissa asked with a preemptive pout. From her seat on a fallen tree, she kicked her feet lazily in the waters of the lake, which had been cool enough to raise gooseflesh on her legs, but retained enough of the warmth of summer to be pleasant once the initial shock had passed.

"By 'everything', do you mean the bit where the Inquisition is on our heels and out for our blood," Keely asked with a puzzled expression, "or just the bit where half the county burned in the night? I suppose I could spoil them both, just to be on the safe side." She'd submerged herself up to her shoulders, having stripped down and hung her clothes on the branches hanging out over the water. Even her boots hung there, though they remained conspicuously within Keely's reach.

"I'd meant the bit about where I'd managed to put all that out of my mind for a few hours," Elissa sighed.

The storm had passed before dawn, leaving behind a mist that held the sun at bay. The muted colors brought back to the world by dawn's first light hadn't brightened noticeably since then, though that dawn must have been three hours gone by now.

Keely and Ulric had arrived in the night with Minda and Doryne, and the four of them seemed to have put their heads together with Nolan and done some planning while Elissa was the only one asleep, but had refused to clue her in immediately for some reason, and had kept their voices hushed. It wasn't until Keely had dragged her down to the lakeside to get washed up that Elissa finally began to get anything out of any of them. So far it hadn't amounted to much more than confirming Nolan had brought them up to date, but at least that confirmation had been made above a whisper.

For the first time since being assigned their bodyguards, Keely and Elissa had actually been allowed some personal space—though not without some convincing. Keely had begged privacy for bathing, and Ulric had finally conceded that they'd be just as safe here with someone standing guard on the bridge as with someone hovering directly over them. And though the threat of pursuit by the Inquisition could not be long forgotten, the chaos of storm and fire pretty much assured that they'd not be picking up the trail in a hurry. As taxing as the last twenty-four hours had been for everyone, better to gather their wits and their strength while they could than to dive still-exhausted back into the fray.

"Riordan said you killed someone," Elissa said, deciding that if the time had come to get serious again, there was no point mincing words. She actually still wasn't sure how she felt about the accusation, even if there was truth to it, but she needed to know.

Keely started to reply, then stopped with her mouth still open, changed gears, started again, then finally closed her mouth and shook her head. "Not really. He meant the rabbit, right?"

"You killed a rabbit?" Elissa looked at her askance. "Why should he...Oh. So he thought...? Gotcha."

"We've got the actual priestess tied up downstairs in the tomb."

"Oh." Elissa nodded. "Oh! You've kidnapped an inquisitrix?!" She buried her face in her hand and sighed deeply. "I can't imagine a single way for this to end well."

"And three months ago," Keely countered patiently, "you couldn't have imagined you'd be all the way out here, helping some mad woman who turns into a cat pull a grandiose con on the Inquisition, right? It always washes out in the end."

"You mean when we're all dead?" Elissa asked.

"Yes, if not before." Keely shrugged dismissively. "Look, I know you *really* don't want to hear this, but we've got even more to worry about than the Inquisition."

Elissa fixed her with a very dirty look. "What have you gotten me into *now*?"

"I wish I knew," Keely said with an uncharacteristic sobriety that set Elissa immediately on edge, "but I've been looking and looking for a chance to warn you—there's something very nasty going on around here."

"How nasty are we talking?" Elissa asked guardedly. "I mean, on a scale of one to Inquisition."

"Not sure." Keely shook her head. "Possible it breaks the scale. Certainly closer to 'Inquisition' than to 'one'. But we can't tell anyone else, because it's local and it's got deep roots. There's some sort of ritual killings going on."

"Ritual? Like a demon cult?" Elissa asked, her glib facade faltering.

"Yeah," Keely said, looking away into the mists. She hadn't put those words to it before, but couldn't imagine what else it could be. "I saw the remains in the water at the bottom of that shaft in the Tooth. They've been piling up there for hundreds of years, and still piling, by the look of it. It...wasn't pretty."

It dawned on Elissa suddenly that for all their weeks together, right here, right now, she was seeing Keely for the first time. The bravado and bluster, the masks and the misdirection that forever swirled around Keely like water around a fish, had all dried up to the point Elissa marveled the woman hadn't begun to suffocate without them. Whatever she'd seen, it had left a mark that would not be quick to heal. "I'm sure it wasn't," Elissa said quietly.

"This stays between us, though," Keely said. "Ulric and Nolan don't know anything about what's going on there, and neither does the countess—none of them batted an eye at my having fallen in the pool. But this thing—whatever this thing is—has got deep roots, and anyone else local could be involved. Each person who knows we know is one more person who can let slip to the wrong ears. And if Earl Haywood himself turns out to be the lord high cultist, don't think our bodyguards won't become our captors."

"They can't afford to let anything happen to us," Elissa countered, "or we wouldn't have those bodyguards to begin with."

"Which do you think would be easier for the Earl to survive? Failing to protect us? Or having the Inquisition find what's in that pool? I mean, if we disappear, he's just one unfortunate accident away from being rid of the one woman who'll care."

Elissa nodded, biting her lip. "Between us, then. And I'll be on my guard against the locals, too. Thanks for the warning."

"Sure you're not coming in?" Keely asked when the silence began to drag.

"Quite sure." Elissa smirked coldly. "The thought's already giving me waking nightmares of Lady Haywood back there interrogating me about my tattoos."

"She's all the way back up at the crypt." Keely chuckled.

"So am I, in those nightmares. It's the whereabouts of my clothes that are in question." Elissa kicked water in Keely's direction. "All I know is that in the nightmare I've lost them again to one of your crazy schemes. I'll be keeping them on, thanks all the same."

The sound of someone crashing through the fallen leaves on the hillside brought both of them turning to see Nolan hurrying their way without any show of concern for what state of dress they might have been in. "Don't ask how," he said before they could question him, "but the Inquisition's already here."

Sabina's first thought was that she desperately needed a drink. Her throat burned so raw from smoke and dehydration that it reduced the terrible aches all over her body to so much background noise by comparison. She would have moaned as she rolled over and tried to push herself up on her hands, but forcing that much air through her throat set off a blindingly painful coughing fit that left her flat back on the ground, whimpering silently.

Finally, after the worst of the pain subsided, she dragged herself over to a hollow in the rock where the rain had collected in the night, and scooped water into her mouth as quickly as she could bear to gulp it down. Then she collapsed again, and indulged in several minutes just listening to her aching body tell her she was alive

The world smelled of rain, with an undertone of ash. The heat of the inferno had gone in the night, replaced with the chill of the rock walls around her. She'd passed out after finding shelter from the fire, but before finding shelter from the rain—and on top of everything else it had left her cold to the bone, her dress completely soaked through. The poor thing was not only ruined; by now it hardly seemed fit for scrap.

Sabina idly wondered if there was any way she could possibly find her way back to Ariadne and the coach, with its nice trunk of clothes, without being seen in public in such a state. Then she took stock of her body to see if there were any other discomforts vying for attention, prioritized its needs, and decided that the first one would be getting up on her feet so the rocky ground would stop sucking so much heat out of her.

With no small effort, Sabina pulled herself up and looked around. Her next priority would be finding a way to actually get warm. Nothing offered itself here short of stripping off her sodden clothes and going naked—a prospect that hardly seemed worth the return for the risk—so that made her next priority getting to somewhere that was not here. That didn't leave a lot of options. She hadn't come far past the wall of rock she'd clambered over to get here, but she lacked the prospect of a fiery death to push her back across it.

What she had instead was aches, stiffness, and a manicure already ruined by the first climb over. She would not attempt it again without at least looking into the other remaining option, which was to continue along the cleft in the rock to see if it led anywhere.

Where it led was a stair, which was promising in and of itself. People did not generally carve stairs into solid rock without the intention that they should assist in a climb to *somewhere* of importance. In Sabina's experience, important places tended to be more warm and sheltered than unimportant places, and they also tended to have more than one way in. In this case, that would translate to more than one way out.

On the downside, important places also tended to serve as magnets for important people, who might then be on-hand to witness her glorious entrance in the guise of a drowned mongrel, but there would be no helping that now. Perhaps if she made the telling of her narrow escape from the fire harrowing enough, she would be forgiven.

Perhaps she should add in a bit about being chased by bandits, or a crazed would-be lover, or even a demon menacing her from out of the flames. Or a demon-possessed bandit king whose unspeakable advances she'd spurned? Might be a bit over-the-top, but tempting. She'd have to think on it.

In the mean time, the steps themselves provided their own concerns, though nothing so ominous as the threat of being seen looking like this. First, there were a lot of them. This climb would be no fun, even if it would be somewhat easier and considerably more dignified than returning the way she'd come. Second, there were the stone skulls.

More scarecrows, Sabina decided, but that didn't stop them feeling macabre, and in some ways more menacing than actual bone. Sabina knew a bit about art, and there was nothing abstract about these representations. These had all been carved by artists who knew intimately well what a human skull looked like, and who had cared enough to painstakingly work that likeness into solid stone. That was miles different from someone deciding to do a quick bit of grave robbing and leave a trophy behind in the middle of a field. This had taken genuine dedication—a devotion to the subject matter.

Sabina took several rests along the climb, sitting on a step and trying not to think too much about the skulls. At least her exertions had started to warm her a bit. Then she came within sight of the top of the stairs, and her heart sank as her nightmares became flesh.

"You there," the man above her called, "who are you?" He leveled a crossbow at her, but that somehow seemed less important than the livery he was wearing. It meant he would be attached to someone's court, and stories of how she'd arrived would start circling through it. Perhaps if she gave a false name? She should have taken time to think of one.

"There's about twenty, best I can tell," Minda said quietly as Ulric, Nolan, and Keely arrived to settle into the cover of rock and brush overlooking the bridge from the island. "Maybe half knights, half blackhoods."

Nolan squinted at the line of riders moving along the trail through the trees on the far shore. "There's a local leading them. Isn't that Evert Fisher?"

"Yeah." Minda nodded. "He was out here yesterday, too, leading some strangers around. Said they were nobles looking for a lost sister, but between this and, well...they must have been Inquisition, too. What do they *want* out here?"

"Evert wouldn't throw in with the Inquisition," Nolan scowled. "Not after..."

"Willingly," Ulric cut him off. "Not *willingly*. The Fishers are a decent family, but that definitely means he's a man with something to lose. I'm sure he's there as the lesser of evils. If this turns into a battle, don't waste a shot on him."

"If this turns into a battle, we die," Nolan said.

"True," Ulric answered dispassionately. Without Doryne—who they'd left with Elissa and the prisoner back at the mausoleum—they could muster a total of three marksmen with as many rifles and one crossbow between them, facing an organized and disciplined force of mounted zealots. Given the amount of time it took to reload a musket, even with an advantage of surprise and then trying to bottle the enemy up at the bridge, he couldn't imagine a scenario where they wouldn't wind up overrun by a dozen bloodthirsty killers who were all better-armed and better-trained than any of them for close-quarters fighting. Even adding Doryne's crossbow into the equation wouldn't make much impact on the cold, hard math.

"Then we don't let this turn into a battle," Keely said.

"How much farther?" Maritine demanded impatiently.

"About two hours, Sister," Evert answered, cool but respectful.

Maritine peered up at the open sky above the lake to their right. "I'd say we've got about three hours until the sun's directly overhead," she said, though in truth she couldn't see the sun at all. "If I haven't seen the witch by then, we'll break *both* your ankles and leave you where we are."

"I dunno about no witch, Sister," Evert said plaintively. "You asked for the one-eyed wolf, and that's where I'm taking you."

"Then you'd best be praying to Seriena you're taking us to the right wolf, hadn't you?" Maritine said. "It's down to where every hour wasted could be a life wasted. One of those lives might as well be yours."

It had galled Maritine more than she could say to stop for a few hours of shelter at the castle while the storm and the fire fought outside. At least there'd been a chapel of sorts to pray at for the goddess to smooth their passage, and it had done an effective job of sheltering them from the witch until the storm broke.

Starting from the castle after the rains, too, had indeed been much better than if they'd been trapped atop the peak the whole time. That hadn't made it easier to sleep while they waited, nor lessened the urgent weight of her divine mission. Seriena had anointed her personally to see this business through, and Maritine would not be able to rest until she had.

Without warning, a shot rang out from across the lake they'd been riding beside. The horses started, and all heads instinctively turned to try to pinpoint the attack, but no second shot followed, and no one showed signs of having been injured. Evert seemed largely unconcerned as well, and Maritine quickly regained her composure.

"Hunter," she announced authoritatively, and beckoned the line of riders to move forward again.

Ahead and to the right, an aging bridge extended out across the lake to an island, and Maritine couldn't help keeping half an eye out that direction in search of the owner of the gun. She was still about fifty yards from it when that half an eye caught sight of a flurry of movement among the trees. Maritine reined up her horse for a better look, and the movement resolved itself to glimpses of someone hurrying down the slope in the direction of the bridge. In a few more seconds, it came clear as a woman clutching a hunting rifle in one hand. Maritine instantly began sizing the woman up as a potential threat.

By tradition, the Inquisition seldom resorted to any sort of long-range weaponry. Demons and witches lacked the usual arrangement of internal organs—or at least lacked a reliance on them—which left them notoriously resistant to arrows and gunpowder, and mortals seldom raised arms against the Inquisition in any numbers.

So the Inquisition specialized at fighting in close quarters, and supplemented their strength with archers and musketeers conscripted from among the faithful when necessary. If by some insanity this woman did take a shot at them, she'd have no prayer of reloading before they rode her down. Still, a gun was a gun, and it would only be prudent to not sit waiting patiently right in front of the thing for it to go off, so Maritine watched the woman approach with alert caution.

For now, the woman showed no sign of noticing them, her attention entirely focused on the ground in front of her as she descended the hill at full speed. Then as the ground leveled and she neared the bridge, she paused, raised her rifle, and took careful aim—not toward them, but directly across the bridge.

Then something small and white came darting out from the end of the bridge. The cat started to take a left turn, saw them, skidded into a complete one-eighty as its back legs scrabbled for purchase in the dirt, then took off back past the bridge as quickly as it could run. The crack of the hunting rifle sounded, and a cloud of dust flew up directly behind the departing cat.

"Witch!" Maritine screamed at the top of her lungs. She held back only long enough to bark orders to the riders directly behind her. "You two find out what happened!" She pointed to where Minda stood at the far side of the bridge, then spurred her horse on, trusting that the rest of her entourage would follow.

Evert was forced to dive off the path simply to avoid getting trampled. By the time he pulled himself to his feet, limping a little from having struck his knee on a tree root, all that remained of the procession he'd come with were the knight and the inquisitrix that Maritine had singled out.

"What happened here?" the remaining inquisitrix demanded, heading across the bridge.

"Are you all right, Lady Minda?" Evert called.

Minda nodded darkly. "Doryne's a squirrel, but I'm all right. I thought I was next, but the witch suddenly turned and ran. She must have seen you lot coming."

"You're the Earl's daughter?" the inquisitrix asked, and Minda nodded again. "You'd best get out of these woods. You can burn a witch, you can behead a witch, but the musket ball would have been wasted even if you'd hit her."

"I need to find my friend the squirrel first," Minda said grimly. "I'll be safe here with you on the tail of the witch, won't I?"

"Probably," the inquisitrix conceded. "It's on you, though. She's a clever one. Come on," she beckoned to the knight and to Evert.

"Can you spare the huntsman, Sister?" Minda asked. "I could really use someone to watch the bridge and make sure my squirrel doesn't try to leave the island."

The knight and the inquisitrix exchanged glances, reaching a silent accord that it would be a blessing to be rid of the baggage so they could properly join the chase. "Very well." The inquisitrix nodded. "But see he stays here with you, milady, until we return. He may still be needed if the witch evades us again."

"So the witch turned Doryne into a squirrel?" Evert asked Minda incredulously as they stood alone on the bridge, watching the riders thunder away.

"Yes," Minda said calmly, never taking her eyes off the riders. "And I suspect she's about to turn you into a fish."

"What?!" Evert asked, incredulity turning to alarm.

"What did they threaten you with?" Minda asked, ignoring the question.

"Broken bones." Evert sighed. "They were ready to work their way through everyone sheltering on the Tooth last night, until someone told them where to find the one-eyed wolf."

"The one-eyed wolf?" Minda cocked an eyebrow.

Evert shrugged. "*Any* one-eyed wolf. They don't seem to know, either. But there's an old rock back in the forest I think kinda looks like that if you squint at it right."

"Grandpa always said it was a fox." Minda nodded.

"Yeah." Evert shrugged again. "I had to do something. My Elly was on the short list to be questioned."

Minda winced and clapped a reassuring hand on the man's shoulder. "You did good. Now in about a twenty-count, the trail should take our friends off into the trees. Then the witch will appear out of nowhere and turn you into a fish."

"So you said," Evert agreed with concern.

"As soon as that happens, run for all your worth to the castle, and tell my mother everything that's happened, and that I said to hide you away until this blows over. Oh, except don't tell her that bit about the squirrel. Doryne's fine."

Evert opened his mouth to start another question, but at that moment the last two riders disappeared into the forest, and Minda gave him a meaningful little shove. "Run!"

CHAPTER TWENTY-SIX

WITCH HUNT

Escape would have been easy if it had been an option at all. No human on foot can keep up with a cat in full flight, and no horse can squeeze into all the little highways and hiding places open to a cat in the deep forest, but Keely had to leave her pursuers *hope* that she could be caught, and that became a very risky business. Multiple times she had to feign fatigue or confusion to let them close the gap, and then trust that real fatigue or confusion wouldn't catch up with her once they did get close.

The horses and their riders were all creatures of the city or the open farmland, but this rocky forest wasn't exactly Keely's home turf, either. She was built to take advantage of it, but that didn't give her an intimate knowledge of the terrain or its idiosyncrasies.

When the heat was on, she would cut across a loop in the trail, bounding over rocky outcroppings and tangled tree roots, but with so many riders able to spread out around her, one wrong turn could leave her pinned up against the shores of the lake. Swimming wouldn't be a problem in and of itself, but swimming fast enough to get out of range of any rocks, knives, or similar unpleasantness was not going to happen.

Convincing Ulric to let her take this chance hadn't been the easiest con she'd ever run. He'd tried to stare her down when she said she'd have no problem at all keeping ahead of the horses, but in the end, four things had forced him to accept her faked sincerity. Two of those things were the dead inquisitrix secreted in a stone sarcophagus in the mausoleum and the live inquisitrix tied up outside that stone sarcophagus. Anyone discovered on that island with the women would be instantly assumed responsible, with all the consequences that entailed.

The remaining two things that forced Ulric to throw the staring contest had been Minda and Elissa. He could no more allow either of them to come to harm than he could Keely, and this plan got them both out of harm's way.

A throwing axe suddenly buried itself in a tree not three inches in front of Keely's nose. It took all of her feline agility just to roll aside and slam into the haft instead of the edge of the blade left jutting out of the trunk. She rebounded, rolled, and scrambled away, losing some time, but remaining relatively unharmed. This, she decided with a sideways glance at the riders racing around the bend she was cutting across, was the time to stop playing coy and get out of the proverbial kitchen, because any more heat was certain to result in roast kitty cat.

Driven by a fear that she might truly have cut it too close to the edge this time, Keely called up the reserves she'd been saving and turned her run into a headlong sprint. She arrived back at the trail just ahead of the riders trying to cut her off, but the woman in the lead had seen it coming and was poised to swing off of the saddle in that moment.

Without hesitation, Sister Maritine threw herself at the ground, knowing full well she was in for some serious hurt. It very nearly paid off in full, less than a heartbeat away from landing on Keely with a force that would have crushed the little cat. As it was, she managed to grab Keely by the tail and hold on tight despite the beating the ground was giving her. Keely screeched in pain as they tumbled together, bouncing off of rocks and slamming into a tree.

A hand closed about her throat, attempting to lift her up and away, where she'd have nothing to claw at but the woman's heavy leather glove, but Keely managed to snag Maritine's collar with the claws of one forepaw and hung on for life while she scratched straight at the woman's eyes with the claws of the other.

Maritine released Keely's tail to protect her face, but Keely had been counting on that. The move freed up her hind claws to rake at Maritine's throat. The sharp sting of the gouges on Maritine's face and neck finally did what the concussive force of the ground couldn't, and she released her grip just enough for Keely to wriggle free and kick away.

Even before Keely landed, a flash of silver at the corner of her eye prompted her to twist in midair. The spear still managed to graze her ribs—drawing blood and jolt of pain—before burying itself in the ground. She landed ungracefully, willed the pain and all questions of how bad the wound might be to the back of her mind, and sprang away in the direction she'd been headed originally.

Maritine was down—unhorsed, bruised, and wiping blood from her eyes—but the knight who'd tried to skewer Keely had released the spear without breaking his mount's stride. Already they were racing around the next bend, trying to cut her off again. More riders came hot behind him, and far too many trailed along after for her to double back.

What she could do, though, now that she'd crossed the path, was veer left, away from the lake. As she did, the priestess right behind foolishly spurred her horse up the treacherous, rocky ground after Keely, and the animal went down screaming for it.

"Don't lose her!" Maritine screamed in a tone that, to Keely, almost made Shoshona's fanatic ravings sound sane by comparison.

Keely bounded nimbly over the rocks and roots, angling her path generally upward away from the lake. Behind her, riders had begun to dismount, crashing through the fallen leaves, fanning out in an attempt to surround her. Farther out along the trail, she could hear horses galloping in either direction, pushing to get their riders further out to close the gap.

One way or another, this was all going to be decided in a matter of seconds. Keely's feline body was a sprinter, and now that she'd pulled out all the stops, it would overload quickly. Her only chance was to evade the jaws of the trap, then disappear into the forest before that happened. She longed to dash up a tree and out of reach, but dared not with the pursuit so close. Leaping from tree-to-tree was the domain of squirrels, not felines, and even with these grand old trees it would be all too easy to find herself cornered in one.

"Don't lose her!" Maritine screamed again. The voice of the woman herself was falling behind, and Keely dared to hope that the inquisitrix had seriously injured herself in the leap from horseback.

Keely crested a rise and looked in dismay down to her right, to where the trail had curled along the contour of the hill back toward her. Three riders had already come into sight that way. If the curve cut back too close to the original trail, they'd be closing in from the other side at any...

Too late, Keely began to swing her gaze back to the left, and the blind-side impact sent her spinning head-over-hind-paws through the air. She landed amid leaves, slick from the night's rain, and skidded into a narrow gully where she lay dazed, staring up at the forest canopy.

"There!" one of her pursuers shouted from nearby as multiple sets of feet crashed through the fallen leaves. "The witch!"

Keely clawed her way weakly to her feet, panting for breath, and pulled herself up to peer out of the gully, trying to decide if there was any direction left to run. This time she saw the collision coming with just enough time to avoid it by pulling her head back down, and the doe that had run into her moments before went sailing over her head.

Keely pressed herself down amid the rocks and the leaves, making herself as small as possible as she watched the ghostly-white deer bound away amid a rain of hurled weapons. Two knights vaulted directly over Keely's hiding place in pursuit of the animal, unmistakably convinced that their shape-changing quarry had transformed itself from a little white cat into a little white deer.

Keely felt a pang of guilt for the animal, but only a rather small one, considering she would probably have made good her escape just now if not for its interference. In any case, she was spent. The collision had finished her, and any attempt to intercede on the doe's behalf would be suicide.

"Wait!" a man shouted. "What are you...?" Abruptly steel rang on steel. "*Get away from my sister!*" the voice snarled.

A moment's leaden silence followed, broken in the end by another man's calm, quiet voice. "Well, that wasn't the right thing to say." Keely swiveled her ears toward the sound in a double-take. That second speaker had been...Prince Tobias? She didn't have time to confirm the thought or to ponder further before someone let out a feral battle cry and steel sang again.

"She's getting away!" a woman shouted.

"Go!" a man yelled from nearly on top of Keely. "Get the witch! We'll handle her minions."

"I am no one's *minion*," Tobias spat. In an ideal situation, the words might have been taken as a defense against his association with any witch at all, much less the one in question, but neither his tone nor the adrenalin flaring all around did anything to encourage that interpretation.

Abruptly, Keely found herself in the middle of a frantic battle, with the sound of blades clashing in all directions, and boots treading so close as the combatants maneuvered for position that she began to fear getting stepped on nearly as much as simply getting discovered.

Keely began an attempt to take stock of the combatants, reflexively looking for escape routes while telling herself she'd recovered enough to dash a few yards if she saw the right opening. Telling one side from another was easy, with the Inquisition all in its team colors. It looked like they had perhaps four knights engaging Tobias and his companions, plus a pair of blackhoods. The women hung back for the most part, circling with their short blades drawn as they looked for openings, while the more heavily armed and armored knights engaged directly.

Tobias had himself, his squire, another swordsman, and a giantess of a woman. Like the blackhoods, the giantess didn't seem so well-equipped for battle as her male counterparts, but she held a pair of knives at the ready and seemed to be making it her business to keep an eye on the circling priestesses.

As the combatants clashed and spun apart and clashed again, it quickly became apparent that they were evenly matched—which was saying something for the outnumbered Tobias-and-friends. They clearly hadn't trained as one coherent team as their opponents had, but they did fight in teams of two—prince and squire, swordsman and giantess—and with an aggressive flamboyance that kept the Inquisition off balance.

They'd also arrived at the scene less winded. Still, first blood went to the Inquisition as a priestess spied her opening and lunged in under the squire's guard. His hunting leathers took some of the impact, but the short sword of the inquisitrix still sliced across his left thigh and came up glistening red. Though the wound was minor, the youth reeled back from it, off balance for a moment—and that was all the knight he'd been facing needed.

A heavy, overhand stroke of his blade came crashing down toward the squire's head. The squire parried the blow awkwardly, narrowly escaping injury, but failing to counter the knight's real intent, which was to disarm him. The youth's blade went clanging off the rocks underfoot and spun wildly away.

Had there been time for Keely to stop and analyze that moment and those that followed from it, her conscious brain would have arrived at the following observations and conclusions: in that one heartbeat, the balance of the battle had tilted sharply against Tobias. He'd been able to hold his own against a superior number of skilled warriors by taking the offensive and keeping them off-balance, like a con-artist who bluffed her way through a hairy situation by denying her mark time to think.

But in this case, Tobias' mark had been suspicious to begin with, and, hunting for the weak link in his smoke screen, had cut through it with unnerving precision. Denying the squire his sword had been nearly as effective as striking him dead, because it put him on the defensive—and going on the defensive sounded the impending death of any con.

Unless Tobias and his friends could do something in the next few moments to restore the balance of power, before their opponents could capitalize on this weakness, the fight would be lost.

She would have gone on to ask herself what the bloody hell Tobias was doing at this very spot at this very moment anyway, and she would have answered that any idiot could see she'd led him to it. Certainly, he'd followed of his own free will, just as any mark would hand over his coin purse or the keys to the castle with a happy smile when she'd done her job right. And nowhere in her agenda had there been anything about luring him to his death in a sword fight with the Inquisition in the middle of a dark, old forest, but such was the nature of her agendas.

They started out as these nebulous, grandiose plans with a definite starting point, a goal that might or might not be concrete, and a whole bunch of "we'll make it up as we go along" filling up the space in the middle. Going with the gut had always gotten her by on a day-to-day basis, but she'd long since passed out of the realm of the day-to-day con on this one.

Four people of arguable innocence, who had gotten tangled up in her web of deceits, were about to die right in front of her for it, slaughtered by the very evil she was working to bring down. A part of her had always understood that there would be a price for victory. It had known that her actions would have ripple effects, and that as the Inquisition hunted her it would surely be taking its frustrations out on whomever they found within reach. It had even told her as much, in matter-of-fact tones, while assuring her that she'd save far more harm than she'd cause if only she could bring down the Inquisition once and for all.

What that bit of her had entirely failed to mention was that she'd have to watch helplessly while the damage played out right on top of her.

As Keely looked on, a young man whose only crime had been to follow his master on an adventure screamed in pain and crumpled to the ground as the knight who'd disarmed him kicked him savagely in the gut. Beyond him, the only woman Keely had ever seen dare take arms against the Inquisition, much less go toe-to-toe with a knight, had just been cut off from her allies and backed against a tree.

The swordsman who'd somehow started this by trying to stand between the Inquisition and his sister held his own for the moment, but looked to have lost track of the second priestess who was now circling around behind him.

And the brash, bloody fool who—in addition to being rather handsome and an amazing dancer—had obsessively followed Keely across half a continent for the privilege of playing her knight in shining armor, now stood with his back all but unprotected between two men who were each nearly his equal with a blade. The preliminaries had come to a close, the bloodletting about to commence. She could talk about the monsters of the Inquisition all she liked, but this was her own idiot fault.

Amidst the swirling chaos of the fight, the only bit of this that actually reached her conscious mind was a blur of images—visions of gruesome deaths about to be. And as she drew in a breath and forced herself up, ignoring the slight twinge at her side and the ongoing panting as she labored to breathe, Keely bundled all the images up together with one of Ulric grimly assuring her she'd turned him into a dead-man walking.

Then she opened The Rules to the next blank page and burned the images onto it, overlaying them all with an echo of her own voice saying, "I'll fix it." Then the little white cat closed her book, tucked it neatly away onto its shelf in her mind, and launched headlong into battle.

CHAPTER TWENTY-SEVEN

True Love's Kiss

The sum of Keely's knowledge of weaponry could be expressed as, "Don't get poked with the pointy bits," but within that specialized sub-field of the subject, she rightfully considered herself an expert. She'd seen a few fights in her day, but almost all of them had been from the vantage point of looking over her shoulder as they chased after her, beckoning her to join in. The concept of standing one's ground belonged to people who possessed ground to stand on. So when Keely launched into the fray, her mind was coldly analyzing the whole thing not so much as a fight, but as a tactical extraction problem.

Priority one had to be the disarmed boy. He mightn't last long enough to be a second priority. Sadly, his very predicament made a direct approach futile, so she veered away from the knight standing over the boy and toward the inquisitrix who'd wounded him. The woman had backed off a few steps and dismissed the squire as dispatched. Now her eyes settled on Tobias. That, at least, would be handy, as it put her back full to Keely.

Keely didn't make a sound until she was already in the air, halfway to the woman's back. Then she let out the most horrible feline screech she could muster. Having stepped clear of the fight, the priestess was at luxury to whip around in alarm, which resulted in her getting a face full of cat. She screamed, dropping her sword as she reached to pull Keely from her face, but Keely had already bounded away after giving the priestess a quick bloodying. "Witch!" the woman howled.

The only knight free to give his full attention to that cry would be the one standing over the squire, and Keely had covered half the ground to him before he could even start to turn. As he spun around to the right, she darted past on his left, and all he saw as he came about was the priestess clutching at her bloodied face with one hand while waving the other accusingly in his general direction. That left Keely free to bound over the fallen squire and between the legs of his master.

She came out in front of Tobias and under the guard of the knight facing him. She leapt once more, but with a much lower trajectory this time, straight at the man's groin. With no time to analyze this sudden threat, the man involuntarily dropped his guard low toward her, and Keely caught the glint of steel flashing over both her head and the man's lowered guard as he did. She rebounded harmlessly off the knight's mail tunic, but still he screamed as she raced away. Keely accepted that as sufficient evidence that Tobias would be free to protect his squire now.

Her next priority could only be the second priestess, who now stood as the greatest threat by virtue of being neither disoriented nor distracted. With no element of surprise left, Keely could never hope to close on the woman, either, so fled past her instead, as tantalizingly close as she dared.

This time Keely didn't fight the urge to escape up a tree. She scrambled up the first one she could reach, ducking behind a great gnarled branch just as a throwing knife flew past. Then she paused, panting. Her heart raced, and her head had begun to swim from the exertions, but she would be safe here for several seconds at least. Below her, the cry of, "Witch!" echoed again.

Before the world had quite stopped spinning, Keely heard the sound of someone scrabbling up the trunk, and she knew she had no choice but to move again. She began to climb in short, determined bursts. Glancing behind, she could see one priestess climbing while the other circled the base of the tree, keeping a careful eye on Keely. Then three knights of the Inquisition fell back to protect the women, loosely ringing the tree with their backs to it.

By Keely's count, that left no one likely to be up and moving to block Tobias and his friends from leaving. Her plan had succeeded masterfully—even ahead of schedule. The one little hitch was that this had been the phase of the plan where the squire picked up the sword of the fallen knight and the two sides had faced off four-against-four, keeping all but the one priestess too busy to chase her. Evading one woman trying to follow her up a tree would have been kitten's play. Evading that woman and a small army camped at the bottom of the tree would...not.

Worse, this woman was a climber, and an inquisitrix out looking for trouble never seemed thoughtful enough to wear her encumbering robes of office to the party. The priestess hauled herself nimbly up branch after branch, quickly closing the distance between herself and Keely.

Winded as Keely was, she judged that if she persisted in trying to escape the woman by continuing to climb vertically, she wouldn't have half a minute before the woman managed to overtake her. From snatches of overheard conversation and the sounds of feet crashing away through the fallen leaves, she also guessed that the unknown swordsman who had provoked the confrontation was already charging off with giantess in tow.

She wasn't sure whether her own presence factored into Tobias's decision to remain behind with his squire, or if they merely intended to buy time for the other two. Hoping for them to fight their way through the wall of fanatics in time to do anything about her predicament—even if they meant to—would be grasping at straws. She couldn't survive a direct confrontation with her pursuer, and she couldn't expect the woman to pause and listen to either negotiation or con. She couldn't go up, she couldn't go down, and she couldn't wait. That didn't leave a lot of options.

Keely paused to survey the branches radiating out from the trunk around her. She'd gotten maybe twenty-five feet into the air, but the limbs of the gnarled, old tree still started out thick as a man's chest at this height. She'd have plenty of room to run along any of the ones she could reach in the next few seconds, but the leaves grew too thick and the branches too twisted for her to know what she'd find when she got out there. Her view of the ground, too, promised to be limited.

With nothing to distinguish one option from another, Keely committed to the branch she'd just reached. She scurried out along it and into an arboreal labyrinth, with a murderously pious minotaur on her heels, and all she could do was pray she'd find an exit too narrow for the creature to follow her through before it could trap her in a dead end.

Three times Keely judged another branch close enough and sturdy enough to risk the leap to it, but so did the priestess. The third time it seemed that the woman's luck had finally run out. The higher branch she grabbed to steady herself when she landed snapped as she put her weight on it.

Overbalanced, the inquisitrix tumbled forward and down. Then one flailing hand caught a branch off the one they'd landed on, and her whole weight abruptly came dragging it down. Keely lurched off-balance herself, scrabbling for purchase with her claws. For a moment she hung there, hindquarters dangling off the branch, just out of arm's reach of the woman.

Then a triumphant grin flashed across the woman's face as Keely saw her reaching with her free hand for the dagger at her belt. In those eyes Keely read the dead-certain confidence that the same motion that would draw that dagger would bury it in Keely's gut. Whether the owner planned to throw it or to simply use it to extend her reach, her eyes and her muscles had already done their reflexive mental arithmetic and deemed the outcome as certain as picking up a spoon from a table. In the mind behind those eyes, Keely had already died.

In the split-second left to her, Keely did the only thing she could do, and relaxed every muscle in her body. Her claws sheathed. Her feet stopped scrabbling. She plummeted like a furry white stone. Leaves and twigs slapped at her from all sides. Her flank glanced off something unyielding. Then her fall abruptly ended in a distressingly thin layer of fallen leaves.

Keely hadn't even had time to properly assess if she was still alive when a rapid series of sickening cracks above her announced the descent of the inquisitrix. The woman landed three feet in front of Keely, staring at her with dead eyes and an unmistakably broken neck. Half a breath later, a flash of silver announced the arrival of the blade-heavy throwing dagger, which sank two inches into the earth between Keely and the dead woman.

Nearby shouts and the sound of running prompted Keely to pull herself to her feet before she could finish taking stock of her own condition. Her body ached, and it moved reluctantly, but at least it responded more or less according to usual expectations. She rose to find a knight and the other inquisitrix bearing down on her. She didn't dare run, and climbing another tree seemed a laughable proposition, so she fell back on the only instinct left to her and bluffed.

She bloodied one paw for effect, swiping it across the still wet wound where the spear had glanced across her rib cage, she hopped up onto the dead woman's shoulder with all the ferocity she could still muster. She arched her back. She hissed. She assumed a stance calculated to say, "Ignore the relative lack of blood. This woman is dead because I just tore her stinking throat out, and I really can't wait for round two to get started. Who's next?" Then she waited to die.

The ploy did buy her a moment, as both knight and priestess faltered in their headlong charge. Then from behind them came the howl of a man who'd just met the business end of a sword. That divided their attention and deepened their moment of indecision, which Keely filled with the most blood-curdling caterwaul she could muster.

Before they'd made up their minds, Tobias came charging at them in a rage, blood dripping from his blade. A sense of self-preservation finally broke through the finely honed fanaticism of the zealots facing him, and the pair fled into the woods, quickly joined by the knight who'd been left facing Tobias' squire, once the man realized he was standing alone.

At least one of the two fallen knights remained alive, judging by the groans of pain, but neither of them seemed inclined toward regaining his feet. The others would no doubt return soon with allies, but right here and now, Tobias and his squire remained as the only two people who might soon try to kill Keely. At the moment, Tobias stood staring at her through narrowed eyes, holding his bloody sword while clearly trying to decide if he would do just that.

This could only go down one of two ways, Keely knew. She could no more fight or flee from him right now than she could have from the Inquisition. She might already be dead if not for the simple fact Tobias had just seen the inquisition jump to conclusions about a similarly colored creature being the witch he'd come looking for.

Seizing on his hesitation, Keely very gingerly stepped down off of the dead woman. Then she sat down with her tail curled about her feet, cocked her head to the side to look up at him with wide eyes, and very eloquently let out a tentative, "Mew?"

"Does that mean you understand me?" Tobias asked, not lowering the sword.

Keely dipped her head down in a semblance of a nod, otherwise remaining where she was.

"And if I ask," he said, "you'll try to tell me you're not a witch?"

Keely nodded again.

"Girl?" he asked tersely. Nod. "Anyone I know?" Nod. "We'll see."

"Conrad!" Tobias barked to the squire, who'd already come up a couple of paces behind him.

"Highness?" the young man asked dutifully.

"Watch her." Tobias strode forward and lifted the unresisting Keely by the scruff of her neck 'til he was staring her in the eye. "Witch or victim? Victim or witch?" he mused aloud. "I guess there's only one way to find out." So saying, he leaned forward and kissed Keely squarely on the nose.

Keely blinked. She wrinkled her brow in puzzlement. She saw Tobias' gaze begin to narrow suspiciously. Then her brain kicked into gear, and she remembered she was dealing with a man lost in his own private faerie story. She twitched. She shivered. She began to blink rapidly. Then when she figured she'd achieved the minimum of necessary theatricality, she shimmered back into her bipedal body and threw herself into Tobias arms.

"You did it!" she cried ecstatically, flattening her body against his. Over his shoulder, she feigned suddenly becoming aware of the slack-jawed Conrad, who had indeed been watching her carefully. "And I'm naked...aren't I?" she asked in a faltering voice. Before anyone could rally to answer that question, she fixed her eyes on a stray lock of her own hair that had fallen in front of her face. "And my hair's white! Why's my hair white?!" she asked in feigned panic.

"I think it's more of a silver, miss," Conrad offered awkwardly.

"And no less fetching than when it was gold," Tobias assured her. He smiled down into her eyes, his nose practically touching hers from the way she was plastered against him. For all that Keely was playing a role, the shiver that ran down her spine was a genuine reaction to gazing into that handsome face and feeling those strong hands cradling her naked back. "You've suffered a terrible fright," he said, voice soft and distracted. "These things happen."

"And you're, ummm...wearing those pretty slippers, at least," Conrad added.

Keely felt Tobias' breath warm against her lips, felt her own tongue run unbidden over her teeth, and felt the heat creep up her cheeks. Was she actually blushing? She thought she'd forgotten how to blush. "I feel...strange," she breathed. "Unreal. Like I could just melt and...find I was a cat again. Maybe the kiss on the nose..."

"Wasn't enough?" Tobias finished for her.

"Mhmm." Keely nodded weakly.

She tilted her face fully up to his, her lips parting gently as Tobias leaned in. Their lips met, warm and soft and tentative at first, but in no hurry to break away. Time took on a lazy, detached quality, and Keely could no more say how much of it had passed before their tongues met than she could say whose idea it had been to introduce them to each other. She did manage to retain enough lucidity to know it had happened before his hands began to wander from their relatively chaste hold on her waist to explore up and down her naked back, but not nearly enough to say by how long. Regardless, she very pointedly failed to object to any of it, and the spell remained unbroken until she finally became aware that the pesky assault that had begun on her senses was someone's frantic cry of, "Wolves!"

CHAPTER TWENTY-EIGHT

DEATH ROW

Sabina prodded suspiciously at the bowl of stew they'd brought her, stirring the viscous, brown concoction with a wooden spoon that had clearly seen better times. On any other day, she would have thrown the whole thing against the nearest wall in disgust and demanded something that actually resembled food, but if she'd ever been this hungry before in her life, she couldn't remember when, and she harbored no illusions that her demands would be catered to. No matter what that stuff in the bowl looked like, her traitorous nose insisted it showed too much potential to be carelessly discarded.

Even though the young man had been apologetic about locking her up, that hadn't stopped him from doing it and disappearing into the dark. In the hour since, no response had come to her shouts save their own echo. He'd left her with the stew, a jug of water, a woolen blanket, and a few candles to keep her company, and not with the impression that she was here to rot.

Nonetheless, he'd been adamant that she was there to stay until Lord or Lady Haywood had time to spare from dealing with the tragedy of the fire to talk with her themselves and sort things out. If she satisfied them she'd come this way as an innocent refugee from the flames, and not some vandal bent on destruction at the cathedral site above, he was sure she'd go free with all apologies for the inconvenience.

The decision, however, was simply not his to make, and that hadn't changed no matter how she'd plead or cried, or how winsomely she'd looked at him. Seriously, after all the leg she'd shown to no avail, she couldn't imagine him taking an interest in women at all.

So here Sabina sat alone on a crude, wooden stool in a dank dungeon cell formed from two walls of solid rock and two walls of unyielding iron bars, staring at something from one of the four basic refuse groups, and earnestly contemplating eating it—when she suddenly realized she *wasn't* alone.

"What are *you* looking at?" she demanded of the wiry, ragged man staring at her from two cells down. He clung to the bars, gazing in her direction with an empty, unfocused expression, and appeared in such a dreadful and bedraggled state that it eclipsed even her own. The word that leapt instantly to mind as she returned his stare was "madman".

The man offered Sabina no reply, and no other acknowledgment of her presence beyond the vacant stare, until she finally gave up glaring at him and turned away in disgust. Hunching under the blanket with her back pointedly toward the man, she returned to contemplating the contents of the bowl in what she knew was a losing battle for her dignity.

"You're *not* the witch," the man said firmly.

"Excuse me?" Sabina asked, glancing over her shoulder with an eyebrow arched in indignation.

"He said you were the witch, but you're not."

"*Who* said?" she asked, carefully setting the bowl on the floor before turning to the man with her full attention. Her heart had skipped a couple of beats to hear it even intimated that she'd been accused of witchcraft, and she fervently began to hope this man was as mad as he seemed. "*Who* said I was a witch?"

"Some high'n mighty lord guy." Her fellow prisoner waved his hand dismissively. "S'okay. When they come for you, I'll tell 'em you're not."

"Where did you hear this?" Sabina demanded.

"Down at the Tankard, just after you threw your silver at me. Fellow barges in asking questions, gets all excited when I mention you, an' takes off looking for his witch. He thought you was the other woman."

"Do I *know* you?" Sabina asked, peering to see past the filth on his face, and past a ragged beard that hadn't been there quite long enough to look like he'd left it by conscious choice.

He gave a cynical laugh. "No. I'm sure you don't. But we met before, in another nightmare. Your dress was all pretty and pink and new, and your hair was shiny and clean, and you was even more full of yourself. You asked about my father and you threw that silver at me."

"Ambleforth?" Sabina furrowed her brow.

"Clay." He nodded. "Nice you remembering. Most of the time people don't, and they tell me I was dreaming or I'm mad, which gets annoying, 'cause I know both by now."

"What are you doing here?"

He shrugged. "Woke up here. It's kind of nice, actually. When I wake up someplace *really* nice, I'm always waiting for that moment when the world turns upside down and things go horribly, horribly wrong, you know? And nobody's showed up here yelling at me to find my father's go'ss-forsaken book yet. It's been...peaceful."

"You mean the Grimm Truth?" Sabina asked.

"The book? I guess so. They're rarely that specific." He sighed. "I'm hoping it'll show up in one of these nightmares and that'll break me out."

"Well, I'm glad you know I'm not a witch," she said, deciding that the man seemed to be clinging to at least a few threads of sanity. "But..."

"Do you remember any of my other dreams?" Clay asked. "I think something's started to change."

"What do you mean?"

"Seriena abandoned me many dreams before the one I met you in, but lately *someone's* been reaching out like she's trying to save me. There's this white lady who shines like the moon. First time I saw her, I was drowning. She took my hand and pulled me out of the water. Did you see that one?"

"No." Sabina shook her head. "I didn't."

"And the last time people started climbing out of their graves, she showed up and drove them away. She caught me once when I was falling, and she's been in a couple other dreams too muddled to make sense of, but I die a lot less when she's around. Sort of thing a guy could get used to."

"She's...is she the witch you were talking about? The one that's not me?" Sabina asked. Then she nearly fell over backwards as a trio of rats burst out of the darkness from the cell behind Clay, scurrying so quickly that they were past her before the reflexive yelp could pass her lips.

For his part, Clay barely blinked, though one of the rats had actually rebounded off of him in its haste. Then they were gone, disappearing into a small hole in the stonework as quickly as they'd come, leaving nothing but an uneasy sense in Sabina that she should perhaps think twice before mentioning witches again.

"Nah," Clay answered Sabina's question as if there'd been no interruption, giving a small, dismissive wave of his hand. "I think she's...probably the moon."

Sabina just leaned her head down on her knees and tried to calm her breathing and the wild beating of her heart. She tried to remind herself that she'd gone *looking* for adventure, and these were the sorts of things that happened to people who did. If she lacked the steel to endure one day in a dark cell, a vile meal, and few vermin, she was not the woman destined to find the Grimm Truth, much less to rule an empire.

The thought hit her like a whole bucketful of cold water, and composure came flooding back to her. Many highborn men and women had already underestimated her steel, and she was only now getting started.

Sabina's ears perked up at a jingle of keys, and she lifted her head to see a big man in ill-fitting livery approaching her cell door. Perhaps this guard would be more easily swayed than the other one by a well turned calf. Or perhaps he wouldn't even need persuading. "Will I be getting to see the earl now?" she asked hopefully.

"She's not a witch, you know," Clay offered matter-of-factly as the man fumbled with the keys, needing a couple of tries before he got the right one. Sabina glowered at Clay, but the jailer only grunted and nodded. Sabina wasn't quite sure whether the man was nodding at her question or Clay's remark, but his going along with either could only be a good sign.

"Top of the stair," he muttered, holding the cell door open for Sabina.

She stopped abruptly halfway there. "A moment," she begged with a genteelly raised hand, and she turned back toward the wall as if facing a mirror as she began to brush off and smooth her dress. It did less to restore her dignity than simply squaring her shoulders did after, but the attempt struck her as important. Then she carefully crouched to retrieve her bowl from the floor and passed it through the bars to Clay.

"Was nice visitin' with you," Clay said, accepting the bowl with a small, genuine smile. "Maybe you'll remember me again next time I see you."

"Maybe." She answered his smile with a similar one and offered him a little parting wave as she disappeared into the darkness with her escort.

With no place to go and precious little else to even look at, Clay watched her silhouette dwindling against the flicker of a distant torch. He allowed himself a bit of a sigh as he savored the first spoonful of stew, and he reflected on just how awful the day hadn't been so far.

He'd settled into the corner, scraping the last of the bowl, when he heard a man clear his throat, and looked up to find that the jailor had returned. "Mind answering me a question?" the man asked.

"Depends," Clay answered suspiciously. "Is this one of those seemin' innocent questions that actually opens the door to the next nightmare? 'Cause I think I've filled my quota on those."

The man gave a little snort. "I just wondered who the other witch was."

"There's no *other* witch," Clay scowled. "There's *a* witch, and like I said, that wasn't her."

"Oh. You did," the man conceded. "So who's *the* witch?"

Clay's eyes narrowed. "I'll give you this much: the question doesn't seem innocent. You're still one of 'them', though. You reek of it."

The man chortled. "Well, one of us reeks, certainly."

"You things never can hold on to details," Clay persisted. "They slip through your fingers like water. Your clothes have changed colors. And they fit now. They didn't fit before."

"I *changed* them," the man said, slowly and deliberately, as though explaining things to a dense child. "They were just...borrowed. Besides, they'd got all bloody."

"*You're just proving my point!*" Clay bellowed angrily. "It always ends the same way, so just stop playing coy and tell me that you killed the pretty girl. Then you can throw her head at me or whatever so I can wake up screaming and we start the whole go'ss-forsaken business over!"

"But..." the man said, taken aback.

"Just do it!" Clay screamed.

"She *said* she was a witch," the man snapped back.

Clay threw the empty bowl at the man's head. It bounced harmlessly off a reflexively raised forearm.

"'The witch you were talking about', she said. 'The one that's not me.'"

"Do it!" Clay howled, lunging for the man's throat through the bars, and coming up a hand's length short.

"We're not going to have a useful conversation right now, are we?" the man asked.

"I said—" Clay's next scream cut off abruptly as Riordan's huge fist struck him squarely between the eyes, and he collapsed to the floor like a rag doll, blood streaming from his broken nose.

Riordan stepped back and sighed, massaging his knuckles as he listened for any sign that the man's ravings might draw someone in to check on the prisoners. He'd only seen the one guard when he'd followed Sabina's trail into this place, and Seriena knew that guard wouldn't be causing any trouble, but he couldn't know who might still be lurking in the maze of tunnels.

At last satisfied that no one was coming, Riordan started off down the corridor away from the cells, but stopped thoughtfully after only a few paces. He turned back to stare at Clay's limp form sprawled on the floor, shook his head, and sighed, before turning away again and walking off. His footfalls faded in the distance, leaving the cells in a silence broken only by a few quiet rustlings and squeakings, until at length they were rejoined by the sound of approaching footfalls.

"Fine," Riordan said, trying to rub the tension out of his forehead with the knuckles of one hand as he drew to a stop. "Have it your way." He lofted the burden from his other hand through the bars, and Sabina's severed head bounced a couple of times before rolling to a stop in the middle of Clay's cell.

Two of the wolves had died by Tobias' sword in the first moments after he'd broken away from Keely's embrace, but the other beasts coming on had barely seemed to notice. In the grips of some blood madness, gaunt and hungry and glassy-eyed, they came rushing on like demons more than wolves.

Keely tried to stumble away, but the fatigue she'd built up as a feline hadn't vanished just because she'd returned to her hardier human body. Conrad caught her as she started to fall. All his awkwardness at her state of undress dispelled by the urgency of the moment, he half led, half dragged her off through the forest while Tobias covered their retreat with deadly steel.

It was not just the three of them beset, though. Shouts, screams, snarls, and howls echoed through the forest all around them, testifying to the presence of dozens of wolves coming into conflict with the scattered agents of the Inquisition. Somewhere in the chaos, Keely became aware that the swordsman and the giantess had joined Tobias in his fighting retreat.

Then it was knights and priestesses of the Inquisition forming up and falling back with them, the deadly enemies of mere moments ago transformed into allies of necessity by a common foe bent on ripping out the throat of anything standing on two legs.

Keely saw one inquisitrix narrowly escape the jaws of a wolf with a running leap to a low-hanging branch. Then she saw a knight and a priestess fighting back-to-back, dragged down under the weight of half a dozen wolves, and in the ensuing moments wished devoutly that she could close her ears as easily as she could avert her eyes. The wolves had achieved a bloodthirsty state of pitiless savagery so intense that it seemed almost human.

Then water came splashing around her ankles...her knees...her thighs. They'd made it back to the lake, and Conrad had led her straight in 'til they were up to their waists. As she continued to lean on him, gasping for breath, his sword would slash at any wolf foolish enough to try to pursue them into water too deep for it to stand and fight in. In another moment, Tobias was at their side, and soon a wall of steel-armed humans stood staring defiantly out from the lake at the larger lupine wall formed up along the shore.

Tense moments passed, the stalemate punctuated by threatening growls from the wolves, while crimson clouds of blood from the wounded spread out through the water and dispersed into the lake. Then shadows stirred back among the trees behind the wolves, and the center of their wall parted deferentially.

Into their midst stepped a woman flanked by two men, all carrying steel-tipped spears, the woman holding a flintlock pistol pointed casually out toward the people in the water. The fair-complected trio all wore their auburn hair long and braided, and a few bits of gold jewelry. Intricate scrollwork tattoos of blood red hue covered nearly half of their exposed flesh—which also worked out to half of their total flesh, because pretty much all of it lay exposed.

"Are you listening?" the tattooed woman asked with a severe scowl and a thick accent that Keely couldn't begin to place. Perhaps it was the setting as much as the sound, but the voice seemed to hold a hint of canine growl.

"The witch!" a bloodied woman three priestesses down, staring pointedly at the newcomer, hissed triumphantly. How many different creatures had the Inquisition declared to be *the* witch in the last half hour alone? Keely began to think she'd need to have Elissa start taking notes, lest they completely lose track of this aspect of the con.

"Shut it!" the tattooed woman snapped, leveling the flintlock at the speaker. "This is not your forest, plains-woman, and we do not have the glyphs you seek. You'll spill not another drop of our blood looking for it.

"You have declared war on the Tuatha. We accept. My people have driven you back to your plains time and again since the dawn of the world, so go huddle behind your walls and pray for the protection of your demon queen. The Lady of the Forest calls for your heads."

"Oh, no," Keely murmured almost inaudibly in the ensuing moment of silence. Around them, all heads of the Inquisition were turning to gauge their leader's reaction. With every nerve in her body on edge and every instinct in her head screaming, Keely kicked at Tobias' leg under the water to draw his attention and mouthed a single word. "Swim!" Without waiting to see his reaction, she shoved all her weight against Conrad, forcing him deeper into the lake. "Get down! Get away! Go!" she hissed in his ear. "Swim!"

Behind her, a howl of defiance erupted from the Inquisition, coupled with the splashing of its charge back toward the shore. A shot rang out.

Wolves snarled. Two feet to Keely's left, an arrow zipped past at the level of her head. The world went even more crazy than before.

It was all she could do to stay afloat, but Tobias hooked an arm around her as he swam past, and he began to pull her along with him while arrows launched by archers hidden in the tree line pelted past. Even dragging her along, Tobias still outpaced Conrad, as well as the swordsman and the giantess trailing after.

The battle was still raging back down the shore when they waded out of the lake some hundred yards closer to the island. Even the sky was getting into the spirit of the moment, growling with the thunder of a returning storm front. Keely had already managed to lose Conrad's cloak, but Tobias forced his on her as they emerged from the lake.

"Never, never, never issue an ultimatum to a fanatic." Keely sighed, glancing toward the bloody battle. She paused for a moment, mentally opening to a fresh page in the Rules and jotting down the insight. Then a stroke of lightning split the air so close overhead that the combination of alarm and concussive force literally knocked Keely off her feet. Even the flicker of light that preceded the thunder had only done so by a split second.

Finally shocked out of their frenzied state, the remaining wolves disappeared into the forest in a heartbeat. Deprived of their canine support, the tattooed folk broke and ran only moments behind. They left a handful of knights and priestesses standing dazed and bloodied on the shores of the lake, amidst a field of the dead, the dying, and the direly wounded. The forest fell briefly into near silence—then a scream cut through the air almost as sharply as the lightning bolt had. The forest had already been ringing with screams for several of the longest minutes Keely had ever known, but this one stood out for its different and entirely unexpected tone. The voice lacked any trace of fear or terror or pain, which really didn't leave it much of anywhere to go except rage, yet it lacked the timbre of either the Inquisition's self-righteous anger or the wood-folks' defiant resolve. What it carried was the fury of a child's violent tantrum.

"No!" the girl screamed. "No no no no no!" Her voice tore through the forest like the wail of a banshee. "I was *using* that!" Then the storm broke all at once, drowning out all fury but its own, and blinding Keely to anything beyond five paces.

"The island!" Keely pointed off down the shoreline as she yelled to be heard above the sudden roar of wind, rain, and thunder. "There's shelter on the island!"

CHAPTER TWENTY-NINE

BONE PIT

"No!" Elissa's voice rang sharply through the mausoleum, even above the thundering downpour outside. "Keely, you are *not* going to do this." All eyes turned to take in her resolute glare. "You came clean with me. You came clean with the Haywoods. Now you are going to come clean with prince charming over here," Elissa said, vaguely waving a hand in Tobias' direction without taking her glare off Keely, "or I will. We're *all* in it up to our necks with the Inquisition now, and he needs to know."

"Know what?" Tobias asked with uncharacteristic caution.

"Fine." Keely did her best to let the resignation in her sigh drown out the relief. She'd been looking forward to a few more of those kisses before putting this particular deception to rest, but had to admit to herself it wasn't just the physical fatigue getting to her. She'd been juggling too many balls for too long, and had started making reckless, over-emotional decisions like the one that had nearly gotten her killed just now. The stakes had gone far too high for her to play this game sloppy.

"Look, your highness...I'm nobody. I'm not noble. I'm not a witch. I'm not even related to a witch. The only witch in this story is in the fevered imaginings of the Inquisition."

"But...you were a...cat," Tobias protested haltingly.

"Yeah. I can do that." Keely shrugged. "I just can. I didn't bargain with any forces, dark or otherwise, for it. Being able to turn into a cat makes it easy to spy on pretty much anyone, so it didn't take long for me to learn how to fake being a noblewoman.

"I'd lived in a backwater fishing town until the Inquisition burned it down and killed practically everyone I'd ever known when I was barely more than a kid. After that, I did whatever it took to survive, until I fell in with a family of...traveling storytellers. We were paid to crash your party and find that book. We didn't have a clue what was in it until I found Elissa to read it for me."

"But the *book* is the real deal," Elissa stepped in. "Jane Carver herself wants us dead just because we know it exists, and the Inquisition is here because this is where the trail to the Grimm Truth leads. I hope you'll pardon me saying this to a man of your station, but you and your friends need to get out now and pretend this whole adventure never happened, while you're still nothing to the Inquisition but nameless henchmen to an imaginary witch. You wouldn't be the first prince Jane Carver's destroyed."

"We're not leaving without my sister!" Baldassare protested hotly.

"But if there's no witch," Evadne asked, "who turned Sabina into a deer?"

"No one," Doryne assured her. "That doe was just a doe."

"But it was—"

"White. Yes," Doryne said. "She was a ghost deer."

Tobias started to muster another question, but Minda cut him off. "No, not an actual ghost. Probably not. I guess. I've never tried to kill one. It's supposed to be bad luck. But they're not that rare in the forest. I've seen them at least half a dozen times myself." She cast a glance at Baldassare. "Your sister's lost in the woods, which is plenty bad, but I think it's safe to say she's still your sister."

"We're not going anywhere," Tobias said, folding his arms over his chest. "We're staying. We're finding her. And the Inquisition can..."

"The Tuatha are going to make finding her a lot dicier, too," Ulric cut in. "Probably a worse danger than the Inquisition, after that skirmish."

"I think I can handle a few savages," Tobias replied, undeterred.

"Who *are* these 'Tuatha'?" Keely asked.

"The hill folk of the deep forest," Ulric said. "Never seen them myself, but you hear stories."

"Never thought they *actually* ran with the wolves," Minda said. "Makes me wonder how many of the other stories are true."

"*None* of which changes *anything*," Tobias said.

"We've got a very important inquisitrix tied up downstairs," Elissa offered helpfully.

"Enough!" Tobias snapped. "*We stay!*"

"And *you*," he added, rounding on Keely, "are *not* getting off with a shrug and an apology!"

"She apologized?" Ulric asked with a smirk. "I missed that."

"You're not helping!" Keely said with a glare.

"I have so many bones to pick with you we could start another graveyard," Tobias growled. "Where do I even *begin*?"

"With a generous display of mercy and forgiveness?" Keely asked hopefully.

Tobias responded with a grab and twist of her ear. "Am I given to understand that the only other available space is currently occupied by an inquisitrix?" he asked of the gathering in general.

"Pretty much," Nolan confirmed.

"Then we shall finish this outside," he said, dragging the wincing Keely toward the door. "I apologize for the scene. And have no concerns. I shall return her to you..." He paused, considering his words carefully. "...in reasonable condition."

"It's kinda wet out there," Elissa observed.

"We're already soaked through," Tobias answered without missing a step.

"I'm not!" squeaked Keely, who had returned the borrowed cloak for her own clothes. They remained mercifully dry and warm right up to the moment Tobias dragged her out into the downpour—a moment which chanced to coincide with that of a nearby crack of thunder.

"Do you know how many kingdoms I chased you through?" Tobias demanded as he pulled her around to the leeward side of the mausoleum, away from the worst of the wind and rain.

"I didn't count." Keely admitted, fidgeting as rain poured off a gargoyle and down over her head. There hadn't exactly been toll collectors waiting at neat little border walls to mark the transition.

"Five! Five kingdoms! And for what?!" Tobias demanded.

When he paused expectantly, Keely—who felt like the earth had been snatched out from under her—prolonged the moment by pushing her sodden hair back from her eyes and shielding her face from the downpour. Taking a deep breath as she did, she opened the Rules to page one and listened to her mother's advice to restore her equilibrium. When she looked up a moment later, it was the prince's turn to be thrown off balance. All traces of the momentarily shaken and cowed creature had vanished as Keely looked him squarely in the eye and replied, with a firmly set jaw, "For me."

Words failing him, Tobias only replied by deepening his scowl while his mind scrambled to regain conversational traction.

"You did it for *me*!" She raised her voice against the storm as she advanced on him aggressively, prodding his chest. "You did it for the crazy girl who crashed your party, fired up your imagination, and ran away without her dress! By the time I sent Elissa to you, you were already turning Serylia upside down looking for me. The witch was never more than an obstacle to you. *I* was the adventure—a riddle to be solved.

"Well, guess what?" she pressed. "You solved me! You win. Quest achieved. Don't like the answers you found? *Tough!* I finally found *my* purpose. Yes, I used you for it. Yes, I lied to you. But you've got a name, a title, power, wealth...and what? You use it all to go chasing after some girl who drops her dress on your front steps?! I've got *nothing* except what I can lure people into parting with, and let me tell you, they don't part with much for a backwater orphan hiding from the Inquisition. I lie or I die or I sell myself for my looks. Which road would you take?"

Tobias started some sort of an answer, but Keely didn't wait for him to get it out. "I *had* a new family of sorts," she said. "It was an odd sort of family, but it was *mine*. Then the Inquisition came barging into our lives, ready to torture and kill every last one of us over a lousy, stinking book not one of us could even read!

"I try not to get angry. I try *so* hard not to get angry. It's *really* bad for business. But I am royally ticked over this, and I am not letting the grudge go until the Angelis herself sees the Inquisition for the abomination it is, and until I see Jane Carver boiled in her own oil. So pardon me, but, yeah. I put myself ahead of you here, because I think my needs are a teensy bit more important in the grand scheme of things. And if you can't forgive me, then get out of here, and good luck finding your friend. I'm sorry she went and got herself lost, but—"

Mid-thought, Keely found herself abruptly unable to speak, owing to Tobias' mouth pressed hungrily against hers. There was nothing tender in the kiss this time, and nothing tentative—no pretense of asking permission. There was only the raw, overwhelming physical need, and she welcomed it.

Her fingers curled unbidden about his neck even as his weight bore her back against the cold, hard wall of the mausoleum. Her tongue sought his as the rain cascaded off the roof in a waterfall around them, soaking them both through and through, and neither of them spared the drenching a moment's thought. A muffled moan escaped her lips as his hand found it's way down over the curve of her hip and thigh.

"You're right," Tobias murmured, finally breaking the kiss. "You're the adventure."

Keely wiped the rain out of her eyes again to smile brightly up at him.

"I honestly hadn't given much thought to witches or to Inquisitions either one before you tangled me up in all this, but the Inquisition did make an enemy of me today—and you may have well saved my life. You were remarkably brave trying, in any event."

Keely couldn't suppress a chuckle. "I don't do brave. I was only running away very aggressively."

"I'm in, Keely," he said, ignoring her attempt at self-deprecation. "Whether it's a witch or witch-hunters that I'm protecting you from, I'm not ready for the adventure to be over."

"It wouldn't just be protection," Keely answered soberly. "I don't know if they've really been chasing me all these years, but I've been too scared all this time to stop running anyway. That's done. I'm taking the fight to them, now. I want blood."

"I won't lie." Tobias shrugged. "I've got some reservations about that, but no one's ever accused me of over-thinking things. My gut says by your side is where I belong right now."

"Really? That didn't feel like your gut," Keely giggled, boldly running her hand over the front of his trousers.

"Then you know I'm not kidding," Tobias said, "when I say I'm going to ravish you if we stay out here any longer."

"And me with a vendetta to organize," Keely sighed. "I guess this isn't the time or place."

Tobias nodded. "The storm has probably driven the Inquisition and the Tuatha to cover, too, but no telling what trouble they'll cause as soon as the rain lets up."

"All right then. Hold that thought. But we've got the rest of this all sorted?" Keely asked him. "Friends?"

"Friends," Tobias agreed.

Keely leaned her head on his shoulder as they walked back toward the mausoleum door, feeling very warm despite the pelting rain. Still, she released his arm before they reached the door and replaced her momentarily contented expression with one of stern resolve before stepping inside.

"His highness and I have worked out our differences," she announced without risking a pause in which anyone else could take charge of the situation. "We've agreed to focus on our new mutual enemy, the Inquisition, and on rescuing anyone we can who needs it. Yes, your sister's on the short list," Keely assured Baldassare, "but I suggest we start with ourselves."

Visions of that grisly aquatic graveyard deep inside the Wolf's Tooth danced through her mind as she continued. "It sounds like none of us knows quite what to expect from these forest folk, but if I know people—and I *do* know people—they'll be as quick to see Inquisition everywhere as the Inquisition is to see witches and demons. This war's just started, and once the rain lets up enough for them to rally, both sides will be back here looking for their enemies along the shores of the lake."

"We can't wait here for them to find us," Ulric agreed. "But let's be clear: this is county Haywood, not whichever far, far away world you folk are from. We play this game by Haywood rules. Right here and now, with the county burning around us, those rules put me in charge. 'Highness' or 'lowness', make your peace with it or we part company, and good luck to you. I'll point the way out of the forest. Otherwise, you're on your own from here."

Baldassare gave Ulric a dark look and seemed on the verge of saying something *someone* was sure to regret, but Tobias laid a hand on his arm. "The man's right. With this downpour, we'll never find the doe we were chasing even if that *was* Sabina. That means your sister's trail has gone cold. Chasing through this wood without a guide was bad enough before. Now it's turned suicidal. So either we throw our lot in with the locals, play nice with them, or we sit at their inn and wait for her unlikely return."

The angry set didn't leave Baldassare's jaw, but actual thought seemed to be going on behind his eyes.

"You're a proud man, true and plain," Tobias said calmly, "but if you're the sort of man who puts his pride ahead of his family, then I'm Miraculata Winnifred."

Baldassare let out a breath and nodded, sizing up Ulric. "Your word as a gentleman that we'll have your aid finding my sister?"

"I'm not—" Ulric began.

"Yes," Minda cut him off quickly. "Yes, you are." When he started to protest further, she grabbed him and pulled him aside. "It'll be hard enough having noblemen thinking they're taking orders from a common knight," she hissed. "You are *not* going to make this worse by telling them you're not even that. I'm knighting you here and now. If we survive to tell the tale, you'll have earned it. You can do the whole kneeling and sword thing with Daddy later, but now you're going to turn around and reassure our guest with your word as a gentleman. Got it?"

"Ah, yes, Lady Minda," Ulric said, turning back and clearing his throat with a cough. "Of course you're right.

"By my word as a gentleman, and by the hospitality of my Lord Haywood, I'll do whatever good conscience allows to help you find your sister."

Baldassare nodded his acceptance, mollified.

"So, first things first," Ulric said. "We need to relocate immediately while we've got a heavy rain to cover our trail, and not just mud to mark it for anyone who might come looking. The ruins of Caer Cacamwri should make our best base of operations in the forest. It's far enough in that the Inquisition should be hard-pressed to find it, but not so far—"

"The one-eyed wolf!" Elissa blurted abruptly. Everyone looked to her questioningly.

"It's the one-eyed wolf we need to make for!" she went on, turning to Minda. "That thing you said the Inquisition was trying to find! Look at this!" She fumbled to produce the damp page of bilge glyphs from the folds in her robes. "Right..." she traced a searching finger over the page. "Right...oh, damn. *Before* it got smudged, there was a glyph I was puzzling out—a wolf's head with one eye a circle and one eye an 'x'. I thought they were talking about a wolf hiding in the woods or something, but I just realized, it all makes sense if the wolf *is* the hiding place. We *have* to beat the Inquisition to the one-eyed wolf!"

"You're sure?" Ulric asked.

"Of course not!" Elissa answered. "I'm trying to sort this out with one part guesswork, two parts hope, and three parts wild and unfounded supposition. But the Inquisition was sure enough about it that they were ready to maim anyone they could reach in order to get there in a hurry. Can we *not* race them to it?"

"You heard our scholar, folks," Ulric said. "We're moving out *now*— two teams. Nolan, take our new friends, Doryne, and the prisoner to Caer Cacamwri to set up camp. Everyone else with me."

Tobias cleared his throat. "With all respect due your current role, I have to protest one thing."

"We don't have time for..." Ulric began crossly.

"I chased this young woman all the way from Serylia," Tobias said. "We've settled our differences. We *haven't* finished our business, and she has a habit of simply vanishing every time I turn my back. I'll follow your lead for everything else, but where she goes, my squire and I go."

"Fine," Ulric snapped. "Let's move."

Heading straight out into the storm might have been necessary, but that didn't make it safe, and it certainly didn't make it pleasant. The clouds blotted out the sun, the treetops blotted out the clouds, and the rain obscured everything. Their little company might nearly as well have been traveling by night—and without Minda's confident guidance, they would have been lost within minutes of leaving the lake shore.

The thought of feline eyesight tempted Keely to change back into a cat, as did the thought of riding on someone's shoulder—drained as she still felt from her earlier exertions—but she feared that to do so would be rubbing her past deceptions in Tobias' face, and spending the day in sodden fur held even less appeal than spending the day in sodden clothes.

Even filtered through the forest canopy, the cold rain poured down steadily on their heads and pooled around their feet in muddy rivulets or standing puddles. The foliage did manage to break the velocity of the rain's fall and to provide them with a wind break, but it couldn't hold back the sheer quantity of the torrent spilling from the sky.

"*Someone* up there's sure upset!" Keely observed, shielding rain from her eyes as best she could as she stared upward. "Do miraculatas ever do storms?" she asked.

"There's precedent," Elissa said. "But this doesn't feel particularly holy—just wet and cold. Maybe angry."

"They say demons up in the hills send storms like this," Minda said between cracks of thunder as she ducked under a low-hanging, wind-blown branch. She cradled her carefully wrapped rifle to her body as protectively as she could, clearly uneasy about having to trust the oilskin to keep her prized weapon safe from the elements.

"It's just the sky gnomes," Conrad said.

"Sky gnomes?" Elissa asked dubiously. "Gnomes are earth elementals."

"Oh, sure," Conrad agreed. "Just not the sky ones."

"His grandmother considers herself something of an expert on the alchemical sciences," Tobias murmured in Elissa's ear. "She's deucedly good at making things explode, just not generally when she means to. In any event, the boy worships her. I'd just let it go."

"Next person to float a theory for who's making it rain," Ulric said evenly, "had better be ready with a theory for how to make them do it somewhere not on top of us."

"This is my chastised face," Minda said, glancing back at him angelically. "You know, the one that exudes contrition together with..." Her sentence ended in a short, sharp shriek, that in turn ended with a very substantial splash. In the blink of an eye, she'd vanished into the puddle they'd been forging through, leaving behind only ripples.

"Minda!" Ulric charged forward, stopping just short of where they young woman had vanished, and raising an arm to hold back the others crowding up behind him.

Before anyone could commit to doing anything more, her head broke the surface, gasping and spluttering, followed by her hands clawing for anything to latch onto. What they found was Ulric, who heaved her up out of the water, ignoring the small, desperate scratches he received for it.

"Artema!" Minda wailed. "She's in there!"

"What? Who?" Tobias demanded.

"Her blasted gun," Ulric explained even as he shed his pack, then plunged feet-first into the muddy waters.

Keely peered after him, seeing nothing, trying not to be concerned. While there was no telling how deep the waters might be, at least they were still, and Ulric—unlike Minda—had gone in fully prepared. Tobias shouldered his way forward to stand beside her, tensed to do something, but clearly uncertain as to what he *could* do.

After many long seconds, Ulric surfaced, hefting his burden into the shallow water at Minda's feet. To Minda's credit, she only backpedaled a couple of steps and said quietly, "That's not Artema."

Ulric wiped the water out of his eyes and stared at the long, solid bone that might easily have been a human femur. "I'm...in a bone pit, aren't I?" he asked Minda flatly.

"Pretty sure, yeah," Minda said.

He swam a stroke over along the edge of the submerged pit and looked up for a moment at Minda's empty arms, clutching at her shoulders as she shivered. Then he looked on up into her eyes. Then he muttered a curse and ducked back under the water.

"A bone pit?" Keely asked from behind her best poker face as the seconds ticked by.

"Tuatha burial bogs," Minda said.

"Imperial," Elissa said, then repeated when all eyes turned questioningly to where she was prodding at the water with a stout stick, exploring the edge of the pit. "Maybe Tuatha threw the bones in, but that pit started out as an imperial-dug cellar."

"Really?" Minda asked archly. "What architectural detail of mud gave it away?"

"Well, there's the nice, straight stonework lines along the edge," Elissa said without looking up from her prodding. "Then there's that." She pointed over their shoulders to the right, toward the towering statue that stood upon a rocky promontory not thirty yards away.

Though it stood half-obscured by rain and foliage, and though its features had been eroded by the passage of centuries, there could be no mistaking the iconic image of the emperor Marcus Lupus astride his rearing horse, sword held low in his right hand, falcon alighting on his raised left hand, and a lioness stalking along the ground at his right.

"Okay," Minda admitted. "I'll give you that one."

"Whatever building rated that statue had to be big and important," Elissa said, finally tossing aside her stick and standing back from the edge of the pit, visibly relaxing as she put some distance between herself and it. "Odds are it came with big and important cellars, and with a whole compound of lesser buildings that may have had cellars of their own. There'll be no trusting standing water around here. We'd best head for higher ground."

Ulric's head broke the surface of the water again, thoroughly muddied and gasping for breath. This time when he tossed Minda's hunting rifle at her feet, it was really Minda's hunting rifle—still wrapped in its oil cloth, for all the good that did it now—but he was grimacing as he crawled up out of the pit, favoring his left arm. "That new title comes with a nice estate, right?" he asked Minda. "A really, *really* nice estate?"

"Only if my father has any sense of justice," Minda said, hugging the rifle fiercely before leaning it against a tree so she could get down and have a look at Ulric's arm. "You're bleeding."

"Probably stabbed it on someone's rib," he muttered. "It's nothing."

"Yeah, right," she said as she watched the blood dripping from his torn sleeve to dilute into the muddy water. "We've at least got to bind it. Get that shirt off."

Especially after those steamy, stolen moments with Tobias, a proper lady would have studiously avoided watching Ulric stripping out of his soaked shirt—but there was nothing proper about any of the claims Keely had ever made to ladyship, so she found herself repaying his earlier appreciation of her legs by taking a moment to look over his well-muscled torso, thoroughly storied with scars. It was, she concluded, a very good torso. It suited him.

Studying the bleeding arm she left to Minda, who—with the help of supplies from Conrad's un-muddied pack—cleaned and bound the wound with business-like detachment.

None of it distracted her for long from thoughts of the bone pit and what it had to say about the pool at the heart of the Wolf's Tooth. Was this pit really only filled with clean old bones, or was Ulric just trying to keep from freaking the rest of them out? In that mud, whatever he'd discovered, he'd discovered by groping around blind. Bad enough searching a pile of bones that way, but her head filled with nightmares of what that would have been like had the pit harbored recent corpses.

And was this really just the odd ritual of a barbarian culture as Minda thought? She couldn't imagine those folk they'd met at the water's edge slipping out unnoticed, across pasture and orchard, to conduct routine burials in that distant cave. But if they didn't do that, had they done this? And if not them, and if there were similar pits scattered around the forest, then who? How? Why?

None of the plausible answers she could come up with were answers she liked, and even the most plausible of those answers seemed improbable. The one thing she felt certain about was that she'd stumbled into something she wanted to stumble out of at first opportunity.

Keely was still staring out across the standing water, in morbid contemplation of the pit beneath, when she saw a faint, flickering swirl of red brighten up the murk from below. She froze in horrified fascination, as in an instant her doubts that the two dreadful pools were connected dissolved, along with her doubts that she'd really seen something stir in the depths beneath the Wolf's Tooth.

When the surface of the water began to bubble, to where there could be no mistake that it was still just roiling from the impact of the rain, Keely finally found her voice, small and faltering though it was. "Run," she said, though so quietly that no one paid it any mind, if they even heard it at all.

Whatever lay beneath still moved in an unsteady meander, but it seemed to be meandering in their direction—particularly toward Elissa, who still stood disturbingly close to the edge of the pit, her back turned to it as she exchanged words with Minda that might as well have been random babbling for all the impression they made on Keely's brain. At last she broke the paralysis and barged forward, grabbing Elissa by the wrist.

"Jenny, run!" she screamed, dragging Elissa nearly off her feet in the haste to pull her away from the pit.

When her outburst was met with more startled queries than action, she grabbed Tobias next and shoved him after Elissa. "Move it, hero! Go! Go! Everyone out of here now!" That got them started. "Away from here," she snapped to Minda, pointing her to take the lead—and now that Keely had broken the emotional inertia, her will brooked no argument. "And straight for high, dry ground!"

A couple of chaotic minutes later, Keel finally allowed the group to stop on a ridge of rock, and she held up a hand for silence as she peered back into the gloom behind them, straining to hear anything above the sound of the rain through the trees.

"There was something there," she said quietly once she felt certain that, if they *were* being followed, at least they weren't being followed quickly. "Something stalking us under the water."

"Are you sure?" Ulric asked her. The subtext of the question implied she could have gotten spooked and imagined it, but at least it didn't go so far as to sound dismissive.

"I'm sure," she said, folding her arms across herself as she shivered. "Please tell me we're getting close to this wolf-rock thing. The rain is actually getting colder."

"No promises," Minda said. "I never saw that statue before, which means we aren't exactly where I thought we were. It might be another fifteen minutes, or we might be totally lost."

"Right," Ulric said. "We should be well away from the Inquisition by now, and they'll be blundering around without a guide. We'll press on, but if we come across any sort of shelter from the rain, we stop to dry off and warm up while we wait for the rain to clear. This is no place to risk getting farther off the track than we absolutely have to."

CHAPTER THIRTY

ONCE UPON A TIME

"There's not going to be a less bad time," Keely said. She pulled the blanket tight around her otherwise-bare skin while rain continued to rattle the leaves outside their shelter. She, Elissa, and Ulric had each brought packs they'd filled in preparation for an extended round of hide-and-seek with the Inquisition, and had managed to keep most of their contents miraculously dry.

Keely had insisted Minda take the simple, sensible outfit she'd packed for herself, on the grounds that she'd been given it by Minda's family anyway, and that between the two of them, she was the one with no qualms to speak of about lounging around in nothing but a blanket in mixed company. With only three sets of dry clothes available between them, Tobias and Conrad had joined her in blankets of their own.

They'd holed up in what could either be called a shallow cave or a generous overhang of rock, but for the moment what they called it was "mostly dry and out of the wind". Everyone had wanted a fire to gather around, but no one had wanted it enough to overlook what a beacon that would make for all the people they were trying to avoid just now, so they'd contented themselves with the simple pleasure of not being soaked to the skin, and their various shiverings had begun to subside.

"Lady Minda," Keely asked, "what do you know about these 'bone pits'?"

"Less than I thought, apparently." Minda shrugged. "Unmarked mires and pools scattered around the forest, filled with ancient bones. I've seen a few. They're plenty creepy, but I don't know they're more dangerous than any other deep pool or mire in the forest. They make great fodder for ghost stories, and they're supposed to be Tuatha graveyards, like I said. Can't imagine who else could be responsible."

"Even the one in the Wolf's Tooth?"

"Wait...what?" Minda asked with a double-take that Keely found very reassuring. Given that she could count on fully four of the six people present to have her back if the scion of Haywood turned out to be some sort of mad cultist, and that Ulric could at least be counted on to be conflicted if it came to that, now was the time for confrontation. If there were answers to be had, she needed them.

"I've been all over that rock," Minda said. "There's no bone..." she trailed off, frowning.

Ulric gave Keely a sideways stare. "Are you saying you've taken your own dive into a pool of bones?"

"That big, central shaft?" Keely said. "Yeah. That pool at the bottom is full of them...and worse."

"Worse?" Ulric arched an eyebrow, turning his gaze on her fully.

She told them what she'd seen, including the thing glimpsed moving in the water. She'd omitted that from her previous telling to Elissa, as she'd still been trying to tell herself she'd imagined that part. "And three of us have been down there with these things now—four, if you count the crazy guy with the shovel—and climbed back out untouched. But back there, it suddenly dawned on me what roused these things."

When her audience waited expectantly for her to elaborate, Keely looked meaningfully into Ulric's eyes and traced a finger up across her temple, following the red line that had been cut on Ulric's head by the rock falling out of Clay's grip and into the pool. Then Keely touched her arm where Ulric's had just been injured. "Whatever's lurking down there in these pits, it's out for blood."

Tobias gave an incredulous cough, but before Keely could even thank him with a dark glare, Minda rushed in. "Don't go there, city boy," she said with a warning tone that dropped the air temperature several degrees. "*You're* the one who came here chasing a witch who was chasing a book most people say doesn't exist. And even if you weren't, this is a woman I've personally seen march out to face the forces of the Inquisition all alone and armed with nothing but her wits.

"Plus, you know, cat? With all the weird things I've encountered in this forest, I'm a whole lot more willing to believe there's some monster lurking in mysterious graves than to believe Keely here's suffering some sort of hysterical delusions."

"Sorry," Tobias said ruefully. "Sorry. You're right."

"Tell me you aren't going to go back now and try to slay it," Ulric said dryly.

"Of course not," Tobias answered, rolling his eyes. "We've got unfinished business. I'm going back to slay it some other time."

"Good to know you've got priorities," Ulric said. "Killed a lot of monsters, have you?"

"Not really, no." Tobias shrugged. "They're harder to find than you might think."

"How many, exactly?" Elissa asked.

"Well...none. But all the more reason to start when the chance comes up, right?"

"Right now I'd settle for knowing who or what filled the bone pits to begin with," Keely said, uncertain she should encourage Tobias, no matter how much better she'd sleep knowing that whatever was able and willing to lurk in sunken graveyards waiting for blood had had its lurking days put to a permanent end. "I don't care *what* these things are, hundreds of people don't just wander into a hidden cave one at a time and accidentally spill blood into a pool to rouse them."

"Well, if the Tuatha using them as simple burial grounds isn't far-fetched enough for you," Minda said with a joyless little laugh, "there's dozens of less-creditable stories to choose from."

"Are my ears playing tricks," a woman's voice asked a little creakily, "or did someone mention stories?"

They looked up to find a gray-haired woman in a faded red cloak leaning heavily on a gnarled wooden staff and peering at them through the rain from under her hood.

"Granny Rowena?!" Minda asked excitedly, hopping to her feet and scurrying the dozen yards down the hill to hug the woman warmly.

"And what brings my little huntress out here with such a rabble of strangers in tow?" Rowena asked, patting Minda affectionately on the cheek.

"Something much more sensible than whatever brings you out wandering in the rain," Minda said, pulling the woman up toward their shelter.

"You know I never waste time on good sense, dear," Rowena said. "Good sense is like wasted rabbits. You never know one 'til it's bit you on the knee."

"Impeccable reasoning as always." Minda nodded. "Come on and get out of the rain with us."

"I'd as soon invite you to my cottage over the hill," Rowena said. "It's a good sight warmer and dryer, and close enough for you to wake me with all your shouting and crashing about, despite these old ears."

No one argued against the invitation, and grabbing their packs and wet clothes, they scurried on over the hill ahead of their slow-moving host, trying to minimize their time out getting wet again. They soon came to a place where the general tangle of the forest had been replaced with an orchard of stout and strong apple trees that still managed to appear as stunted dwarfs next to the towering old growth that surrounded them.

Though poorly tended and somewhat overgrown, to the extent that the line between orchard and forest tended to blur, the trees hung thick with lustrous red fruit grown impatient for the harvest.

An old path, recognizable even if it was neither well-kept nor well-marked, led them through the orchard into a rocky hollow, where a weathered old shack presented itself as the only thing in the area that could pass for a cottage. There they waited on the covered porch as Rowena and her staff patiently made their way through the rain behind.

"Much as I hate to say, you might want to douse your fire, Granny," Minda said, observing the smoke rolling out of what was actually a rather splendid chimney for such a house. "The Inquisition's back, and about in the forest. You know you're the first sort they like to accuse of witchcraft."

"I shouldn't worry about that lot," Rowena said, though she wrinkled up her nose and actually spit at the mention of the Inquisition before stepping up to open the door and usher them inside. "They've been poking about for a week or more, stirring up trouble, but they've got other things on their mind than witches for once. The fools are actually here looking for a...book." At that last, she wrinkled up her nose again, as if she'd just bit into something truly ghastly.

"All the same," Ulric said. "It doesn't pay to take chances."

"They should've thought of *that* before they started poking around in the forest," Rowena said crossly. "If they want to get themselves killed, it'll not be me standing in their way." She pulled up a stool by the fire and eased down onto it carefully. "Spread your things out to dry, and I'll tell you a story. I do believe I overheard someone asking about the bone pits?"

"Yes," Keely said. "I believe you did."

"There were bone pits in these woods long before there were Haywoods," the old woman began, wanting for no further prompting. "When old Marcus Augustus first marched his armies this way to do battle with the Tuatha, there were bone pits. And when the Tuatha first came to these lands, there...was one little pit, sitting alone in a dark corner of the forest, filled as much with animal bones as the bones of human folk." She paused a storyteller's pause, allowing her words a moment to work on the imaginations of her audience before she took a deep breath and went on.

"Once upon a time, at the edge of this very forest—though its edge has moved a great deal since then—a little girl lived with her mother and her sisters. Don't ask about their fathers, for indeed each girl came of a different father, each man of whom was a right nasty little git, and no one gave fathers much thought in those days in any event. The mother raised her daughters on her own, and glad they all were for it.

"The family was well-loved indeed, for they were all charming and pretty to a fault—and were hardly ever cross with anyone who didn't vex them—but not one of them was more loved or more beautiful than the little girl herself.

"The little girl had a favorite sister who was her best friend in the whole world. While their older siblings would venture out into the wider world and seek what trouble they could find there, the two sisters would retreat together into the shadows of the forest to play and explore and just generally be adorable. Many a secret and many an adventure they shared there, and it was during one of these adventures that her sister came by a fine, crimson cloak so brilliant that it glowed like fire. The sister wore it everywhere, and came to be known for it far and wide, which is why everyone called her..."

"Scarlet?" Elissa ventured.

"...Ruby," Rowena finished, giving Elissa a dark look. "I'm sorry. Did *you* want to tell the story?"

"No," Elissa said hastily. "Sorry."

"Anyway, in those days, no one had even heard of the upstart goddess, and the most-feared spirit for leagues around was Cu Carraig, who haunted the spire of the Wolf's Tooth. Cu Carraig would hoard precious stones like a dragon, and he would demand regular tribute of them and of other things from all the folk and all the lesser spirits who lived in the shadow of the forest.

"A cruel and petty lord, Cu Carraig was as despised as the girl and her family were loved, and one day it happened that he set his sights on acquiring the fairest gem of all—little Ruby—to add to his hoard. And the next time they were playing hide-and-seek in the forest, the little girl discovered her sister's hiding place to be right out in a clearing by a lovely, still pool, frozen into a statue of pure, red crystal. She also found Cu Carraig, who had worked this evil magic, still standing there as a towering mastiff, fifteen feet at the shoulder and made out of rock.

"When she discovered what had befallen her sister, the little girl fell down weeping. She begged and pleaded with Cu Carraig to restore her sister and set her free, but the wicked spirit would have none of that, until at last she offered to trade him any treasure he wanted if she would only return Ruby.

"'Any treasure I want?' rumbled the hound. 'Fine. Go off and fetch me the best treasure you can find before the sun sets. If you're not back here by then, I shall take your sister back to my rock. But if you bring a treasure that I like well enough, I will trade you for her.'

"The little girl ran off, desperately searching for anything that Cu Carraig might value even more than her sister. In her adventures in the forest, she had come across many forgotten treasures, and she raided them all until she had a sack so full of actual rubies that she could barely lift it, and she had to drag it all the way through the forest back to the clearing. She barely made it before sunset, but make it she did, and she dropped the great sack at the feet of the hound, and she said, 'There, Cu Carraig. That is what I shall trade you for my sister.'

"Cu Carraig nosed into the sack, opening it, and the rubies spilled out, gleaming all the more red for the light of the setting sun. Clearly, the covetous spirit liked what he saw, but glancing back at his prize, he shook his head and growled, 'No'. So saying, he grabbed up the sack in his teeth and callously tossed it into the pond, which was dreadfully deep, and the sack full of precious treasure sank quickly out of sight.

"'I have so many cold stones already. I want a pretty, warm stone to keep me company. Bring me something warm and red and precious, and I will still consider a trade. You may have until the sunrise.'

"So the poor, desperate little girl set out at once, cold and hungry and alone, into the dark forest. Had she not known the forest as well as she knew her own dear sister, she could never have gotten far. But she did know it, and she knew all the things that lived there, and so she arrived back by morning.

"'Here is what I will trade you,' the little girl stammered, blinking the tears out of her eyes. She held out in her hands the most adorable little rabbit you have ever seen, and it was as red as red could be, because its mother had been a rainbow. The little girl's hand trembled as she held forth the little rabbit, because it was one of her dearest playmates in the forest, and she felt treacherous indeed for even offering it up. But she had to have her sister back. She simply had to.

"The rabbit hopped out of the little girl's hand, but that was all the courage it could muster, and it stared upward, frozen in terror as the great hound leaned down to carefully sniff at it. At last Cu Carraig cocked his head and sat back on his haunches. Then he brought one great stone foot down on top of the rabbit, turning it in an instant into a bloody mess of fur and bone.

"'No,' Cu Carraig growled, sweeping what remained of the rabbit away and into the pool. 'How could such a little thing ever keep me company? Bring me a fair trade, or there will be no trade at all.

"'I shall give you one last chance,' Cu Carraig growled. 'Bring me a *fair* trade. Bring it to me by sundown. And do not get it into your head that some other little girl can take her place, because she would be worth two or three at least. Bring me a *real* treasure!" And with that Cu Carraig chased the little girl away back into the forest with much growling and impatient snapping. She fled in despair, weeping uncontrollably until not a tear remained inside her to let out. She knew she would have only one more chance, and she hadn't a clue where to begin. She also felt a wretched monster for what had happened to the little rabbit, though what she most regretted was that it had accomplished nothing. Though it hurt to think, she knew she would have done it again if only it would save her sister.

"Something broke in the little girl that morning. Her fragile little heart cracked into a thousand pieces. What she replaced it with, I can't say, but it was something made of sterner stuff. For when at last she returned to the pool, with the sun sinking low over the forest, she came leading a troop of little girls from the nearest village, all trailing along behind her in a chain with blindfolds on, for they thought they were playing a game.

"'You said she was worth two or three,' the little girl announced. 'Here are nearly a dozen. Now give me back my sister!'

"At this the girls all tore off their blindfolds, and looking upon the terrible countenance of Cu Carraig, they all fell to screaming and to running in terror. But with a growl from the great hound, rocks burst up from out of the forest floor, walling the girls in so that their only way to go was toward Cu Carraig himself. Rather than dare that, they cowered back against the wall in fear.

"'Well, this certainly is a lovely treasure,' Cu Carraig chuckled with satisfaction. '*Quite* lovely, and indeed large enough to keep me company. Nevertheless, I shall not trade you for them, for they're clearly not yours to give. In fact, they'd be long gone already—and you with no means to hinder them—had I not trapped them myself. And as I trapped them myself, the entire claim on these girls is mine. You've nothing with which to trade.'

"'Cheat!' the little girl cried. 'I could so have stopped them!'

"The hound snorted in derision, then rumbled, 'I think not. And I should choose my words carefully were I you.'

"'I could too have stopped them,' the girl howled. 'You never gave me a chance, and that's cheating!'

"Cu Carraig narrowed his eyes at the little girl, a deep rumble like rocks grinding together rolling out of his throat. 'Then prove it,' he growled, 'right now. Or I'll break *your* body and cast it into the depths.'

"The little girl had truly spoken in desperation and anger, without thinking, and truly had no plan in mind to prove her point. Suddenly more desperate still, she cast wildly around her for any inspiration. 'You think you're the only one who can play tricks with rocks?!' she cried at last and bent down to heft a rock from the edge of the pool that was nearly the size of her own head. It weighed even more than she'd expected, but with both hands and bent knees, she managed the trick.

"For his part, Cu Carraig only snorted again, and rumbled, 'And what will you do with *that?*'

"The little girl just turned her back and walked away to the wall where the other girls cowered, then with all her strength she heaved the rock over her head and up onto a small ledge. Then she scrambled up after it, and again she heaved the rock up, 'til she'd climbed up high enough to turn and look Cu Carraig in the eye.

"'I'm waiting,' Cu Carraig said impatiently.

"Without saying a word, the little girl gave the hound a curt nod. She closed her eyes and she drew in a deep breath. Then she gave her great rock a shove. For a moment, it seemed to hang in the air. Then the pull of the world caught it, and it fell straight down upon the head of one of the cowering girls. For one endless moment, the screaming suddenly stopped, and the entire clearing went dead silent. 'There,' the little girl said coldly, without a glance down at what she'd wrought. 'She's not going anywhere now, is she?'

"'Nor is she anyone's treasure,' Cu Carraig growled, and—with his patience quite exhausted—he launched himself at the little girl with a snarl. Now it was the little girl's turn to scream. If she'd also been one to cower, that would have been the end of her, but instead she dove from the wall and narrowly escaped being crushed. The wall itself did not fare so well, and shards of rock shattered in every direction. One of them collided with the little girl, who had aimed to land on the grass and flee for her life, and it carried her straight out over the deep pool instead. Down she plunged and down she sank, down, down, down under the weight of the stone, and she too stunned to even wriggle out from under it.

"Down in the dark, even with her final breath fading, the little girl found the she was not alone, for there waited the little rabbit she had sacrificed to Cu Carraig. Now a luminous spirit swirling through the water, it would not speak to her, but only glared at her accusingly. The rubies she'd offered the hound waited there, too, glowing a dull, blood red as they floated lazily about her. The further she sank, the more of dead rose to join her. Fellow victims of Cu Carraig whose remains he'd been consigning to the pool for years, they'd felt nothing of the little girl's treachery, and they watched over her in her final moments, welcoming her into their sunken realm. And the little girl spat in their faces.

"'Is it me you want,' she screamed in her head, her blood burning with hate, 'or is it Cu Carraig?!'

"Cu Carraig had turned one of the girls into a statue of emerald by the time the waters of the pool began to boil unnoticed. He'd turned another girl into a statue of sapphire before a small, muddy hand broke the surface of the pool, and the little girl clawed her way up onto the grass, clutching a single mud-caked skull to her breast. For her bedraggled state, you might have thought her already dead were she not gasping so loudly for breath, yet even that did not catch the hound's notice beneath the screaming of all the other girls.

"Finally, the little girl found her voice, and she yelled out at the top of it, challenging Cu Carraig. 'Cheat!' she repeated, holding aloft the skull. 'Thief! Give me back my sister!'

"Cu Carraig turned, mightily surprised to see the little girl, but only annoyed by her shouting. 'Forget her,' he told the little girl. 'You have no sister.'

"Then you have no life," she hissed. And with that the eyes of the skull glowed red, and the entire pool lurched out of its pit and rose up in a great black mass of mud and bones and tortured souls. It engulfed Cu Carraig and dragged him howling back into the depths with it, never to be seen again. But if you stand beside the right pool deep in the heart of the forest and you listen carefully, you can still hear his tortured howls to this day.

"As for the little girl, she turned her mind immediately to thoughts of finding some magic that could free her sister, but in the struggle between Cu Carraig and the tortured souls, the great hound had fallen on the statue and crushed it into crystal shards. The little girl fell down on her knees and wept inconsolably over the shards until the next morning. The other girls left her to it and fled into the dark forest without a word.

"When the sun at last rose over the forest, after the longest night the little girl had ever known, she got up and she bathed in the pool, which welcomed her now like her only friend in the world, and while no one could imagine her contented, at least she could take some small comfort in the lulling sounds of Cu Carraig's torment bubbling up from below. When she was done, and her clothes were as clean and dry as she could manage, she dressed.

"The last thing she pulled on was the glorious red cloak that was all that remained of her sister. Then she set out to find the other girls, who she knew would have only gotten themselves even more thoroughly lost in the night. And when she found them, she killed them in horrible ways. She killed them to be sure that her family would never hear of the choices she had made. She killed them in horrible ways because they'd done nothing whatever to help her save her sister, and because that gave her something to think about *besides* her sister. But most of all, she did it because now she'd been both the hunted and the huntress, and she'd decided that between the two, she rather liked being the huntress, thank you very much.

"What remained of the other little girls, she dumped into the pool, to hide what she'd done and to keep Cu Carraig company. And when she returned home, she told the horrible tale of how Cu Carraig had lured thirteen girls to their doom, and how only she had escaped by grace of the guardian spirits of the forest who'd ended him. Everyone mourned, and no one suspected, for though the little girl was never the same again, how could anyone expect her to be?

"As to the skull she'd dragged out of the pool, she'd chosen it from all the remains because it had belonged to a great warlord Cu Carraig had crushed, and because it's the skull where the spirit resides and power lies. Through the skull, she could call upon the warlord, and it had been through him that she was able to rally the other dead to take their revenge. She cleaned the skull up and she kept it for herself, wrapped in a blanket in a box under her bed. It would be the first skull of many, for as she grew up and came into her proper magic, like her mother and her remaining sisters, she never forgot how useful a skull could be, or how satisfying to collect them.

"Although she didn't kill again until she was a woman grown, she would come to learn that what she'd first done out of desperation came naturally. It became easy for her. Then it became fun. It snowballed, as these things will do, from taking lives to save herself, to taking lives to protect others, to taking lives to protect things or ideas, until even *she* had to admit to herself she'd started doing it merely for sport. No matter who she'd kill or why, she'd keep the skull, and she'd toss what remained in after Cu Carraig.

"After many, many years, the bones had piled so deep that you could see them during a dry year, so she found another pool to dump them. Then another. So it went, on, and on, and on, for though her family hadn't been able to stand up to Cu Carraig, that didn't make them mortal. Generation after generation of those who *were* mortal learned to fear her, then worship her, then demonize her. But love her or despise her, no one could get rid of her even when she seemed a helpless child, and certainly not after. Bloody Scarlet haunts the forest still, biding her time, waiting to take her vengeance on the upstart goddess who would see Scarlet forgotten, and to consign all her simpering worshipers to the bone pits."

The fire had begun to burn low, and the room had fallen into shadow by the time Rowena finished her story. Silence hung over the cottage—broken only by the patter of the rain outside and the occasional rumble of distant thunder—as she rose stiffly.

"Well, then," Rowena asked, "would anybody like a biscuit?"

CHAPTER THIRTY-ONE

SHE DIDN'T SAY NO

"I don't simper," Elissa said crossly. "I definitely do *not* simper."

"Of course not, Jenny." Keely gave her an encouraging pat on the arm. "I'm quite sure she meant that Scarlet only has it in for those Serinians who *do* happen to simper and bears no ill will for the rest."

The rain had passed, the sun had come out enough to play hide-and-seek through the forest canopy and through the patchwork blanket of clouds still overhead, and their little expedition had been able to return to its journey in a relative lack of discomfort. Most of them had been quietly certain they'd pay the price for taking the time to get dry, but with Rowena's cottage most of an hour behind, they'd still no reason to think that either Inquisition or Tuatha might be anywhere near.

"I'm sure she didn't mean anything by it," Minda agreed as she clambered up a rocky rise to lead the way around a thick brier. "Just one more touch for the ghost story. There's people out here who'd take offense if you tried to say they weren't proper Serinians, but even among those there's no love lost with the church. It never takes much more than the Inquisition noticing they exist for accusations of witchcraft to start flying."

"Tell me about it." A woman sighed as they crested the rise. She sat in a sunny patch on a large rock that did indeed look quite a bit like a one-eyed fox, perched on what would have been the muzzle. "You certainly took your time getting here."

Keely, Elissa, and Tobias all froze for a moment. Age her a decade or two, and the young woman could have been a ringer for the lovely, disconcerting visitor who'd crashed that dinner party back at Denecia. She wore a voluminous, crimson traveling cloak over a dress of dark red velvet, and her long, coppery hair hung in splendid curls over her shoulders.

"We...did?" Minda asked guardedly.

"But I *do* accept your apology." The woman beamed. "Besides, who could walk away from *that* story? Oooo...creepy!" she said with a happy little shiver. "Never gets old. Couldn't have torn yourselves away even if you'd been rude enough to try, I'm sure. So I forgive you, even if you could have tried walking a bit faster after."

"Who *are* you," Ulric demanded, politely but firmly.

"I'm Scarlet." She smiled sweetly, then rolled her eyes at the various expressions that played across their faces. "I know. I know. I get that *all* the time. I've thought about changing the name, but, well...I don't want to. It's a perfectly nice name, and red's kind of my thing." She gestured self-referentially at her hair and outfit. "Anyway, a little badger told me you were here looking for a book of all things, so let's look for it together. Then—since I'm so darn cute and you're so darn nice—you can give it to me. Won't that be fun?"

"I'm sorry," Ulric said. "You clearly think you know us, but we do *not* know you, and this is *not* a healthy time to go trusting strangers."

"But you didn't say no!" Scarlet sang brightly, hopping up off her rock. "That's a start. Look, you know and I know that you've got no call to go traipsing through the forest like you own it, but I like you. Well...like-*ish*," she corrected herself, waving one hand in a waffling gesture. "It's the black-hoods I've got a score to settle with, and as they say, the enemy of your enemy's got the most gorgeous blue eyes that totally offset her hair and her stylish red cloak."

When no one seemed to know how to respond to that, Scarlet smoothly stepped into the conversational void in their place. "So where do we start looking? Yes, I eavesdrop. I know it's a rude habit, but I never put my elbows on the table, so I'm allowed one, right? Point being, I've already searched all over this rock, and it's just not *here*. We need a 'plan B'."

"'Plan B' is you let *them* have a turn searching," Ulric said calmly, indicating his companions with a nod of his head, "while you and I sit and talk so I can keep an eye on you."

"I've *been* sitting," Scarlet sighed, "but I'm up for a stroll. I can play along if you want to make your young lady jealous."

"Yeah," Ulric said, "that'll work." He turned to his companions to urge them forward and to roll his eyes meaningfully in their direction. Still, Keely was glad to note that he'd also laid his hand on the hilt of his blade. Even if the move gave the appearance of a casual, unconscious gesture, to her it spoke of the man's unwillingness to trust the stranger or what lay behind her unhinged demeanor. That was good. The woman gave off exactly the same skin-crawling vibe that had sent Keely scurrying away from her older look-alike, only intensified.

"So, which one am I supposed to be hamming it up for?" Scarlet asked with her own backward glance as she slipped her arm into Ulric's and they wandered away. She'd posed the question in what Keely would have considered a stage whisper, if only the woman hadn't seemed to genuinely believe she wouldn't be overheard. Either that, or she was enough of an actress to be even *more* trouble than Keely had estimated.

As the group spread out to search, Keely laid a hand on Elissa's arm and held her back. "Let's make an honest go of it, Jenny," she said quietly, "but the trail can't go cold here. If we don't find anything else, we find our decoy book. And be sure you sell it to the others. Ulric's the only..."

Elissa waved her quiet and gave a nod of understanding. "Got it."

Under rock and tree root and carpets of dead leaves, in rocky niches and in tree branches and hollows, they searched with a purpose. At first, they mostly seemed to be trying to leave few traces as they went, but Ulric called back, "Quick and messy! Ransack the area. It's been searched once, and daylight's wasting. We'd best be done and gone before sundown!" They took him seriously.

"So," Ulric said conversationally, "you're Scarlet, but not 'Bloody Scarlet'?" He carefully steered their wanderings in a wide circle around the others that always kept at least one of them in sight, though he made no effort to dislodge Scarlet's grip on his arm. It left him certain of where at least one of her hands was at all times and trapped her even more effectively than it trapped him.

Though she wasn't a small woman, he still had considerable mass on her, much of it solid muscle. The closer he kept her while he was evaluating her, the easier it would be to subdue her if it became necessary.

Some part of his brain accused him of justifying and nagged about the danger of close-quarters surprise moves from the woman—a dagger to the belly, a poisoner's ring, and all those other tricks that storytellers will warn you about—but for all his stoicism he was a man, and she *did* have the most gorgeous blue eyes. The other bits weren't easy to push away, either, despite her clearly unconventional grip on reality.

"Do I *feel* like a ghost?" Scarlet giggled, cocking an eyebrow.

"Can't swear I've ever felt one." Ulric shrugged.

"I thought only kids believed in Bloody Scarlet, anyway," she said.

"I believe in what's in front of me," Ulric said, "and I believe careless, overconfident men lead short lives."

"Fair enough." Scarlet nodded.

"So stop evading and give me a straight answer."

"I seem to recall," Scarlet sighed, "that *you're* the one who said we should play this game with our cards close to our chest. So, no, I'm not going to start giving plain, straight answers before you do. Besides, *is* there a straight answer to that question?"

"I suppose not," Ulric conceded. He'd heard at least half a dozen distinctly different legends by now about who exactly Bloody Scarlet was and where exactly she'd come from.

"So let's not quiz each other," she said, looking up at him with a sly, sideways smile, "and get back to making your young lady jealous."

"I'm sure she's quite jealous enough as is," Ulric said.

Scarlet shrugged. "It *is* a fine line to walk, this sort of thing."

"May I ask why you want this particular book?" Ulric asked, pausing to offer her a helping hand across a little stream bed that intersected their path.

She shrugged again. "Why do people want gold? I mean, it's not particularly useful, is it? But it's kind of pretty, and there's not a lot of it lying around. That seems to be enough for kings to raise an army with it and go to war over it. People are already lining up to go to war over this book when they're not even sure it's real or what it's got to say. Maybe it's all shiny and sparkles pretty colors? Anyway, no matter what's inside it, the book is a weapon, and I'd rather have some choice in which direction it's pointing."

Mud flew. Fallen leaves flew. Any rock that didn't seem completely anchored down got overturned. With Tobias and Conrad working together, even some small boulders got shifted. Perhaps a quarter of an hour into the chaos, after receiving one too many face-fulls of soggy leaves, the librarian in Elissa took over and she called for a halt.

"We need a filing system," she said sternly, brushing a clod of earth out of her hair. "The debris is going everywhere, and I can't tell where I've searched from untouched ground that someone's just happened to throw mud on.

"We start over, working out from the rock. I'll go this way." She pointed as she bent down to pick up a fallen branch. "Keely, you go the other. Your Highness, if you and your squire would search out to our left and right respectively? Everyone scoop debris inward toward the rock." She shoved the branch into Minda's hand. "Your ladyship, would you prod the ground and the debris for anything with straight, man-made edges to it, wherever we leave you opportunity?" It was a good librarian voice. No one argued.

Of course, no plan survives contact with the enemy, and a forest full of great, big rocks and towering trees makes for an implacable enemy when what you're trying to do is cover ground in a systematic manner. Still, the organization worked well enough that they could generally tell where they'd been, even if they weren't spreading out in neat, ninety-degree arcs, and hardly anyone got a face full of mud after that.

Despite the chill of the day, they all started overheating from the exertion. At one point, Keely turned into a cat to start scrambling up trees and exploring the branches, and when she came back down after a fruitless search, she only bothered slipping back into her chemise.

Elissa had gotten so used to Keely's casual relationship with clothing that she barely noticed. Tobias arched an eyebrow, but Keely simply countered it with an angelic smile, and he just chuckled to himself and moved on. Conrad clearly noticed, but just as clearly decided it wasn't his place to comment. Minda smirked, but actually seemed to decide Keely was onto something—not that she exactly stripped down herself, but she did wind up shedding what bits seemed extraneous, and loosening laces on some of the rest.

They were in a war zone, now, in the embrace of an untamed forest just off the outskirts of civilization, where propriety and class structure seemed generally willing to bow to expediency to begin with. On top of that, the adventure had already made drowned rats of the driest of them, and silent consensus appeared to be that the motto of "practicality über alles" was fully in effect.

Of course, Keely wouldn't have cried foul regardless when Tobias opted to follow her lead and stripped off his shirt. He definitely sported the musculature to make it scenic as well as practical.

Deepening shadows in the forest had just begun to hint at the approach of evening when Keely, Elissa, and Minda—all filthy and moving with leaden weariness—came picking their way down a rocky slope toward Ulric and Scarlet. The less-than-pristine book clutched to Minda's chest immediately drew their eyes.

"Is this the book you were looking for?" Minda asked, solemnly holding out the weighty, weathered tome.

Scarlet studied the thing distastefully, making no move to reach for it. "You tell me."

Minda shrugged. "All I know is that we got what *we* came for. Sister Jenny has already copied out all the bits we need from this book. You're welcome to take the original as a gift from the house of Haywood, and to go in peace."

"Really? That's so sweet." Scarlet smiled. "Uh...If it's a gift, would you mind wrapping it up for me? I'm not so sure I want to actually touch it."

"Are you sure..." Ulric began.

"Quite," Minda cut him off with an authoritative voice.

"We got what we needed," Elissa said, nodding reassuringly.

A few minutes later saw the book wrapped back up in an old oilskin and Scarlet giving them each a grateful kiss on the cheek. "I really am very touched." She beamed. "Most people are so difficult and unreasonable." Then she glided confidently off into the shadows of the forest, her bright red cloak billowing around her.

"We just slipped her that decoy you made, didn't we?" Ulric asked quietly, never taking his eyes off the retreating figure.

"Yeah," Elissa agreed. "I don't think we'll be needing it after all. Did you ever find out who she was?"

"Not really, no."

Riding back up the Wolf's Tooth, Countess Violet Haywood did her best to remain stoic as she surveyed the devastation. From here, it looked as if the fire had consumed a full tenth of her domain—if not more—in a matter of hours. How many had died? She had no idea, and would likely have no idea for days. At least her own, immediate family was accounted for, thank go'ss, since Evert the huntsman had arrived not an hour earlier with word of her eldest daughter. Not that it sounded like Minda was actually safe, but at least she'd survived the night.

Evert had also brought word of what had been happening up at the cathedral site, so they'd left their younger girls to coordinate relief efforts from the castle while she set out for the Wolf's Tooth and Darby ventured into the Crimson Forest to bring home Minda.

As always, discerning the full truth of what happened remained a guessing game. She'd grown up believing—like most anyone, probably—that being put in charge of something endowed one with a magical insight of the workings and goings on within one's jurisdiction. For her, at least, it hadn't worked out that way. Someone had neglected to inform Seriena when Violet had been anointed lady protector of the shire, because she'd been left bluffing her way through from the very first moment.

Each day dawned as a brand-new dice game, and each new decision felt as if it had to be made more on gut instinct than wise counsel. Looking down upon the countless acres of scorched earth spread out below her, Violet couldn't help but feel that gut instinct was failing her. Had she brought this mess upon them by trusting in a confidence woman?

But, no. That way lay madness. Reliable witnesses had placed Sir Riordan at the site of the first fire when Keely had been with Ulric, and then placed him again at the farm where the inferno began. That the man was an arsonist was a variable they'd had no way to foresee. She would have to cling to the comfort that Seriena had not forsaken them entirely, and had sent rains to douse the inferno before it could take any more from them than it had. Perhaps she'd known this was what they'd needed, to let it go this far and snap them out of their complacency.

Down on the dirty brown line wandering between two patches of ash, she could make out a procession of red and black that could only be the bulk of the Inquisition's force returning to the cathedral site. Best not to dally, then. The longer this went according to their plan instead of hers, the harder it would be to get it all sorted. Violet turned her horse back to face up the winding road, and motioned for the half-dozen men she'd brought with her to move out.

A knight of the Inquisition stood to meet them as they crested the final rise to the construction site, flanked by his squire and a couple of Violet's own men who seemed to have been conscripted by the Inquisition. She could feel her teeth grind at the realization, but she attempted to school her expression.

"Countess Haywood," the knight greeted her—not antagonistically, but far from deferentially—as she slid off her horse. "I'm going to have to..." He trailed off, suddenly aware she had a wheel lock pistol leveled between his eyes from five feet away.

"Yes," Violet said evenly. "You will. This is the second time you people have tried to wage an undeclared war on me and mine. To my eternal shame, I let you get away with it once."

CHAPTER THIRTY-TWO

Bread Crumb

Nolan held up a hand in warning, and the small expedition following him shuffled to a halt. He turned his head this way and that, listening intently and peering into the damp, arboreal gloom.

Doryne now led the ponies that she and Minda had ridden into the forest—one carrying the bound, blindfolded, and gagged Shoshona, the other burdened with the dead inquisitrix. The crypt might have been the perfect place to leave the latter to her final rest, but Minda and her gun had been solidly linked to that island by witnesses from the Inquisition, so they dared not risk it.

Though nothing could be seen moving through the dark forest, at last as Nolan listened, he could make out a sound in the far distance that might have been someone laughing hysterically. It was a chilling sort of laugh, generally reserved for madmen, or at least for men flirting with the prospect of madness. The best thing that could be said for the sound was that—if the echoes in the hills could be trusted—it lay somewhere behind them, and it didn't seem to be drawing any closer.

Taking the sound as a reminder that they weren't alone in the forest, Nolan used the pause in their progress to unsling his arquebus and load it, now that the downpour had passed. Then he nodded and they moved on again to the sounds of leaves rustling underfoot and raindrops still pattering off the trees.

Perhaps Nolan should have let Doryne take point. He was no great woodsman, and she'd certainly passed more hours in the forest than he had. Something about not taking point himself didn't feel right, though. No matter how he'd wound up nominally in charge of this lot, he was no more a leader than he was a woodsman. What he was was a guardsman, and in his experience, standing behind one's charges was not generally the most effective way to get between them and danger.

At least he actually did know the way to Caer Cacamwri, even without a well-worn trail. The trees had been marked after the disaster of the last visit from the Inquisition. He'd been out to the old hill fort a few times since then.

Still, he had no memory of the macabre sight that greeted them at the top of a rocky ascent. Half a dozen human skulls hung there with vines laced through the eye sockets, swaying in the breeze like an undertaker's wind chimes. When Nolan first saw them, he recoiled with such a start that he nearly slid back down the ascent onto the giantess coming up behind him, but Evadne caught him with a steadying hand.

"*More* scarecrows?" Evadne sighed, wrinkling her nose.

"I wouldn't think it's crows they're meant to scare," Baldassare said. "The forest folk made it clear we're not welcome here."

Nolan snorted in a manner that he hoped conveyed disdain as he ducked around the skulls and forged on. From somewhere not quite so distant, the insane laughter echoed through the forest again.

They'd all managed to lose their horses one way or another. Two or three of the animals had broken their legs in the rugged terrain. At least a couple had been torn apart by wolves. The balance had simply run off. With luck, most of that last group would have returned the way they'd come, and could be rounded up once this business in the forest had been handled, but for now, Maritine and her companions forged on afoot toward where she had to have faith she would find the one-eyed wolf.

In all, she'd managed to regroup with eight of her companions—five knights and three priestesses—who'd been fit to carry on into the forest. Despite the rain and the mud and the blood and the cold and all their tragic losses, not one of the eight had intimated for a moment that they should turn back.

Any among them who might have possessed wavering faith had already been weeded out by the attack of the savages, now either dead or fled when their trust in Seriena faltered, so Maritine's resolute nine trudged ever deeper into the dark heart of the forest with grim determination.

We nine, she mused. Yes. It was right. Nine was an auspicious, holy number. Yet again, Seriena had sent a sign that she was on the right path—a path to glorious victory in her name, and to...well, a little girl?

Draped casually over a tree that had fallen across the path, the freckled little redhead lay on her stomach, using a stick to prod at the pages of a book that lay on an oilskin on the ground in front of her, next to a wicker basket. A striking red cloak hung across the girl's shoulders.

"Oh," she said, glancing up to Maritine and her companions. "Hi. I thought you should see this."

"See...what, girl?" Maritine asked suspiciously. She laid a hand on the hilt of her favorite short sword as she advanced, bells of alarm ringing in her head. Adopting a guise of innocence was, after all, a favorite tactic among witches.

"The book you wanted," the girl said, casually discarding the stick and swinging around to bring herself up on the log in a sitting position.

"*That*," Maritine asked with a cocked eyebrow, "is the Grimm Truth?"

"Sure," the girl answered. "I guess that's what you call it. *I* call it 'Fiendish Plague Upon Creation Number Five Hundred and Seventy-Three', but I know that's a bit...wordy."

Maritine edged forward and crouched, her eyes flicking back and forth between the girl and the book as if trying to decide which one was a powder keg about to go off, but the book just lay there and the girl's posture remained relaxed and unconcerned. Tentatively, Maritine reached out and picked the book up off the ground. Nothing went boom.

Marginally reassured, she took a step back and held the thing up for examination. She closed the book, studying the cover and the spine. "Hidden Truths and Perilous Predictions," it read, "from the pen of Miraculata Antonia Grimm." Maritine had pictured something a little more grand or a little more ominous—perhaps both—but the book did appear quite aged. She glanced back at the girl, who sat idly kicking her feet.

"You don't get to keep it," the girl said. "I just want you to know I have it, so you can stop looking for it."

Maritine peered around her into the dark forest for any sign that the confident little witch had accomplices lurking in the trees. In her mind's eye, a scenario quickly played out of herself simply taking the book, the girl transforming into a hideous wolf thing, and a horde of tattooed savages leaping from the trees.

In the desperate battle that ensued, she emerged victorious by Seriena's grace, but many of her companions fell due to her miscalculation of overconfidence. In the end, there would be only three of them. Then, perhaps, only she herself would finally stagger out of the forest, clutching the book, if any more dangers lurked to waylay them as they went.

She shook her head to clear the vision, glancing over her shoulders, left and right, studying the faces of her companions and putting names to them in order to ground herself, placing each in that narrative in place of the nebulous, faceless warriors who had died at her side on that first run-through. Maritine sighed, then squared her shoulder and steeled herself. Yes, she decided. This would work.

She opened the book and began, leafing through it, carefully calculating how she would slam the book into the monster to buy herself enough time to draw her blessed blade. "I'm sorry," she said at last, "but the book's leaving with us, and so are you, on suspicion of..." Her voice trailed off. "What game are you playing, girl?"

"What game am *I* playing?" the girl said with a scowl. "I told you the rules. You're the one trying to..."

Maritine discarded the book contemptuously in the mud. "This is nothing but the Exemplar Serinitas bound up in an old cover." She drew her blade, pointing it accusingly at the girl. "What did you do with the original pages?"

"The ex-whosa which?" The girl's scowl deepened.

"Oh, definitely a 'witch'," Maritine growled, the men and women flanking her taking the cue to draw their own blades, "who can't even utter the name of a holy book."

The girl rolled her eyes, but didn't stir from where she sat. "*This* is what I get for trying to play nice. I really, truly, honestly was going to let one of you leave the forest. But you're saying this *isn't* the book all the fuss is about?"

"Of course not," Maritine spat, stepping up to place her blade against the girl's throat. "I won't ask again. Where are the pages?"

The girl sighed, eyes darkening, though if she gave the blade at her throat any thought, it didn't show. "And here I thought they were being so sweet. Not that it would have made much difference in the end." Finally, the girl seemed to notice the sword as a thin trickle of crimson blood ran down her neck. "Right," she said, casting her eyes in the direction of the wicker basket that still lay on the ground. "In there."

"The pages?" Maritine asked.

"No," the girl replied in a tone of unconcerned sarcasm. "It's goodies for my sick granny."

"You think this is a joke, girl?" Maritine snapped, letting the blade slide lightly across the girl's throat, not deepening the wound, but allowing the blood to flow more freely.

The girl blinked. "You don't?"

"Open it," Maritine said, flicking the sword in the direction of the basket. "Slowly."

Not bothering about the blood trickling down her neck, the girl shrugged, and slid down off the fallen tree with the unhurried, deliberate sort of movements one might employ to avoid spooking a skittish animal.

"Though when I say my granny's sick," she said, unlatching the basket and lifting the lid, "I don't mean she's bed-ridden." The girl reached into the dark interior of the basket with one hand, and slowly withdrew a sun-bleached human skull. "Do you like him?" she asked, holding the skull up proudly for inspection. "I call this one Fenton." She turned the skull slightly so that she could study it herself. "He just looks like a Fenton, don't you think? I brought Bess and Irving, too. Would you like to meet them?"

"Tie the little witch up," Maritine snapped. "We're taking her with..." They were the last words she ever spoke.

Two priestesses and two knights—one of them a dwarf of all things— was all the manpower that the Inquisition had left behind at the cathedral site. Once Violet had reasserted her authority over everyone else on the Wolf's Tooth, it completely broke their spell, and the outsiders found themselves surrounded by three times their number in armed men, backed by a barely restrained mob. The force that had blinded the locals to their present power over the inquisitors in their midst now worked to blind them to the perils of retribution from the rest of the Inquisition.

When Violet had publicly shoved a gun in the face of a knight of the Inquisition, she'd been leaping from a cliff and trusting that the rest of Haywoodshire would leap with her. Now all that remained was the long, blind drop, and the best she could hope would be to find turbulent waters of civil unrest waiting to receive them, instead of the unyielding stone of the known world united against their one small county.

Had the Inquisition really been singling them out all these years, or had they sown the seeds of desperate resentment far and wide throughout the kingdoms? Go'ss, she hoped it was the latter. First, though, she had to make sure they lived long enough to find out.

She'd talked this all out with Darby. The earl had been no less incensed than she that the Inquisition had begun to scale up its bullying once again, and they'd agreed that this time they would not wait around for it to get lethal. But she was the family politician, while he was the family soldier.

That's why she'd set out for the cathedral site with the handful of men they'd judged would be enough to overpower the token guard the Inquisition had left behind on the Wolf's Tooth, but not so large a force as to be instantly spotted as aggressive, while he took the larger force into the forest after their daughter and the bulk of the Inquisition's local manpower.

They had not counted on the Inquisition returning from the forest so quickly. From the look of things they might have made it out before he ever went in. No plan survives contact with the enemy. What she absolutely could not afford to do, though, was allow them to regain the cathedral site.

Quite aside from the location's strategic value as the most defensible point in the county, from there they would be able to hold the construction itself hostage, and make up any story they liked when Pontifine Augusta returned to find the Haywood family laying siege to whatever remained of her cathedral.

This was going to be touch-and-go now, regardless of how she played it. Even adding together the guards she'd brought just now with the guards they'd left at the site before, the Inquisition would have them badly outnumbered and would certainly have them out-trained. She'd never pull it off without an ambush, and there'd be one chance to hit the Inquisition so fast and mercilessly that they wouldn't have a chance to retaliate.

Part of her quailed at the thought, but the main advantage of facing a group with zero tolerance was that you quickly found yourself in a position where nothing you did could make things go harder for you.

"Things are about to get really ugly," she said, addressing the gathered collection of guards, workers, and refugees. "Pretty much every man and woman of you has some memory of the treatment we can expect from the Inquisition, and has been waiting ever since they got here for the other shoe to drop. Well, we're done waiting. This time, no one's going to pretend that their open threats and a few broken bones will be the end of it.

"We all knew someone that the Inquisition put to death last time. Most of us *loved* someone the Inquisition put to death last time. Could you truly gaze into the Eyes of Seriena right now and convince yourself it won't be *you* they're coming for now? Can you look around you and convince yourself that everyone important to you will still be there to see next week if the Inquisition has its way? Can you look out there," she asked, thrusting an accusing hand out at the blackened landscape, "and convince yourself that the Inquisition didn't do *that* to us?"

That last the crowd greeted with an angry chorus of dissent. Facts didn't matter to any man, woman, or child within earshot. The moment any one of them had paused to wonder how the fire had started, his thoughts had rushed to the same inevitable conclusion as swiftly and surely as water running downhill.

"The rest of the inquisitors are on their way back as I speak. They'll be here before the bell tolls the next hour. But they still think we're sheep. They think we don't understand that they've declared war on us. They think we're going to just roll over and let them keep kicking us until we die. But we will not. Never again!"

Violet anchored herself against the giddy wave of feedback as her people allowed her to transform their fears into anger and determination. It came in the shouts and cries of a people suddenly drunk on the hope they needed desperately and hadn't dared allow themselves to reach for before this moment. They were ready to do crazy, stupid things. She needed them ready to do crazy, stupid things.

But she would have to remain the grown-up in the room and not get swept away in the tide of emotion. This would all go for naught if they didn't make the most of the next half hour, preparing for the arrival of the Inquisition.

Slowly, the cheers subsided until only the slow, measured clapping of a single pair of hands remained, drawing her eyes upward to a slender, dark-haired priestess robed in blood-red who was nonchalantly ascending a pile of stone blocks with easy grace. "Well said, child," the woman said with a small smile. "Not that I ever have doubts, personally, but if I *did* have any, they would most certainly have been laid to rest after that."

Violet's emotional anchor abruptly vanished as a whole sea of emotions threatened to capsize her reason in the span of a few heartbeats. Even without the trappings, even through the haze of a decade's worth of memories, she knew that face and she knew that voice in an instant.

The last time that woman had walked into her life, it had cost Violet her only son. He'd been young and hot-headed and unwilling to stand by and watch the Inquisition do its "work". By the time Violet knew what he'd gotten himself into, it had been too late to do anything but try to preserve the rest of her family. She'd remained as calm and rational and calculating about the whole thing as any mother could have managed under the circumstances, and she'd hated herself for it every minute of every day since.

So it was with a resigned sort of helplessness that the clinical portion of her brain stood back and watched as ten years of loathing pulled the pistol from her belt and raised it toward the woman. In the instant before Violet pulled the trigger, she could hear herself scream out one single-minded order, "Kill Jane Carver!"

Caer Cacamwri made the old hunting lodge—where they'd found Minda and Doryne holed up—look like Keely's shiny metropolitan townhouse by comparison. Little remained of the old hill fort beyond patches of crumbling stone wall perched atop concentric embankments of earth that seemed for all the world like natural hillside at this point in their life.

The place must have been abandoned centuries before the first stone was laid for Castle Haywood. The biggest protection it afforded against anything at this point was run-off. The earthworks managed to trap broad, shallow pools of brackish water, creating an upland marsh that Keely approached with considerable unease until Ulric assured her the site was clear of pits, bone or otherwise.

After that, she approached them with only moderate trepidation and a reflexive sense of dismay when her boots would sink to the ankle into the soft mud. It might have been considerable dismay if she hadn't known her boots would manage to clean themselves soon enough. That had actually been her first hint to the nature of their magic.

She also had enough experience with marshes to finally be thankful that the weather had taken a cold turn. During the summer months, the remnants of Caer Cacamwri were surely miserable with biting insects.

Nolan's group had holed up in what seemed to be the one intact structure on the site, a cabin built half into the side of the topmost embankment. Despite its primitive design, the cabin looked sturdily built and couldn't possibly have been part of the original construction. Keely suspected she could count on her fingers the number of years of weathering the little building had seen. It offered only one cramped room to crowd everyone into to get out of the elements, though, and their expedition numbered eleven now, counting the inquisitrix.

Pondering the book she still held close to her chest, Keely reflected that everything was finally coming together now. It was coming together in unexpected ways, yes, but these things always did. That was the fun bit.

They left Shoshona tied to a chair in the cabin under Ulric's watchful eye while Keely led everyone else around to the far side of the hill, where large patches of sunlight managed to make it down through the trees. While the others sat soaking up what warmth they could, Keely held their new prize aloft.

"For those of you who don't already know," she said, "this is *not* the Grimm Truth we found." Keely lowered the book and lofted it toward Elissa, who managed to catch it with only a token amount of fumbling. "It's just another go'ss-forsaken bread crumb." From another woman, that would have probably come out sounding of bitter disappointment, but Keely somehow managed to deliver the curse with such easygoing good nature that it sounded like she'd have been a bit surprised to find the book had been anything else. "So the race isn't over, but now we *do* have a vital clue that the Inquisition knows nothing about. That changes the nature of the game. Jenny?"

Elissa started by clearing her throat and looking sheepishly at the small crowd. "My name's Elissa, actually," she said apologetically. "Anyway, Vyncent Amberford died the same year as the last entries in that journal that started all this. When he stopped writing abruptly after claiming he found the Grimm Truth, I assumed he was killed over it. In fact, it seems he stopped writing when he did because that journal was stolen from him, along with the Grimm Truth. What we have here is the new journal he kept after that, detailing what remained of his life over the next couple of months.

"According to this, he'd 'liberated' the book from what he described as 'a coven of witches who haunted the marshes at the north edge of the Crimson Forest' along the Sanguine River. The coven found him and liberated it back. When he led an expedition back to deal with them, he shattered the coven and its 'brigand supporters'. One of the witches escaped with their 'library of heresies', and the Grimm Truth was last seen headed downriver aboard a small pirate ship."

"Wait," Keely said, blinking. "You said the *Sanguine* River?"

Elissa nodded uncertainly. "Why?"

"The Sanguine River that empties into Lake Etherea?"

"I think so," Elissa said with a hint of exasperation, then rolled her shoulders and angled her back toward Keely. "You want to check my map?"

Keely let the offer pass, much to Elissa's relief. "I once met a pirate queen of Lake Etherea," Keely said, a dark expression crossing her face. "Before the Inquisition murdered her, she implied that magic ran in her family."

"You did? She did?" Elissa asked, thoroughly taken aback.

"Right. No time to get distracted with theories," Keely said, waving a hand intended to be dismissive. "The point is, we're back to dealing with the Inquisition without the benefit of having the Grimm Truth in hand, so our first line of offense will need to be deceit. Jenny's starting to show real promise there..."

Elissa buried her face in her hand. "You are a bad person, Keely," she muttered from behind her fingers.

"...and Ulric seems to have a flare for thinking on his feet. Who else? Don't be shy. A lot of lives are riding on this, including our own." No one hurried to speak up. "Well?"

Finally, Evadne raised a hand—so that she could use it to level a finger at Baldassare. When he cocked an offended eyebrow her direction, the giantess smirked. "If you are no scoundrel, sir, then surely I am a dwarf."

"Excellent," Keely nodded. "I'll take all the scoundrels I can get right now. Anyone else adept at telling tall tales? Keeping a poker face? Leading a double-life as a masked outlaw with a heart of gold?"

Tentatively, after another long pause, Minda raised her hand, and nudged Doryne into guiltily doing the same.

"All of the above?" Keely asked with a hopefulness that just might have been genuine, but then shrugged without waiting for a response. "It's a pity that..." Suddenly her eyes lit up. "The rest of you go ahead and make camp or whatever. Ladies, you and I need to talk."

CHAPTER THIRTY-THREE
GHOST STORY TOO

Hunger, thirst, her bindings, and even the call of nature had done little to chip away at Shoshona's resolve during her captivity. She'd wet the horse she'd been riding when they dragged her through the rainstorm, rather than give her captors the satisfaction of seeing her indignity. And they'd at least poured water into her mouth a couple of times discounting the storm, in a bid to keep her alive for whatever nefarious purpose they needed her for. She'd even been guided on a couple of blind, circuitous walks since dismounting the horse, so had been able to stretch her legs a bit and get the circulation back. Things could have been much worse.

They'd kept her blindfolded, and they'd said little when within earshot of her, but she'd done what she could to learn their individual voices to help her settle accounts later. She'd also done what she could to work out of her bindings, but the witch's foul henchman seemed to be well-versed in knots. She'd made no appreciable progress by the time the blindfold was finally removed, and she found the white-haired witch in the tattered red cloak staring her in the face from much too close for comfort.

"Oh, good," the witch said, "we're awake."

Outside the open door of the small cabin Shoshona found herself in, she could see that the shadows were beginning to deepen toward dusk. She sat tied to a crude wooden chair in the middle of what seemed to be the building's only room. The infuriating henchman who'd pointed a gun at her stood flanking the door on one side, and another man who looked like a one-time gentleman exiled from somewhere stood on the other. In her head, Shoshona ran through numerous curses to hurl, but settled for her best glare, thanks to the gag.

"Thought you'd like to know, I found the book," the witch said, smiling—for lack of a better word—sweetly. "Now I just need a righteous woman to donate for the blood ritual. Oh, wait." Any hint of sweetness drained from her smile. "I've got one."

Behind the witch, a hooded figure glided into the room, and Shoshona felt her hatred redouble to see it was a woman in the silver robes of a priestess. It seemed that the witch's poison had already infiltrated the rank-and-file of the church.

"All those stories about 'Miraculata Grimm', martyred for your church? That was a cover-up, you know," the witch said. "They found out too late where her power came from—that it wasn't holy miracles she was performing. Antonia Grimm was the first real witch, and my great, great, great, great..." She trailed off, counting in her head, then shrugged. "I'm her direct descendant."

Shoshona glared harder.

The woman in silver glided up, stopping a pace to the witch's left and standing silently, her face obscured beneath the hood of the robe.

The witch studied Shoshona's face for a minute, then sighed. "You were more fun when you were yelling at me," she said, reaching up to undo the gag. "This whole 'silent treatment' isn't nearly as satisfying."

"How mortifying," Shoshona said sardonically, spitting the taste of the gag out of her mouth. "I can't believe I've been so rude."

"We can't all be perfect," the witch said cheerily.

"Who's your friend?" Shoshona asked, tilting her chin toward the woman in silver.

The witch swung her gaze past the woman, without stopping, to look back toward the door. "Him? I never can keep track of their names. I just call them Hench One and Hench Two, or whatever."

"I mean her," Shoshona said.

The woman raised a conspiratorial finger to her lips and shook her head.

"Her who?" The witch turned her gaze on the woman, but seemed to be looking right through her.

"They can't see me," the woman said. "I came back to help."

"Came back from where?" Shoshona demanded. "Who are you?"

"Pardon?" The witch turned back to stare pointedly at Shoshona. "I'm the witch you chased across half a dozen kingdoms. I didn't think introductions were necessary."

"They can't hear me, either," the woman said, pulling back her hood to fully reveal the features of...

"The Haywood girl?" Shoshona blinked in surprise. "But..."

"Okay, this is even worse than the silence," the witch said, rolling her eyes with a sigh. "Did Hench Three hit your head on the stone sepulcher last night, because your insanity usually sounds more lucid than this."

"But they killed me, yes," Minda Haywood said with a serene smile. "It's lovely. *Your* work isn't done, though, so I was sent back to make sure you live to complete it. Now hush up about me."

"I..." Shoshona started, but trailed off uncertainly. "I do have quite the headache," she said at last.

Suddenly, from outside came the sounds of clanging and shouting.

"What now?!" the witch asked in exasperation. "Do try to pull yourself together so I can gloat properly," she said as she turned on her heels and stalked out the door. "Hench One, with me," she beckoned, then started shouting herself. "Am I going to have to turn somebody into a newt?!"

Minda sighed. "I was hoping that would draw all of them off. No help for it. It's taking a lot out of me just being here, so listen. She can't be allowed to complete that ritual tomorrow night."

Shoshona nodded her understanding and agreement.

"But you're the key to the whole thing. You're the only woman righteous enough that she'll be able to get her hands on before it's too late. So no heroics. Not until the dawn after tomorrow night. Survive that long, and it will be weeks before the stars align properly again. It won't go well for her, either. She's got unholy bargains to keep. She'll lose some of her support, and her powers will be on the wane."

Shoshona nodded again.

"I'm going to free you, but don't let on until I can go create enough to distraction to draw the other guard out. I don't know if I'll be strong enough to manifest again, but go grab the first horse you find. It will be able to see me even if you can't, and I'll lead it out of the forest. Rally your followers and come back to strike in force two mornings hence." She paused as if rolling a thought around in here head. "Yes, hence. Two mornings. That's a really odd word. Anyway, do you understand?"

Another nod.

"Hold very still," Minda said, disappearing around behind her. "Handling physical objects is turning out to be tricky."

Shoshona felt cold metal against her wrists and a tug against her bindings, then suddenly they parted.

"I'll leave to handle the rest. Good luck, warrior." There came a faint rustling sound, then light streamed in softly from above and behind Shoshona for a few moments before the room subsided back into its previous gloom.

Somewhere outside a gun went off. "Hench Two!" the witch bellowed, and the other guard dashed out the door, leaving Shoshona unguarded. She wasted no time in undoing the rest of her bindings, then looking around for the Haywood girl, but behind the chair where she'd been tied, Shoshona found nothing but featureless walls and a disused fire pit. Tracing the eye of Seriena on her forehead in silent thanks, Shoshona headed for the door.

Keely arrived at the hilltop above the cabin just in time to join Minda, Evadne, and Nolan in watching Shoshona disappear into the forest on her stolen pony.

"Do you think she suspects?" Minda asked.

Keely shrugged. "Doesn't matter. The important thing is she isn't sure you're *not* her divine intervention. That'll be enough to keep her on the path of least resistance for the moment. You did good."

"That pony really knows the way back to the castle?" Evadne asked.

"From here? Ananda could find her way with both eyes shut if she didn't have to worry about tree roots and such," Minda said. "The lantern I left on her saddle is almost a formality. Help me with this." She got down and tugged at the tarp they'd used to cover up the smoke hole over the fire pit, both before and after lifting her out. Evadne set to helping Minda, while Nolan began to wind the rope.

"After our last visit from the Inquisition," Minda said, "Mother and Father laid out an escape route through the forest, clear to the other side, over Whitecliff Ridge, and they made sure their girls knew it by heart. This is where they set up the first supply cache. Ananda there's probably made the trip as many times as I have."

Keely led the way back down to where the others had gathered on the far side of the earthworks. "The wheels are in motion," she announced. "With any luck, she'll spend tomorrow rallying the troops, then lead them into a Tuatha ambush the next morning. Without luck, this still buys us some time."

"We stay the night here," Ulric said, "and set out at first light, heading for the Wolf's Tooth. From there we'll..."

"I'm not leaving the forest without my sister," Baldassare cut in.

"Right, then." Ulric nodded. "Where do we start?" When Baldassare hesitated in answering, Ulric pointed off to his left. "You think she's that way? Or would we have better luck over there?" He pointed to his right. "We've got thousands of square miles of forest out here. Any traces of your sister's passing that weren't obliterated by the storm are currently in peril of being trampled out of existence by one of our warring factions. So we head for the Wolf's Tooth.

"From there, we'll replenish supplies, make sure Earl Haywood is appraised of the current situation, and probably split up to pursue separate missions. One of those missions will be finding your sister. If we assume she's still alive at this point, we should also assume it's because she's taken shelter with someone who lives in the forest, so we'll find you a guide to help you make inquiries among them. Worst case, you wind up with scores of eyes who know the terrain who'll be keeping an eye out for her. Fair enough?"

Baldassare nodded his capitulation. "That'll do."

"We don't have a strong defensive position here," Ulric said, "but we do have enough people to stand watch in five two-person shifts. Let's get that sorted, then get some sleep. It's going to be a long day tomorrow."

The nightmares started again almost as soon as she closed her eyes. It was astounding, really, that they hadn't already hit her the night before. Perhaps she simply hadn't let down her guard yet, even in her sleep, but between having successfully uncovered the secret of the bilge glyphs and seeing Shoshona safely on her way to move things to the next stage of the con, she seemed to have breathed a mental sigh of relief, and everything she'd been holding back came rushing in.

For better or worse, at least it wasn't the usual nightmare. Instead, she found herself on the deck of a ship being tossed on a stormy sea while a squid in an eye-patch struggled to keep the helm under control. Towering apple trees grew where a waking person might have expected to find masts, each growing nearly so fast as the fire that threatened to consume them, so that rather than being reduced to blackened husks, they seemed to melt and flow like candles, raining down cinders and flaming fruit that would crash into the deck or plunge into the sea like fiery cannon balls.

The crash of another ship being tossed sidelong into hers threw her from her feet while timbers screamed and splintered. When she looked up, Keely was there, holding out a hand, her dark hair plastered to her head by the downpour.

"Get up, Jenny!" she demanded. "Move!" Jenilee took Keely's hand automatically and allowed herself to be pulled to her feet. Figures in black, dripping with blood and outlined by dancing flames, had begun to pour over the side of the second ship, blades hacking indiscriminately at anyone or anything within reach. A third ship crashed into the other side just in time for Keely to make the leap over the rail to it, pulling Jenilee after her as the ship they'd been on was swallowed in waves of shadow and flame.

Then they were running and jumping together from ship to ship to ship. Hundreds of apple-tree sailing vessels, large and small, had been caught up in the storm, spreading out endlessly into the darkness with barely ever more than a dozen paces between them even when they weren't being smashed together.

Flames danced across the deck and rigging of most of the ships, and battles raged across even more of them. The dead fought alongside the living, while gruesome things with tentacles and antennae tried to claw their way up out of cargo holds.

"There!" Keely shouted suddenly above the din, pointing accusingly toward a lone figure draped in brilliant red. Stalking across the wildly tilting deck of a nearby ship, she somehow seemed to walk as effortlessly erect as if she were walking across a tavern floor. Keely pulled a pistol from her belt and leveled it at the woman.

"This will never be over so long as that woman draws breath," Keely hissed. She took her time in aiming. "You're a dead woman, Jane Carver!" she yelled as she pulled the trigger. Despite the torrential rains, the powder sparked without missing a beat.

The crack of the pistol echoed in Jenilee's ears—then utter calm and silence fell over everything. Steel ceased to ring. Thunder ceased to rumble. The wind ceased to howl. Not one shot or scream echoed through the night. Combatants stood frozen between heartbeats, their blades half-swung. The ships had stopped rocking. The waves had frozen into glassy green hills. Raindrops hung unmoving in the air.

Nothing moved except the woman in red, who turned and plucked up the lead ball from Keely's pistol, where it had stopped just an arm's length from the woman's head.

"Jane Carver?" The woman spoke quietly, but her voice carried perfectly through the silence. "Who in the bloody hills is Jane Carver?"

"The butcher of Hart Cove," Jenilee growled, finding that she was the one who stood holding the smoking pistol, even as she realized it was the woman who'd called herself Scarlet that she'd nearly shot.

"Huh," Scarlet said. "Never met the butcher, but I did know a few fishmongers in a casual sort of way."

Jenilee frowned, becoming aware of the disjointed state of her own thoughts. "This isn't making sense," she said. "None of this is right."

"Don't blame me," Scarlet said, casually strolling across the lack-of-ground between them. "This is *your* dream. I hadn't even nudged it before you decided to point a gun at me."

"Wait," Jenilee said. "You know Hart Cove?"

"Oh, sure," Scarlet said. "Nice enough place until it went up in flames." Then the ships and the sea were gone, and Scarlet was walking toward Jenilee along the fire-lit streets of Hart Cove, a bloody axe clutched in her hand.

The too-familiar nightmare had returned—they'd just jumped in at the end this time—and in a moment of lucidity, it suddenly dawned on Jenilee that although she'd never seen the face of the butcher of Hart Cove, she had seen the woman's red hair spilling out from beneath her hood. Jane Carver's hair was black.

"You?" Jenilee gasped. "All this time, *that* was you? Why? Why would *you* help the Inquisition hunt down Blackwater Molly?"

"I *never*!" Scarlet snarled, bridging the remaining gap between them in the literal blink of an eye, her free hand closing cruelly on Jenilee's throat. "I never!" she screamed. Jenilee clawed uselessly at Scarlet's hand as the woman lifted her effortlessly off the ground and tossed her like a doll. Jenilee hit a wall hard and sprawled onto the cobbles. "You pathetic little brat! How *dare* you!"

Head swimming, Jenilee fought her way to her hands and knees, only to find Scarlet's boot connecting with her nose. The cartilage gave a sickening crunch and her head slammed back against the wall again. When her eyes swam back into focus, it wasn't Scarlet looming over her with the bloody axe, but the old storyteller, Granny Rowena.

"I was killing inquisitors before you were born," Rowena hissed. She swung the axe viciously so the blunted back of the head impacted the side of Jenilee's knee, eliciting a scream of agony. "I've ended more of your upstart goddess's simpering followers than you could begin to count."

Then Rowena was gone, and it was a little girl standing over Jenilee, wearing that same crimson cloak and holding that same bloody axe. "I let you live as long as I did because you were amusing," the child said, glowering. From somewhere beneath her cloak, she produced a bundle and threw it at Jenilee's feet. Elissa's decoy book tumbled out. "This," she said, burying the blade of the axe in the book, "is *not* funny."

Jenilee kicked out at the book with her uninjured leg, sending it skidding away and carrying the axe with it. As Scarlet glanced away, tracking the movement of the axe, Jenilee rolled over onto hands and good knee, then scrambled away around the corner as a little white cat. With her weight on three legs, she didn't make the time she normally would have, but it went much better than trying to hop away on just one leg would have.

"I don't know which is more interesting," Scarlet called as she strolled into the alley after Jenilee. "That you didn't roll over and die, or what you decided to do about it."

"If you think that was interesting," Jenilee called from out of the shadows, finding her human voice even in her feline shape and despite the broken nose. "Stick around. I heard tell somewhere that this was *my* dream, and I'm done letting my own dreams push me around."

"It *was* your dream," the little girl chided as the bloody axe came whirling out of the darkness to land neatly in her outstretched hand. "Mine now. You're just along for the ride."

"Now who's insulting who?" Jenilee laughed mirthlessly. Scarlet glanced around, clearly trying to pinpoint the source of the voice, but it echoed confusingly off the walls of the alley. "Don't even *try* to play me. This is only your dream if I let it be. Get of my head. Now!"

"Here, kitty kitty," the little girl sang undeterred as she wandered down the alley, eyes still scanning for Jenilee. On down the alley, a pile of crates toppled with a bang and a crash, and a little white blur darted away. Before it vanished, Scarlet just had time to make out that the blur was a scurrying white rat and knew it at once for the distraction it had been.

She spun in time to raise her arms defensively at the hurtling ball of white fury descending on her from the roof behind. Scarlet shrieked as a little girl, but landed on her back as woman, the weight of the snowy leopard dropping full on her chest and stomach. The axe went flying again. Blood spattered as the leopard raked with its claws. Then the leopard was Jenilee, delivering a solid crack across Scarlet's jaw with the side of her fist.

"My dream!" Jenilee howled. "My head." She reached out and plucked a well-worn journal out of the air. "My Rules." The book clutched in both hands, she used it to slam Scarlet's head into the cobbles. "You like books, don't you? Let's add a page," Jenilee snarled, slamming the book down on Scarlet's head over and over. "You *never* come into my head again!"

Elissa laid a hand on her shoulder. "Keely!"

"Not now!" Keely snarled at her.

"Keely, wake up! You're having a nightmare."

And there Keely was, back in the cabin, drenched in sweat, tangled up naked in the nest she'd made of her clothes when she'd curled up in the corner to sleep as a cat. Everyone in the cabin had come awake, staring at her with concern by the flickering light of their little fire, while Elissa bent over her.

"It's okay," Elissa said soothingly. "Calm down. It was just a dream. A real doozy of a dream, from the sound of it, but just a dream."

Keely nodded shakily and fought to get her breathing under control. She rolled over, trying to sort out the tangle of her cloak, and shrieked as her knee landed on the floor, pain lancing through her body. Without a thought for all the eyes on her, she curled up into a ball and proceeded to whimper until the worst of it had subsided. By then she had felt the trickle of blood down her lip and over her wrist where it was pulled up close to her face.

"Keely...?" Elissa prompted, her voice heavy with worry.

At last Keely made another, more careful effort to roll over. "Is my nose broken?" she asked.

"Oh, go'ss," Elissa gasped. "I don't know. It's sure bloodied. What did you do? Someone get a lantern over here."

After several minutes of fussing and cleaning, Elissa assured Keely that the basic structure of both nose and knee seemed to be intact, but nasty bruises had already started to form. "I know you were thrashing around something awful," she said. "Even so, banging yourself up like that took some real talent."

"It wasn't me," Keely said, sagging back into the corner with the tattered cloak pulled around her. "It was her. She got in my head."

"Her who?" Elissa asked, her eyes betraying the number of additional questions lurking behind the one that had actually come out.

"Bloody Scarlet," Keely said. "She's here, she's real, and she's not happy with us." The number of questions in Elissa's eyes seemed to keep growing. "Oh, don't look at me like that," Keely scowled. "You're sitting here talking to a woman you think turns into a cat, for go'ss sake."

"You bring that up a lot," Elissa said, but nodded in concession of the point. "What happened?"

"I was having a lovely nightmare; then she just walked into it and started hammering on me. She knows we gave her the wrong book," Keely said.

"You're saying that really was *the* Bloody Scarlet?" Ulric asked.

"She thinks she is," Keely said. "She might as well be. Whatever she is, she's what the Inquisition is supposed to be fighting. Heck, maybe there used to be things like her all over the place and the Inquisition managed to get rid of most of them, so it moved on to seeing monsters wherever it could rather than go out of business."

Minda frowned. "Just hours ago, you enlisted me into tricking an inquisitrix into thinking I was come back from the grave to help her on a holy mission, and now you're trying to convince *me* that a nursery bogey is real."

"I know. I know," Keely said, waving a hand in frustration. "I'm a liar. But a few of you should know I don't waste my lies on practical jokes. What's my angle here? Why should I care if you believe in a 'nursery bogey'? Is there one person here who doesn't already believe this forest is a dangerous place where odd things happen? All I'm saying is—"

From outside the cabin, what started as a faint sound quickly built into a woman's ear-splitting shriek of terror. It ended more abruptly than it had come as something hit the front of the cabin with a resounding crack that rattled the timbers and shook dust from the rafters. The room fell into silence.

"Rifle," Ulric said, recovering first and pointing to Minda. "Crossbow." He pointed at Doryne. "Flank the door and be ready for if you're needed to take a shot at anything. Everyone else who knows how to fight, be ready for close quarters. Elissa, douse the fire so we don't make pretty targets standing in front of it in the doorway. Keely, go feline and be ready to scout. Nolan and Tobias are with me. No one else goes out until we've got some idea what's happening."

All remained still and silent outside until the cabin went dark, and then for the thirty count after while they waited for their eyes to be ready for the deep night. Then Ulric threw open the door, or at least tried to. It bounced off of something before it had gone a quarter open. He started to give it a kick to force the issue, appeared to think better of it, and settled for opening it back just enough to slip quickly through with Nolan and Tobias on his heels.

Moonlight illuminated the bloody, broken mess of what must have been an inquisitrix before she'd impacted the stout wall of the cabin at some terrible speed. What remained of her could mostly be identified by the robes, her actual body so mangled that she might have gone flying from a runaway carriage before being crushed beneath it— though they'd heard no such commotion and no carriage would have had room to build up that sort of speed back here, even if it could have gotten this far into the forest. Still, nothing stirred.

"Keely," Ulric hissed, peering into the darkness. "Cat eyes."

Keely trotted out the door and promptly froze, gazing in horror at the details of the grizzly scene that the night had thoughtfully muted for the others.

"Sorry," Ulric whispered, wincing apologetically as he realized what he'd failed to prepare her for. "Any sign of how she wound up here like this?"

Keely scanned the forest until her gaze fell on the same little girl who'd just been stalking her in her nightmares, sitting atop an enormous coal-black destrier that made the girl look even smaller by comparison. Netting holding dozens of human skulls hung across the horse's back like saddlebags, alongside a couple of freshly severed heads and an executioner's axe so large it looked like it would send the girl toppling to the ground if she tried to lift it.

Scarlet herself looked somewhat the worse for wear, with a split lip and other scratches on her face, and with her hair badly mussed, but still she wore a wicked grin of satisfaction as she watched them from at least fifty yards away at the bottom of the earthwork hill.

The good news was she didn't seem to know she was being watched, as her gaze never wandered down to Keely's feline eye-level. The bad news was the way Scarlet's gaze tracked the others. She could make them out in the moonlight as clearly as Keely could see her, despite their precaution of dousing the fire.

"My forest!" the girl called. "My rules! See you in your dreams." With that, she urged the horse about and rode off into the trees.

Keely scurried back inside and crawled into her clothes, returning to her human form. "That was her," Keely said leaning back against the wall, trying her best to sound calm and steady. She doubted it was working. "She's leaving."

"Right," Ulric said, leading the others in after her. "Whoever or whatever Bloody Scarlet may be, anyone who still thinks she's just a con or a story or a delusion gets to go clean the priestess off the wall right *now*. Anyone? No? Good. She wants this forest? She gets it. Pack up. Sitting tight is no longer an option. We're trusting to cat eyes and to Lady Minda to see us well on our way out of here before sun-up."

CHAPTER THIRTY-FOUR

GET OUT

Caer Cacamwri became the final resting place of the inquisitrix who'd run into Minda's line of fire. There would be no going deeper into the forest to cover up the incident now. With any luck, even if she was discovered at this point, she'd be taken as one more casualty of war with the witch and the Tuatha

At Minda's insistence, they did take time to build the woman a quick, crude cairn on the lowest tier of the old earthworks. After all, despite the woman's line of work, she'd not had a chance to prove herself inhumanly sadistic or anything. Perhaps it had all just been a job to her, and Minda couldn't entirely absolve herself of guilt in the woman's death. A battlefield burial seemed the least she could offer by way of penance.

"There are no innocents among the Inquisition," Nolan assured Minda as he saw her staring pensively at the last stone being placed. "At best, she stood by while terrible things happened, and she just let them. She probably did worse, though. She was trusted enough to come out here operating on her own. If you want my guess, we just buried the woman who pushed the Tuatha into declaring war."

Minda nodded but remained pensive. They let her.

No one suggested that they should try to bury what was left of the other priestess. Bringing it up would have been tantamount to volunteering for the job. Instead, they just hauled everything out of the cabin past her in a single trip, and left nature to take its course, trying to think as little about the woman as possible.

The worst effects of Keely's nightmare-induced injuries had already begun to melt away by the time they set out, and she took a meandering path as the rest of the group made their way through the dark forest by lantern light. To keep that lantern light from killing her night vision, Keely circled it at a distance, pausing occasionally where the others could see her flick her tail in a signal of "all's well" before disappearing back into the shadows.

The net effect was for her to cover the ground in a sort of drunken looping pattern, but she still had no trouble keeping pace with the big, clumsy folk inching cautiously along treacherous ground almost blind, especially knowing she'd be free to recuperate after sun-up by hitching a ride on the back of the remaining pony. She had little concern for any humans she might encounter during her scouting. Even in Scarlet's case, if they could count her as human, Keely's small size made it likely she'd see the woman before the woman saw her.

What Keely did worry about was stumbling into the path of a larger four-legged predator, although she was likely safe enough from them as well. No natural beast would have stuck around to get close to her while she remained within a stone's throw of such a large and relatively noisy expedition of humans.

In the end what still had her jumping at small sounds and random shadows was the same thing that had sent her scurrying away in the night when she'd first encountered Scarlet on that stormy night in Denecia. Despite the woman's slightly different features, that *had* been the same...person? Creature? Keely was sure of it.

Physical age seemed to be nothing but a state of mind to Scarlet. It was obvious that she didn't play by the usual rules, either physically or mentally, and what you couldn't predict you couldn't outwit or evade, and that robbed Keely of most of her favorite options right there. Dealing with something like that, either you got lucky or you got hit head-on by whatever they had to throw at you.

Worse, Scarlet wasn't the only thing out here that didn't play by the rules. There had also been that presence in the bone pit, and even the wolves weren't acting like wolves.

A few times before dawn, a sudden movement among the trees nearly startled Keely into shifting back to human form, but it always turned out to be some creature retreating before their advance through the forest. She was relieved to have managed to stay feline on more than one account.

First on the list, it would have blinded her instantly until she could stumble back to the lantern light. Second, there was no guarantee that whatever they ran into wouldn't be predator enough to try tackling a human, even though there would be fewer of those than of the ones willing to take on a cat.

And although years of practice had allowed her to make the transformation look easy, the shift still took its toll. A muscled laborer might make it look effortless to throw a heavy sack across his shoulder, but after doing that a few dozen times, it could still start to slow him down. Operating on a short night's sleep like everyone else, she needed to pace her exertions to make sure she was out of the forest before mental fatigue caught up with her.

Dawn arrived without real incident, and Keely retreated with relief to perch on the pony while it ambled along through the trees. They seemed to be passing near the lake again, now. She could smell it, and a thick morning fog had rolled in off the water to keep the forest obscured in a dismal, gray blanket long after the sun should have started dappling the forest floor.

But provided this really was the same lake as before, that meant they were most of the way back to the hedge that marked the outer boundary of the forest. Passing through the hedge would hardly mean they were safe, but it would offer one less immediate worry and should afford them a chance to take stock and regroup.

The down side to riding, resting her legs, was that it left Keely without much to do but think. Up to now, she'd been largely managing to distract herself from mulling over that latest nightmare. She recalled this one better than most, even if most of what she remembered was a confusing jumble. On top of all the other worrying bits, it had left her with the nagging feeling that Scarlet was...that Scarlet had...

Suddenly it all made sense. Everything about the night of page thirteen was so fractured and confused because Scarlet had really been there and had messed with her head. There was no telling what magic like that could do once it started rattling around in your skull. That explained why she had memories she couldn't have, and why it could become so hard for her to sort her own thoughts out from Jenny's when the world went topsy-turvy.

It also explained the nomadic sort of borrowed existence her friends had been stuck with for so long. Maybe that's what happened to people Scarlet killed in a dream, given the way the dream injuries Scarlet dished out had partly followed Keely back into the waking world.

Only two details continued to nag at Keely's mind. One, clearly, was the timing of having this monster and the Inquisition both show up on a rampage in the same backwater town on the same night. It stretched the credulity of coincidence to the breaking point. So if she ruled out coincidence, then...

"We've got to take her cloak!" Keely blurted out. When the others just stared, she began to muster her thoughts to explain, then realized they were *actually* staring because she'd just gone back human without thinking about it. She hastily grabbed for her clothes where they'd been left on the front of the saddle, and she pulled them on before continuing.

"Scarlet's magic tricks are all in that bright red cloak of hers. We take the cloak, she's just a girl. Or a woman. Or maybe she crumbles to dust from old age. The point is, she's powerless without her cloak."

"And you know this because...?" Ulric asked, cocking an eyebrow.

"Because it makes too much sense not to be true. I'm not asking anyone to hunt her down and steal her cloak. I'm just saying, if push comes to shove, that's how to take her down. The cloak is her power and her weakness."

Ulric nodded slowly. "If push comes to shove, I'm still going to try driving a sword through her heart. If *that* doesn't faze her, the cloak is worth a try."

As if the forest thought this all a good joke, a peal of mad laughter echoed distantly through the fog.

"Same guy from yesterday?" Evadne mused.

"Not sure it's a guy," Doryne said. "You know those wild dogs that are supposed to 'laugh'?"

"You mean hyenas?" Elissa asked.

"That laugh *did* have a 'beastly' edge to it," Tobias agreed as he turned slowly about, trying to pinpoint which direction the sound had come from.

"Don't bother," Minda said, noticing what Tobias was up to as she glanced back over her shoulder from the front of the expedition. "The way sound bounces around back in these hills, something that sounds two hundred yards to your right might be coming from four hundred to your left."

"I've never heard a hyena," Elissa said. "There shouldn't be one for many hundreds of miles around here, but I suppose one could have been brought in by a traveling carnival and got loose."

"Or two got loose," Minda said, as an answering laugh sounded considerably closer. "I'm definitely with the animal theory now. The echoes don't shift quickly enough for that to have been the same person. And there can't be two madmen out here who sound like that, can there?" She hefted Artema and inspected the rifle's readiness. "Doryne, be ready to toss me my backup."

Silence descended again as they pushed on through the mist-shrouded forest with the entire group back on heightened alert. Even Tobias seemed a bit grim and on-edge, doubtless helped along by the mess Scarlet had left on their doorstep in the night. They'd gone on for another quarter hour or so and started following a discernible trail along the shore of the lake before finding the way blocked by a figure appearing through the mist.

A faint breeze gently rustled the figure's tattered red cloak as it stood silently in the middle of the path. A dozen or more human skulls lay scattered randomly on the ground in front of it.

"The forest is yours, uncontested," Ulric said, stepping up beside Minda. "We got the message, and we're leaving as quickly as the light will allow."

Baldassare shouldered up past Ulric. "Where's my sister?" he demanded. "I know you took her. You were the little girl who led her here in the first place. Some of us wouldn't have come here at all if you hadn't done that."

The figure remained still, silent, and impassive.

Behind them, Evadne sighed, and suddenly a rock came sailing over their heads, knocking back the hood of the cloak and sending the skull beneath spinning on its post. "I'm so sick of scarecrows," she said, without any surprise in her voice.

"Who puts a scarecrow in the middle of a forest?" Conrad asked.

"Whoever strung up the skulls we had to duck around getting to Caer Cacamwri," Doryne said. "The Tuatha probably put it here after their fight with the Inquisition. Go'ss, I hope they've gone back deeper into the forest."

Minda crouched down to inspect the ground. "This isn't that part of the lake," she said. "No fight, and not a lot of traffic here recently."

"We need to assume this means they're nearby, though," Ulric said. "Territorial marker. Lady Minda, is there a good route that won't take us on through..." Ulric trailed off as the skull rotated slowly back around and paused as if regarding them with the points of red light that had begun to flicker in its eye sockets.

The ensuing silence was broken by the ring of steel and a guttural snarl as Tobias drew his sword and came charging forward. The jaw of the skull dropped open, appearing against all reason to emit an animalistic shriek—which then died abruptly as Tobias' sword connected in a two-handed sweep that shattered bone, snapped the top off the post, and sent the whole business spinning away into the lake, the tattered cloak trailing behind like the tail of a comet.

"I am leaving this forest," Tobias said, kicking one skull after another out of the path and into the lake, even though they otherwise remained unmoving, "to see everyone out safe. I am not *running* from anything, and I will not be herded *anywhere* as anything's prey. If this is the best way out, this is the way we're going."

"You're right." Ulric nodded. "If the forest is going to be that way, we're done treading lightly. Everyone, this is the final push. We're making straight for the hedge, and we're rolling over anything that gets in our way."

They formed up with Ulric at point now, Baldassare flanking his left and Tobias on his right to lead with a wedge. Behind came Minda with her rifle, Doryne with her crossbow, and Conrad following them with the ammunition and Minda's back-up hunting rifle.

Elissa, who was tiring more than anyone, and whose idea of a fight was to debate the virtues of various systems of library cataloging, found herself on the pony along with Keely, who rode as a cat once more. Nolan and Evadne came last as the rear guard. So organized, they broke into a quick step that had them covering ground nearly twice as fast as before.

The first thing that got in their way, not five minutes later, was clad in black and red. A company of knights of the Inquisition appeared abruptly out of the fog and opted to forgo the traditional threats and rhetoric in favor of an enraged battle cry and a headlong charge. Ulric, Tobias, and Baldassare all ducked aside, and Minda dropped the lead knight with a bullet between the eyes before he'd gone two paces. The man sprawled face down into the muddy earth, his sword clattering away off a tree root as it slipped from his grasp, and he lay still.

Doryne lacked Minda's deadly precision, but she still managed to punch a crossbow bolt through the armored shoulder of the second man, and it sent him reeling away in pain. Conrad had begun to toss Minda her back-up rifle even as she spun around for it. She grabbed it out of the air one-handed, using the other to toss Artema to him, and she finished the smooth motion by pulling the new gun up to sighting position as she came back around to face the onrushing knights.

Haste and the idiosyncrasies of the less favored weapon combined to throw Minda's aim off, and instead of hitting the next man between the eyes, her second bullet entered his skull through the left eye socket. The net effect remained the same.

That left seven armored knights charging toward them, and no time for another volley. Ulric, Tobias, and Baldassare stepped back in to meet the charge with a charge of their own, metal ringing through the forest as the two sides clashed.

"This is wrong," Doryne said, her eyes dancing across the battlefield as she did a quick head count. "Something's wrong."

Nolan and Evadne charged past on either side to join the fray, Nolan tossing his rifle into Minda's hands on the way past.

"What's wrong?" Elissa asked, clutching Keely to her chest in alarm as she might a pet.

"Go'ss, she's right," Minda said. "There weren't fifteen knights of the Inquisition in the county when we left the castle. After yesterday, they couldn't have had even ten in any sort of fighting shape, but not one of these men showed up bloodied. I don't recognize any of those shields, either. They've had reinforcements already. Very, very not good."

For all that the Inquisition had shown up ready for a fight, it didn't appear that they'd actually expected to get one. They'd only kept charging despite their losses because charging was what the Inquisition did, and now they seemed a bit disoriented by the fact that the enemy hadn't turned and fled.

Perhaps no one had informed the reinforcements yet that they were in a desperate struggle with a ruthless witch, her army of henchmen, and forest full of heathen savages? Whatever the ultimate source of their confusion, and however small the impact on their reaction time, it wound up costing the knights dearly.

A parry that only came late by the blink of an eye did a man no more good than a parry that was never executed, and Tobias and Baldassare both possessed the speed to capitalize on that fact. Before the knights knew what was happening, another of their number lay bleeding out on the ground and one had been thrown from his feet, affording Nolan the moment needed to step in and finish the man with a well-placed thrust before he could rise back up in his heavy breastplate.

Then Evadne managed to slip past the guard of a third knight to close with such force that her momentum carried them both off of the trail and down the steep embankment into the lake, where she landed on top of him, snarling, and forced his head beneath the water with one hand while she pinned his sword arm down with the other.

As had been discovered the day before, even the most devout fanatic has his breaking point. The remaining men turned and ran.

Minda had just finished reloading Artema when Evadne came wading out of the lake, dragging the limp form of the man she'd either drowned or nearly drowned. Grim, drenched, and bedraggled, with her hair all a mess and someone's blood from the fight spattered across her face, the giantess suddenly struck Keely as one of the last people she ever wanted to cross. It wasn't just the woman's size or her skill in a brawl, but the pure savage abandon with which Evadne threw herself into a fight, completely at odds with her apparent station as a gentlewoman.

"Want a hand with..." Nolan began to offer Evadne, then stopped short as the shaft of an arrow stopped, quivering in the ground, not two inches from his foot. All eyes turned to see scores of other arrows arcing high across the mist-shrouded lake.

No one needed Ulric's hastily barked order to pull back into the trees, which was good, because the deadly hail of arrows was already pelting down around them in earnest before he could get it out. Minda's marksmanship may have paved the way to an easy route of the Inquisition, but it had also announced loud and clear to the Tuatha where to find armed intruders in their forest.

In the time-honored tradition of battlefield archers, the Tuatha weren't worried about the fact they couldn't target individuals through that fog, they were just filling the air with countless pointy things and trusting to the odds that some of those would wind up trying to occupy the same space as their enemies.

The pony screamed and stumbled, spilling Elissa and Keely onto the ground. Keely landed lightly on feline feet, and Elissa rolled away as expertly as any equestrian could hope, but there was no pretending that the animal was going to make it out of the forest alive, or carry a load any further for them. With a grimace of regret, Elissa turned away from the pony and continued scrambling for cover, only just thinking to grab Keely's clothes from where they'd tumbled in the mud.

The mad rush stopped about twenty yards back from the shore, where the trees of the forest offered sufficient cover to shelter behind with confidence. A scattering of arrows continued to pelt in from across the lake, but any that got near sunk harmlessly into the trunks of the great trees.

"Are we all here?" Ulric demanded.

"Mostly," Baldassare answered through gritted teeth, clutching at his sword arm. Blood already drenched his sleeve and the chest of his tunic where an arrow had cut a deep gash across the bicep and a shallow line across his chest.

"On it," Doryne said, stepping smartly in and holding a knife up to Baldassare's ruined tunic until he nodded his acquiescence. Then she set to cutting it off him and using strips to bind the wounds.

"Where's Keely?" Elissa asked in a panic. "Keely?!"

Several long heartbeats passed before the little white cat came scurrying up, not waiting to get into her clothes before transforming.

"Hush!" Keely said urgently, taking the bundle from Elissa. "Those knights were just the vanguard. We've got more Inquisition coming in fast, and I'm pretty sure there are Tuatha headed this way around the lake." A burst of unnerving laughter echoed through the forest again, this time disturbingly close—as was the answering laugh, and the one that followed on its heels. "Then there's that."

"Of course being caught between two armies wasn't bad enough," Nolan muttered.

"My turn again," Minda snapped. "Come on!"

"Hold on!" Doryne called, hurrying to finish binding at least the deep cut across Baldassare's arm, but Minda was already moving out. Urged on by Ulric, the others fell in to single file behind Minda, stringing out in a tail to keep her in sight while lingering as long as possible to keep Doryne and Baldassare from being left behind. Ulric stayed 'til last, waiting for Doryne to finish her work on Baldassare, then shooed them on ahead.

Every fifty feet or so, Minda paused, inspecting the trees before taking off at a run again, often in a new direction. The pauses allowed the rest of the group to form up again fairly well before Minda stopped at one of the larger, more gnarled trees and slung Artema across her back.

"Up up up," she ordered as she began to scramble upward herself, the tree providing hand and footholds so numerous that even the wounded Baldassare was able to climb it with some help from Evadne. Forty feet above the forest floor they reached a sturdy plank walkway suspended from thick ropes, heading off through the branches in two directions. "The Haywood family doesn't stint when it comes to backup plans," Minda said. "I would have pointed us this way sooner if it wouldn't have meant leaving Doryne's poor pony to fend for herself."

Shouts from down below in the direction of the lake announced that the Inquisition and the Tuatha had come face to face.

"How far will this take us?" Ulric asked as they set out. The plank bridge swayed constantly underfoot, but had been fenced in with enough rope to keep anyone from becoming overly concerned about their footing.

"It starts at the postern gate into the forest," Minda grinned. "It'll take us straight to the castle."

"Not my first choice of destinations right now," Ulric said, "but as long as we're sneaking in the back, it'll definitely do."

They hurried on as quickly as the swaying bridge would allow, leaving behind the confrontation that sounded like it had become a pitched battle. What they weren't leaving nearly far enough behind was that laughter. It kept coming in bursts, at shorter intervals and from more and more sources, until it had practically turned into a chorus. Sometimes one of the voices would erupt directly underfoot, its owner unseen through the mist and the thick foliage.

"Nothing's *that* funny," Conrad muttered.

During one particularly loud bout of laughter, the plank bridge began to shake wildly as off through the mists, shadows began to emerge, rushing toward them along its narrow pathway through the trees. Currently at point, Tobias pulled his sword and prepared to meet the charge, while everyone with a crossbow or rifle at hand took aim.

Even so, the ensuing shrieks caught them all off guard by being neither bestial nor monstrous, as half a dozen children came to a screeching halt, staring wide-eyed at their weapons.

"It's all right!" Minda said, slinging her rifle and pushing past Tobias, rushing to meet the children. "Wenna! Siani!" she said, throwing her arms around two of the girls and pulling them to her. "What are you doing here?!"

"We're playing hide-and-seek!" the older of the two declared as the shock of thinking they'd been waylaid in the fog began to fade.

"Oh, no," Minda gasped.

"This is no time for games, children," Evadne said kindly, coming to kneel where she could look some of them in the eye. "The forest is a dangerous place right now."

"Well, it's really not that bad, I suppose," Minda said, laying an arm on Evadne's and shooing her gently back toward the others. "Not so long as we're keeping to the trees."

"Lady Minda? Is that you?" A buxom, young, brown-haired woman came hurrying out of the fog behind the children. It took a moment before Elissa was able to place the woman as Nolan's friend they'd encountered on the Wolf's Tooth.

"Oh, good," Minda said, looking up with a bright, brittle smile. "Just the woman I needed to talk to. Hello, Nessa. Kids, sit down a moment and catch your breath while you can. The game can wait a minute, can't it, Nessa?" she asked with a questioning eyebrow.

"I...think so," Nessa said hesitantly.

With a glance and a nod, Minda beckoned to Nolan, and he slipped past the children, catching a quick hug from Nessa on the way past.

"How bad is it?" Minda asked quietly when they'd pulled back away from the children. Most of the others gathered around, and neither woman made any attempt to discourage them.

"It's bad, milady," Nessa sighed miserably. "Is your father with you?" When Minda shook her head, Nessa added, "He led a search into the forest looking for you after the fire. No word from him yet."

"He'll be all right," Minda said unhesitatingly. "It's just a really big forest."

"Then that's my only good news," Nessa said. "Jane Carver's here. She's declared reverential law."

Minda blinked. "She...?"

"She's denounced the entire county for heresy, milady. She took the cathedral site by force of arms, then came for the castle. She already had people inside, and it was barely garrisoned, what with all the emergencies pulling the men away."

"What about my mother?" Minda demanded.

"Dead or prisoner," Nessa said, tearing up. "I'm not sure. She sent me to see your sisters to safety when the fighting started, since I was no use in a fight but I knew the tunnels well enough to get out on my own. She knew the castle would fall if she did, the way things were. I'm sorry, milady. The war's come and gone. We lost."

"No!" Keely cut in. "The war's not over. I'll make it right!"

Nessa stared coldly at the silver-haired apparition in the tattered red outfit. "There are scores dead already," Nessa said flatly. "Burned in the fire or cut down by the Inquisition. How will you make that right?"

"I..." Keely faltered.

"How?!" Nessa demanded loudly, forgetting herself.

To Keely's horror, she was saved from answering when a sinuous gray tendril—barbed and about two fingers thick—lashed out of the fog. In the literal blink of an eye, the tendril had wound twice around Nessa's throat. Bright blood welling where the barbs pierced her flesh, the young woman had time for one futile attempt at a scream, a heartbeat to raise her hands in an effort to claw at the tendril, and then she was gone, yanked headlong off the walkway and plummeting toward the ground.

Nessa vanished into the fog without a sound almost before anyone else could raise a hand.

CHAPTER THIRTY-FIVE

WHIPLASH

For one long, stunned second, silence hung in the air. Then the children started to scream. From below, the insane laughter erupted again, and in such a cacophony that it began to sound like the baying of hounds. Most of the children turned and fled back the way they'd come.

"They can't go back!" Minda shouted.

"And *none* of us can stay here," Ulric barked.

Nolan swung himself between the ropes and began to lower himself toward the branches below.

"What are you doing?!" Ulric demanded.

"We can't leave her," Nolan snapped.

"Whatever she hit, she hit it headfirst," Ulric said, grabbing for Nolan's arm. "She's dead, and *they* aren't." He thrust a finger in the direction of the children. "Keeping them that way comes first."

Nolan grimaced and banged his head against a mercifully yielding support rope before wordlessly starting to haul himself back onto the plank bridge with Ulric's help. He was halfway on when an alarmed look came over his face, and he suddenly shot a foot backwards before their combined grips jerked him to a stop.

Unslinging Artema again, Minda leaned out and fired. Her uncanny aim severed the slender tendril wrapped around Nolan's ankle, freeing him from its grasp, and Nolan came lurching back up. Multiple helping hands quickly had him full onto the plank bridge.

"They heard us!" Elissa hissed urgently. "They didn't see us, they're just lashing out at the noise!" She glanced meaningfully after the fleeing children. It wasn't at all hard to hear their retreating screams or the clattering of the planks under their feet, even in competition with the baying laughter from below.

"Up!" Minda pointed her sisters and the two other children who'd remained with them toward the nearest tree trunk. "And for go'ss sake don't make a sound until I tell you it's safe."

Another tendril whipped at them from out of the fog. This time Tobias was ready and waiting, severing the thing with a flick of his blade before it could touch anyone.

"You're going up with them," Ulric told Minda. "You, too, Nolan." Before releasing Nolan's arm, Ulric added low enough to be sure that Minda wouldn't hear above the eerie baying, "Pretend that's everything left of house Haywood up that tree. If it's not and we *don't* bring them home safe..." He let the sentence trail off unfinished, but Nolan nodded his understanding.

When Ulric looked around, he found only Baldassare and Evadne standing there, back to back, peering into the fog warily with their blades drawn. The others had already taken off after the fleeing children.

There was no right way to do this, Keely observed as she dashed to catch up with Elissa and Doryne. If Elissa was right, whatever had yanked that woman off the bridge would not only be chasing after the children as they screamed and clattered away; it would be targeting the clatter and shouts of anyone who might be following the children, trying to get them to quiet down.

Worse, "running" on the suspended planks wound up being more of a drunken dance, with as much energy spent in staying upright as in moving forward. Even without a clear, uncluttered path on the forest floor, whatever was down there shouldn't have much trouble keeping up with people on the plank bridge, or even overtaking them.

That left Keely as the only one qualified to actually follow the children under these conditions. As a cat, she could easily overtake the children, and do it in total silence. The problem arose once she got there. In their panic, they'd either totally ignore a strange cat or be further spooked by it.

On the other hand, if they saw a strange, naked, silver-haired woman stepping out of the fog in this dark forest, it could *only* make things worse. On top of every other factor, they would have been warned all their lives against the woman who lurked here, just waiting to take their heads.

Keely thought she'd recognized Addie, the girl from the castle chapel, among the children, but seriously doubted they'd built enough of a rapport for Keely to reach even her through the current insanity. Maybe she could get them to stop running, but not to stop screaming, and to have them stand still while they kept screaming would be about the only way to make things worse.

At least her clothes hadn't been left totally behind when she'd gone feline this time. Tobias—with Conrad at his heels—had chased right after her and had been thoughtful enough to scoop her clothes up as he did. Still, it wouldn't be any plus in getting the children to calm down if, instead of showing up naked, she showed up in a tattered costume meant specifically to conjure up thoughts of the very woman they'd been told to steer clear of.

Keely darted around the legs of Elissa and Doryne with her brain still racing furiously to come up with a plan, but it was getting nowhere fast. The children had gotten enough of a head start that it was hard to see them through the fog, but a sudden shriek pitched a couple of levels of panic above the others announced that she might already be too late.

Those children who could be made out through the fog skidded to a halt and headed back toward Keely, heedless of how close they came to trampling her on the narrow walkway. The first girl to reach Doryne threw herself into the woman's arms, while the other children began crowding past to huddle behind her. Doryne just had time to set that first girl down with the others, then ready her crossbow, before an odd, flailing shadow loomed from the mist.

It resolved itself into the form of Scarlet—wearing the face and body of the young woman they'd met her as—holding a struggling child aloft by the throat in each hand. The boy in her left hand was a sandy-haired youth of maybe seven or eight, probably a courtier's son to judge by his clothes. The girl in her right hand was Addie.

Scarlet clucked her tongue scoldingly as she advanced toward them, her cloak billowing around her though no breeze swirled the fog. "I'd say something about how you can't leave yet, and a party," Scarlet sighed, "but I just have the nagging feeling that one's been used. How about, 'Don't go away before I tear your arms off, because that would be rude?'"

"How about you put the children down before I put a crossbow bolt through your chest?" Doryne offered, taking careful aim. Elissa and Keely both froze, trying to be not in the line of fire. Even Tobias coming up behind them slowed to a wary advance.

"You see, that doesn't work for me." Scarlet rolled her eyes as she continued unhurriedly forward, still holding the children aloft with no apparent effort. They clawed desperately at her arms, trying to free themselves, or at least to relieve the pressure on their throats, but Scarlet showed no sign of noticing the bloody scratches they'd managed to gouge around her wrists. "I can't imagine what you think I'd get out of it. Whether it's before or after I put them down, that's still a crossbow bolt through my chest."

"You know what I meant!" Doryne snapped.

"I'm not sure she does," Elissa hissed.

Scarlet kept advancing, the planks creaking under her feet, the bridge gently swaying with each step. "Listen to the simpering lackey," Scarlet told Doryne, smiling a smile that, under other circumstances, might have been called disarming. "I *excel* at misunderstanding people."

"Drop them!" Doryne screamed.

Scarlet sighed again. "Oh, whatever." With a casual flick of her wrists, she released the children, but with so much effortless strength in the gesture that they went arcing up and away from the bridge in opposite directions, easily clearing the ropes and sailing out into the empty air. Then things started happening very quickly.

Doryne screamed in dismay and released the crossbow bolt. The bolt flew straight and true, burying itself deep in Scarlet's chest just to the left of her sternum. Scarlet's eyes flew open wide, then she simply folded in a heap without a sound.

The moment Scarlet had released the children, Tobias's instincts and combat reflexes short-circuited his brain, taking it out of the equation. Before Scarlet hit the ground, his sword had flashed out, severing one of the supporting ropes of the bridge, freeing the rope to drop loosely into his waiting hand. He released the sword before the arc of the slash had fully completed, allowing the blade to spin away into the forest canopy—because if he'd had even half a heartbeat to spare he'd have spent it looping the rope about his wrist before he jumped.

He didn't, but his grip held as he caught the falling girl in the crook of his free arm, and it reversed his trajectory. He still fell, but swinging under the bridge when he did, rather than plummeting away from it.

Keely had started to leap toward Addie even before Tobias had, but the same reflexes that had allowed her to get moving first allowed her to notice when Tobias began to move, and to quickly change her own trajectory. Despite her first impulse being to save the child she actually knew, she'd had to trust Tobias to pull off a miracle for the girl, or there'd have been no one even trying to scrounge one up for the boy. Only she possessed the combination of reflexes and proximity to make the attempt thinkable.

In her diminutive form, Keely slipped easily between the ropes and launched gracefully into the air despite the sudden lurch of the planks beneath her feet as Tobias severed the supporting rope and launched himself. In mid-air she melted back into human shape so she'd have the mass to carry the child with her when they collided.

With no rope to grab for, all she could do was angle them toward the least of the available evils, and they crashed together into a stout branch, at least two feet in diameter and less than ten feet down, rather than into the rocky ground at least four times as far away. She managed to twist so that she bore the brunt of the impact, and so that they landed lengthwise along the branch.

It hurt like blazes—cutting bloody scrapes across her bare skin in several places, on top of the blunt force—and she probably would have screamed if she hadn't had the breath knocked completely out of her, but at least she didn't hear the sound of any bones snapping.

About the time Keely hit the branch, the full weight of Tobias and Addie came down on the rope, sending a shockwave through the plank bridge that overshadowed the lurch that had come when Tobias first leapt. Doryne was knocked completely off her feet, her crossbow sent sailing after Tobias's sword.

Most everyone else on the bridge was only saved from going down by having their hands free to grab for the ropes. Only a quick grab from Conrad kept one child from sliding beneath the ropes and over the edge. Tobias's leather hunting gauntlet kept the rope from tearing his hand open as his weight hit. It didn't keep his hand from slipping. As Tobias lost his grip, Addie managed a shriek despite the abuse her throat had taken, and they plunged together into the fog, her voice choking off abruptly a moment later.

"Come on," Conrad said, taking charge of the stunned children while Doryne still lay peering off one side of the bridge—where Tobias and Addie had been—and Elissa stared down off the other, at where Keely lay trying to re-inflate her lungs. "Climb and be quiet. We have to wait out whoever's listening down there."

The baying laughter below had never let up. Conrad had nearly led the children to the nearest climbable tree when another tendril lashed out behind them, wrapping around the rope Elissa gripped to support herself, just inches from her hand. The bridge swayed as something tugged from below, but the tendril remained where it was, and Elissa got a good look at one of the tendrils for the first time, even as she backed away with a start. She'd been expecting something along the lines of a slaver's lash, but what had anchored itself to the bridge was a vine—gray, gnarled, and covered with wicked thorns.

Beginning to backpedal, Elissa nearly tripped over Doryne. That brought Doryne's attention around in time to see another thorny vine whip up from out of the mist and wrap around a branch above the bridge. Elissa glanced between the vines and Keely, and with an agonized expression began to back away toward the tree the children were climbing.

Even without the thorns sprouting between her and Keely, the gulf between them was clearly something Elissa had no illusions about being able to leap. As Doryne and Elissa watched, the vines began to twist and writhe like snakes, the far ends slowly coiling upward, drawing a single voice up out of the chorus of dreadful laughter with them.

"Well...*ow*." Before whatever it was could emerge from the mists, Scarlet's voice dragged their eyes away to where she sat up, frowning at the bloody crossbow bolt that she'd pulled from her chest. "I *told* you it was a lose-lose for me," Scarlet sighed, then rolled casually over into a predatory crouch, like a jungle cat perched high in the trees, ready to pounce.

"Not again," Elissa whimpered, staring in transfixed horror.

Scarlet's eyes glinted blood red from beneath the shadow of her hood. For three dreadful heartbeats, Scarlet stared them down—then her gaze flicked to the tree the children had begun to climb.

"No!" Doryne screamed, launching herself forward at the same moment Scarlet leapt. Doryne caught Scarlet in mid leap, arms locking around her waist in a full tackle that sent both women tumbling together over the security ropes and down toward the forest floor.

That left Elissa standing alone on the narrow bridge when a skull rose up out of the mists, laughing like a deranged jester fit for entertaining in Jane Carver's torture chamber. Twin points of light glowed in the darkness of its sockets, the same blood red as the glint from Scarlet's eyes. Where a neck would once have supported the skull, an array of stout, thorny vines sprouted, coiling about like tentacles and pulling the skull through the trees like it was some sort of macabre arboreal octopus.

Elissa stood transfixed for a moment, the glow from the eye-sockets drawing her gaze almost hypnotically. Then she turned and fled, stumbling over her own feet as the bridge swayed erratically beneath her. Blind panic took her past Conrad and the tree full of children without even seeing them. Conrad spun to face the onrushing...thing...meeting it with sword drawn and a desperate battle cry. One thorny vine lashed out from the thing, drawing a stinging trail of blood across his face before he countered with a furious swing that severed the vine.

Elissa yelped in pain and surprise as one of the other flailing vines caught up with her, wrapping around her unprotected ankle and pulling her unsteady feet out from under her. Desperately she gripped the planks, fighting against being yanked toward the thing, while Conrad grappled with the remaining vines. He managed to lop off a second and third before one finally caught a solid grip on his sword arm and forced him to drop the blade.

Back the way they'd come, Elissa could just make out Ulric and Evadne headed quickly their way through the mist, but not nearly so quickly as she seemed to be losing her grip on the planks. Then Conrad's sword clattered to a stop beside her. She gave up her grip and made a lunge for the sword, just managing to snatch it up as the vine hauled her into the air. Gripping the weapon in both hands, she swung out blindly. Once. Twice. Three times. The thing let out an ear-splitting shriek just before she felt the sword slip from her hands again.

Then Elissa found herself in free-fall for one sickening moment, only to be snatched up in another thorny embrace that pinned one arm to her chest. Up above her hung the bridge, a good twenty feet away. The spot where she'd just been could be easily picked out by the pair of vines there still flailing spasmodically about.

Not two yards from her face, though, another skull hung in the air, suspended from the vines it sprouted. The skull's decrepit jaw snapped at Elissa even as another of its vines snared her free arm, and another grabbed one of her helplessly kicking feet. She couldn't suppress a scream as a fourth snaked about her neck, then tightened, gouging her flesh and choking off any hope of sound or breath.

Her world shrank to the hideous sound of the thing's laughter and the bloody light in its eyes. Then just as she was sure she would black out completely, another skull came arcing in out of nowhere to smash with a bone-shattering crunch into the skull holding her. The vines uncoiled, and she fell all of five feet before landing in Tobias's arms.

"There!" Tobias pointed as he eased her down onto the branch he was standing on, but Elissa couldn't look. She was too busy gasping for breath. Rather than allow her time to recover, Tobias wound up half-dragging Elissa down the limb to the trunk of the tree, then helped her wedge herself into a large crevice where the ancient tree had gnarled itself into a shape that offered some minimum of shelter. "I'll be back for you," he assured her before heading out.

By the time Elissa's head had stopped spinning, she had become gradually aware that she was sharing the space with Addie, who was wedged even further back into the crevice and whimpering quietly, arms clutched in a death grip around Elissa's waist.

Though badly scratched and well-bloodied, Tobias remained otherwise intact. The worst of what he'd suffered was pain, and more than once in his life he'd managed to block out considerably worse and keep right on moving. While he remained mindful of the terrible things happening around him, something inside him sang along with the rhythm of his pounding heart. He was in his element, and he still had a damsel to rescue—or at least a rather attractive con-artist who would eventually, but inevitably, be replaced with a damsel in someone's retelling of the story. That seemed close enough to tradition to work for him.

Like Elissa, when he'd fallen, he'd found himself snatched out of the air by one of these abominations. Unlike Elissa, he'd been prepared to deal with it. Even without his sword, he'd had a dagger in easy reach. It couldn't slice through vines nearly so neatly as a sword, but it had bought him the chance to slip out of the thing's grasp and onto a sturdy branch along with the girl. After that, well, the skull-things had proven their own worst enemies.

When another vine lashed at him from out of the fog, Tobias stood his ground and raised his gauntlet, allowing the thing to snare his wrist. Then he promptly spun in place, whipping the vine in a violent arc that evoked a shriek of protest. The move also threw off the aim of the next vine that came whipping drunkenly at him, and Tobias managed to parry it with the same gauntleted wrist, quickly twining the two vines together like the start of a braid. He took one more moment to be sure of his footing on the broad tree-branch, then spun back the other direction, slamming the skull-thing into a tree trunk.

However unnerving and ghoulish the things might be, however nasty their grip, they could not be mistaken for tactical geniuses. Certainly it had never occurred to them that someone might choose to take the skull by the thorns. Given a moment to realize what was happening, they could anchor themselves fast in place. Denied that moment, well...

Tobias cracked the whip, snapping the hapless skull at the end upward, where it wound dizzyingly around a branch in a spiral that inevitably led to bone cracking once more into tree. Then he kept a firm hold on the vines as he leapt from his own branch, using the vines to swing to the tree where Keely had landed. Once he'd quickly tied them off to make sure that the stunned thing would have no easy time recovering, he scrambled up through the branches to reach Keely.

The boy she'd kept from falling was cowering against the trunk of the tree, too small to reach a handhold for the next branch up. Tobias boosted him, and the boy scrambled gratefully away. There would be no perfect cover from what they were facing, but downward lay disaster and upward lay allies. It was the best Tobias could do for the lad at that moment.

Keely, for her part, was finally beginning to push herself unsteadily upright, and the sight frankly took his breath away. This was hardly the first time he'd glimpsed her without her clothes on, but she'd never seemed more vulnerable than at as this moment, nor more primal and wild, and to stay alive in this scuffle he had already handed over authority to his base emotions.

For that one instant, the cultured, chivalrous prince vanished, and only the sure knowledge that they were all still fighting for their lives kept the animal inside from trying to outdo the moment he and Keely had already stolen together in the rain outside the mausoleum. Grinding his teeth, he tore his gaze away on the pretext of scanning the trees for more threats, even as he extended a hand to help Keely up.

"Did we win?" Keely asked unsteadily as she brushed back the wild tangle of hair that had fallen into her eyes.

"Both children are alive and whole, just terrified. It's not over, though. You need to get moving. Perhaps as a cat?" he suggested. "I'm, uh...not sure whether your clothes are up on the bridge or scattered through the trees at this point."

Keely nodded in response, leaning on a hand for support while she attempted to chase the wool from her head. After a few moments she gave a muttered expletive, then sighed heavily. "Not sure whether I'm just too scatterbrained still or I've burned myself out. I don't think I've ever switched back and forth so much so quickly."

"I should have known you'd land on your feet, your highness," Conrad said as quietly as he could manage, while still feeling confident he could be heard over the maniacal baying of the rest of the things below them. He had leaned out from the bridge above, but now leaned back, respectfully finding other directions to look, much like Tobias had, on spying Keely's current state of dress. He'd managed to retrieve his sword, and held it firmly at the ready. "What about the others?"

"Our scholar and the girl I caught live, if a bit banged up," Tobias said, finally thinking to strip his tunic off over his head and pass it to Keely. "Keely seems unbroken, and the boy..." Tobias nodded toward the climbing child.

"I'll find a way to get him to the others," Conrad said. "Dame Evadne's with them, and Sir Ulric's gone to see how quietly he can get the others caught up with us so we won't have to split ourselves guarding everyone. Did you see what became of Lady Doryne and the witch?"

Tobias shook his head. "Did they fall, too?"

Conrad nodded.

"I'll have a look after I get the others up here. In the meantime, make sure everyone knows what we're up against with these deadlings," Tobias said.

"You mean these...skull things?" Conrad asked.

"That's what I said." Tobias nodded firmly. "Deadlings." It was the first name that he could come up with. Tobias knew that his grasp of the finer human motivations and emotions could come up short, but fear he understood. If he seemed fearless to the world, it was only because he'd devoted so much of his life to understanding, channeling, and controlling fear. Fear killed. At its best, it incited unpredictable panic that could get you out of a scrape where all other hope had failed, but in a fight, that was just rolling dice with your life.

The man who consistently survived and overcame was the man who kept his head, and nothing instilled fear and paranoia like being stalked by a nameless foe. They weren't getting those children out of this forest alive without giving these things a name first. "They seem to be relentless, but nearly mindless."

By the time Tobias had turned back to Keely, she had pulled his tunic on. It could have used a belt on her, but otherwise made for a very serviceable dress. She wasn't making any apologies for studying his bare chest. "A girl could get used to this kind of chivalry." She grinned.

Tobias chuckled. "Can you climb? I need to..." A girlish shriek from the direction he'd just come cut him off. He gave Keely a quick, questioning glance, and she just shoved him lightly away.

"Go!" she demanded.

Tobias went, hopping lightly down the branches to where he'd left the deadling's vines tied off. They remained that way, and the thing hadn't managed to unwind its skull from around the branch, but it did thoughtfully find a spare vine to lash out at him with. Again, he let it grab his wrist and used the vine to launch himself back across the gap between trees.

He was already in the air before he spied the flash of red from Scarlet's cloak, where she came clawing her way up the tree toward Addie and Elissa. The woman's movements were halting and uncertain, as if several of her bones had been cracked and joints dislocated, yet she made surprisingly good progress all the same.

It wasn't good enough to get out of the way when Tobias's boot connected with her jaw. The astounding part was that even though it snapped Scarlet's head back precipitously, the impact did nothing to loosen her hold on the branch, and she didn't go flying. She just swung her head back and grinned unnervingly at Tobias as he landed agilely a few feet away.

"Now this is living," Scarlet sighed wistfully as she pulled herself up onto the branch and shoved a dislocated shoulder back into place with an audible pop. "I haven't had this much fun in ages."

CHAPTER THIRTY-SIX

DOWN TO GOBLIN TOWN

Addie shrieked again. Elissa already had the girl out of the crack they'd been wedged into and was hustling her higher as fast as they could manage.

Tobias did some quick mental estimates of the amount of force Scarlet had managed to exert even in her current state to keep herself firmly anchored to the tree branch. He cross-referenced that with the velocity that the inquisitrix must have hit the outside of the cabin at Caer Cacamwri for the impact to have turned her into the mess she'd wound up as, factored in Scarlet's apparently complete obliviousness to pain, factored in the landing she'd been able to crawl away from, and observed the sinuous movements of two more deadlings emerging from the fog as they homed in on Addie's shriek.

It all added up to this being no time for one nearly unarmed man to press his luck trying to capitalize on Scarlet's injuries. Grinding his teeth in frustration, Tobias bypassed Scarlet by leaping to the next branch, then hurried to join Elissa and Addie. "Up!" He hissed at them. "Up!"

"Down!" Keely insisted, dropping onto the branch beside him. "Down!"

"How did you...?" Tobias began.

"I was very motivated," she said, pointing up and away toward where he'd left her. No less than a dozen of the deadlings swarmed through the trees there, headed this direction. "We're cut off, and 'up' has stopped helping. Worst case if we take to the ground is that we're drawing the pack away from the others."

"What about Scarlet?!" Elissa demanded.

"I get the feeling Scarlet can take care of herself," Keely said. "Move!" She ran out along the branch, beckoning the others to follow. Tobias urged Elissa after Keely, then scooped Addie up and carried her. The fog no longer obscured the ground from here, and a fall didn't look like it would be deadly; but it was sure to be painful, and would invite broken bones that—under the circumstances—would bring death along as part of their entourage.

At last Keely spied what appeared to be a thoroughly muddy, rock-free patch of ground passing beneath them, and quickly rolled down to dangle from the branch, getting her feet a full body-length closer to it before letting go. Making a quick exit had always been easiest for her as a cat, but she'd had the wits to never count on being able to do it that way, so she was able to roll neatly into the mud now as she landed. She came up a total mess, but otherwise no worse for the fall.

"Addie!" Keely beckoned, and held out her arms. Tobias, who was still carrying the girl, didn't leave a moment for Addie to protest or freeze up. With the deadlings closing in behind them, that would have been a moment they didn't have. He just dropped flat on the branch and let her dangle from his extended arm long enough to break the momentum.

"Let go now," he hissed, "or they catch us all."

Elissa added her steady gaze to his, looking Addie in the eye, and said one word. "Faith."

Addie let go of Tobias's wrist, and dropped into Keely's waiting arms. What resulted was no heroic catch. Keely didn't even try to stand firm, just to divert the force of the fall into a tumble that sent her sprawling together with Addie back deep into the mud.

"Your turn," Tobias said, taking Elissa's arm and swinging her down while he held on as tightly as he could to a fork in the branch. "Protect your head," he ordered her. "Knees bent. You don't have to stay on your feet. Just twist to the side."

Elissa nodded. She fell. She created a rather spectacular splatter of mud, but she did climb back to her feet under her own power.

As Tobias fell himself, he felt a thorned vine graze the top of his head, closing just an eye-blink too late on the space where he'd been. Elissa and Addie were off and running before he had grabbed Keely's proffered hand and let her help him to his feet. The next vine lashed out while they were still in the middle of that maneuver, and Keely let out a yelp of pain as the thorns dug into her unprotected wrist, binding it fast to Tobias's gauntlet.

Tobias cursed himself mentally for allowing this to happen. Unable to lash the deadling about while his arm was bound to Keely's, he fumbled with his off hand to draw dagger and slash at the vine. He couldn't manage the leverage to severe the thing with a stroke this time, and before he could try a second, Keely let out another yelp. The deadling had snapped a vine around her ankle and yanked her feet out from under her. She hung suspended upside down for a moment, his tunic falling toward her shoulders in a manner he deeply regretted lacking the circumstance to enjoy.

Then as he redoubled his efforts to hack through the vine, Keely screwed up her face in intense concentration. The little white cat fell completely out of his tunic and scrambled desperately away through the mud. With the first vine nearly hacked through anyway, the sudden disappearance of Keely's arm from its grip allowed Tobias to yank his own arm free and to follow close on her tail.

He didn't waste the moment grabbing for his tunic, or even for a glance back over his shoulder. He just shifted the dagger to his good hand and ran. The deadling would already be recovering for its next strike, and with another ten or so coming up fast behind it, that didn't leave many options beyond "get out of its reach" or "die".

Ahead of him, Addie shrieked again, and Tobias found the reserves to push just a little harder, catching up with the others.

"No no no no no," Addie was whimpering, staring in shock at the sight of Doryne's broken body sprawled in a still-spreading pool of blood on the rocky outcropping where she'd landed—final confirmation that the young woman had given her life in defense of these children. Before Tobias could finish closing the distance between them, Elissa had scooped up the unresisting Addie and began carrying her along, but Tobias finally did risk a moment to look around.

With the body for a reference point to where they'd fallen from the bridge above, he was able to quickly spot the metallic glint of his sword, lying in the mud nearby. With a dive and a roll to evade the crack of another whip-like vine, he came up within reach of the blade and hefted it as he spun to face the next attack.

With a defiant roar, Tobias charged back at the closing deadling. Thorns ripped a fresh line of blood across his bare shoulder, but by then he had closed with the thing, catching the skull with a two-handed swing that smashed it up against the trunk of a tree with bone-shattering force. What fragments remained of the skull bounced and rolled away. The vines fell limp.

Then Tobias was forced to counter the lash of the next deadling with a desperate defensive stroke that allowed it to twine a vine around the sword. He barely managed to wrench the blade around and bring it to bear, severing the vine before it could yank the newly recovered weapon out of his hand. The next lash he countered with more grace, and he lured its owner into grabbing his gauntleted wrist again. He swung the skull about with such force that it completely circled the trunk of the tree he still stood beside.

Before it could orient itself, he'd pinned it there and shattered the skull with the pommel of his sword. That eliminated the closest threats, buying the others some time to get further away and himself the luxury of turning his back to flee after them once more.

Addie had started stumbling along beside Elissa again under her own power, while Keely trotted just ahead of them, scouting the way with her sharpened senses and moving fast enough that she could pause now and again to make sure no one had been left behind.

"Here," Tobias said, pressing his dagger into Elissa's hand. She would surely be carrying a knife on her for its pure utility, but the larger blade honed for combat might buy her a precious second or two if she had to cut herself—or the girl—free of their pursuers. Then he scooped up Addie again and urged the others to move faster. Even burdened by the girl, he had no trouble keeping up with Elissa's best speed.

"We can stay ahead of these things for a bit," Tobias said, "but I'm sure they'll run us down eventually, and I'm betting we can't outrun Scarlet at all once she's finished putting herself back together. I might be able to take on the witch by herself, and I can handle a couple of deadlings at a time, but we can't let ourselves get swarmed. We *have* to get out of the forest and away from the trees."

Keely paused directly in front of him and gave a sharp nod, raising one paw in the air, then she turned away again, beckoning him on with a jerk of her head. They'd become disoriented in the fog, she didn't know the forest, and there was no way for them to even keep to a straight line while navigating the maze of rocks, gullies, and massive roots and tree trunks.

For all that, Keely knew exactly how to find the edge of the forest: the world beyond the hedge reeked thoroughly of ash.

They pushed hard for the next couple of minutes, focusing on lengthening their lead while Keely veered their course steadily toward the source of the ashen smell. Then they eased up from the mad dash and tried to set the best steady pace that could be kept up by a small cat, a sedentary scholar, and a burdened swashbuckler, who'd all already seen more than their share of exertions in the past few days. It was no remarkable speed, but at least it seemed to be one that would buy them several more minutes.

Beyond those minutes, their future remained anyone's guess. The ghastly baying of the deadlings constantly reassured them that the pursuit hadn't broken off, but the erratic and echoing nature of it left little clue to the relative speed of their pursuers.

"There!" Elissa cried as they found themselves skirting along the top of a rocky outcrop, looking for a way down. Through a break in the trees and a thinning of the fog, they could make out the distant-but-distinct silhouette of the Wolf's Tooth. Keely wavered for a moment between deliberately leading them straight for it and deliberately leading them wide of the Tooth.

By the time she hit the muddy ground at the base of the rock, she'd made up her mind, and angled their course to the right, toward Castle Haywood. Yes, that would be leading these things straight to where the others should emerge from the forest, but it was at an exit currently held by the Inquisition—and as page seventeen clearly said, "When in doubt, unleash chaos."

Landing directly beside Keely and still carrying the unresisting Addie, Tobias slipped in the mud and went down along with his burden. He managed to roll to take the brunt of the impact himself and let out a mangled curse as his elbow connected solidly with a jutting stone. He skidded nearly two body lengths before coming to a stop.

Addie had recovered enough of her senses during the flight that she reached for Elissa's proffered hand and scrabbled to her feet so Tobias could gnaw, unimpeded, at the wrist of his gauntlet while the initial rush of pain passed. "Anything broken?" Elissa asked.

"Don't think so," Tobias finally managed to hiss; then he leaned on the arm to push himself up. The ground beneath him collapsed, and the three humans found themselves swept away in a sudden avalanche of mud.

Only Keely, with her light frame and feline reflexes, managed to leap to solid ground on the rock face behind them before everything else collapsed. What remained was only a gaping hole in the ground, filled with a darkness that even cat eyes couldn't penetrate from their vantage in the relative brightness above.

Hero? Keely yowled plaintively. *Jenny?* Nothing stirred in the darkness, and the only sound to be heard above the cacophony of the approaching deadlings was the echoing roar of rushing water. Icy dread fell over Keely, and she suddenly felt more alone and helpless than she could ever recall feeling since those first days after Hart Cove. She gave a mewl that sounded pathetic even in her own ears.

If she ran for it now, straight for the edge of the forest, she had no doubt she could make it out alive. The others were probably dead already, anyway. It was now or never. Cut and run to save her own skin.

She'd done it before—abandoned them for dead. Or...no. It had been Jenny who'd...Jenny who'd...

It didn't matter now. The point was they'd all pulled through, and she'd long-since forgiven Jenny. It wasn't Jenny's fault she was a pathetic little coward, useless in a fight. You had to accept your friends for who they were, or they weren't your friends.

Truth to tell, Keely had only survived that night because Jenny had needed her to—because Jenny never would have had it in her to soldier on on her own. Of the two of them, Keely was the clever one, the resourceful one, the survivor. Jenny had never been anything more than, well...Jenny.

Only now, Jenny was...and Hero was...back at the castle! Keely sighed as best a cat could and rolled her eyes. Typical for her to be left with the dirty work of leading the monsters astray. Well, she'd held up her end of the plan and bought them some time. All she could say is they'd better actually be waiting at the rendezvous this time, or she'd give them a proper piece of her mind when she *did* catch up with them.

With a last look at the gaping hole she'd so narrowly escaped, Keely shook the fog from her brain and took a series of hops across the rock face to solid ground, then darted away toward the edge of the forest and the rendezvous with her friends.

CHAPTER THIRTY-SEVEN

OOBLY YECH

Tobias hadn't been aware he'd stopped breathing until he woke suddenly, gasping desperately for air. It must have taken ten or fifteen seconds with him aware of nothing but the panicked need to fill his lungs before the pain crept in. It came slowly at first, then in a rush that threatened to make him black out again as nerves all over his body began fighting with each other to make their complaints heard.

"Hush! Hush! Hush!" Elissa hissed, urging him to choke off the scream he hadn't even been aware of starting, while she continued to work at clearing the mud away from his face. He was only peripherally aware of her skyward glance, but it did just manage to focus his attention enough to hear the laughter of the deadlings as its echoes grew steadily louder from that direction.

"Is he...?" Addie began tentatively.

"He'll live," Elissa said dismissively.

Tobias himself didn't feel nearly so certain at that moment, but either the young priestess was well-convinced or she was a damn-good liar. Through the haze of pain, he took a mental head count. "Keely?"

Elissa just shook her head. Her face remained impassive, but another tear joined the few that had forged trails down her cheeks.

"I think your cat's buried under the mud," Addie said. "I'm really sorry. I could tell she was special."

Somewhere in Tobias's head, a gate slammed shut, and a cold wind howled through the castle of his mind. There was no way he could possibly process the import of those words right now on top of everything else. Locking them away was the only option. Finish the fight first, then assess the cost. "Dig me out," he said flatly. "I have to..."

"You have to nothing," Elissa said in a voice of cold steel. "You're done, Your Highness. I only said you'd live. I'm not promising anything else. And unless a miraculata happens to stroll by, *not dying* is the *only* thing of consequence you'll be fit to do for weeks. If you're feeling like passing back out, don't fight it. I've got a handle on things here."

"You do?" Tobias asked.

"Absolutely." She tugged his gauntlets off, one at a time, causing currently misplaced bits of bone in his arms to shift in unintended ways. By the time she was done, he *had* passed out again.

"Then why are you shaking?" Addie asked.

"Because we're in a cave," Elissa said, pulling the over-sized leather gauntlets onto her own hands. "And it's bloody cold. Keep digging him out, but try not to jostle anything. I need to look around."

"This is the Oobly Yech's cave," Addie said, peering miserably at the light far overhead. "There's no way out." It wasn't that the walls of the cave were sheer. It was that they leaned inward as they rose.

"Nonsense," Elissa said. "You're not going to get eaten by a slimy monster, and there's always a way out."

"Don't treat me like a baby. How can you say the Oobly Yech doesn't exist when we're being chased by Bloody Scarlet?" Addie demanded angrily.

"I never claimed it doesn't exist." Elissa sighed, picking her way down the heap of mud and stone they'd landed in. "I said it's not going to eat you. Do you have faith in Seriena?"

"I...She didn't save Sister Petra," Addie said. "And the Inquisition..."

"You don't believe for a moment that the Inquisition *actually* has her blessing, do you?" Elissa said without looking back. "And as to Sister Petra, she was a woman grown, fully responsible for her own life and her own choices. Plus, I seriously doubt she spent her last moments praying. You're more devout than that. Leave off digging long enough to make sure Seriena knows exactly where things stand. She's not going to let a pious little girl get eaten by monsters."

"Really?" Addie asked tremulously.

"Absolutely," Elissa said. She was moving with a serious limp after the fall, but her voice remained unwavering. "There's a pool down here that'll pass for a mirror if you want to come say your prayers at it."

This was no cramped little cave they were in, but broad and twisting, with a ridge of fallen stone down the center where the ceiling had given way to leave a crevice in the forest floor some thirty feet above. The new collapse they'd rode in on had extended the existing crevice by at least fifteen feet in the process of depositing them here. Most of the floor not mounded with rubble lay submerged beneath a muddy stream, swollen and roiling with runoff from the recent downpour.

While Addie knelt and said her prayers, Elissa walked downstream along the banks, disappearing around a curve of the cavern for what felt to Addie like an eternity, but realistically must have been only a couple of minutes. Even so, by the time Elissa did return, the laughter of the deadlings seemed to be coming from directly overhead. Addie remained kneeling until she found Elissa standing over her, offering a hand up.

"You believe." This time there was no question in Elissa's voice. It was a simple statement of fact.

Five minutes before or five hours before or five days before, Addie couldn't have honestly told herself what she believed. But here and now, with the world collapsing around them, the unvarnished conviction in the voice of the only woman standing between her and a nightmarish end filled up the doubts.

"You know she will stand with us," Elissa said, keeping Addie's eyes locked on her own steady gaze. "And you know she will deliver us."

Addie just nodded as the racing of her heart began to ease—not completely, of course, but substantially.

"Now dig," Elissa said, nodding her head back toward Tobias. "The next time you hear my voice, if I'm not telling you the danger's past, hide yourself and Prince Tobias under your cloak as best you can and be still. Understood?"

Addie nodded again and scrambled away back up the debris to where she'd left Tobias. She was still scooping mud away from around him when the insane laughter overhead abruptly ceased.

Without thinking about it, Addie stopped digging and froze, her eyes wandering back and forth between the ribbon of light overhead and Elissa, who had started exploring upstream along the cavern when Addie had returned to digging. When the deafening silence fell, Elissa sat down calmly on the nearest rock, pulled out the dagger Tobias had given her, and started using it to clean mud from under her fingernails.

An interminable minute passed before the shadow appeared at the hole in the ceiling, then Bloody Scarlet came gliding serenely down on the thorny vine of a deadling like she was an acrobat descending from the wires. At first, Elissa's only reaction to Scarlet's appearance was to stop cleaning her nails. Then as Addie watched, the young priestess rolled up her sleeve, gritted her teeth, and very deliberately cut a long gash down the inside of her left arm, most of the way from elbow to wrist, and simply allowed it to bleed as she rinsed the blade off in the stream.

"And you complained about *us* taking our time," Elissa said as the crimson-cloaked figure neared the floor. Obediently, Addie quickly ducked down and hid under her cloak—but not so thoroughly down or hidden that she didn't leave herself a gap to watch the proceedings.

"In my defense, you did indeed take your sweet time," Scarlet sighed, stepping lightly to the floor. Gone was the broken creature that had clawed its way up the tree toward them, replaced now with a wholesome, rosy-cheeked woman who'd have had an easier time at convincing passersby she'd never been ill a day in her life than she'd have had at convincing them she was a day over twenty. Even her long, lustrous red hair peeked coquettishly out from under the pristine hood of her cloak.

"I've got to say, I never imagined you'd be the one standing to face me. Sitting. Whatever. What happened to prince charming? I was looking forward to snuffing out a final, gallant display of chivalry."

"He's buried under about five tons of rock and mud, I expect." Elissa shrugged, giving a nod toward the new mound on the cavern floor. "Just me left, and I'm not even scared of you. Sorry to disappoint."

Scarlet half-stifled a chuckle of amused disbelief. "City girl, you're terrified. I could smell the fear rolling off of you even if you *hadn't* wet yourself."

"Oh, yeah, I'm terrified," Elissa agreed, her voice still clear and level. "But I believe that what I *said*, is that I wasn't afraid of *you*. I know a thing or three about monsters. And as monsters go, you're a rank amateur."

"So...what?" Scarlet asked, unperturbed. "You're trying to goad me into going all, 'How dare you?' so I'll leave myself vulnerable for prince charming to get a free shot? Like it *matters*. I've put myself back together more times than you've even bathed," Scarlet said, beginning to amble in Elissa's direction. "Get it through your wispy little head, girl: I...don't...die."

"Eh." Elissa shrugged. "But you do get bored, don't you? All that time on your hands, and you don't even know how to spend it? You're not even really angry with me, and you sure don't think I can inconvenience you. You just decided you'd kill me to give yourself something to do, never for a moment thinking about the rollicking good time you're throwing away."

"Don't tell me you're into girls." Scarlet smirked even as she flared out her cloak in a frivolous little pirouette that showed off a figure custom made for being shown off in frivolous little pirouettes—perhaps *literally* custom made, given what the woman sporting it seemed capable of. "Been there. Done that. Not looking for another pet."

Elissa shook her head. "I'm into hunting monsters."

"You?" Scarlet snorted.

"Big time." Elissa nodded. "*Real* monsters. I had a plan going with a friend of mine, but as we seem to be sitting in her mausoleum, I'm going to need a new partner. Feel like taking down the Inquisition? Permanently?"

"Oooh." Scarlet stopped. "*Now* I'm surprised. Not amused yet, but I'm surprised. One of the upstart's own offering to help me sunder her sword and shield? Aren't you afraid of what I'll do to your precious church without them?"

"Not really," Elissa said with a dismissive shrug. "Theologically speaking, the Inquisition serves no purpose. They'll tell you themselves that their power and wisdom pales before that of the divine, so what good are they—especially weighed against all the damage they do? They're no one's sword or shield except their own.

"That's what this whole book thing has been about, you know," Elissa went on, seizing on the grain of interest from Scarlet. "The Inquisition is running scared because they know what it has to say can finish them once and for all. I don't have the muscle to take advantage of that myself, and *you're* never going to find someone else who can read it and understand what she's seeing as well as I can—not someone who's actually *eager* to help you use it against the Inquisition.

"Plus I know full well you don't even have the morals of cat. Just as soon as I'm done being of use to you, you'll kill me anyway. At this point I just don't care. My friends are gone. My family's gone. My future was well and truly out the window before we met. All I want is to take the Inquisition down with me."

"Huh," Scarlet grunted, a thoughtful expression playing across her face as she stood with hands on hips. "You actually sound like you mean it."

"Well, to be *perfectly* honest," Elissa said, climbing a little unsteadily to her feet, "there is *one* other thing I'd like."

"Oooh!" Scarlet beamed, clapping her hands. "Is this where you spring the clever trap?"

"Can we maybe just call it a 'mad gambit to hedge in case you weren't in a listening mood'?" Elissa asked. "'Clever trap' makes it sounds like I was doing more than grabbing any dice I could reach and rolling them, in the desperate hope that *something* would change the game."

"Fair enough." Scarlet shrugged. "Tell me your punch line."

"Not that the 'mad gambit' seems to have panned out, mind you. But I still want to know what's lurking in the bone pits."

Scarlet blinked. "That's rather a disappointing punchline. Anyway, I thought I already told you. It's the vengeful dead."

"Like from your story?" Elissa asked. "I wasn't sure how much credit to give any of that."

"Oh, it's all absolutely true," Scarlet assured her. "Excepting the bits I made up, of course."

"Certainly." Elissa nodded.

"They can't kill me, either," Scarlet said matter-of-factly. "Mother *knows* they've tried."

Elissa answered with a "fair enough" shrug. "So what do you say? Shall we dismantle the Inquisition together?"

Scarlet stood for a few moments, rolling her eyes thoughtfully while tapping a foot and drumming her fingers on her folded arms. "Still not convinced I need you for that."

"Obviously, you're at the advantage in a skirmish with them," Elissa said. "But you've been fighting skirmishes with them for...how long? They just keep coming back for more. And, if I may make an observation, you don't actually have to decide right this moment, do you? Nothing's to stop you from going back to finish *this* skirmish with them, then seeing how you feel. I'm clearly going *nowhere*." She gestured expansively to the cave around them, and to the only exit, high overhead. "All the same for you whether you kill me now or leave me to stew for a day or two before you come back to kill me."

"You have a point," Scarlet conceded. "All very reasonable."

"Thank you."

"I don't do reasonable," Scarlet hissed abruptly, crossing the remaining distance between them in a blur and lifting Elissa off the ground by her already abused throat. "And I'm not keen on this whole 'delayed gratification' business, either. I'm more your basic spoiled brat type."

Elissa's composure cracked. The only thing that stopped her from letting loose a piercing shriek as she kicked and struggled uselessly was the hand around her neck.

"I *am* a storyteller, girl. I know how these things work," Scarlet went on, completely unperturbed by Elissa's struggles. "Plucky young nobody cleverly leads powerful adversary into underestimating her—granting said nobody time to rally, learn from her mistakes, and come back with a plan to exploit her opponent's fatal flaw. I tell that story over and over and over and over and over..."

Scarlet's eyes rolled, then they went out of focus as her voice fell into a monotone loop that seemed like it would persist longer than Elissa's breath would. Then as Elissa thought she was going to black out, Scarlet abruptly released her to crumple on the rocky floor of the cave.

"And do you know why I tell it that way all the time?" Scarlet asked, dropping down beside Elissa and pulling her head into her lap. "Not because it *happens* all the time. That would be nonsense." Scarlet began stroking Elissa's hair in a manner that might have been soothing, had she not also been effortlessly pinning Elissa's shoulder in a way that actually hampered her desperate attempts to get her lungs working properly again.

"It's because a head without proper stories is like a body without bread, and because a wolf who tried to deny food to the deer would soon find herself an ex-wolf. There's only three ways to tell a story, and two of them don't work. One's like gorging yourself on honey 'til you're sick, the other's like trying to live on a diet of rocks. Proper stories are important. They tell you how to live your life. They tell you why to live your life. The trick is to keep from confusing them with your actual life.

"In *actual* life, for every plucky little girl who overcomes impossible odds, you could build a mountain out of the little girls who tried and failed. *I'm* the little girl who managed the impossible. That makes *you* just one more body on the heap. Because no matter how much I enjoy playing with my food, I never let it crawl away alive. When I do leave this cave, it will be after removing your pretty little head," Scarlet said, grinning and laying a finger to Elissa's nose like a mother telling her child a silly story, "from your pretty little shoulders. Won't that be nice?"

Scarlet suddenly blinked and her eyes widened as a stone collided with the back of her head, then bounced harmlessly away. Relinquishing her grip on Elissa, Scarlet slowly turned to see Addie glaring down at her from atop of pile of rubble. "Leave her alone," the girl demanded, her body shaking in rage and terror, her face stained with tears.

"See?" Scarlet grinned at Elissa, who was laboring to rise. "I knew you were lying about *something*." Then Scarlet turned her grin on Addie. "Hello, little girl. Were you wanting to play? I could show you what big teeth I have." As Scarlet's grin widened, it did indeed bare a rather nasty-looking set of fangs.

Still disoriented, Elissa took a blind swing toward Scarlet's ankle, but all she connected with was trailing end of the woman's billowing cape. Scarlet had already begun stalking toward Addie. With a shriek, the girl turned and ran, dancing downstream along the top of the ridge of rocks. Elissa attempted to hiss out a threat at the retreating Scarlet, but the attempt only devolved into a painful coughing fit.

"Come now," Scarlet chided the girl as she strolled unhurriedly after her along the less-treacherous ground on the banks of the swollen stream. "*You* started this. Well, okay, *I* started this first, but then you came back and started it some more. What did you think would—"

Scarlet's question died unfinished when all at once a great muddy black mass lurched up out of the stream and came crashing down on top of her. There was no way of properly saying what size the thing was, given how it undulated and oozed, and how it seemed to extend back into the water like a gigantic worm, but to liken its girth to that of an elephant or a small cottage would give some account of its scale. Whether or not it was truly made of mud was hard to say. It might have been glistening black mud. It might have been tar or dark, coagulating blood. It might have been all of them mixed together, or something else entirely. Whatever that core component of the nauseating, viscous mass might have been, it smelled of decay and bristled with bones of all sizes and kinds—with the possible exception of jawbones and skulls. The thing made no sound beyond the splat of it hitting the cave floor, then it squirmed back into the water, leaving no trace of Scarlet behind.

"Oh dear," Elissa breathed. "I hope—"

About ten yards downstream, the floodwaters exploded with such violence that they knocked Elissa off her feet and spattered her with black ooze. There was no way to catch a glimpse of Scarlet in the midst of that, but her head must have broken the surface, judging from the deafening, primal scream that echoed off the cavern walls. Then the scream died as quickly as it had come, leaving behind just the background roar of the flood.

"Addie!" Elissa screamed, beckoning to the girl who remained frozen, staring at the spectacle. Then Elissa pointed toward the thorny vine Scarlet had rode in on, still dangling there, unmoving.

It took the girl a moment to get her brain working again, then she was running back the way she'd come, heading for the vine. Before they reached it, a series of smaller explosions broke the surface of the stream. Here, a blackened hand clawed its way momentarily above the surface. There, chunks of bone and ooze went flying out of the water.

"But how do we...?" Addie asked, arriving at the vine only to stare up at the nasty array of thorns spiking its whole length.

"You didn't ask 'how' before, did you?" Elissa asked, gripping the vine firmly with one borrowed gauntlet. It failed to react. "I'll handle the thinking. You handle the praying. Don't stop. And hold onto me."

While Elissa fiddled with the vine, Addie cast a sideways glance in the direction where Tobias lay hidden in the mud. "Pray for him, too," Elissa said. "We'll be back, girl. Faith." Elissa stabbed the dagger about half an inch into the stout vine. It shuddered, but no more. "Come on," she muttered as another scream erupted farther down the stream. "You've got to have *some* sense of self-preservation left in that skull."

She stabbed again. And again. The vine jerked and danced, nearly pulling her off her feet. It did not, despite Addie's fervent prayers, rise.

Something came staggering out of the darkness downstream, making its way laboriously along the banks, dripping water and mud and slime as it came. What hair remained on its tattered scalp hung in limp, auburn strands. What flesh hadn't been flayed from its bone had been blackened and burned. Its clothing had fared no better than its flesh, but the ragged remnant of a red cape and hood still hung tenaciously to its bony shoulders. The thing cast about blindly, for no trace of eyes remained in the sockets of its skull.

Perhaps its lungs and throat remained intact, though, for it screamed out in an unmistakable semblance of Scarlet's voice. "Kill her!"

Addie yelped and held on for life as the vine wrapped firmly around Elissa's arm and yanked the two of them upward. They hung for a moment, dangling over the mouth of the cave, staring at the permanent grin of Scarlet's macabre servitor. Then it let go.

Elissa grabbed desperately with both hands, doing her best to ignore Addie's continued shrieking. Somehow the girl held onto her, and she held onto the vine, but when simply letting go didn't finish the job of killing them, the deadling brought its other vines to bear, tangling Elissa's limbs and throat.

In the midst of all that chaos, Addie blinked, abruptly aware that the deadling and its entire pack of compatriots were paying her no mind whatever. With an exultant surge of hope and a reaffirmed belief in the power of prayer, she leapt straight at the skull. The thing let out an unearthly shriek as she locked her arms around it and it tumbled through the air with her. Just clearing the edge of the crevice, they landed and rolled together across a muddy slab of rock. Then Addie was on her feet again, bruised and battered and feeling thorns tear into her flesh, but ignoring it all. No monster was going to eat her today, and no monster would eat Sister Elissa, either.

With the skull tucked under her arm, Addie scrambled up the slippery stone, putting distance between herself and the cave mouth. Between trying to anchor itself and keeping Elissa entangled, the captive skull seemed to lack either the vines or the mental faculties to foil Addie.

After a few moments, she looked back to find that Elissa—having been dragged along with them—had come clear of the cave mouth as well, and Addie smashed the skull down on the rock underfoot with all the strength she could muster. The skull shattered. The lights in its eyes winked out. It vines went limp, and Elissa fell to the ground, gasping for breath.

The the rest of the pack of the deadlings resumed their insane laughter and converged, single-mindedly intent on carrying out the orders of their mistress.

Addie charged to Elissa's aid, only to find herself drawn up short. In shocked disbelief, she realized too late that the things had been ignoring her not because of divine protection, but because they'd considered her irrelevant. She'd made herself relevant by directly interfering with their mission, and now they had her tangled as thoroughly as they'd tangled Elissa.

By whatever grace remained, none of them was throttling her, but still she struggled and screamed in pain and in helpless frustration, unable to do anything but watch as the vines twined once more about Elissa's neck.

Then all at once there was a giantess at Addie's side, slashing about her maniacally with the short blade in one hand, smashing skulls into whatever rocky surface came to hand with the other. Then Ulric, of the Earl's own guard, appeared as out of nowhere, laying about him no less viciously as he fought to reach Elissa with the aid of the young man who'd seemed to be Tobias's squire.

Soon Addie and Elissa were both free, grabbing whatever stones they could find and joining in the desperate fight. When the chaos died down, the five of them were all well bloodied by the thorns, but still standing amid the fragments of skull and the lifeless vines. It might almost have been peaceful for a moment, were it not for the enraged and incoherent howling of Bloody Scarlet still coming from below.

"Everyone catch your breath," Elissa commanded as she started gathering up vines and tying them together. "This isn't over. Ulric, I know we're nearly to a gate in the hedge. Can you point us at it?" When he nodded, she passed him one end of a vine. "Find a tree to tie this to. Secure it like a life depended on it."

"You're not seriously going down there?" he asked.

"No." Elissa shook her head. "But if Scarlet doesn't come out, Tobias is dead. She'll find him down there eventually if she's cooped up for long."

"Right." Ulric nodded and headed toward the nearest likely looking tree.

"Conrad, I know where your duty lies," Elissa said as she finished tying off her knots, "but we're not getting him out of there without something better than thorny vines. As soon as we're clear of the forest, the best thing you can do for him is to round up help and equipment. He's in bad shape, so send someone for a healer, too."

"Don't say I never did anything for you!" Elissa called down the sinkhole as they finished up. She tossed the free end of the vine down the hole, then turned to limp away as quickly as she could manage, with Ulric and Conrad on either side to support her.

Addie ran ahead with Evadne, babbling excitedly to her about what a hero Sister Elissa was, and how she'd pulled one over on Bloody Scarlet.

"What happened down there, Sister?" Conrad asked, somewhat awed by the account even after making allowances for its source.

"I forgot to simper," Elissa said grimly.

CHAPTER THIRTY-EIGHT

DEALING WITH THE DEVIL

They wasted no more breath on talking, and only ran as best they could until they reached the gate Elissa had come through with Nolan, which—by a stroke of luck—now stood unlocked, and no one had to clamber over anything. They simply ran on through, and they kept running until they reached the gate in the hedge at the far side of the pasture. It was there they finally stopped, breathing with varying degrees of difficulty as they all kept an eye on the forest hedge from the nagging fear that pursuit would come exploding out of it at any moment.

It was also there that Elissa, after spending some minutes staring at the forest with a lost expression on her face, abruptly collapsed onto the ground and began to cry, quietly but uncontrollably. When it became clear this wasn't just a passing moment, Evadne settled down beside Elissa and silently laid a hand on her shoulder, while Ulric pulled Addie to the side and reiterated Conrad's earlier question. "What happened down there?"

"I think Sister Elissa's going to be a miraculata," Addie managed, though she was clearly having trouble processing her own collection of deferred emotions. "Everything happened so fast. But Scarlet...got Lady Doryne, and she must've got the sister's postulant. There was a nobleman with them who rescued us, but then we all fell into the cave. That nearly killed him, and it killed the sister's cat. Then Scarlet came down after us, but Elissa kept her talking until the Oobly Yech came, and we got away." Her halting explanation trailed off, and that seemed to be the end of what she was going to offer.

"Keely's, dead...?" Ulric asked, suddenly going a little numb himself. When Addie nodded, Ulric found himself sinking down beside Evadne and Elissa and pulling the little girl into his lap.

"I need to go find help for Prince Tobias," Conrad insisted.

Ulric pointed through the gate and down the lane toward the right. "Nearest farmhouse will be that way," he said. "Tell them I sent you. Just remember, no matter how much you want to rush back, we need to give plenty of time for Scarlet to get clear."

Conrad nodded and took off, leaving Ulric with the two women, the little girl, and his thoughts.

The foremost, overwhelming thought was that he'd failed miserably. He could make all sorts of excuses about having been handed an impossible challenge to begin with, but to what end? His whole life had been about protecting Haywoodshire in general and the house of Haywood in particular. Now half the county lay in ash while the Inquisition terrorized it without restraint.

They might lack the political authority to choose the successors to the Haywoods, but they could destroy the family by excommunication, turning them outlaw—and apparently already had. From the sound of things, they'd declared a holy war on the entire county. The earl and the countess must already be dead or worse. Their girls, though likely alive for the moment, had been effectively cut off from the carefully planned escape routes by a homicidal nursery bogey.

And now that the only woman presumptuous enough to claim she could set everything right lay dead in a sinkhole full of monsters, he discovered that despite all his protestations of cynicism, some small part of him had been waiting for Keely to make good on her promises.

Without noticing when it had happened, Ulric found that Addie had her face buried against his neck, the tears flowing freely as he rocked her in what had probably started as much as an effort to sooth himself as one to sooth her.

Time ceased to matter as they remained like that, aware of nothing much except that nothing had yet come bursting out of the forest looking for their blood. Then Elissa left off her crying to let out a blood-curdling shriek.

In a heartbeat, both Ulric and Evadne were on their feet with blades drawn, casting about for the source of the threat. What they found was Elissa backing away from something unseen, scooting through the grasses of the pasture more quickly than they would have imagined possible. Ulric attempted to step defensively between Elissa and whatever her horrified gaze had fixed on, but still he saw nothing, and still Elissa kept screaming.

He was lowering his guard and debating whether she'd simply gone mad when, turning around, he spotted what her eyes were tracking: a palm-sized pink-and-white butterfly, flitting in what might generously be called Elissa's direction. The only thing at all remarkable about the creature was that Ulric couldn't recall seeing one with those markings before, but the same could probably be said for half the butterflies in the county. Butterflies weren't a thing he spent a lot of time contemplating.

With no better options coming to mind, and with the slight twang of regret natural to destroying anything pleasant, Ulric stepped forward and smashed the butterfly between his hands. When Elissa's eyes continued to track the colorful, lifeless form all the way to the ground, Ulric ground what remained of the wings under the heel of his boot. Elissa's panicked screaming immediately trailed off into hyperventilating.

"Better?" he asked.

Elissa nodded weakly. "I...butterflies..." she managed.

"Are more scary than all the forces of the Inquisition and the goblins of the forest combined?" Ulric volunteered.

"Oh, yeah." Elissa nodded, roughly wiping away her tears with the heel of her hand. "Thank you, Ulric." She climbed unsteadily to her feet and dusted off her robes, then limped determinedly out into the lane beyond the hedge.

"Where exactly are you going?" Ulric asked.

"Away," Elissa said simply. "Lake Etherea, I expect. I'm sorry everything's gone so terribly wrong. I can't fix any of it, but I can still make it count for something. I'll be damned if Jane Carver's getting her hands on the book we found."

Ulric nearly slapped himself for forgetting about the thing that had started this whole mess. Wherever the Grimm Truth had ended up, it surely would contain the leverage he'd need to restore the house of Haywood. If not, it would at least position him for a messy revenge on the Inquisition. He'd lost the battle, but the war still stretched out ahead of him. Cold comfort, but a reason to get up and get moving again.

"I'm with you," Ulric said, "but I've got people trapped between Bloody Scarlet and Jane Carver that I can't abandon."

Evadne nodded. "I have to get to Baldassare. Then, go'ss willing, we might still find Sabina."

"All right, then." Elissa stopped and unslung her pack, passing it to Addie. "How's that faith of yours?" she asked the girl.

"Strong," Addie said firmly.

"Then you're on a special, secret, holy mission, protecting the book in this pack. Keep it hidden. You're going to pretend to be a page to Prince Tobias now. Pick out a boy's name to hide behind, and ask Conrad to help you in your masquerade to get you away from the Inquisition. If we don't make it back, leave with him when he goes. If that happens and Prince Tobias lives, give the book to him and *only* to him. He's a good man who'll take care of you. If Prince Tobias dies, tell Conrad I need him to take you to Miraculata Cosima in Serylia. Give the book only to her, and tell her my last wish was that she find a place for you in the church. Can you remember all that?"

In the great hall of Castle Haywood, Jane Carver sat slouched in her chair with Sir Riordan flanking her, leaning on his great axe. With fingers steepled, Jane regarded the couple seated across the high table from her. Dried blood covered much of the right half of Earl Darby's face, which had already begun to bruise badly. Countess Violet's left arm hung limply in a sling. Her complexion pallid, she seemed somewhere on the edge of either being violently ill or passing out—perhaps both.

"This is the *last* time I will ask," Jane said coldly. "Do you take sugar with your tea?"

Darby and Violet remained silent and unmoving.

"Fine," Jane huffed. "Sugar for both of them." Her eyes flicked briefly to the kitchen girl standing at stiff attention nearby, and the girl pounced immediately on the eye-contact as permission to see to her duties by going somewhere that wasn't here.

"Right, then." Jane sighed. "I know we got off on the wrong foot, but no one ever accused me of holding a grudge. There were extenuating circumstances. Your whole county's become ensorcelled under the foul spell of the witch, etcetera, etcetera. I'm quite inclined to let you off with blood spilled and land devastated. You've paid your penance."

"Just like that?" Earl Darby asked suspiciously. "After...everything that's happened?"

"Oh, no," Jane admitted. "Not 'just like that' of course. There will be speeches and confessions and accusations and repentance. Much wailing and gnashing of teeth. The usual showmanship. And you'll need to hold up your end. Politics can be a dreadful bore, but I wouldn't complain about that too much, because—let's be candid—I've decided we can be politically useful to each other."

"How would you like it," Jane asked politely, "if I not only gave you a clean slate, but I also took care of your little vandalism problem and got Pontifine Augusta forever off your backs about the cathedral? From what my people tell me, you're rather in an untenable position with *her* now even if *I* clear you of all charges. Her emissaries have both gone missing, and between us and the vandals, we've left the cathedral site a total mess."

"And what is it *you* want?" Violet asked through gritted teeth. Jane seemed to overlook the countess's demeanor of bad grace as purely a matter of pain, though there was no telling whether that was truly the case.

"All I want is the Tooth." Jane shrugged dismissively.

"We've told you—" Darby began, but Jane cut him off.

"The *Tooth*," Jane repeated, stressing the lack of an "r". "The Wolf's Tooth. It's lovely. I want it. It's got such wonderful...atmosphere. Such history." She sighed wistfully. "I'm going to have it one way or another. Eventually. Pontifine Augusta doesn't 'get' the Tooth. To her, it's just a lofty place to sit, but she's dreadfully set in her ways, and she isn't going to give it up willingly. Your political pull as worldly caretakers of this county added to mine as head of the Inquisition should expedite matters quite wonderfully, though.

"Before you say anything brave or defiant or otherwise stupid—anything at all, really—I'm not asking you to agree to anything. I don't *need* your support. It would just be convenient. That's the only tenuous reason you're alive—and why I won't hesitate to remedy that situation the moment I decide my magnanimity was wasted." Jane Carver smiled a bright, cold, empty smile as she gracefully rose from her chair. "Political circus aside, you and your entire county are pagan scum. I will never be your friend. Still, many people find it quite motivating to simply not have me as an enemy. Enjoy your tea."

Brushing a wayward lock of graying hair back from her face, Jane turned and walked unhurriedly from the hall with Sir Riordan falling neatly in step to flank her. When the serving girl returned bearing the silver tea service, a little white cat ducked unnoticed from an alcove near the doors, and then through them before they could be closed. From there, it scurried away, following the sound of Jane's voice.

"That went well, don't you think?" Jane was asking.

"I'm sure they'll be no more problem, Sublima," Riordan's voice responded, "and probably useful."

They were exiting into the courtyard when Keely caught up with them. Following the pair across the courtyard offered no challenge despite the presence of several of Jane's followers doing their best to secure the site. The Inquisition might have won the battle, but it had been no easy victory, and even the freshest of the sentries looked fairly haggard.

Add in all the clutter left behind by the refugees who'd sheltered in the courtyard while the fire was raging out of control, and there was really no way they could spare the attention it would take to notice a small feline attempting to go unseen.

"Let's have a complete tour of the tunnels inside the Tooth day after tomorrow, as soon as the witch is dealt with. Excellent work finding those, poppet," Jane said, in a tone Keely found unnervingly close to sincere affection.

"Thank you, Sublima," Riordan said simply.

"That spire actually sings with divine power," Jane said, falling into a rapture not unlike a child contemplating the imminent arrival of a beloved sweet. "I could hear it calling to me from miles away. Do tell me you hear it too?"

"I wish I could," Riordan said. "There might have been a tickling at my ears. I could feel...something, though. Heady. Raw. A little intoxicating."

"Ah, well." Jane patted him on the shoulder. "Dulled senses are better than no senses. And how is our Shoshona? Still sleeping it off?"

Riordan nodded.

"I'm quite gratified she survived her ordeal, but even given her portents, we must go into those woods expecting a dreadful battle. There's power in them, too, and demons ancient beyond reckoning. Dealing with them will be our next great crusade, and the Wolf's Tooth our holy fortress to operate out of." Jane Carver stopped suddenly, spinning around as she scanned the courtyard. "The witch is searching for our Shoshona, poppet. I can smell her spying on us."

For all Keely could tell, Jane might as easily have been imagining things, have come down with a case of showmanship, or have genuinely noticed she was following them. Regardless, Keely wasn't about to wait around to find out whether that phenomenal run of bad luck she'd had getting away from Jane at Belgrimm Abbey had been anything more than coincidence.

She bolted at once from hiding place to hiding place, until she could scramble up to the roof of an out-building, thence to the parapets, and finally up onto the roof of the keep, where she remained carefully hidden for the remainder of her spying. It made listening in on the rest of the conversation difficult, even with feline ears, but that didn't last long in any event. Jane ordered an extra guard sent into the keep to watch over Shoshona, then mounted up and left the castle with a small entourage that included Sir Riordan.

"Your daughters are all alive and well," Keely announced the moment the doors to the great hall closed behind her. Clad in a borrowed tunic she'd found unguarded, she'd arrived to discover Darby and Violet alone with their untouched, cooling tea. "At least they were when I left them this morning."

Violet sat up abruptly, putting on her best facade of a stately noblewoman who had *not* just been crying into her husband's shoulder. The effect got rather spoiled by the yelp of pain she gave at the sudden shifting of her arm. "All three of them?" she asked, instantly discarding all concerns of a non-motherly nature to grasp at whatever hopes she was offered.

Keely nodded. "At least Minda had a couple of young ones there acting like they were her sisters. Her friend, Lady Doryne, was killed this morning trying to keep them all safe, though. Whatever honors you can heap on her family after this is all done, she earned them. We may not have long, though, so I'm going to try to keep this brief.

"I owe you like a million apologies, but I can't give them yet because there's a lot I can still salvage. Once the battle's over, I'll break down in the whole self-recrimination thing if you like, and probably even if you don't. Point is, we've managed to convince the Inquisition to march into the forest with all the force they can muster come tomorrow morning, and the forest has become an insanely dangerous place."

Darby snorted. "You got that much right, girl. I went looking for Minda and lost three men to a Tuatha ambush before we could pull back. I was counting myself lucky to make it out alive when Carver's men fell on us."

"The Tuatha are just the tip of it," Keely said earnestly. "I'm an unreliable witness to begin with, so I'm not even going to try to go into the details, but the ancient horrors everyone talks about in the forest are waking up, and they're not happy—both in general, and with the Inquisition very specifically. I wouldn't lay money on anyone walking into the Crimson forest tomorrow wearing red and black making it out alive, no matter what force they go in with."

"The bad news is that your daughters were still in the forest when I left them. The good news is that Hero, Jenny, and I were leading the dangers away from them when we split up. The girls could be showing up any time at whatever postern gate the young ones snuck out of here through."

"Hero? You mean Ulric?" Darby asked.

"Oh, right. You haven't met Hero. Different guy. I expect Ulric's still with them. Anyway, they can't stay out there, so you need to make sure that gate's safe for them to return through, and try to find them someplace safe to hide out here for a day or two. *I* have to go find a way to keep Jane Carver from going into the forest, no matter what becomes of her lackeys."

The countess blinked. "Whatever for?" she asked incredulously.

"Because if the Grand High Inquisitrix goes off to get herself martyred fighting witches, demons, and pagan forest savages," Keely said, "we will *never* be rid of the Inquisition."

She retreated at once to her lofty hiding place on the roof of the keep and began to contemplate. She had absolutely not considered Jane Carver showing up in time to be the reinforcements she'd sent Shoshona to find, and she certainly hadn't known what she was luring them all into the forest to face. She'd been counting on some bloody fighting with the Tuatha to sap their strength.

The thought of luring militant extremists into a fair fight had seemed a sort of poetic justice. Luring them to face Bloody Scarlet and her macabre hounds felt more like cold-blooded murder. If she told them point blank what lay waiting for them and they believed her, they'd probably still charge in. This was the very sort of job they were supposed to exist for.

But even if they charged in believing, they'd charge in not understanding. If the rank-and-file of the Inquisition really did go around dealing with monsters like Scarlet, they'd have their hands too full fighting actual threats to wage all those cloak-and-dagger wars on people whose only crime was being inconvenient.

On the other hand, they *did* wage all those cloak-and-dagger wars on people whose only crime was being inconvenient. Maybe the Inquisition and Bloody Scarlet deserved each other. Maybe she was underestimating Jane's resources—spooky woman that she was—for a fight against the likes of Scarlet, even if the rest of the Inquisition remained clueless and helpless.

All the maybes had her head swimming. The one certainty was that regardless of who walked away from a fight between the Inquisition and Bloody Scarlet, the world would be a safer place without whoever didn't walk away.

Keely knew she was over-thinking this, but so much had already gone so wrong. Riordan had lit that fire, not her, but she couldn't wash her hands of it either. She hadn't pushed Violet into armed rebellion, but she'd planted the seeds of hope that the Inquisition *could* be overthrown. She hadn't roused Bloody Scarlet, but...

No. There was no wiggle room on that one. She *had* roused Bloody Scarlet. She'd never meant to, but in her own cleverness trying to make everyone believe that the Grimm Truth was really out there, up for grabs, she'd caught the attention of a monster. Everything that had gone wrong after could either be traced directly back to that night in Denecia, or to her own hubris in underestimating the Inquisition.

Or was that more properly said as "overestimating her own cleverness"? For years, no matter how many balls she'd tossed into the air, she'd always been right on the spot to catch them as they fell—until now. And where in Seriena's name had Jenny gone off to? She and Hero had, of course, missed the rendezvous. They were starting to get predictable that way. But now of all times, why couldn't she keep from getting distracted?

Whatever faults Jenny might have, she'd always been Keely's rock. Without Jenny's stabilizing presence, Keely knew she would have long since come unhinged. She'd probably already have been dropping those balls left and right.

Then Keely saw them: three thoroughly muddied and bedraggled figures trudging through a pasture on the outskirts of Weasel Gap, even now approaching the castle at an oblique angle. The woman towering head and shoulders above the others *had* to be Evadne. Keely's own reinforcements had arrived.

If she hadn't already been a cat at that moment, she would have allowed herself a triumphant grin. Things being what they were, she simply hopped down and began hurrying to meet them as quickly as her fading reserves of energy would allow.

Along the way, she lucked onto someone's washing and a dress that very nearly fit. She was particularly glad it came close enough to wear, because it took two full minutes of concentration to find her way back to human this time. No telling how long she'd be stuck this way now. Every bit of her needed a few good weeks of sleep.

Keely was waiting when the trio slipped through a gate in the pasture hedge. "Hero!" She pounced, throwing her arms around his neck, heedless of the mud, and kissed him hungrily in greeting. That her sudden appearance caused them all to freeze didn't faze her, but when the seconds dragged on and on without a sound or movement from even the man she was kissing, Keely finally stood back grinning at them. "No worries!" She laughed. "You're forgiven."

The next thing Keely knew she was lying on her back on the ground, staring up at Jenny's livid face, her jaw aching and her mouth tasting of blood. Jenny was trembling and incoherent with rage, her mouth working in a vain attempt to make words come out while she thrust an accusing finger in Keely's direction.

Keely, for her part, was too dumbfounded to contribute to the conversation either, and shock seemed to have rendered the others mute as well. Finally, Jenny's voice began to work, and every other shock vanished into insignificance.

"You...left...me...to...die!"

CHAPTER THIRTY-NINE

You Broke Her

"You broke her," Evadne said, crouching over Keely's limp form.

"Good," Elissa snapped, refusing to even look their direction.

"Serious," Evadne said, waving a hand slowly in front of Keely's face. "The girl's breathing, but nobody's home. She not even blinking. It's...creepy."

"I didn't hit her *that* hard," Elissa muttered.

"She was broken before we got here," Ulric said. "No sane person would mistake me for that prince who's been mooning over her. If you want my guess, she hit her head when the ground collapsed and Scarlet got inside again. That would certainly explain why she left you there."

"Thank you," Elissa sighed. "A big helping of guilt is about the only thing that could have made this day better."

"She never struck me as all that balanced to begin with," Evadne said.

"Yeah. Right. Okay. Let me think." Elissa rubbed at the ache in her forehead.

"You think," Evadne offered. "We'll keep on to the inn. Time's wasting."

"Yeah. Go." Elissa nodded when Ulric hesitated. "We can't leave her, and we can't drag her through the street. Get cleaned up and see if you can come up with a plan more specific than, 'Find someone to help us sneak past the Inquisition.' Safe is in short supply today, but I'll be as safe here as any of us."

When the others had gone, Elissa stood pondering Keely for a moment where she lay, then took a deep breath and sat down cross-legged, pulling Keely's head into her lap in an effort to at least make her *look* less uncomfortable. Keely, meanwhile, remained an unresisting rag doll. "All right. Maybe I overreacted," Elissa said grudgingly. "I don't know what happened to you, I can't swear I would have played the hero if *you'd* been the one trapped down a hole with a bloodthirsty demon, and you never pretended to *be* a hero. I just...let myself think we were a team, after all we've been through. I know you're a crook and a liar, but you were *my* crook and *my* liar, watching *my* back when I didn't have anyone else to do it. I hear there's one born every minute. I just didn't think I was that one. I guess no one wants to think that. Anyway, we still need you here, and I promise to have more sensible expectations if you'll come back and finish what we started."

The gentle rise and fall of Keely's chest remained the only proof she wasn't dead.

"Or I could just take your boots and walk away," Elissa offered. When even that failed to elicit so much as a blink, Elissa sighed again.

"Is this what happens when Scarlet gets in your head and wins?" she asked. A series of emotions fought for control of her face, but in the end it was simply biting her lip that came out ahead. "No. That's a cop-out. *I* broke you, didn't I? But that's good news, right? If I broke you, I should be able to fix you." She sat quietly for several minutes, lost in thought, her fingers combing through Keely's hair.

"Bookend?" she asked finally. "Are you in there? There's butterflies loose in the garden. Lots and lots of butterflies. I'm freaking out here."

Nothing continued to happen in great quantities.

"Orange ones...blue ones...pink ones...I could really use a rescue. What are you hiding from, silly cat? There's fish in it for you."

The great quantities of nothing maintained an admirable level of consistency. Elissa gave it up and began humming a lullaby, punctuating it with what lyrics she could call to mind. When the song trailed off, she pulled her thoughts together again.

"Why 'Jenny'?" she asked. It might have been her imagination, but she thought perhaps this time she was actually rewarded with a blink. "I can correct you a million times, and still it's 'Jenny', 'Jenny', 'Jenny'. Why 'Jenny'?"

This time, Keely did blink. She drew a deep breath. She calmly opened her eyes, rolled over and sat up, all without any show of recognition that Elissa was there at all. She looked down at herself, spread her arms, and inspected what bits of herself she could see before rolling her eyes and finally glancing up at Elissa—who had already risen halfway to a crouch, and looked poised to run.

"Relax," Keely said evenly. "I'm not Scarlet."

"Maybe," Elissa said, not relaxing. "You're not Keely, either. You're using her voice, but you don't sound like her. You're wearing her face, but she's not behind it. You don't even move like her."

"I am *not* Keely," Keely agreed, unperturbed. "She is, as you say, broken. Sorry."

"Then who *are* you?" Elissa asked warily.

"I'm Regula," not-Keely said.

"*What* are you?" Elissa demanded. "And what have you done with Keely?"

"She's broken," Regula repeated. "I thought we'd established that. I don't expect I'll be able to fix her, either. She was such a patch job to begin with."

"Wait," Elissa said. "You're saying this is *your* body?"

"Of course not," Regula said dismissively. "This is Jenny's body."

"Ooookay. Maybe you should lie back down," Elissa suggested. "Or maybe *I'll* have a lie down."

"Seriously?" Regula asked. "All you've been through, and *this* is what makes your head spin?"

"Can we at least take this from the top?" Elissa asked.

"Fair enough." Regula shrugged. "I'm Jenilee's imaginary friend. I help her keep track of stuff—or at least I used to. Jenny kind of 'checked out' on me a few years back when, well, *everybody* died. She couldn't cope, so I did my best to resurrect the one person we knew who *could* cope, and that was our best friend, Keely. I thought she'd make Jenny feel safe enough to come back, but it never really worked, and I'm more 'support personnel' than an actual person, so it's been Keely's show ever since."

"So all this time she's called me Jenny because she's mistaken me for herself?" Elissa asked.

"Sort of. Well, basically."

"Do you have any idea how twisted that is?" Elissa fell back on the grass with her arms spread wide, staring at the sky.

"Probably not," Regula said. "Anyway, Jenilee checked out on me when she couldn't live up to page twelve, and now..."

"Page twelve of what?" Elissa interrupted.

"Of me," Regula answered patiently. "I'm really just a book."

"It's only fair to warn you," Elissa said, "if this is just some game to see how credulous I can be, we either end it now, or I kill you when we do." When Regula showed no sign of being perturbed, she asked, "All right. What's page twelve?"

"Fight for what you love." The words came out of what Elissa had always thought of as Keely's mouth, but this time they didn't even pretend to use her voice. Elissa had often enough heard Keely change tone and inflection—even accent—to better play a role. It didn't seem to be a specialty or anything, but she did it well enough that she could hold her own on a theatrical stage.

Actual mimicry—changing her voice to completely disguise it as belonging to someone else—was something Elissa had never even heard Keely attempt. Yet the voice that somehow emerged from her mouth now, unhesitatingly and with crystal clarity, should have issued from that of a man grown and at least ten years her senior. Gentle sincerity and paternal conviction filled the voice, sharing space with a tangible weight of years. For the briefest moment, Elissa could have sworn she heard gulls crying in the distance, and smelled the faint aromas of fish and of pipe tobacco.

"The poor thing tried." Regula said, returning smoothly to Keely's voice as reality came crashing back through the surreal sensations. "She made a real effort to stand up to the Inquisition, but, well...apparently this isn't the first time we've been caught between them and Bloody Scarlet."

Elissa, who'd almost had time to think she'd finally run out of reserves of surprise, blinked again. "It's not?"

"We didn't have a name for her, but I recognized her face when Scarlet showed up in Denecia. *Keely* didn't, and we don't really talk, but the bad gut feeling she had that night was me telling her to get out of there. And before you get to asking about the why's and the how's, it all went down a lot like this. The same thing that brought the Inquisition to town had brought Scarlet to town, and between them, they managed to kill pretty much everybody. Between an army of the Inquisition and an entire town several times the size of Weasel Gap here, I can only vouch for five people having walked out of the wreckage of that night. Worse, three of them walked out of it in this one body."

"And the others?" Elissa asked.

"Scarlet, of course," Regula said, "and at least one knight of the Inquisition. I suspect the Inquisition could claim some other survivors, but their losses were obscene in any event. If any other locals lived through the night, I don't doubt they died later in the dungeons of the Inquisition. Our friends did nearly get out intact with us. We escaped Scarlet once, and we got out into the swamp while she and the Inquisition were busy with each other, but she was on an absolute rampage.

"As best I can piece together, the Inquisition killed her sister that night, and she held all of us responsible. Once the town had been emptied, she came scouring the countryside with those 'hounds' of hers. In the end, they tore our friends apart while Jenny cowered behind a rotting log, too terrified to move. That's the only reason any of us made it out, but still, she broke the rules. When push came to shove, she didn't fight for what she loved. On top of all the other horrors, that knowledge shattered her."

"Wait," Elissa said. "You said the Inquisition *killed* Scarlet's sister? How?!"

Regula shrugged. It seemed to be one of her favorite gestures. "Holy horseshoes, I expect. They trampled her in the street."

"You're sure she was dead?"

"She certainly looked the part, but given what we've seen Scarlet come back from, if they really were sisters, maybe not so much," Regula admitted. "We didn't stick around to check to see if she was some sort of minor goddess. She was just 'Aunt Molly'."

Elissa had never risen from where she'd collapsed back onto the ground, yet she somehow gave the impression of doing it all over again. "What have I gotten myself caught up in?" she asked.

"Wish I could tell you," Regula said. "Sharing living quarters with Keely is confusing at the best of times, and I'm doing a lot of guesswork here. I'm not omniscient. I'm just observant. It's a rare day I don't get to devote to just watching and thinking about things. Blackwater Molly said she was Jenny's aunt on her mother's side, and I think she believed that. I was born of a few words from Jenny's mother, but that's all the memory Jenny ever had of her.

"The night of page thirteen—when everyone died—Molly said her sisters were in town, and Jenny was supposed to finally get to meet her mother, but everything went south before that could happen. And in the middle of it all..."

"Scarlet shows up," Elissa finished for her. "And just now, I threw it in Keely's face that *she* broke the rules like Jenny had, and so she's broken, too?"

"Just so. She's not one for letting it show when she's under stress, but it's there. It's always there, and this whole thing has been spiraling out of control."

"And on top of everything else, she's afraid now that this monster who destroyed her life and killed her friends right in front of her is actually her own mother?" Elissa asked.

"In a manner of speaking, yes," Regula said with a nod. "Words are never simple when you're trying to sort out the pronouns and antecedents concerning three minds in one body, plus Keely has only confused and fragmented memories of how that night went down. She didn't exist at all as you know her until after it happened. They're actually Jenny's memories, and when they do start to coalesce, Keely shoves them down as hard as she can and shatters them again."

"Sounds like just the sort of treatment that *would* keep Jenny from returning."

"I suppose it is," Regula agreed. "At this point, it's all moot. Keely's gone. Jenny's gone. I'm just a book..." She shrugged. "About all I'm good for is getting what's left of us out from underfoot."

Elissa snorted. "That's what this whole mess is over, you know: just a book. And you're *not* just a book. You think. You have agency. What that makes you is a librarian—and if you *dare* to tell me you're 'just a librarian' I promise I will slug you again."

"What exactly do you want from me?" Regula asked, cocking an eyebrow.

"Bring me Keely," Elissa said.

"I told you..."

"And I told *you*," Elissa said, pulling herself up off the ground, "*bring me Keely*. That's not a request."

"Even if I was willing to accommodate you," Regula said, "I don't know how you expect me to comply. She's gone."

"She can't be gone," Elissa snapped. "It's against the rules."

"That doesn't make any sense," Regula said.

"The hell it doesn't," Elissa growled. "If it's so bloody important to her that she curl up and die because she abandoned me, then there's no way you can *stop* her from coming back. We need her. *I* need her. This is her one chance to atone for all of it. You're so bloody observant, but do you even hear that?"

Elissa pointed off in the direction of the forest, from which a distant cacophony of unearthly laughter was just becoming audible. "It's happening again. We're all caught between the Inquisition and a hard place, and Bloody Scarlet is coming for us. She's coming for us, and she's going to single *me* out for special attention because of what I had to do when Keely ran off and left me to her.

"Swords aren't going to stop her. Guns aren't going to stop her. All my luck and pluck and cunning only slowed her down for a couple of hours. It's going to take nothing short of a miracle for me to live through the day, and Keely is the closest thing to a miraculata we've got. Keely didn't just mistake me for her best friend, I *am* her best friend. I'm the one who put my faith and trust in her when no sane woman would. I'm the one who stood by her across half a continent, no matter what she put me through, all for the sake of a crusade we both believed in. For love of me and of Jenny and...and 'Hero'—however he fits into all of this—she is going to get herself back here right now and *fight*. Because that's the rules!"

"Ow." Regula winced.

"Well it was supposed to hurt," Elissa said. "Now get in there and get her."

"In *where?* Get *who?* And for go'ss sake, what did I do to deserve that sucker punch?" Between voice, mannerisms, and context, there could be little doubt that this was Keely sitting there, rubbing her jaw.

"If you really don't remember," Elissa said earnestly, "just trust me that you earned it."

The inn had been too crowded with refugees to hold a proper council of war at, and Keely had been too conspicuous without a wig at hand to hide her hair, so they'd wound up holing up instead in the attic of the village stonemason who lived on the edge of town. As a friend of Ulric's and the owner of a major grudge against the Inquisition, the mason had no qualms with harboring a few fugitives long enough for them to get cleaned up and sort things out.

Evadne had managed to get through the crowds to reach her luggage, and she had also raided the luggage of her traveling companions, so the four of them didn't just look clean at this point; they looked like clean gentry, in visiting from the Heartlands.

The attic had one window, looking out in the direction of the forest. Most of the locals that hadn't become casualties of the skirmish with the Inquisition or taken prisoner after it were currently sequestered in their homes, praying to escape the Inquisition's notice, but what few did dare to venture out seemed to be queuing up in small knots to stare off at the trees. They could be seen whispering among themselves, speculating about the distant, unnerving laughter drifting out from beyond the forest hedge. The deadlings hadn't come rushing out into the settled lands, but did seem to be massing just back among the trees.

"So, Lady Doryne is gone." Keely sighed. "Hero is out of the fight and Conrad is looking after him. Nolan, Minda, and Baldassare should be okay in the castle but would seem to be trapped there by the Inquisition. That's everybody who's not here accounted for, right? It's down to the four of us to sort this mess out."

"And I'm not sure how much good I'm going to be for anything," Elissa said. "I hobbled this far mostly on willpower."

"For that matter," Keely said, "I seem to have pushed the whole shape-shifting thing to its limits and beyond. That's another resource we're out. So we're looking at two battered and fatigued warriors, a scholar who's more or less off her feet for the duration, and a trickster everyone knows not to trust. With that, we take on both a small army that makes whole kingdoms cower and a sadistic, unstoppable madwoman."

"Yeah. That's pretty much the size of it," Ulric agreed. "And if I'm any judge of these things, Scarlet will be holding off 'til nightfall for maximum chaos when she lets go the leash of her deadlings, and so everyone can get good and on-edge listening to them all day. We've got no longer than that to figure this out."

"If you're trying to talk me into grabbing a horse and riding out of here," Evadne said, "keep talking. You've got my attention."

"I won't ask you not to," Keely said. "This isn't really your fight."

"Actually, it is," Evadne corrected her. "I can't give up on Sabina, and—if only for her sake—I can't abandon Baldassare. If I don't see this through, we'll never be able to mount a proper search. I'm just waiting for you to give me some thread of hope to clutch at."

"Hug away," Keely said, pointing Evadne toward Elissa. "There's our secret weapon."

"Me?" Elissa asked, managing to sound aghast.

"Like it or not, Jenny, under pressure you're a natural-born charlatan. I don't know if *I* could have talked my way out of that cave with Scarlet. And even counting the folk who can't be here right now, every one of us has been compromised with the Inquisition—identified and possibly reported as being a witch or her associate or just plain dead—except for Nolan and you."

Keely paused, allowing the others a moment to compare that statement with the truth of their memories. "Even Nolan will be considered a heathen rebel until proven otherwise, since he's so obviously a local boy, but you, Jenny..."

CHAPTER FORTY

THAT WHOLE BREAD THING

"Thank you for seeing me, Sublima," Elissa said, curtsying subserviently in the torchlight before straightening up to lean on the walking stick Ulric had scrounged up for her. It was Sir Riordan, though—not Jane Carver—who caught her eye when she looked back up. He remained remarkably unruffled for someone she was certain had been trying to kill her so recently.

There could be no doubt, though, that those eyes were watching her carefully. Even if she walked out of this interview alive, what she said during it would surely determine whether she would meet an unfortunate accident on her way out.

What walls remained standing of the cathedral construction would be ripe for random collapse. A body who wandered too close to any number of sheer drop-offs would have a long fall ahead of her. Any number of things could conceivably go fatally wrong on the long, winding trail back down the Wolf's Tooth.

And all those dangers assumed he didn't just volunteer to escort her out of the tunnels and break her neck in a dark corridor. It was horrible to consider the number of ways her body could just disappear into a mass grave in the near future, and to consider how missed she *wouldn't* be. All in all, the circumstance seemed slightly less intimidating than facing down Bloody Scarlet had been. Things were looking up.

Jane Carver, meanwhile, continued for some time inspecting the ancient, skull-themed carvings on the chamber wall. Several kegs of powder and a pyramid of stockpiled cannonballs that must have been obscuring the view lay carelessly tumbled across the floor near her. A part of Elissa kept hoping the woman would lose track of where those cannonballs had been scattered and stumble over them, yet somehow

Jane continued to step effortlessly over and around them without giving any obvious sign of looking down.

It was just as well, though. Conceptually amusing as it might be to watch the Grand High Inquisitrix take a well-deserved pratfall, anyone so accustomed to casually abusing power as Jane Carver would not hesitate to turn generalized annoyance and embarrassment over her own carelessness into a very specific nastiness against the nearest expendable target. That, of course, would have been Elissa.

When Jane finally did look up and turn to Elissa, she scowled. "*Where* is this priestess who asked for an audience?"

"Right here, Sublima," Elissa responded quickly. "It's me, Sublima."

Jane's scowl only darkened. "I see no priestess. What have you done with your robes, girl?"

Elissa looked down, flushed. "They were hopelessly damaged in the fire, Sublima. I'm afraid I shan't be a priestess for much longer, in any event."

"Oh, yes." Jane nodded. "I imagine Augusta shall be none too pleased with the mess you made of things here."

"So I imagine," Elissa agreed. "Strictly speaking, it's not my mess. She'd only appointed me to the job a few days before you arrived, so I hardly feel guilty about it all, but I understand that's a technicality. My job, my responsibility, and I can hardly complain that the Inquisition arrived to do what needed to be done. In my brief tenure, I saw enough heathen practices to doubt I could have set the locals down the right path given ten years. Giving me ten weeks or ten months would have accomplished nothing but allow the rot to continue, so thank you, Sublima."

Jane acknowledged the gesture of gratitude by allowing her scowl to soften to a business-like frown. "Is that all you came for, then?"

"No, Sublima. Earl Haywood also asked me to draft these up, as his legal representative to the church, and deliver them to you," Elissa said.

Producing a set of neatly folded documents from up a voluminous pink sleeve that had come from Sabina's wardrobe, she offered them up to Jane Carver. "He wanted me to say that he accepts the terms of your mercy with only two reservations. He wants me to sign as witness on your full absolution of all charges and heresies, with your verification as Grand High Inquisitrix that the blame for them and for all vandalism to date of church properties in the county by parties previously unknown lies solely in the enchantments of that witch of the Crimson Forest known locally as Bloody Scarlet.

"In return, I am to witness his gifting of sole and unrestricted stewardship of the Wolf's Tooth to the Inquisition, in gratitude for its

363

heroic assistance in freeing his county from the ensorcellment of said witch, and because he has deemed that the curses and corruption the witch laid on the spire have rendered it unfit for any other purpose. It will require an extended cleansing by true experts in the matter, which will surely take many years even so.

"Oh, and I took the liberty of adding a few words of my own to make explicit that the recent, tragic fire was part and parcel of the witch's sins." Elissa paused to catch Riordan's eye again. "I'm sure no one wants to risk that getting dredged up later as a separate matter with all the childish finger-pointing that could ensue."

"Hmmm..." Jane accepted the proffered papers and began leafing through them. "I mistook Haywood as having a bit more mettle than that. My read was that he'd at *least* sleep on it before letting reason overcome his pride."

"I believe that comes down to his second reservation," Elissa said. "I'm given to understand that the Sublima will be leading an expedition into the forest to hunt down the witch come the morning, but it appears the witch is too impatient to wait for you. There are strange sounds coming out of the forest, and the earl believes the witch is conjuring an army of demons to come sweeping down on us tonight. His hope is that the writs can be signed immediately so all prisoners can be pardoned and released and all travel restrictions and curfews lifted, that he may evacuate his people and make ready what remains of his army."

"The man's a fool as well as a heretic if he thinks I'll be re-arming him tonight," Jane said with as dismissive snort. "But he can evacuate his people, and 'what remains of his army' with them if it pleases him. There's no more sense allowing the innocent to be trampled than in allowing the guilty to linger at my back, ready to cause more trouble. Just give me a few minutes to look these over."

"Of course, Sublima. May I borrow Sir Riordan while you do?"

"I'm sorry to even bring this up, but I hope you've caught Ryan," Elissa said as they walked, the sounds of his heavy footfalls and the clacking of her walking stick echoing quietly through the tunnels of the spire. "I had to throw in the bit about the fire because of him, you know. You seemed to think he could have been involved, and I couldn't stand to have him causing your family any more embarrassment. It's hard enough even thinking about him at all."

"Not yet. I'd guess he's out there with the witch, but just put him out of your head, Littlebrook." He gave a dry chuckle as he tousled her hair. "To quote someone who's sounding atrociously all grown-up, that's my job, my responsibility. Still, thank you for your concern and your discretion."

She offered him a wan smile. "I'm sure you'll get it all...sorted."

"What happened to your leg?" Riordan asked with a concern that could have been genuine.

"Same thing that happened to my robes. I took a bad fall in the night, rushing around trying to take care of everyone else. I feel stupid, but also feel like I got off lucky. It could have been so much worse."

"I do seem to recall telling you to be careful out there," he admonished her. "Still, I may have to repent of calling you Littlebrook any longer. You have *definitely* grown up. Wasn't it last week you were a gangly little tag-along? Now here you are, looking every inch the lady, rushing around taking charge of things and owning mistakes. And that cool-and-responsible act with the Sublima? I could see you were nervous, but I've known grown men to literally wet themselves because she looked at them funny. She was going easy on you—I think she actually *likes* you—but still..."

"She seems nice," Elissa said with a little shrug. "You hear the stories, of course. 'Oh, what a monster.' But she's got a tough job. *You've* got a tough job. I don't know how you do it."

"Ever thought about doing it yourself?" Riordan asked.

Elissa let out a sputtering burst of laughter. "I am *not* in your league."

"Well, I wasn't thinking in terms of getting out and grappling with demons yourself. Certainly not right away." Riordan grinned. "But I do recall you getting on quite well with books. I'd feel a lot better next time I find myself chasing down a witch if I knew you were there to feed me information about her. Knowing the strengths, weaknesses, and habits of a particular witch can make a huge difference in how long a witch-hunter stays alive. Besides, the church will be the poorer if you let this setback end you just as you're getting started. I've got no pull with Pontifine Augusta, but I can certainly open doors for you in the Inquisition."

"Thank you, Riordan. That *is* a sweet offer. Perhaps you'll repeat it if we both survive the night?" She smiled endearingly.

"I need a bath! I need a bath! I need a bath!" Elissa moaned, reining up the horse Evadne had borrowed for her from Baldassare's retainers. "I need a bath and I'm going to be sick."

"Be sick later," Ulric said, patting the horse's flank. "Did she sign it?"

Elissa nodded.

"Then you're done with the dangerous stuff. Just finish your bit, get everyone clear you can, and get out of here with them. You can have your bath down the road at Fodderen while you're waiting to see if the rest of us survive."

Elissa nodded her acknowledgment again and urged the horse on down the street toward the castle. Ulric watched her go for a few seconds before retreating into the stonemason's house to rejoin Keely and Evadne.

"We're free to move," he said.

"Good," Evadne said, shaking Keely awake. "The more sitting still I do, the harder it is to forget how exhausted I am." At Ulric's urging, they'd risked curling up on the attic floor in shifts while Elissa was out, keeping an eye for any signs of restless sleep in case Scarlet tried to get into someone's head. Whether they were currently beyond her reach or had just gotten lucky, they each managed an hour or so of rest out of it. That was a lot less than they owed themselves, but it couldn't be helped.

One more change of clothes, arranged courtesy of the stonemason's family—with a full-length cloak and concealing hood for Keely, and masculine attire to help Evadne pass for a really tall man instead of a towering woman—and they were ready to blend in with the crowd when the alarm bell began tolling from the castle once more, urging the locals to evacuate. Riders galloped out from the castle toward each local crossroad, directing the evacuation toward nearby Fodderen—which herded it through the shadow of the Wolf's Tooth.

"Be warned," Elissa said, pulling Earl Haywood aside into an alcove as the evacuation preparations swirled around them, "I know you didn't agree to do anything for Jane Carver, but to arrange this, we had to make her think you did. Fortunately, she doesn't know your seal *or* your signature, but I'd think very carefully before contesting the documents ceding the Wolf's Tooth to the Inquisition. You know what happens to people who thwart her."

Darby cringed but showed no inclination to chastise Elissa. His pride had already taken a thorough beating and he'd passed the point of thinking in terms of politics and deep into the territory of seeing this for the survival situation it was.

"We both know that having the Inquisition up there will make it insanely dangerous around here," Elissa nodded her understanding. "Even if there *was* another way, we didn't have time to figure it out. Even if I could undo any of the damage, I don't have a clue how I'll live to see another sunrise, so just...go, and don't look back. I know you've had plans in place for getting your family out of harm's way for years now, so follow them. Disappear. Only don't go through the forest. Minda can tell you how much you do *not* want to go through the forest.

"Wherever you go, whatever you do, *get away from the Crimson Forest*. It's got a mind and will of its own. Her name is Bloody Scarlet. She's no less sadistic or insane than Jane Carver, she's infinitely more powerful, and she just doesn't die. Whatever nursery stories you grew up hearing about Bloody Scarlet, she's worse. Do not even try to laugh her or me off, or I will slap you. You stood on the parapet and you listened to the forest. She's coming. You go. Got it?"

"And to think I took you for the mousy one." The earl gave a dry chuckle and a shake of his head.

"I *am* the mousy one," Elissa insisted. "Go!"

The earl inclined his head in polite acquiescence. "I would not challenge the authority of our beloved pontifine *or* her duly appointed representative."

Elissa accepted that as a win and spun away to go hunt down Shoshona. It didn't take long. The inquisitrix was already out querying the castle denizens about the tolling bell, and those who weren't pointing her to the great hall were pointing her directly to Elissa. Elissa had caught plenty of attention on her way in simply by virtue of being able to enter un-harassed, carrying authorization of passage during this crisis that came directly from Jane Carver.

"There you are, Sister!" Elissa greeted Shoshona with convincing relief. "The High Inquisitrix asked me to deliver this to you with all haste."

Shoshona took the proffered missive and read it, her scowl deepening as she went.

"Is there anything I can do to help?" Elissa offered. "Obviously, I'm lamed up, but still, if there's anything...She confided enough in me to know that we're abandoning the castle. Smart considering what I've seen the witch do. She'd be over the walls in a heartbeat. Anyway—"

"Who *are* you?" Shoshona interrupted with a querulous glare, looking up from the letter.

"Oh. Sorry. Secular dress. Right. I've seen you, but why would you notice me?" In keeping with last-minute advice from Keely, Elissa kept up the patter as best she could with barely a gap between sentences.

"My poor robes didn't survive the fire. Gotta get in and try to save the flock, right? Mucked up my leg the same way. I'm Sister Elissa. Pontifine Augusta appointed me to the castle just before you got here. Such a lucky thing you did, too. I mean get here. When you did. Providence really. I knew we had a witch problem the moment I showed up. I can smell them a mile off, can't you? Of course, I'm no inquisitrix. Wouldn't stand a chance against a real witch. So I prayed and prayed for her to protect us, and here you came! Miracle!" Elissa beamed.

"Do you ever breathe, girl?" Shoshona demanded.

"Not so much," Elissa said, finally inhaling properly. "Sorry," she added, shuffling her feet. "Nervous. Real inquisitrix. Jane Carver herself. Wow. Witch hunt. Miracles. One of your sisters who headed into the forest after you even joked she thought *I* was miraculata material just because of that whole bread thing."

"*Bread* thing?" Shoshona just managed to wedge the incredulous question into the tiny space between Elissa's sentences.

"I know, right? I did make priestess young and all, but it's so stupid. She *had* to be joking. She *was* joking, right? Had silly me going a moment, though. Wanted to slap myself. Anyway, big day. Big week. Bouncing off the walls. I'm babbling. I know I'm babbling. I'm just going to go now before I make myself look any more an idiot, right? Right. Her strength protect you! Take down that witch!"

Elissa scurried away with her head down, muttering to herself, and nearly tripped over a hurrying servant as she rounded a corner.

"Sorry, milady," the woman apologized, picking up and returning Elissa's walking stick from where it had clattered to the floor. "I'm on business for the countess, packing up to go. I haven't time to draw you a bath."

Out in the courtyard, Elissa found Nolan tending to her borrowed horse. "Baldassare's in place," he told her quietly. "Minda's slipped off to join Ulric before Shoshona could get a chance to spot her."

"I thought surely you'd talk her into going with her family," Elissa said.

"Tried," Nolan said. "Couldn't. Doryne."

"Right," Elissa said. "Are you coming with us?"

"Can't." He shrugged. "Minda. Ulric. Keely. Nessa. Doryne."

"Then promise me you'll take care of yourself."

"Can't," Nolan said. "Scarlet." He studied her face for a moment. "And don't go getting any noble ideas. You're no fighter, and you're lame besides. Baldassare's in no shape to fight either, but I suspect the fool would come back to save face if he wasn't escorting you out of here for your own protection. Let the man have his pride."

"What..." Elissa began, but Nolan cut her off.

"Heads up," he said. "She just stepped out of the keep."

Elissa nodded without looking around and allowed Nolan to help her onto her horse. She took her time getting her walking stick settled across the saddle, then urged the horse carefully through the crowded courtyard toward the gate while Nolan headed back toward the keep. He was about ten feet from Shoshona when he suddenly stopped, listening intently for a moment, then spun to turn to the nearest man passing him. "Did you hear that, Kavan?" he asked.

"The bell?" the man asked him, puzzled. "Those hound-things in the forest?"

"It was like...like a cat hissing, only..." Nolan spun slowly in place as if scanning the courtyard for something until a moment before Elissa exited the castle gate. "There!" He suddenly shouted, pointing in her direction. "It's..."

Elissa shrieked as Keely suddenly leapt as if from out of nowhere, vaulting into the saddle behind Elissa, her silvery hair and tattered red scarecrow's cloak billowing behind her. No sooner had Keely landed than the horse veered sharply off its path. Picking up speed, it disappeared from view to the side of the gate, carrying the fake witch and the still-shrieking ingenue with it.

Behind them, Ulric tucked the voluminous traveling cloak that had been hiding Keely's costume under his arm, and he turned to disappear into the crowd before Shoshona could fight her way through the gate. Shoshona shouted orders for someone to bring her her horse, shouted orders for her subordinates to rally to her on the street in front of the castle, and stood seething at the unavoidable delay as she watched her quarry riding away.

"You!" Shoshona stabbed a finger at an inquisitrix. "Ride to the Wolf's Tooth and let the High Inquisitrix know that the witch has her sacrifice and we're giving chase down the road toward Axminster. The rest of you," she added as she swung up into the saddle, "we're giving chase."

"That old stone circle on the hill south of Axminster!" Nolan shouted. "She's headed for the stone circle!"

"There's a stone circle near Axminster?" Kavan asked.

Nolan threw up his hands with a "search me" expression on his face as he quietly withdrew around the corner of the stable.

CHAPTER FORTY-ONE

TAKING A STAND

As it approached the edge of town, the horse bearing Keely and Elissa cut between buildings, and Keely hopped off almost before Elissa had reined it to a stop in front of Baldassare and the horse he was leading. While Elissa dismounted, Keely switched out cloaks with Baldassare, trading him the tattered red one for his serviceable traveling cloak.

Baldassare tossed Elissa a similarly serviceable cloak to slip into, then unslung the hastily assembled straw dummy in another of Sabina's pink dresses from the horse he'd brought. He draped the dummy across the saddle of the other horse, then mounted behind it. The dummy wouldn't pass for a woman for any more than an eye-blink of inspection, but then neither would Baldassare.

Hopefully the horse would be going fast enough that if he kept low in the saddle, all that anyone would really see would be the billowing red cape and the billowing pink skirts, and they'd fill in the details appropriately if the Inquisition stopped to question them.

Elissa was no slouch as an equestrienne but had been willing not to argue when Baldassare assured them he was the best rider they had available. Keely had shut down any arguments before they got started, anyway. Too much of the con had already rested on Elissa's shoulders, and too much pressure in playing her role, without also knowing she'd have to transition right into this sort of chase.

Baldassare gave a gallant salute. "I'll meet you behind the inn once I'm clear to double back," he told Elissa. Then he spurred the horse away, leaving Keely and Elissa to go the other direction around the buildings leading the horse he'd brought for Elissa.

Keely tied back her hair to make sure it remained hidden under the hood, and they arrived back onto the street, merging with the stream of refugees just in time to see the first riders of the Inquisition go thundering past.

"He'll be all right, won't he?" Elissa asked, watching them go.

"At this point," Keely said, "I give him much better odds than I give me. Go see if you can find Hero, Conrad, and Addie, and get out of here. Oh, and Jenny...?"

"Yes?" Elissa asked. Still leading the horse, she planned to actually mount up once they passed the castle. Even with the walking stick, traveling afoot was currently a slow and painful process, but she didn't want to risk drawing attention yet by giving herself the high profile of a rider.

"I told you you had the makings of a great liar." Keely grinned. "No telling how many lives you just saved. Of course, nothing else is going to go wrong from here on in, but just in case: It's been an honor."

"Bloody Scarlet!"

Time was growing short. The shadows had begun to lengthen. Silence hung heavy over the deserted town and pastures and orchards, disturbed by little more than the creaking of forgotten shutters and an occasional nervous snort from the few horses left in the castle stable. Dark clouds had begun to roll in on rising winds, muting the sun.

Given the timing, and given what had been going on the last time the weather went berserk, Keely couldn't believe that was a coincidence. Even the skies above the Crimson Forest seemed—if not under Scarlet's direct, conscious control—at least to answer to her moods. If Keely had had any doubts about the prediction that Scarlet would strike at sunset, they were dispelled now as she watched the storm build.

"Bloody Scarlet!" Keely shouted again from the tower battlements overlooking the forest. "I know you can hear me!" The trees of the forest seemed almost animate as they swayed back and forth together, their wind-tossed autumn leaves shimmering with color.

"You want a story?" Keely screamed against the wind. "I'll tell you a story! Years ago, the Inquisition came chasing you and your sisters to my home. You didn't care. You knew you could slaughter them. And I *know* you didn't care about what happened to *us*. You laid the sins of the Inquisition on my friends and neighbors, and you murdered them as freely as you murdered the loathsome creatures who had come for you.

"Hardly anyone walked away that night, but I *did*, and now here I've led the Inquisition to *your* door chasing *me*. That whole book thing is nonsense. Rubbish. It was my lure to get them here. This was never about you and them. This is about you and me!"

"Really?" Ulric asked quietly beside her.

"Enough of it," Keely said. "Now hush."

"I tricked you good," Keely started shouting again. "I've chased off all the toys you were going to play with, and I'm ready to settle scores! Don't bother waiting for dark! I can see in the dark, too! Come on out and fight!"

"You really think she heard you?" Ulric asked as they descended the tower stairs together.

"You're just full of questions today, aren't you?" Keely said.

"Can't help it. I get all question-y when I'm staring at probable, painful death."

"There's the spirit." Keely grinned. "Too many people would already be looking at this as a certain painful death. I am buoyed by your optimism.

"You know, if I live through the night," she added, "I'm going to have to hire a new maid. Seems like Jenny's finally over her whole 'sidekick' phase, and you've seen how hopeless I am keeping track of my own clothes. Speaking of which, I'll catch up with you. I need to go see if anyone left me proper clothes to wear for playing the feisty underdog in Scarlet's story. Jenny said Scarlet didn't believe in them, but that was just before Jenny gave her a bloody nose, so maybe that's a seed of doubt I can exploit.

"Anyway, go'ss knows we're already stuck cast as underdogs, and the only underdog who *ever* wins is the feisty one, so what's to lose? And no way am I showing up to a showdown dressed as either her understudy *or* a pink princess."

When Keely walked into the great hall to join the others, she was feeling more like herself—whoever that was. She'd found nothing serviceable to wear in her signature color of look-at-me red, but she had found a man's tunic large enough for her to wear as a dress, and in a shade of red she could accept if not love. Cinched with a decent belt, it hardly looked second-hand at all.

Ulric, Nolan, Evadne, and Minda had all taken time to get cleaned up and dressed for the occasion as well. Ulric and Nolan each even wore a proper steel cuirass to protect their torsos.

"I had a hard time thinking what we could do to prepare for Scarlet herself," Ulric admitted, "but we've got options to make her deadlings less deadly."

He gestured at equipment he'd spread out for them on the high table. "This," he said, pulling a small arrangement of leather and steel from out of the first pile, "is a gorget—an armored collar. It was meant to keep anyone from slitting your throat with a blade slipped between helm and breastplate, but it will give the deadlings a whole lot less real estate they can take advantage of. Find one that fits. Buckle it on. Anyone who dies tonight because they got throttled will have to answer to me for it."

He walked down the length of the table, pointing out the different stacks of equipment. "Helms—open-faced, but trust me you don't want to wind up fighting half blind—leather gauntlets...doublet...breeches...boots. If you can find a set that fits, wear it—unless you just *like* the feel of quarter-inch thorns biting into your skin."

He stopped at the last pile at the end of the table and hefted a hatchet. "These are our weapons of choice," he said. "Short and light for close quarters." He held the hatchet out demonstratively. "Blade for severing vines." He flipped it. "Solid, blunt back for shattering skulls. If you find you have a free hand when there are deadlings about, you're doing this wrong. Have one in each hand at any time you can manage it, so you can use either one to free the other when it gets pinned. Expect to lose at least one hatchet during the fighting, so carry a third on your belt.

"Remember that the real danger of the deadlings lies in the swarm. From the sound of their baying, we've got to expect scores of them to be coming out of the forest. Five people isn't much to fight off a swarm of these things. If even a couple of us go down, the rest won't be good for much except to stand fighting back-to-back, and if it comes to that, we've already lost. Any time Scarlet herself isn't an immediate concern, job one is making sure *no one* stays pinned by a deadling. They're not cunning, so if we're armored up and they can't pin us, they can't beat us.

"They should also have more limited mobility without something to grab and swing from, so we steer clear of the trees.

"Take a few practice swings with the hatchets once we get out where there's something to practice on, just so you'll have some feel for them, but don't wear yourselves out. We can't expect much recovery time before they come at us.

"That's everything I've got. Zero for dealing with Scarlet herself. But I'm not backing down. I could list all sorts of selfless reasons I have to put this un-killable monster in her grave, but in the end, I'm doing this for me. She was in my dreams when I was trying to nap this afternoon, and I still don't know if it *was* her or I was making her up. I'm never going to know—never going to have a rest worth anything again—as long as I know she's out there. I'm facing her now, on my terms, to escape what will likely be a short life of constantly looking over my shoulder otherwise. So, Keely, please tell me you've got a real plan for dealing with Scarlet, and that you're not just going to be making this one up as you go along."

"I've always got a real plan," Keely assured him. "Some of them are just more nebulous than others. So, Nolan says he can drive a cart in a pinch. They did leave us one, right? Lady Minda's our best remaining equestrienne. Does anyone have experience with the castle artillery?"

Ulric and Nolan pointed in unison to Minda, who smirked in response. "Hey, I like it when things go boom," she said.

"Perfect." Keely nodded. "Now remember what I said about Scarlet's cloak? It's possible I got over-optimistic saying it had *all* her power, but still..."

Lightning was flickering across the black clouds mounting overhead by the time Keely and Ulric returned to the battlements. Thunder grumbled, and the wind that had been creaking shutters was now banging them vigorously.

"I really thought she'd take the bait," Keely muttered. "Well, I hoped she'd take the bait. I can't actually see in the dark without my cat eyes. Being stuck in one shape stinks."

"On the plus side, I spend a lot less on clothes than you do," Ulric said, scanning the rocky ground between them and the forest. "She's hanging back for the sake of theater, though, not for tactical advantage. She's not afraid of us, and she'll come over these walls as easily as she dropped into that sinkhole. This castle's just a nice big target for her, and taking it will be symbolic.

"When she comes, her deadling will swarm down the most convenient hedge, but otherwise it'll be straight from the tree line and into the courtyard without bothering to go around to the gate. Even the keep's not defensible, unless we lock ourselves in an interior room— and then we're just waiting for Scarlet to batter down the door and come at us where we're trapped.

"With the light failing, we can't stand out in a meadow and wait for them. We won't see them coming at us from all sides until they're on top of us, and then they'll just keep us pinned down again until Scarlet can finish us. Torches or bonfires could help there, but even if we could

is supposed to be,"
don't know what a r...
ve got this covered,
...at's no loss, but the cou...
...swallowed up by the forest, j...
blackmoon Lake, and we'll never get it b...
her horse. "I never said I'd defer to a...
"It's my call, anyway," Minda said, g...
monster from the forest; just in fig...
land, my home. I wouldn't let the In...
pontifine have it, and I'll be damne...
bogey without a fight. We stick to...
to work."
Not waiting to allow time for a...
the stable doors just as Evadne...
"Odd," Evadne said, turning...
...st thing Sabina said, horse...
remaining hors...
...stless as th...
...ould d...

...ad

...llected skulls
...kest heart of the
...just in time to make
...the setting sun vanished behind

them

"Oh, ...ly swallowed. "That's theater."

"Minda. Ulric shouted down to the walls. "Light off whatever cannons you've managed to load and go!"

Keely and Ulric ducked back into the tower, grabbing the torch they'd left burning just inside, and hurried down the stairs. Outside, one by one, the forest-facing cannons of Castle Haywood began to roar. As thick as the deadlings were coming, the cannonballs were sure to crush a few skulls, but no one in the castle doubted the effort was mostly for show: a token roar of defiance, meeting theater with theater.

Minda arrived down at the stables at the same time as Keely and Ulric.

"Leave the rest," Ulric snapped to Nolan, who was still loading barrels onto the back of the cart.

"It's bad," Keely said. "Worse than bad. Probably not too late to just run, though. Jane and her friends will double back when they realize they're chasing geese, and handling this sort of thing is supposed to be their job."

"Do you think they stand a chance?" Minda asked soberly.

"Not really," Keely admitted.

Nolan said, "the truth is
...eal fight looks like. They'll
...hey'll try a frontal assault,
...nty will be. The whole thing
...st like Caer Cacamwri and
...ack."
...abbing a lantern and mounting
...yone when it came to fighting a
...ting the Inquisition. This is my
...quisition have it, I wouldn't let the
...d if I'll give it over to some nursery
...your plan, Keely. It will work. It has

...n argument, she spurred her horse out
...returned from lighting streetlamps.
...s to watch Minda go. "That sounded like
the la... ...re she disappeared."

The two... ...s, hitched to the cart, grew increasingly
nervous and re... ...e baying of the deadlings approached. It
became all Nolan co... ...o keep them under control as they left the
stable and headed for th... gate with everyone on board the cart.

The flickering oil lamps Evadne had lit on the street outside kept the darkness enough at bay for the horses to step surely, and would hopefully buy them a couple of seconds warning of approaching deadlings, but they still seemed woefully inadequate against the deepening night. The cart rattled on down the hill from the castle, nearly reaching the bottom before all at once the dreadful baying stopped.

"How anticlimactic," Scarlet called. She stood in the open gateway off the castle, watching them from above. Around her swarmed more deadlings than the eye could count, their vines writhing together like a wall of tentacles. "I thought I'd been invited to a fight."

"Of course you were!" Keely called back, standing up in the cart. "No one ever said it would be a fair fight!"

Somewhere in the darkness, Minda's rifle cracked. The oil lamp nearest to Scarlet shattered. Flames rained down on the cobbles, then raced along the oil Evadne had spread while she was lighting the lamps, drawing Scarlet's eye with them to the powder keg Evadne had left just to the side of the gate. Things started going boom. The horses drawing the cart took off without waiting for permission, and Keely would have been thrown from it if not for Ulric's quick grab at her belt.

"Too much theater!" he snapped at her. "Sit down!"

Behind them, deadlings shrieked. Oil blazed. The second powder keg went up, then third. Fragments of bone and thorny vine went ricocheting off the castle walls and raining down out of the smoke-filled air. By the time the sixth and final keg blew, the entire length of the castle wall had been engulfed in smoke and flames.

The horses ran for all they were worth, taking full advantage of the one lit avenue out of town that Evadne had left them, but just before they rounded the corner that would take them out of sight of their little inferno, Keely caught sight of a solitary figure standing tall as it stepped from the flame, cape billowing around it.

"Well, that's...what? A couple hundred deadlings we won't have to beat with hatchets?" Keely asked.

"Something like that," Ulric agreed. "If she'd just keep lining them up for us like that and we just had a few hundred kegs of gunpowder and time to place them all, we'd be set."

Once they passed the last streetlamp and found themselves reduced to the light of Nolan's one lantern to guide them, the horses were forced to slow down. After the initial mad dash, they'd needed to, anyway. The streetlamps had done their job, too, buying the cart a substantial head start and leaving an unmistakable trail for Scarlet to follow.

The galloping of a lone horse coming up fast behind them heralded Minda's return. "That was pretty," she beamed, slowing her horse to match their pace. "Everyone all right?"

"So far," Ulric assured her. "Go do what you have to do. We'll catch up."

"That'll be bloody nose number two," Ulric reflected as Minda rode ahead. "Scarlet ought to be getting fairly annoyed by now."

"I hope so," Keely said. "I'd hate think of her hunting us down with a clear head. And speaking of clear heads...what did Minda mean, she wouldn't let the pontifine have it?"

Ulric opened his mouth to answer, stopped halfway, started again, then finally just shrugged.

The cart rattled on down the road as quickly as it dared by lantern light—and while that was quicker than they'd seen Scarlet or the deadlings travel, the road didn't follow a straight line, and their pursuers very well might. Keely and Ulric kept peering nervously into the dark behind them and kept watching the hedges for any sign that they were being overtaken.

They heard the signs before they saw any, though. In the aftermath of the explosions, the deadlings had remained quiet, but now they resumed their baying, sounding more than ever like a pack of pursuing hounds, and unmistakably drawing closer. Then came the hoofbeats.

"Isn't Minda supposed to be in front of us?" Evadne asked.

"Oh, bloody—" Keely pounded the heel of her hand into her forehead. "Scarlet's got a horse! I saw her on a horse in the forest. Oh, go'ss, I forgot."

"Scarlet!" Nolan shouted in a panic.

"Yes!" Keely said. "She's riding up behind us!"

"No!" Nolan insisted. "Scarlet!"

Keely, Ulric, and Evadne spun just in time to see the billowing red cloak flash in the lantern light as a figure standing in the middle of the road appeared out of the darkness.

CHAPTER FORTY-TWO
THE BEST-LAID PLANS

In a split second, the consequences of the horses colliding with a firmly braced Bloody Scarlet played out in Nolan's head, and he pulled hard on the reins in an attempt to veer around her. The cart bucked and tilted dangerously, forcing all of its occupants to grab whatever they could hang onto to keep from being thrown out.

In a moment, the figure in red was blurring past just inches off the left side of the cart. Keely had time to catch the fleeting impression of a skull grinning at her from under the hood of the cloak just before the deadling's thorny vines lashed out, wrapping around her throat. Their speed yanked the deadling free of the cloak and of the post it had been resting on, both to disappear behind in the darkness, but the deadling itself clung tenaciously to Keely and to the side of the cart.

The cart righted itself enough for Ulric to free up one hand, and then he was there, hacking away at the thorny vines. "I will never...trust...a scarecrow...again!" he managed between swings and fending off vines.

Keely wasn't able to manage a hatchet herself while clinging to the cart and trying to avoid a face full of thorns, but she finally managed to grab the skull and slam it down to the floor of the cart, where Evadne finished it with a blunt-side blow.

"Were they *all* hers all along?" Ulric asked as Keely carefully unwrapped the limp vine from around her throat, thankful beyond words for the gorget. The metal collar had certainly done its job. She actually seemed to have emerged from the whole episode without a scratch. The next episode, coming up fast, however, didn't look so promising.

While they'd been busy with the scarecrow, she'd appeared out of the darkness behind—at first just that fiery red cape, almost glowing with

379

a light of its own. They still heard the horse rather than saw it, a black silhouette against the night, obscuring parts of the cape.

"We should have brought the guns. We should have brought the guns," Keely said in a panic, scrambling to press herself as far as she could toward the front of the cart, away from the pursuit that was closing much too quickly.

Ulric pulled a pistol from his belt and leveled it at their pursuer. "I said 'think twice'. I didn't say 'don't bring them'." The pistol cracked. Nothing changed. Presumably, firing in the dark from the jostling cart, the shot had gone wide. "Reload!" he ordered Keely, tossing her the gun as he reached for a second pistol.

"With what?!" she demanded.

Ulric ignored her, bracing himself and taking more time to aim.

"Deadling!" Nolan shouted from the front of the cart.

The second pistol cracked.

The cart jolted. The horses screamed. Thorny vines flailed wildly all around the cart for a moment, then vanished behind them into the darkness, along with the broken wooden cross-piece and tattered red cloak of a scarecrow where they'd been trampled into the dirt. The last they saw of the deadling was a fragment of its skull being crushed under a hoof of Scarlet's great black horse, fully illuminated for a moment by the crackling lightning.

In that moment, Scarlet too could be properly seen, her flesh torn and blackened by the explosion and flames, but any more serious damage she might have suffered seemed to already have repaired itself. Neither horse nor rider showed any more signs of being troubled by the second shot than they had by the first.

The first drops of rain started falling, almost unnoticed in the chaos.

Keely passed the pistol to Evadne, pulled a hatchet, and started hacking at the nearest barrel. Striking in the same location twice wasn't easy under these conditions, but wood began to splinter and securing ropes began to fray.

"What are you doing?!" Evadne shouted.

"Improvising!"

"Rifle!" Nolan shouted. "Behind the barrels on the left!"

Ulric shoved the expended second pistol back into his belt and dove to dig behind the barrels while Keely kept hacking, and he came up with the rifle. He dropped low in the cart—if not to steady the rifle, at least to synchronize its shaking with the jostling of the cart—and took careful aim. The rifle cracked. Scarlet's horse stumbled. The securing ropes on the barrels parted.

Free to bounce and jostle along with the cart, the barrels began to roll off the back. The first slammed into the legs of the already-stumbling horse. The beast went down, taking bloody Scarlet with it, straight into the path of the second barrel.

"Lantern!" Keely screamed to Evadne, pointing at the barrel just now bouncing off the back of the wagon. "That one's been breached!"

Evadne waited for a moment to gauge her throw and to let that barrel join the bone-shattering pile-up. The lantern flew true. The glass shattered. Flaming oil spattered. The force of the initial blast threw Ulric, Keely, and Evadne into a jumble up against the front of the cart, and nearly flung Nolan from the driver's seat. Several secondary blasts followed as later powder kegs bounced into the flaming wreckage.

"Well, there goes your rockslide," Ulric said, watching the flames retreat behind them.

"Don't you military men have a saying about plans and contact with the enemy?" Keely asked. "I'm honestly surprised it took that long for things to start unraveling. Anyway, we lost that rockslide as soon as she brought in the horse. We'd never have wrestled the kegs into position with her so close on our heels."

The rain began to pour in earnest. Thunder sounded so close that it rattled the cart. "This storm's only going to get worse," Nolan shouted as he urged the horses to a halt. They'd begun to slow as they winded themselves, anyway. "And we're nearly blind as it is. What's left of the cargo isn't worth it."

Ulric nodded his assent. "Cut the horses loose. We're on foot from here."

"Is it too much to hope that the second explosion was too much for her?" Evadne asked.

"The storm's still growing," Ulric responded. "The deadlings are still howling. We assume she's alive."

They each grabbed a lantern, though Nolan had the only lit one, and the wind and rain put aside all question of pausing to try to light the others. They simply made a dash through the cold rain toward the looming spire of the Wolf's Tooth.

Mud and ashes squelched around their boots as they picked their way through the charred remnant of the copse in front of Skull Crevice. A little torrent was already pouring out of the crevice, and water cascaded down the walls as they made their way inward.

Clambering over the barricade of fallen rocks while it was an active waterfall proved an adventure in itself, and a trio of deadlings caught up to them before they could descend the other side. A brief, slippery battle ensued, with Ulric and Nolan making efficient use of their hatchets and full armor of steel and leather, while Keely and Evadne scrambled on down to the floor of the inner crevice.

Then the women stood ready to respond with a hatchet in each hand while the men took their turns climbing down, but no more pursuit showed itself, and they hurried on down the crevice.

Soon they were climbing the stone staircase while water poured around their ankles. The realistic skull carvings had seemed macabre enough to Keely in the full daylight and her previous, blissful ignorance. Now, they appeared nothing short of sinister, verging on diabolic, yet seemed almost welcoming compared to the prospect of turning back toward the baying of deadlings that had started to echo cacophonously up the crevice.

It hadn't dawned on Keely until this very moment, but this had all been a temple once, long ago, to the Skull Collector, Bloody Scarlet. Then the empire had come, and...and, what? What powers had that first emperor had under his command that could have driven this monster back to spend centuries skulking in the shadows of her forest? Was this how Miraculata Antonia Grimm had really died, in the miracle of binding Bloody Scarlet to her forest? Had those enchantments been wearing off?

Honestly, Keely decided, she could live without knowing the answers—just so she actually lived.

They burst through the waterfall at the top of the stair and stumbled at last out of the rain and into the tunnel that led to the heart of the Wolf's Tooth. Nolan stood, blocking the entrance with hatchets at the ready, while the others took the time to light the remaining lanterns. Two deadlings came howling into the tunnel while they were at it, but Nolan smashed one against a stone wall the moment it appeared. Spinning on the other, he severed a vine that had wrapped harmlessly around his leather-clad arm, cracked its skull into the opposite wall with the wooden haft of a hatchet, then finished the thing with a clean smash from the metal head.

The waterfall blocking the tunnel entrance behind them drowned out what howling of the deadlings wasn't already being lost to the wind and rain, but somehow the relative silence seemed worse. They still knew the deadlings were out there. They were just blind now to how close the pursuit might be getting.

"This is the bit of the plan where we seal the tunnel behind us with the explosives we no longer have, right?" Evadne asked.

"Pretty much," Keely agreed.

"What do you suggest instead?"

"Run."

With the four lanterns lit now, they did run, splashing through the half-inch of standing water already accumulated on the floor of the tunnel, until at last they burst through the waterfall cascading over the exit into the central shaft.

Leading the way, Keely had a split second to see the gleam of the axe descending toward her head. Her first instinct—to become a small feline with its head several feet below where it was now—only managed to evoke a sensation akin to putting weight on a torn muscle. She screamed a scream that was only saved from dying in her throat by the sudden appearance of Evadne, hurtling through the waterfall behind her and tackling Sir Riordan with all her considerable mass. Evadne had seen the man's silhouette through the waterfall just in time to throw him off his feet, causing the axe to miss Keely's head by a hand's width.

What Evadne hadn't seen at all was the sudden drop-off just a few paces past the opening of the tunnel. She and Riordan went over it together, vanishing through yet another sheet of falling water as they did. The only trace of their passing by the time Ulric and Nolan burst through was Evadne's lantern, rocking on the floor where it had somehow managed to survive being dropped without smashing.

"You know," Jane Carver shouted over the thundering water cascading from the summit of the Wolf's Tooth into the pool behind her, "when it's overused, even cunning misdirection becomes predictable." The numerous figures around her in black and red didn't even wait for a signal. They just began to close in with their blades drawn.

"All right," Keely said. Taking a careful step forward, she set down her lantern and slung her hatchet on her belt. "Hench One, Hench Two?" She turned to make eye contact with Ulric and Nolan. "Follow my lead. Put away your blades."

"I really don't know that I'm feeling merciful enough to accept a surrender," Jane said.

"That's okay." Keely turned back to her. "I'm not really feeling stupid enough to offer." She took two steps and leapt with a shout through the inner cascade. Ulric and Nolan hesitated for a heartbeat, but only just, seeing no alternative. They leapt after Keely before the knights and footmen of the Inquisition could close the remaining distance.

Keely hung in the air for a dizzying moment, blind to everything but the glow of a few flickering lights just visible through the rain and sheeting runoff. The roar of the cascade filled her ears. She just had time to reflect that the woman she'd been only the night before would have done *anything* to avoid leaping back into the dark pool waiting below to embrace her.

Then the pool did. Still submerged, Keely hurriedly doffed her metal helmet as the easiest weight to divest herself of, then she stroked for the surface, imagined decaying hands reaching out of the depths to drag her down with them. Then a hand really did grab her ankle, and she freaked out. She grabbed for a hatchet, floundered futilely to use it beneath the surface of the pool, bobbled it, and felt it tumble away into the blackness. All the while she could feel the iron grip and feel herself being dragged down, other bodies closing in around her.

Then abruptly the grip released and she found herself kicking again for the surface. When she came to her senses, Evadne was there, helping her stay afloat while rain poured down around them.

"Are you all right?" Evadne gasped once she was sure Keely could keep her own head up. "If that fool man doesn't stop struggling and unbuckle that metal breastplate, he's going to be no more concern of ours."

"Oh, go'ss," Keely gasped. "Ulric and Nolan!" Panic surged again as she tried to peer through the dark and the rain, but she could barely even pick out a hint of Evadne right there in the water beside her. "I forgot they had on that metal armor."

"Had," Ulric's voice assured her from nearby. "We went into the water a bit less disoriented than Riordan. Still can't tread water like this for long. We need to find the stairs."

"Over there!" None of them could see Nolan pointing, but they did all look around and spied the lanterns of the Inquisition starting to wind their way down toward the surface of the pool. Using the lights to orient, they made their best guess to where the stairway entered the pool and struck out for it with a sort of terrified relief at the prospect of what constituted less danger at this moment. "I don't see how we're better off, though," Nolan added.

From up above, someone screamed. Then the laughter of the deadlings made itself heard again over the storm.

"Oh." Nolan said. "Forgot for a moment."

"Stay close, follow me, and be ready," Ulric said, dragging himself up onto the steps. Even without a torrent pouring directly down from above, there was no dry here. Rainfall still cascaded down the stairs. "There'll be no getting out of here without some sort of fight." He readied his sword in one hand and a hatchet in the other.

All too soon, the lead lantern drew clearly into sight around the curve of the staircase, illuminating the knight of the Inquisition holding it.

"This one's mine," Nolan said.

Ulric fell back to let his fellow guardsman through, and Nolan stood for a moment, silhouetted against the lantern glow while he hefted a hatchet, testing its weight as the well illuminated target drew nearer. Then the little axe flew, tumbling gracefully end over end, and came impressively close to striking the man in an unprotected eye—but in the end, it bounced off the nose-guard of his helm, even the clang of the impact drowned out by all the other noise going on.

The force of the blow was enough to shift the man's weight, though, which turned his step into a stumble. The slick stairs then turned that stumble into a slip, a fall, and a slide right off the open edge and into the pool below.

"That'll do," Ulric observed as he resumed his lead to charge at the next man, who'd been coming close behind the first.

While Ulric closed with the knight, Keely slipped the gauntlet off her left hand and flung it in a high arc over Ulric's head. "Pixus poxus!" she shouted—the first nonsense to pop into her head—and struck what she hoped was a threatening pose. The ruse did its job, distracting the man into swatting away the flying gauntlet he was certain carried a terrible curse, and allowing Ulric to slip in under his guard.

Ulric's sword clanged harmlessly off of the knight's armored torso, but he'd taken his cue from Nolan's stroke of luck and was swinging to unbalance, not to cut. The man staggered just enough for Ulric to slam the haft of the hatchet into the knight's knee, then yank the weapon back toward himself. The axe head caught the crook of the man's leg as handily as a hook. His feet went out from under him, and he tumbled away into the pool like the man before him.

Nolan's hatchet and one of the lanterns had gone over the edge with the knights, but Ulric had managed to catch the second lantern and Keely was able to recover her gauntlet as they splashed past.

From above came the frenzied sounds of battle as the deadlings engaged their unprepared opponents. If anyone from the Inquisition had actually engaged a deadling in the forest and returned to tell the tale, they'd managed to come back without useful information from the encounter. More likely, none had returned at all.

From the sound of things, too, few of Jane's followers had ever come face-to-face with anything more supernatural than an old woman with a bad squint. They were not, as a unit, holding together gracefully. Still, whether chasing Keely or fleeing from the deadlings, several more lanterns were headed their way down the long curve of the staircase.

"Through here," Ulric commanded, ducking into a side tunnel just as a knight and an inquisitrix came splashing into view.

Clay wasn't terribly surprised when he heard the eerie chorus of deadlings begin to echo through the tunnels. What had surprised him was that it had taken the next nightmare so long to arrive.

For several hours after he'd woken up to find Sabina's head in his cell, he'd left it untouched—certain that it would either spring back to life or transform into something worse if he did reach for it—but eventually he'd broken down and slipped it back into its former owner's cell without incident. That had seemed the least indecent option available to him.

After that, excepting the fact that he'd begun to get hungry, his captivity had become blissfully dull again until the untended lights had sputtered and gone out, leaving him alone in the pitch black with his imagination. When the howling started, he had felt around for the stew bowl—the closest thing to a weapon he had available—and settled in to wait with his back against the wall.

He was still crouched there, listening to the howling growing louder and louder, when lantern-lit chaos burst out of the entrance to the cell block. No less than half a dozen men and women appeared amidst a mass of writhing, thorny vines peppered randomly with red-eyed skulls. Some of the people seemed to be fighting the rest of the people while the vines seemed to be trying to throttle and ensnare all of them.

Blades flashed. Skulls smashed. Now and again, blood spattered from slashing blades or lashing thorns. One woman in black got pulled completely off her feet by a throttling vine, and she hung there choking while the battle raged around her.

Then in the midst of the chaos, he saw her—his silver-haired guardian—and something that he'd once thought of as hope timidly smoldered up in the embers that remained of his soul. She and her companions seemed to have allied themselves in a desperate fight against the people in black and red.

She had dressed all in red, too—the *other* she, the real witch who'd started this all. He'd barely seen that monster at all since the silver-haired one had shown up, but he'd never be able to forget the witch's torments even if he had a dozen lifetimes to do it in. It didn't take much for him to conclude that the combatants in red and black were minions of the monster, and that any aid he could render against them would be fighting for whatever fragments might remain of his own sanity.

So when the vines pinned one of them up against the bars of his cell, Clay helped himself to the cudgel hanging from the man's belt and started beating on him through the bars. It didn't seem to do much. The man was well-armored. Still, it felt good to be making even a token gesture to fight back, and the man was far too busy dealing with the vines to retaliate against Clay.

Clay got so into taking his petty vengeance that he failed to notice when the vines came for him, too. He didn't even notice he was having trouble breathing until after he noticed the blood dripping into his eye from where the thorns had left a nasty gash across his forehead. He clawed reflexively at the vine that had wrapped around his throat, wondering when he would wake up again, and where.

Then the silver-haired woman was there, laying about her with a pair of axes, dismembering the vines that held Clay fast, shattering any bodiless skulls that came within reach.

"Evadne! Evadne! I'm so sorry, but we have to go!" Keely tugged at the arm of the big woman. Evadne was kneeling in front of what had been Sabina's prison cell with her head resting against the bars and her hands gripping them so tightly that part of Keely was waiting for the iron to break.

They'd come through the fight only slightly bloodied, more by virtue of being prepared for the deadlings than by being able to directly overpower the knights and black-hoods that had caught up with them. Ulric and Nolan were capable fighters, but this hadn't been like it had been when Tobias and Baldassare danced with the Inquisition. For a strictly fair, one-on-one fight, the forces of the Inquisition were better-trained and better-prepared than the Haywoodshire guardsmen.

This skirmish had been won on little things, like most of the opposition fighting with only a single weapon—leaving them easier for the deadlings to pin—and gorgets having become less-valued equipment for the modern knight as gunpowder on the battlefield reduced the relative value of a pound of armor.

In this fight, too, the Inquisition had expected speed for countering a witch's hex to be more important than steel armor to repel a blade. Some of the knights had simply chosen to forgo gorgets, and blackhoods rarely wore them anyway.

"Who did this?" Evadne demanded of Clay through gritted teeth.

"I think it was one of that lot," Clay said, surprising even himself at this point with his relative clarity of thought and speech, especially given the state of his nose. "They're Inquisition, ain't they? I remember a man. We thought he was the jailer. Took her away. Then he came back without her, dressed like them, talkin' about witches, and he..." He waved a hand toward the mess of his face. "When I woke up, he was gone, and...I'm sorry. She was nice."

"Big man?" Keely asked. "Dark hair? Neat beard? Handsome devil?"

"Yeah. Yeah. Yeah," Clay said. "I expect you'd call him that. Know him?"

"Riordan," Keely said. "It was Sir Riordan. With any luck, he drowned back there."

"If he didn't, he's mine," Evadne hissed, pushing off the bars to force herself back to her feet.

"I promise I've got more claim on him than you do," Keely said, "but if he *is* still alive, I'll share." She shoved a hatchet into Clay's hand, re-arming herself with a short sword one of the priestesses had dropped.

"We haven't seen the last of these things," she said, gesturing toward fragments of skull and vine scattered across the floor. Protect your throat, try to keep your hands free. If you see a chance to get out in the open and run, take it, and don't look back. Just make sure you're running *away* from the forest."

The sound of more deadlings coming up fast spurred them to action, and the group resumed its flight through the tunnels of the Wolf's Tooth with Clay in tow. A quick right and a couple of lefts brought them back out into the main shaft. Lightning still flickered and thunder still rumbled and water still sheeted down from above, obscuring the central part of the shaft from where they stood on the stair.

"What's that sound?" Evadne asked, straining to distinguish a new thread that had joined the chaotic chorus of storm and conflict and howling laughter.

"Anchor me," Keely said, grabbing Evadne's wrist tightly and leaning out through the waterfall. At first, all Keely could see was the glimmer of torches and lanterns scattered randomly up and down the stairwell, their glow left dispersed and hazy by the surrounding curtain of water. Some of the lights were clearly being born by people in various stages of haste. Others remained unmoving, probably either mounted on the wall or dropped by people fleeing from—or overrun by—the deadlings.

She could hear this new sound more distinctly, though—a low, agonized wail coming from somewhere below. Then the lightning flash directly overhead, lighting the entire shaft for one flickering moment, and it illuminated the toxic mess that surged below as if showing it in a series of still images.

As best Keely could piece together in that moment, the deadlings had come bursting in through the tunnel faster than they could get clear at the end of it, forcing a steady stream of their number over the edge and into the central pool. The blind flailing of the deadlings who'd wound up in the water hadn't had much success grasping anything but the vines of other deadlings, dragging them in after and creating a writhing green mass that buoyed up the already-flooding surface of the pool.

From there, things had gotten ugly. There was no guessing how many of Jane Carver's lot had wound up in the pool with the deadlings, but several surely had, bleeding profusely from gaping, thorny lacerations. Once they'd fallen, they'd have found themselves drowning in a merciless wall of rending thorns, and bled out completely, feeding their lives to the hungry dead in the great bone pit that lay beneath the surface.

Keely's imagination had already conjured all manner of terrors emerging from that sunken graveyard, and done so quite vividly, but it still hadn't prepared her for the sheer, enormous horror of the reality.

Bone-riddled, black mud geysered upward in columns, punching gaping holes in the writhing thicket of deadlings. Decapitated corpses clawed from the muck, grabbing blindly at any skull they could find to sloppily replace their missing heads. Others had started erratically swarming up the shaft like drunken spiders.

A few still-living knights and priestesses could be seen caught up in the mess, all either being torn apart by bony hand and thorny vine or simply dragged down screaming—not that Keely could actually pick out individual screams above the cacophony of raging storm and howling dead.

She'd been feeling already that she'd been thrown into a waking nightmare, but at this moment she found herself looking straight into the abyss.

CHAPTER FORTY-THREE

THE LAST WALTZ

For a dreadful heartbeat, Keely realized she'd inadvertently let her grip on Evadne's wrist slacken, and would have surely fallen had Evadne not been gripping *her* wrist so unfailingly. She wheeled for a moment, trying clumsily to grab Evadne's other wrist, but Evadne sensed her distress immediately and hauled Keely back in through the rushing water.

"Lovely, isn't it?" The little girl in the red cape beamed as she paced up the curve of the stairs toward them, casually tumbling an over-sized axe back and forth between her hands. "You really *did* surprise me. Teaming up with the Inquisition? I never figured you could set aside your differences that long. And that High Inquisitrix girl's tougher than you'd think, just to look at her. She's got some serious blood in her. Still..."

Bloody Scarlet paused in tumbling the axe to spread her arms and gesture at herself. "...here I am. Don't let it get you down. You had a good run. Best hunt I've had in a hundred years, easy."

"We're not done running, if it's all the same to you," Keely said, then turned to point the others on up the stairs. "Go!" They did. It was a voice that brooked no arguments.

"You know what happens to people who make noble last stands?" Scarlet asked as Keely turned back to face her, sword and hatchet in hand. "They die. You're a clever girl, but we've gone completely off script now, I think. You can't top the Inquisition for brute force. You've got some strong blood too, but not that strong. Think maybe you can improvise another explosion? I'll come back. Think you can throw me to my leftovers down a pit again? I'll come back. I *always* come back, little girl. It's what I do."

"Have you ever considered...I don't know...tapestry weaving?" Keely asked. "It may not have the glamor of this whole 'revenant' thing', but it'll keep out the drafts over the winter."

"Huh." Scarlet stopped, leaning on her axe as her eyes rolled back and forth thoughtfully. "Never thought about it. You're right, though. Terribly good for drafts."

"Keely!" Ulric bellowed. "Get up here, you idiot!"

Keely turned and ran.

Behind them, the little girl continued up the stairs in no particular hurry, mumbling pensively to herself. "Hmmm...Tapestry weaving?"

With Ulric in the lead, they arrived at the tunnel leading out to what remained of the cathedral site, more than slightly winded from their rapid ascent. When he paused and looked to Keely, she glanced over her shoulder and found that they'd left Scarlet too far behind to judge where she might be. Keely nodded, and they hurried on out into the storm, trying to move as briskly as they could through the dark and the drenching wet while still recovering some breath.

Around them, everything lay in ruin. All that remained of the tents that had once sheltered supplies and workers was a few rags of canvas that had gotten too caught up in the rubble to blow away in the storm. Scaffolding and other timbers lay blackened, broken, and hopelessly mingled with the chaotically tumbled stones that had once been the start of walls, columns, and buttresses.

This hadn't been the devastation of a pitched battle, but systematic and deliberate destruction, doubtlessly orchestrated by Jane Carver to pin on the locals and deny them any hope of support from Pontifine Augusta. Not a single standing structure cast its silhouette against the lightning that flashed across the sky.

What did cast silhouettes was the deadlings swarming up off the only trail to the site and crawling over the ruins in a thick mass.

"Yeah," Nolan said. "Not getting out that way."

"Looks more inviting than going back down the way we came," Keely assured him. Her eyes lit on the freshly bloodied remains of a horse out among the ruins—almost certainly Minda's horse—but she kept the observation to herself. Minda would be alive, because...well, she had to be. If Minda hadn't finished her job, there could be no doubt now that Scarlet would finish hers.

"We go up," Ulric said grimly. "Now, before she cuts us off from behind, or we die right here."

The distance remaining to be climbed up the central shaft to the summit of the Wolf's Tooth seemed unfairly long, given how far they'd already come. On the other hand, once they reached the summit, that was it—no way up, no way down, no way out—so each aching step represented another precious second of life. Not exactly a cheerful thought, but the best Keely could come up with to console herself while she pushed the burning lungs and aching legs past what she normally thought of as their limits.

They passed a few more openings on the way up, but the narrowing spire of the Tooth didn't leave much room for tunnels near the top, and even Keely had done enough exploring here to know those only led to store rooms where the Haywoods had laid in supplies for the anticipated siege.

At last, they emerged once more into the storm, this time standing at the pinnacle of the Wolf's Tooth and its moss-covered ruins. The slightly concave structure of the pinnacle had been too subtle to notice the first time they'd been up here, but the shallow, bowl-like shape surrounding the central shaft collected every bit of water the storm poured at the top of the Tooth and funneled it straight into the shaft. By the time the water got there, it had already picked up enough depth and speed to threaten to drag anyone who managed to slip and fall straight over the edge with it.

"We've really got to stop meeting like this," Baldassare said, stepping out of the shadow and shelter of the ruined watchtower.

"Oh...my...go'ss." Keely gaped. "Baldassare, what are you even doing here?!"

"We had to come back and warn you," Baldassare said. "The Inquisition's doubled back."

"We?" Keely asked darkly. "Where's Jenny?"

Huddled in her cloak against the rain and leaning on her walking stick, Elissa stepped out behind Baldassare and gave a sheepish wave. "It, uh...sort of didn't work out like we expected. You've already figured out the Inquisition's here, haven't you?"

"I was starting to suspect," Keely admitted, her words punctuated by a crack of lightning and thunder.

"We took a couple of wrong turns coming back," Elissa said. "Then we nearly ran into the Inquisition ourselves. Then the deadlings..."

"Okay. Okay. Got it," Keely said, cutting off the explanations with a wave of her hands. "All right. No one's dead yet," she said to no one in particular. "Well, okay, a lot of people are dead, but at least they're not us. Mostly aren't us. I'm babbling. Stop it. Anyway..."

"Tick-tock, tick-tick!" Scarlet called up the stairway. "Sands through the hourglass. Sundial's...running out of sun, I guess."

"Your plan's still on track, right?" Baldassare asked hopefully.

"So far, exactly one thing went like it was supposed to," Keely said. "Where's Minda? Is she here, too?"

"Was she supposed to be?" Baldassare asked.

Keely threw her head back and screamed. The effect was very dramatic for all of a second or two before the scream was choked off by the rain falling into her mouth, and it turned into more of a gurgle. "Gimme," she said, yanking Baldassare's sword out of its sheath and pressing the smaller one on him to replace it. "We're all going to be dead before you're fit to use this again, anyway."

"Do you even know *how* to use it?" he demanded.

"Sure," Keely said. "Hit her with the pointy bit."

"I thought and I thought," Scarlet said, stepping up and out into the rain with them. Once more looking the grown woman in her prime, she casually twirled the enormous axe like a weightless extension of herself. "The thing is, I don't actually *like* tapestries. Sorry."

With a scream of incoherent rage, Keely hefted the sword and ran straight at Scarlet. Unperturbed, Scarlet stopped spinning the axe, planted her feet, and braced to receive the charge. A part of Keely had expected she wouldn't have time to actually feel the incoming blow, but what caught her really off guard was that when it landed, it came from behind and while Scarlet still stood twenty feet away. Baldassare's sword skittered away and she hit the ground hard as Ulric landed heavily on top of her.

"You do *not* get to die doing *my* job," Ulric shouted angrily, leaving her lying there gasping for breath as he stood up to draw his sword. Multiple pairs of boots splashed past her at eye-level—Evadne and Nolan charging to join Ulric, and Baldassare scrambling to rescue his sword before the shallow current could find enough purchase to slide it toward the pit. Then Elissa and Clay were at her side, trying to drag her away from the sound of ringing steel.

"No!" Keely screamed, struggling to rise, but at Elissa's command Clay was holding her back. Keely's eyes held a glazed, far-off look as if trying to take in a reality that gone out of focus. "Keely! Axy!" she screamed. "Run!"

Though outnumbered three to one, Scarlet actually looked to be toying with her circling opponents. She moved swiftly, fluidly, effortlessly, and decisively, with a constant awareness of her surroundings that by itself marked her as something other than human. Even when a blade came in from behind her, the only time it didn't pass through empty air was when she knocked it artfully aside with the head of her axe. Any dancer at a king's court would have gone mad with envy of such grace.

"I get it," Elissa said fiercely, shaking Keely. "You think it should have been you that died. But you didn't throw your life away then, and you don't get to now. Stay with us, and do what you do best. You still owe me that."

Jenilee closed her eyes to the nightmare replaying itself out in front of her and tried to muster her thoughts. "We can't kill her, but we can buy time by hurting her." Her words fell into a rhythm as though she were reciting a memorized speech.

"If we can buy time, we can take her cloak. I'm sure there's power in her cloak. If we can take her cloak, I'm sure it'll cripple her. We can't hurt her unless we can touch her. We can't touch her with a blade, because she can always outrun it. She couldn't outrun Doryne's crossbow, but we don't have a crossbow. She wouldn't be able to outrun a pistol, but all our powder's been drenched and ruined. Unless Baldassare...?" Jenilee asked hopefully.

"No chance," Elissa said. "We got drenched to the skin getting this far."

"There's powder downstairs!" Jenilee said abruptly. "Dry powder in the storerooms, remember? We've got to get past—" A shriek from Elissa drew her up short, and Clay's grip on her arms went abruptly slack. The ringing of steel had suddenly stopped.

Jenilee opened her eyes, pulled herself halfway up, and followed Elissa's horrified gaze to where Ulric's head had rolled to a stop not five feet away from them. "But...I have to fix it," Jenilee said feebly, staring at his unseeing eyes. "I have to fix it."

"All right," Clay said, carefully picking up the fallen head and carrying it to nestle in the nearest pile of rubble, where the water couldn't carry it away into the pit. "It'll be safe there." Even Scarlet— who had stepped back theatrically from the fight to let the moment sink in—seemed a bit taken aback at the man's complete detachment from the context of what he was doing.

"I have to fix it," Jenilee repeated.

"You do *not* have to *fix* it," Elissa hissed. "You have to get dry powder loaded into a pistol before she kills everyone fit to aim a gun."

"Yes," Jenilee agreed, less feebly.

"Do you need Keely for that?"

"Yes," Jenilee nodded. And then she wasn't Jenilee anymore. "All of you stop!" Keely screamed. "Get over here! Now! This is *my* job!"

"Hey, whichever order you feel like," Scarlet said dismissively. "Talk amongst yourselves."

Dragging Ulric's body, they came to her with the normally easy-going Nolan visibly tottering on the edge of the same unreasoning rage that had moments ago taken Keely. If she didn't act swiftly and decisively, she knew he would die next and it would be the final straw to break the rest of them. She pulled the discharged pistol briskly from Ulric's belt and pressed it into Nolan's hand.

"You know where to find dry powder. None of us will be able to get to it faster or to load the gun faster, and I doubt any of us has a truer aim. You will get exactly one shot. If Bloody Scarlet takes a lead ball through the brain, I may still salvage something here. If she doesn't, we *all* die tonight at the top of the Wolf's Tooth. Do you understand? I'll make the opportunity. Be ready to take it."

Keely straightened up and brushed the rain-slicked hair out of her eyes. "Oh, and Jenny?" she said to Elissa. "Thanks for talking things out, but there's one big flaw in your logic." Without pausing to elaborate further, Keely reclaimed Baldassare's sword and stepped forward grimly to face Bloody Scarlet through the pouring rain.

"Ready, dear?" Scarlet called, smiling as she gave her axe a twirl.

"Ready." Keely nodded. "I just have one last question."

"Sure." Scarlet shrugged affably.

"What about ballroom dancing?"

Scarlet blinked. "Ballroom dancing?"

"Yes. What do you think about ballroom dancing?" Keely asked. "Have you tried it? Miles better than tapestry weaving, and the way you move...? You've got the knack."

"Huh." Scarlet pondered. "Can't say I really know anything about ballroom dancing. Sorry." She began twirling the axe again.

"I can teach," Keely said. "I'll never be as good as you could, but I've got the experience. I know the steps. What say? You, showing off all that grace in front of Seriena's simpering nobles just before you seal the doors and start the slaughter? Imagine it."

"Well..." Scarlet lowered the axe again, her face working expressively as she clearly *did* try to imagine it.

"Come on. One free lesson, no obligation. If you're not thrilled with it, you go ahead and kill us. If you do like it, you let us live and I teach you everything there is to know about blending in among Seriena's elite. Heads rolling. Blood everywhere. Entire noble lines wiped out. Entire kingdoms in chaos. Just *try* it." Keely carefully laid down the sword where it couldn't float away, then took another step forward and held out her hand toward Scarlet. "What do you say?"

"I...hmmm."

"Come on." Keely grinned. "Live a little."

"You're right." Scarlet laughed girlishly as she dropped her axe with a careless splash. The heavy weapon showed no inclination to budge in

395

the current. Scarlet took a few steps closer to Keely, holding out her hands. "So teach. How do we do this?"

"Well, first..." Keely closed the remaining distance between them and took Scarlet by the hand. The touch was electric—literally electric. Thunder cracked directly overhead and lightning lanced downward, striking both figures directly and blinding everyone on the summit of the Tooth. When vision cleared, though, neither of the women appeared so much as frizzled. The lightning had dissipated harmlessly around them, and Scarlet was actually laughing giddily.

"You...you're...you're..." Scarlet stammered.

"Leading," Keely assured her, taking one hand firmly and placing the other on Scarlet's hip. "Just follow me and try to move your feet with mine. Da da dum, da da dum, one two three, one two three...See? Anyone else would be stepping on my feet at this point. One two three, one two three..."

"This is amazing!" Scarlet laughed.

"Knew you'd like it." Keely grinned as they splashed together, spinning through the rain.

"No! I mean, yes! But you're..."

"No," Keely said, bringing the dance up short to tap Scarlet merrily on the nose. "I'm *not*. You've got me confused with Jenilee."

"Jenilee?" Scarlet cocked an eyebrow.

"No one, really." Keely sighed. "Just a girl I once was." Before Scarlet could even *try* to make sense of that, Keely suddenly gasped. "Your cape!"

Scarlet's eyes went wide with alarm as the wind whipped the cloak from her shoulders. She spun and made a desperate lunge for the fluttering red cloth, only to find that it wasn't there. What *was* there, just in front of her, was a gaping black hole plunging straight down into the heart of the Wolf's Tooth. She landed two feet short of it and scrabbled for a non-existent handhold as she skidded the rest of the way, the water pushing her with it.

Whether from fear or simply from frustration, Scarlet screamed as the edge of the shaft crumbled beneath her and she vanished down into the dark pit.

"It's okay!" Keely yelled after her. "I caught your cloak!" She whipped the sodden red material about her shoulders and carefully secured the clasp she'd undone when she reached up to touch Scarlet's face, then looked up to find the others staring at her, stunned. "Well?" she demanded, fixing Nolan with a pointed gaze. "Gunpowder?"

"But..." he stammered.

"I'm a *liar*," she said pointedly, "but we still need the gunpowder, and we need it fifteen minutes ago. Run!"

With Nolan in the lead, they ran—at least as much as anyone could and would dare to run through water cascading down a rail-less stone staircase directly beside a hundred of feet of nothing. He took the tunnel off the first landing they came to, charged through the open door, and skidded to a stop in front of a frozen tableau.

There, by flickering lantern light, Sister Shoshona stood with the knife in her hand pressed right up against the throat of Minda Haywood, while Minda stood with her back to the wall and a pistol pressed to Shoshona's temple. At the sound of the running feet, a triumphant grin spread slowly across Shoshona's face. Then Minda's eyes flicked up to see who'd arrived, and she aimed one slow shake of her head at Shoshona as a grin of her own appeared.

With smile faltering, Shoshona shifted in an attempt to look over her shoulder. In that instant, Minda's pistol cracked.

"Thank you *so* much for not being the Inquisition," Minda said, using her own cloak to wipe the blood from her face. "This would have been a lousy time to spoil my perfect record of never being on the losing end of a standoff." She stared down for a moment at what remained of the inquisitrix and shuddered.

"Are you hurt?" Keely demanded.

"Not really. Hey, is that...?"

"Yes. It's Scarlet's. Did you...?"

"All set," Minda said. "She caught me after I finished. Now?"

"Now."

"Then run! I'll be right behind you."

Back out in the stairwell, the storm had gone berserk. Lightning sizzled not merely overhead, but straight down the shaft. Over and over again it arced downward, each strike coming so close behind the last that the deafening thunder never found a chance to die away. The hurrying group found itself forced to descend the stairs with eyes turned to the wall and hands clapped over their ears.

At each landing they passed, Minda ducked briefly into the tunnel there before hurrying back to rejoin the others in their descent. The roar and the brilliance got so intense that none of them actually knew when Minda's charges started going off. All they could say after the fact was that it had started late enough for all of them to clear the mouth of the tunnel at what had been the cathedral site and dive for cover beneath an overhang.

At the pinnacle of the Wolf's Tooth, fire roared upward in answer to the lightning, and countless tons of rock began to collapse inward at the summit of the spire. Yet somehow, above it all rang the clear tortured note of one woman's scream.

CHAPTER FORTY-FOUR

AFTER THE BALL

The chill light of dawn found Keely, Elissa, and Minda standing on the newly lowered summit of the Wolf's Tooth, surveying the rubble. None of the others had managed to fight their way back to consciousness yet after they'd collapsed from exhaustion.

"I told you I like it when things go boom." Minda smirked.

"It was you tearing down the cathedral all along, wasn't it?" Keely asked.

"I had help," Minda said. "But yeah. I never agreed with my parents' decision to kowtow to the church. There's a lot of people around here who felt the same."

"I was hoping maybe we could break loose a few big slabs on her," Keely said. "This...wow. You know your demolitions."

"She's still not dead, you know," Elissa said.

"You're sure?" Keely asked.

"Listen."

They listened and they heard it, faint but unmistakable. Filtering up through the crushing weight of a crumbled mountaintop came the tortured sound of a woman's screams. Shivering—and not just from the damp and the morning chill—the three of them turned and started back down to where they'd taken shelter during the night.

The deadlings hadn't politely fallen still and silent when the Wolf's Tooth came down on Scarlet, but had all vanished one way or another before dawn. Where they had been swarming across the construction site, it was now hard to tell they'd ever been there. Of course, it was hard to make anything out of that mess.

The unfortunate horse Keely had spotted wasn't the only one to be found dead amidst the rubble in the morning light, and there were human remains as well—mostly in the livery of the Inquisition, but not all. Some of the dead could have been left there from the battle the day before. Others clearly hadn't been—at least, if you knew what you were looking for.

They paused on a rock overlooking the devastated construction site, staring out at the damage and the blackened landscape beyond.

"Is this my fault?" Keely asked pensively. She wasn't actively crying, but a few stray tears had managed to find their way unnoticed onto her cheeks. "Did I do this? I practically begged the Inquisition to come here."

"It's your fault the Inquisition was here," Minda said, "but where would they have been if they *weren't* here? What would they have been doing? I won't lie. I'm still trying to absorb what's happened, and I know I'm going to be in a bad way when it sinks in, but I don't blame you. You could as easily blame the whole thing on me. Sister Petra wasn't supposed to die. We didn't even know she was up here before the walls started coming down that night.

"But she did die. That's on me and my carelessness. My arrogance. Up 'til then, I thought it was all a game I was playing with the pontifine. An innocent woman died because of me, and you never would have lingered here if not for that. So don't go there."

"The Inquisition was already hunting for the Grimm Truth before you got involved, Keely," Elissa said. "And there's no way you could have accounted for Scarlet getting involved. No one could have."

"Think about it," Minda said, "every one of those skulls crawling over the Wolf's Tooth last night probably represented someone Bloody Scarlet killed personally. Between us, we just managed to lock away one of the worst murderers in the history of...history...in her own personal dungeon. It doesn't undo the wrong, but start counting the skulls, then imagine a future where the woman who did that is wandering free. If preventing that future's not a serious start on atonement, I don't know what is. I'll try to cut myself some slack if you will."

"I'll try," Keely said. "No promises."

"It sounded like Jane Carver was still alive the last time Scarlet saw her," Keely said. "Do you think she got out?"

"Either way, it's trouble," Keely said. "If Jane got out, she'll be trying to take credit for vanquishing the most horrible witch ever. If she didn't get out, her next-in-line will be painting her as the fallen miraculata who vanquished the most horrible witch ever. Either way, we've got to get moving and find a way to steal her thunder. I didn't go through all this to lend justification to the abuses of the Inquisition."

"Hey there, Hero."

Tobias hurt everywhere, but he'd managed to piece together enough memory to be pleasantly amazed he was alive to hurt at all. To find Keely's concerned-but-smiling face hovering over him made opening his eyes seem nearly worth the effort.

"Hey," he managed. His jaw ached horribly, but at least it didn't seem to be broken. Based on how much trouble someone had gone to to immobilize various parts of his body, he was sure he owned several major bones he couldn't say that about. From the look of things, he was recuperating in a private room of an inn somewhere. "How long have I been out?"

"About a week," she said. "You've tried to wake up a few times before now, but I'm not surprised you don't remember it. That's the first really lucid sentence you've managed. I'm very glad you made it this far. I've been assured you'd live if you did."

"My body may yet have other ideas." He grimaced. Then his eyes lit on her cloak. "Is that...?"

"Oh, yeah." She grinned, stepping back and twirling for him to show off the brilliant red cape. "We won. You were a big part of that, even though you checked out early. Your adventure is sorry she nearly got you killed."

"It'll look *amazing* with that red dress of yours," he said.

"It will, won't it?" Keely's grin broadened, and she leaned down to kiss him gently on the lips. "You keep that dress safe for me, and I'll promise to wear it to another dance with you. But for now, there's like a million things to do, and it's going to be weeks or months before you're up to any of them. Looks like Jane Carver's still at large and still looking for the book. I've got to beat her to it, or none of this matters. Okay, ending the thousand-year murder spree of an insane goddess matters, but you know what I mean."

"I think so, yeah."

"I'll be leaving you in good hands," Keely assured him. "Conrad's got a handle on things, and Baldassare is recovering nicely. He'll make sure you get wherever you want to be before he heads home himself."

"What about the others?" he asked.

"Let's see...we got Addie out alive, but she's got no family and she lost everything. I'm trusting you to make sure she gets her shot at becoming a proper priestess. She'll make a fine one."

"I can handle that," he said.

"The Inquisition technically owns the Wolf's Tooth, but I can't imagine they're going to do anything with it. No one wants to go back to Haywoodshire. I'm afraid it's going to be a haunted wasteland for a while. I'd take it as a personal favor if you'd do whatever you can to help out the refugees, including Minda's family. We managed to swing them a full pardon from the Inquisition, and they still technically own land, but they're going to have problems."

"I'll do what I can," Tobias promised.

"Minda's decided to stay dead. She says there's going to be too many things that could go wrong if Jane Carver starts asking questions about what happened to her. She's coming with me to look for the book and bringing Nolan. Seems if his life's going to be turned upside down regardless, he'd rather be hanging out with people who've seen what he's seen, not tagging along somewhere he has to pretend he hasn't seen it in order to feel normal.

"Evadne's coming, too. Baldassare wanted to come with us—turns out the Inquisition killed that sister he was looking for, and I'm sure they made an enemy for life there—but he says he owes it to her to go back home and figure out how to salvage their family fortunes. He's going to bide his time and trust Evadne to make things difficult for the Inquisition in the short-term."

"Sounds like quite the little army," Tobias smiled.

"Oh, and there's one more guy. I don't think you've met. Name's Clay. Not from around here, but Scarlet dragged him into this and tore up his mind something awful. Best I can tell from his ramblings, he was an undertaker some—"

"Clay Ambleforth?"

"You *have* met him?"

"I'm afraid I must have led Scarlet *to* him." Tobias sighed. "He's a descendant of Lord Vyncent Amberford. Yes, leave him to me. I'll see what I can do for him, and he may be able to tell me something he didn't before when I was looking for you. I was in a hurry, and not too concerned what he could tell me about the book at the time."

"Excellent." She favored him with a brilliant smile. "I couldn't leave without knowing if you'd be all right, and saying goodbye. I owed you a goodbye. But time's wasting. I'll do my best to stay alive, and I think we both know that staying alive is a specialty of mine." She leaned down to kiss him again, and this time he managed to return it gingerly.

"You know I'll be coming to chase you down again," Tobias warned her as she turned to go, her lovely new cape billowing around her.

"I know," Keely said. "And when you do, I promise not to run as fast as before. What I *don't* promise," she said, looking back with a wink, "is not to lose my dress again."

The Wolf's Tooth still loomed in the distance as they headed out from Fodderen in the direction of Lake Etherea to follow their scant clues to the fate of the Grimm Truth.

"It does make a helluva monument," Nolan said, looking up at the tower of rock. "As ends go, it's one Ulric would have been okay with."

"I know I'm pretty pleased with how I died," Minda said. "Of course, I get to have it both ways. I hope Doryne and Nessa like it up there with him."

"I hope they all like being the heroes of the song Tobias commissioned while he was asleep," Keely said. "I thought the minstrel showed a lot of promise."

"At least they don't have to actually live with it," Elissa said dryly. "I thought you were going to drop that bit about me being a miraculata once it got the Inquisition out of the way."

"Well, it didn't get the Inquisition out of the way, did it?" Keely asked. "We might as well make it count for something."

"You know I've had to convince three different people already that I'm not a miraculata?" Elissa asked.

"Did it work?"

"No!" Elissa cried, exasperated. "That's the worst part!"

"Excellent." Keely grinned. "Only a true miraculata would deny her holiness. Keep it up. No one's going to believe it was an unknown girl like you and not Jane Carver who rid the world of a monster like Scarlet if they don't buy into the story of you being a miraculata."

"And what happens when they start asking me to perform actual miracles?" Elissa demanded.

"That's the great thing about miracles," Keely assured her. "They never work by request. But here's something that might cheer you up, Jenny: It's not just you that was wrong."

"Oh?" Elissa asked archly.

"You did get so caught up in the notion that hurting Scarlet would inconvenience her, you forgot to consider all the other ways she could be inconvenienced. But *I* was actually wrong about a couple of things, too."

"*You* were wrong?" Elissa asked, sincerely shocked by the admission.

"In the end, I couldn't fix everything." Keely sighed, her face falling. "I had to settle for keeping things from getting worse. Not sure yet how I'm going to deal with that."

"And the other?"

"Apparently," Keely said, a shadow of a smile returning, "you *can* con crazy."

Made in the USA
Monee, IL
25 May 2021